Also by Steven Voien

In a High and Lonely Place

Black Leopard

Black Leopard

Steven Voien

Alfred A. Knopf 🐆 New York 1997

This Is a Borzoi Book
Published by Alfred A. Knopf, Inc.

Copyright © 1996 by Steven Voien

This is a work of fiction; any resemblance to actual events or people is
entirely coincidental. Denkyara and Terre Diamantée are invented countries.

Library of Congress Cataloging-in-Publication Data
Voien, Steven.
Black leopard / by Steven Voien. — 1st ed.
p. cm.
ISBN 0-679-44072-4 (hardcover : alk. paper)
1. Revolutions—Africa, West—Fiction. 2. Biologists—Africa,
West—Fiction. 3. Americans—Africa, West—Fiction. I. Title.
PS3572.O327B53 1997
813'.54—dc20 96-15696 CIP

Manufactured in the United States of America
First Edition

To the memory of my father

A number of people provided valuable assistance and encouragement during the writing of this book. My warmest appreciation goes to real-life biologists Christophe and Hedwige Boesch, Marcel Alers, Louise Emmons, John Seidensticker, Pascal Gagneux, Karl Van Orsdol, and Skyli McAfee.

Thanks as well to former diplomatic colleagues Tom Price, Ken Brown, Gerry Hamilton, Doug Hobson, Lee Litzenberger, and Vince Rizzo. Gratitude and appreciation to Esther Newberg and Ash Green, to good friend and critic Beth Foote, and to my brothers Dana and Derek.

Finally, my heartfelt thanks to Lydia, who made sense of it all.

Black Leopard

1

Trowbridge spun slowly, in complete darkness, resisting the urge to put on the night scope. If he were ever to become practiced at this—ascending and descending by feel, working confidently in an absence of light—now was the time.

He leaned back in the harness, straightened his legs before him for balance, and looked up. The slender Kevlar line, which he knew ran twenty meters straight up, disappeared barely an arm's length over his head. The darkness around him was so rich with sound and life, so warm and tangible, that it was nearly liquid. Katydids sang and frogs pinked in a steady chorus; some other creature made a hollow *tock-tock* that echoed strangely; a high scream erupted, was cut short, and erupted again. Then a series of deep, weird howls, coming faster and faster, culminating in a breathless screech.

It was like being in a vast cave, he thought.

Only there wasn't this much noise, this much life, in a cave. It was like being in the great, dark, beating heart of Eden—whistling and trilling and croaking around him—if Eden had been created before the sun.

He relaxed his senses and aimed his eyes forward, attempting to sift out the information he needed. He was accustomed, by profession, to being intensely aware of his surroundings, to listening for the tiniest crack of a twig or skitter of a stone, to seeing the slightest shift in an otherwise still landscape. Here, there was so much input it was overwhelming.

Something. There, in the darkness. A few seconds later, there again. Past his boot tips, dimly, an enormous column—the straight-trunked *iroko* from which he hung suspended—sweeping through his field of vision.

Good, he thought. That's a start. Now it's time to stop the spinning.

He pulled up the crossbow which hung from his harness, set a dart into its firing niche, and coiled the eighth-inch line so it wouldn't tangle as it paid out. Raising the crossbow, he steadied it against the taut climbing rope. He waited till the dark column came into view again, and squeezed the trigger.

A small hissing. The tight sound of metal penetrating wood. He reached behind himself, clipped the line to a carabiner on the back of his harness, and cinched in the slack. There was a gentle tug at his back, and the spinning stopped.

He was still, now, and floating, suspended over an invisible abyss.

Taking a deep breath, he pulled the night scope down over his eyes—making the darkness instantly claustrophobic—and turned a switch by his right ear. With a click, and a humming that sounded like a distant television set, a world made up of pale yellow halftones sprang into being. He'd spent three hours in this clearing before darkness fell, and knew more or less what to expect; still, the sight was spectacular enough to send a thrill through him. The forest floor six meters below, with the exception of a small clearing, was thick with undergrowth. Around him was mostly empty space, but within that emptiness, rising massive and straight, bearing the immeasurable weight of the canopy above, was the physical body of the forest, the trunks of the great emergent trees. Their massive columns rose perfect and still, like the pillars of a temple beneath the sea.

He reached into his bag for another dart, a blunt-tipped practice dart this time, and slipped it into the bow, taking careful aim at a dark outline on the forest floor. He'd laid out this target in daylight, using leaves and vines; it was about the size and shape of a small man. The bow jumped slightly in his hand as the dart released, and he saw that he'd missed. Too high. The darkness, and the scope, had thrown him off. He put in a second dart, compensated, and did a little better. On his third shot he hit the object within the outline he was aiming at, a grapefruit-sized piece of fruit with a pithy outer shell.

He shot six more times, using up his practice darts, making small adjustments on the crossbow until he began to feel confident he could do what he needed to with this weapon. Then he took a flat plastic case from his pocket, opened it, and removed a syringe dart. Easing the tiny cork from its tip, he held the dart close to the scope, needle up, and pushed the plunger up slowly until a squirt of water jumped from the tip. He slipped the dart into place, raised the crossbow, and aimed. Releasing a deep breath, he squeezed the trigger.

A moment later the syringe dart appeared in the piece of fruit, only slightly off center. Very nearly a perfect shot.

Yes, he said quietly. Apologies, and sweet dreams, and may you never know what hit you.

⊞　⊟　⊞

He was about to begin his descent when he noticed a faint feeling of unease, a prickling at his neck that had nothing to do with the physical discomfort of the scope. Something was different. He peered around, seeing nothing in the blanched yellow light. Vegetation, tree trunks, a vertical spray of bamboo at one side of the clearing. Methodically, he checked the knots and buckles of his harness. Everything seemed secure. What was it?

He clicked off the scope, raised it, and listened, realizing that the sound of the forest had changed. The katydids and frogs had lowered their volume, and the other, more mysterious creatures were no longer sounding off. Wondering why, he saw a distant flicker of light, and felt disbelief, then a slow burn of anger. This was supposed to be a protected park.

The light disappeared, then came into view again, shifting wraith-like between tree trunks and high, buttressed root systems. Closer than before, and moving in his direction. He felt the anger drain away, displaced by a sense of his own vulnerability. The only people likely to be in the forest at night were poachers—and he was suspended above this clearing like a piñata.

He reeled in the climbing line which hung beneath him and tied it off on his harness. The irregular flickering moved nearer, becoming steadier and more distinct. He could hear the sound of bodies now, pushing through vegetation. The light flared, and divided in two, and then a pair of human shapes entered the clearing.

The two men wore miner-style carbide headlamps and ragged but practical forest clothing—tennis shoes, long pants, shirts buttoned to the neck against insects. Probably Ebrio, members of the tribe that bordered the northern and eastern boundaries of the park. One of them carried the limp form of a duiker—graceful even in death, with slender legs and tiny horns—across his shoulders; both had muzzle-loader shotguns. Not much of a weapon, but effective enough when a duiker froze, transfixed at the sudden light.

Equally effective, fired upward, point blank, at a biologist in a sling. Trowbridge felt his heart thudding in his chest, and told himself that they would walk right by and disappear into the trees. There was no good reason for them to look upward.

Almost directly beneath him now. One of the men glanced left and stopped, saying something in a low voice to his partner, who stopped as well, and swung his gaze. Trowbridge had forgotten about the target at the edge of the clearing, illuminated now by twin beams of light.

The two men approached the target slowly, as if it were something alive, not a crude outline of leaves and vines. He had a moment of incomprehension before he saw the scene through their eyes. This was West Africa, birthplace of the dark magic which had been exported in the holds of slave ships to the Caribbean to become voodoo; it was the middle of the night, in the middle of a tangled forest, and the two poachers beneath him were staring at what looked like a human shape on the forest floor. Within that talismanic outline, a single piece of fruit, bristling with darts.

He'd assumed they would look at the target and see science. Maybe start flashing those headlamps around in search of the scientist. But what they were seeing was *juju*, and very bad *juju* at that.

He concentrated on silence, on not making the slightest sound or movement. One of the men knelt beside the target. The other, in a frightened voice, said something; the first man rose, and they backed away and moved on quickly through the clearing. Their solid shapes pursued the wild, leaping shadows cast by their headlamps until soon there were only the two lights, fluttering like a pair of moths through the trees; then even those disappeared and he was alone again in darkness.

He released a deep breath. The unaccustomed quiet, which had moved along like a kind of envelope with the poachers, began to fill with a normal array of croaking, trilling, and buzzing. He brought the scope down, clicked it on, and studied the clearing where he'd intended to spend the night. Then he leaned back in the harness and looked up. In the lower reaches of the canopy, that wild riot of darkness, he made out the heavy limb of the *iroko* tree from which he hung suspended.

The forest floor seemed a less secure place than it had a few minutes ago, and the air was warm enough that he wouldn't need the light sleeping bag stowed in his pack. Anyway, the chimps did it every night.

He reached behind himself, unclipped the anchor line from the carabiner, and reeled himself in until he could place his boots against the trunk of the *iroko*. Grasping the dart, he worked it slowly out of the wood, stowing it in his bag as he swung away from the tree in a gentle arc. He slipped his foot into the sling attached to the lower of his two ascenders—devices developed to climb mountains, not trees—and took a high, one-legged step, sliding the top ascender up as he went. Shifting his weight back into the harness, he raised the lower ascender and took another upward step. The *iroko* was sacred to most of the people who lived around the park; he had the unscientific thought, as he ascended into darkness, that it might be good luck to spend his first night here within its high embrace.

2

The rain began at twilight, quietly at first, then gathering weight and strength until it drowned out the evening cacophony. Even now, during the relatively dry month of December, the forest got several inches of rain. Trowbridge, warm and dry amidst the great washing, sat on an old couch, a beer in his hand, facing out into the forest as the light failed, glad he was not spending a second night in the treetops.

He was alone at the *paillote*, a round slab of concrete perhaps fifteen meters across with a high thatched roof held up by support beams. The platform was sufficiently elevated to discourage snakes—there were no steps—and to stay dry during the rainy season. Aside from the beams, the *paillote* was open to the grass-filled clearing before it; there was no enclosing wall except at the back, behind a kitchen which consisted of a propane stove, a rusty refrigerator with a lock to keep monkeys out, and a sink which drew its water from a fifty-gallon drum on stilts. On one side of the kitchen a narrow door opened onto a small private room. A few meters away from the *pail-lote* was a smaller enclosed structure with shuttered windows—Jean Luc's quarters, the place where he and his family had spent most of the last ten years.

The station was airy, clean, and austere, but also clearly a settled place, a place where people lived. If you had to stay in one location for such a long time, Trowbridge thought—lighting a nub of candle which sat on the low table before him, then sitting back and looking out at the rain—you could do worse than this. His own quarters in the forest, once he established them, would not be so comfortable.

It was fully dark when three narrow figures, moving in single file, appeared out of the trees. Each wore a dark green poncho, fatigue pants, and rubber boots. Reaching the shelter of the overhanging *pail-lote*, they began pulling off ponchos. Two of the faces were white—intensely so against the surrounding darkness—and the third was black.

The first person boosted himself up, glanced at Trowbridge, and snorted quietly. "So, the world-famous biologist actually showed up," he commented, then headed toward the back of the *paillote*.

The second figure hopped more heavily up onto the concrete and put out his hand, a broad smile lighting up a young face. Speaking English with a thick French accent, he said, "You must be David Trowbridge. I know your work—I mean, *of course* I know your work. My name is Guy."

The young man's name, in French, rhymed with *tree*.

Before Trowbridge could reply, Guy looked past him with a panicked expression.

"*Je l'ai!*" he called out in French. "Jean Luc, I'll get it!"

The only answer was a hollow pumping noise, the sound of a gas lantern being pressurized.

"*Merde,*" Guy said. The lighting of the lantern, apparently, had been his job. He looked at Trowbridge ruefully, moved past him, and began struggling out of a wet shirt.

The third figure was leaning against one of the pillars. He flashed a swift, gentle smile at Trowbridge, but made no move either to introduce himself or to get out of his wet clothes, which dripped quietly on the concrete.

The familiar sounds of the lantern and the rain filled him with an unexpected nostalgia for earlier days, earlier studies. I'm getting older, he thought, seeing himself suddenly through Guy's eyes. And even here, buried in an obscure West African forest, I'm someone a young biology student has heard of. What a strange idea.

From the back of the station came the sound of a match being struck. There was a pop, and a steady hissing, and the station filled with light. Squinting against the brightness, Jean Luc reached above his head, hooked the lantern on a piece of line, and began shucking off his wet clothes. He was as lean as a marathon runner, narrow waisted and without an ounce of fat; he didn't look much like a father with two small children, which he was, or a distinguished scientist, which he was on his way to becoming. His features were handsome, almost boyish, and as lean as his body, but his skin was rough and pitted, scarred from the acne of younger days.

After twelve years, Trowbridge thought, he doesn't look a day older. And he hasn't gotten any easier to deal with.

"Difficult to get any work done, we have so many visitors these days," Jean Luc said conversationally. "Wouldn't you agree, Guy?"

He spoke English, apparently for Trowbridge's benefit, which Trowbridge—who spoke more than passable French—found annoying.

Guy, wringing out his trousers at the edge of the platform, looked over his shoulder apprehensively.

"Hard to imagine you get too many visitors," Trowbridge said, "given the condition of the road."

"I keep it that way on purpose."

"Ah," Trowbridge said. "Good idea."

Jean Luc disappeared out the back of the *paillote*, reappearing a few moments later in a clean T-shirt and cotton pants of some bright African fabric. He began conferring quietly—speaking a musical, West African French—with the man who leaned patiently against the post. Trowbridge studied Jean Luc's face, only half listening as the two men discussed plans for the following day. Jean Luc's expression was generous, almost intimate. The African, apparently, was someone of whom he approved.

"*Merci*, Gregoire," he finished quietly. When he held his hand out, Gregoire, instead of shaking it, brushed his own hand past Jean Luc's in a quick touch of fingers, then pulled up the hood of his poncho and jumped down into the rain.

Jean Luc glanced at Guy, who was furiously chopping some kind of meat in an attempt to redeem his failure with the lantern, then said to Trowbridge, "You're not vegetarian, are you?"

"No."

"Good. I wouldn't have let you come if you'd had special requirements."

Trowbridge said nothing. He hadn't, in fact, needed Jean Luc's permission to come to the park; what he'd needed, and received, was permission from the Ministry of Waters and Forests. Jean Luc had the title of associate park director, but he was Belgian—a citizen of the former colonial power—and was thus allowed to serve only as a *conseiller technique*, not a true administrator. This placed him in the position of having responsibility for much of the park's management without the authority to make real decisions; that power, as stipulated in the constitution, was reserved for citizens of Terre Diamantée, an independent country since 1963.

On the other hand, this pleasant island in the forest—the *paillote*, with its propane refrigerator and its shelter from the rain and its comfortable couches—*was* entirely Jean Luc's, because his university in Antwerp had funded its construction.

Jean Luc swung one leg over a rough-hewn bench, sat in a smooth motion, and studied Trowbridge with a certain disapproval, as if he were a poor-quality museum exhibit.

"So," he said finally, "still chasing cats, and still haven't managed to settle down and stick with anything, is that it?"

"Roughly," Trowbridge said, wondering why someone as rude as Jean Luc should be in that small group of people whose opinion he cared about.

"The reasons why no one's ever succeeded at studying leopards in the forest haven't changed. You think you can pull it off this time?"

Another figure came in out of the rain, the second of the two grad students Jean Luc had working for him. A young woman, probably around thirty, and nearly as slender as Jean Luc; Guy, with his comfortable belly straining the waistband of his shorts, looked almost obese compared to the two of them. In further contrast to Guy, she carried herself with quiet confidence, and was wise enough not to make any particular fuss over Trowbridge's arrival.

"Claire Fournier," she said, shaking his hand briefly.

"How is Odysseus?" Jean Luc asked her, reverting to French.

"Testing Lucifer again. Three full displays."

Jean Luc considered this a moment, then stood and moved into the kitchen. With a critical expression, he looked over Guy's shoulder into a pot filled with eggplant, onions, red peppers, and what smelled like mutton.

"Salome?" Jean Luc said, turning back toward Claire.

"Rejected Lucifer's advances twice. He looks desperate."

"Ah," Jean Luc said. "Hunting activity?"

"None," Claire said. "How's the new group doing?"

Jean Luc shrugged elaborately. "Well, they didn't scatter when Guy caught his camera strap on a branch, and lost his footing, and nearly hung himself. I suppose that must mean they're habituating."

Claire shot a quick glance of sympathy in Guy's direction, then ducked briefly into the room beside the kitchen and disappeared behind the station. Trowbridge wondered how long Guy had been here, and if he would last; Jean Luc had a reputation for going through two or three assistants for every one he kept. He heard a shower running above the sound of the rain, which seemed paradoxical. A few minutes later Claire reappeared, wearing jeans and a clean white oxford shirt, and began slicing tomatoes in the kitchen.

When she was finished Jean Luc pronounced dinner to be ready and ferried the cast-iron pot to the table, summoning Trowbridge with a nod. The four of them ate awhile in silence before Jean Luc launched into an unsolicited rundown of the situation in the park.

"The local park *directeur* is an idiot, and rarely visits the park, but thinks well of himself nonetheless. His boss, *l'Administrateur des Parcs Nationaux*, is worse; fortunately, he never leaves the capital, so he's a non-issue. The number two at *Parcs Nationaux*, Alain, is fairly good, but powerless; still, he's the one to talk to if you need something."

"I know Alain."

"That's right, you mentioned that. What else? Half the forest guards are corrupt, in their own individual ways—"

"What do you mean by 'corrupt'?"

"I mean they hunt the animals they're supposed to protect, and take bribes to let other hunters do the same."

"Not all of them," Claire said.

"No, some are too lazy to go into the forest, a quality they share with the park director. What else can I tell you? The local *magistrat* dines on poached bush meat every night in the best *maquis* in Kisanga, and has a fresh leopard skin—I thought that would get your attention, and yes, it's illegal—hanging over his fence to dry. He lets off the rare poacher who is actually arrested with a suspended sentence, then accepts an honorarium in his office, usually bush meat poached from the park."

"What about the locals? The Ebrio, and the immigrants?"

"The locals are hopeless, and the immigrants are worse. Africans have no feeling for animals—you ought to know that by now. We have to ram conservation down their throats. Aside from that, things are going fairly well. By West African standards this park is a raging success."

"The chimps?"

"The Ebrio have a taboo against hunting them. They say chimps are too similar to human beings. I suppose that's an insult to my study animals, but so far it's protected them, so I'm grateful."

"I wouldn't mind spending a day or two out with the chimps."

Jean Luc, pointedly, said nothing; Claire, with no change of expression, continued to eat. Guy was unable to restrain himself.

"I could take him out, Jean Luc," he volunteered, voice trailing off when he saw Jean Luc's face.

Jean Luc was staring coldly at Trowbridge.

"There won't be any kind of predator-prey study conducted in this park. I thought I made that clear."

"You did," Trowbridge said. "And I wouldn't undertake that kind of study without your cooperation. But I'm not going to ignore any data I find which might establish a leopard-chimp relationship."

"And I suppose you won't share such data with me unless I let you go out to see the chimps."

Trowbridge stood, carried his plate to the kitchen, and began to wash it.

"You make it sound like blackmail," he said.

"Leave the dishes. Gregoire's niece comes tomorrow. All right, Claire can take you out. I have my hands full trying to habituate twenty-three new chimps—*and* Guy—at the same time."

"Not tomorrow," Claire said immediately. "There's a lot going on right now. I don't want some newcomer out there screwing up the data. Sorry," she added, glancing at Trowbridge.

Her English, he noticed, was perfect, although her accent was hard to place.

"Science wins," Jean Luc said.

Claire added, "Even three or four days from now would be better."

"Maybe when I get back from the capital," Trowbridge said.

Claire nodded. Jean Luc carried his plate to the kitchen and stood staring out into the darkness. The rain was lashing down more heavily than ever; it looked and sounded as if the station were directly under a waterfall.

He said, "It's hard to believe, but it rains less these days than before. They've cut down so much forest in this country the weather's changing."

He motioned to a low cot at one side of the station.

"You're sleeping there, for as long as you're with us. There's no mosquito net, but you won't find many mosquitoes in the forest. As for you, Guy, go to bed, and no reading those trash novels. If you fall asleep tomorrow with the chimps I'll ship you back to Belgium."

3

The following morning Trowbridge spent three straight hours slogging through wet vegetation before he saw his first mammal, a banded duiker which broke from cover not three meters away, eyes wild and slender legs pumping as it dodged off in a low rush and leaped through a gap of yellow sunlight. For a split second the solid, terrified little forest antelope was lit up like a watercolor; he had a clear vision of its dark haunch stripes, the scent-gland slashes on its cheeks like scarification, its finger-sized, swept-back horns, and then it was gone. In its absence the forest seemed a bit more alive, a bit more promising a place.

He had another good moment an hour later when a dove exploded from its place of cover nearly beneath his feet, and he tipped his head back, shading his eyes, seeing the flash of pale blue head above cinnamon-colored wings as it labored upward through the forest's interior space. The canopy, delicate and infinitely green, seemed to wheel down to meet it; he wondered if the dove would roost somewhere in the treetops, but it slipped out through a delicate gap between branch tips and disappeared. This gap was known as crown shyness, the reluctance of trees—which looked, at first glance, to be incredibly tangled—actually to touch one another.

He stared a moment at the intricate pattern of leaves, the cloudless sky behind it like pale blue lace, feeling vertigo and a slight sense of loss. Then he lowered his gaze, and pushed on. Unfortunately, healthy bird and duiker populations didn't add up to evidence of leopard. He hadn't seen a single sign, throughout the course of the morning, that leopards lived in this park. Not a scrape on the forest floor, not a trace of scat, not a claw mark on a tree. Nothing.

And the forest was incredibly tough to move through, choked and tangled, impossible to navigate in anything like a straight line. Buttressed root systems higher than his head surrounded the bases of the larger trees; vines and lianas hung from the canopy, twining into downed logs to make impenetrable curtains of vegetation; thin, insidious creepers, adorned with sharp tiny thorns, tore at his legs.

It was nearly noon when it came to him why this forest was so difficult. He stopped, transfixed by the simple explanation. He'd assumed it was just different vegetation. But it was more than that. There were no elephant lanes.

Unfortunately, in the course of this revelation he forgot one of the prime rules of the forest: Watch your foot placement. His thoughts were broken into by an odd whisper of feeling on one knee; when he looked down, he saw a dark rope of driver ants flowing up his leg into his shorts. Driver ants, which moved across the forest floor in columns as thick as a man's arm, attacked almost anything that lived, and were clever enough to cover some distance before announcing their presence by a vigorous piercing of the skin—a process which began the moment he flung off his pack, dancing and swearing and stripping off his clothes, and began knocking the ants from his lower body.

⁙ ▯⦂ ⁙

Notes for the day, he told himself, stepping out of the outdoor shower behind the station, ruefully inspecting the damage before pulling on a pair of shorts: *Leopards a question mark. Healthy population of driver ants.*

He resisted the urge to scratch the several dozen welts between his knees and waist; they would be bad enough as it was during the course of a long drive to the capital. He opened the refrigerator, found some leftover rice and sauce, ate quickly, then grabbed his bag and stepped down off the *paillote* and walked toward his truck, tossing the bag in the cab and popping the hood release.

Claire emerged from the forest and came around the concrete island of the station. He raised a hand in greeting. Unbuckling the webbed belt which held her canteen and notebook, she dumped it onto the couch, and ran her hands through sweaty, tousled hair as she watched him raise the hood and check the oil. Her face and chest were sunburnt; above the top button of her khaki shirt, a small "V" of pale skin showed, emphasizing the green of her eyes.

"Jean Luc never mentioned the two of you had met," she said. "Much less that you knew each other."

"We didn't get along all that well."

"Somehow that doesn't surprise me. What were you studying?"

"Leopards."

"And it didn't work out?"

Trowbridge slammed down the hood of the truck.

"I had trouble finding them. When I did, and managed to collar a couple, tracking them with a radio antenna was cumbersome work. I wasn't getting enough data, and the foundation refused to extend the grant."

The Ituri, an inaccessible forest in northeastern Zaire, had been his first field study after getting his Ph.D. As the study came apart around him he'd been increasingly desperate, terrified it would mean the end of his career. As it turned out, the Ituri had been his only real failure as a field biologist—and the only extensive work he'd done in tropical forest; most of his work since then had been done on the open plains and in the mountains.

"I thought of something that might help you. You're going to be working in the interior of the forest, right? Not just near the station."

"Yes."

"You should talk to Alberto. He's Italian, runs the sawmill you passed coming down from Sandoukou."

"A sawmill?"

She heard the skepticism in his voice.

"Alberto's been here twenty-five years, and he's spent a fair amount of time in the park. He collects orchids, and he's interested in elephants. Of course you're free to maintain your professional purity and snub him because of what he does for a living."

He studied her. She was straightforward to the point of being blunt, and displayed no commonly female traits of accommodation or willingness to compromise. He appreciated this, but it wasn't necessarily going to make her any easier to deal with.

And she was nice-looking, he realized. Fine pale features, something quick and watchful behind those green eyes. She didn't make a point of being attractive, and he hadn't noticed it particularly last night, but it was true.

"Alberto has a plane," she added, "and he likes to fly. He might take you up. Give you a better sense of the park."

"Where do I find him?"

"He lives behind the mill—you can't miss it on the *piste*. Jean Luc and he don't get along, so you don't need to mention I suggested this."

"Deal," he said. "Your English is flawless. How—"

"Swiss mom, American dad."

"Where'd you grow up?"

"Everywhere, after they got divorced. Are you driving all the way to the capital? The roads are pretty bad after dark."

"I'll spend the night in Sandoukou."

"There's only one hotel there. It's pretty awful."

He shrugged, somewhat annoyed at the presumption behind that statement. "This isn't my first time in Africa. And I'm used to something less than four-star hotels."

"It's your funeral," she said.

⚏ ⚎ ⚏

Twilight, this close to the equator, came early and short, catching him on the dirt track between Jean Luc's station and the main *piste*. The track was still muddy from the morning rain, and seemed to gather the darkness from the sky and intensify it; he felt as if he were negotiating a low green tunnel through the trees.

The French term—*forêt dense humide*—was more accurate than "rain forest," he thought, flicking on the headlights as he launched the Toyota into a body of water that hadn't been there when he drove in. A root scraped the skid plate; foliage whacked his elbow and the side of his face, and scraped loudly along the body of the truck. When he reached the first of three makeshift bridges he stopped and got out to make sure the crossbeams were spaced evenly, then drove slowly across, heart in his throat as the truck bounced and jumped and the bridge seemed to sag to one side. It was only a couple of meters down to the narrow watercourse, but it would be a lousy place to get stuck—particularly since the Toyota would probably go in upside down.

Fifty meters farther on he saw something profiled in his headlights. Something small, perhaps twice the size of a house cat. He let the truck roll to a stop, expecting whatever it was to disappear into the brush, but it made no move to do so. Instead—as the engine idled quietly and he vowed never to leave the binoculars at the station again—it continued washing its face.

The head shape, even in twilight, was too elegant for a civet; it was a cat of some kind. In this part of the world, that meant he was looking either at an adult African golden cat, or a subadult leopard.

The cat paused in its washing and swiveled its head to look at him. Green eyeshine, a reflection from the headlights, seemed to leap from its face. A golden, he decided, making out the ears—small and sharp, almost pointed—and the narrow, rounded face. Probably a solitary male, taking a break from his twilight hunt.

And I'm about to lose him, he realized, watching the nervous tail movements.

With a bound, the cat was gone. Trowbridge let the truck drift forward and sat staring into the forest. Golden cats, reclusive and little known, had a mysterious habitat connection to leopards; they were known throughout West Africa as *le frère du léopard*. No one knew why, but where there were goldens, there were usually leopards.

In theory, that should be extremely encouraging. On the other hand, he'd just spent two totally unsuccessful days looking for cat sign. A sighting like this, coming when least expected and through no effort of his own, was a pointed reminder of the difficulties of studying predators in the forest. One didn't make a systematic study of a species by spotting an individual animal on a muddy road at twilight—no matter how much of a pleasure such a sighting might be.

He put the truck into gear and drove down a long slope through the high trees.

☷ ䷜ ☷

Black Leopard

The study, as he had proposed it, and as the Society and a well-heeled scientific foundation had funded it, entailed radio-collaring six leopards with contiguous home ranges, then remote-tracking them in real time for movement patterns, interaction, and behavior. Six months from now, if things went well, he would have a detailed portrait of a small population of wild leopards, information you couldn't get in a lab or a zoo. As studies went, this was ambitious in its scope, but not revolutionary in its aim; what made it unusual was the location. Virtually all the data on African leopards had come from east or southern Africa, where leopards were easy to find—pressured by lions, their arch enemies, they spent a fair amount of time draped in thorn trees or on rocky *kopjes*—and easy to habituate, because the biologist doing so was enclosed in a nonthreatening, box-shaped vehicle. In addition to the technical advantages, the savannah was a congenial environment in which to work—the air was dry, temperatures were reasonable, sunsets and sunrises were spectacular, and there was a comfortable tent to retire to in the evenings.

The forest, by contrast, was arguably the most difficult working environment in the world, especially if you were studying a ranging predator like a leopard, not tree shrews or butterflies. Visibility was so curtailed that simply *finding* a study animal, as he'd discovered in the Ituri, could be an insurmountable challenge. Leopards had phenomenal hearing and sight, and the gift of silent movement; they simply slipped away when a biologist came blundering along the way he had this morning. Habituating a forest leopard to human presence was assumed to be impossible, given the density of vegetation and the fact that you couldn't use a jeep. And working without a jeep had safety implications; leopards, on the whole, were more likely to flee than attack, but there were plenty of attacks on record, many of them fatal.

For all these reasons, biologists knew a good deal about the behavior of savannah leopards—and a fair amount about leopards in the Kalahari Desert, and even in the Himalayas, where they shared terrain with snow leopards—but virtually nothing about their forest cousins.

The several boxes of electronic gear awaiting him in Pont Noir made up a system he hoped would let him surmount the difficulties posed by the forest. If he succeeded, he would have papers not only on ranging patterns and behavior, but on new tracking techniques a generation of researchers could make use of. A very strong upside, as one of his colleagues had remarked. But a *chasm* of a downside; the system was untried, and the technology had been expensive. The Society would have been happy to fund a traditional binoculars-and-notebook study, but computer gear, custom-built radio collars, and satellite time meant writing a grant and approaching one of the big foundations. When a proposal like this came in, foundations sent it to the other names in the field for comment; in his case every reviewer had expressed cautious interest in the research, but serious doubts about the viability of his methods. It had taken all his persuasiveness, and all the scientific weight of the Society, to convince the foundation to go ahead. He wouldn't lose his job if the study failed, but he—and the Society—would lose a good deal of credibility. It would be harder to ask for money next time around.

Moonlight appeared abruptly around him. The canopy became ragged islands of darkness, then opened to the sky, and he found himself driving through a cleared field. He passed a sign which marked the boundary of a *Parc National de la République de Terre Diamantée;* hunting and gold mining were declared to be illegal.

That'll stop them, he thought.

A smell of wet soil filled the truck; around him were rows of waist-high cocoa plants. You rarely smelled dirt in the forest, where leaf litter covered what little soil there was. It occurred to him for the hundredth time that the predator-prey study would have been a potentially saving addition to what he was doing here. Two long-shot studies gave better odds of success than one; the foundation cared less about *what* he produced, than *whether.*

Never mind, he told himself. Focus on this one, and do it right. Six months, three solid papers, you've justified the study budget, and you're gone.

He slewed around a tight corner, downshifted into first, and climbed a muddy hill. As he crested the hill the track dead-ended into what Jean Luc referred to as "the main road." This was something of an overstatement; the *piste* before him, threading north-south within the strip of land between the park and the border with neighboring Denkyara, was unpaved, but had at least been graded since the last rainy season, mainly so lumber trucks could thunder up and down it. With a fair amount of faith in one's luck, and a willingness to beat hell out of your vehicle, you could do sixty or seventy kilometers an hour on this road.

Twenty kilometers to the south was Kisanga, a town of several hundred people with a market he would visit later for supplies. Eighty kilometers beyond that was Granville, a small city wrapped around a rare opening in the stretch of coast known in slave days as the White Man's Grave. A steady stream of timber and rubber and bananas went out of Granville, and not much came in; most imports went to the capital city, Pont Noir, two hundred kilometers west, where the politicians reigned and people had more money. He imagined the long breakers of the Atlantic pounding in darkness on the beaches near Granville. It might be a nice change, after a while in the forest, to take a few days off and see some open space.

At the moment, his destination was Sandoukou, at the northeastern corner of the park, where he hoped to find a meal and a bed. He turned left and accelerated up the *piste*, which moved in great sinuous curves, like a dark riverbed, through the ragged, depleted forest. The villages he passed were lit by orange firelight, not electricity; fire-lumined figures walked here and there between mud-and-wattle huts. He nearly hit a short-legged goat which ran out before him, its alert, diabolical face shining like a pie pan in his headlights; then he drove past the sawmill, a high dark shape set back from the *piste* with a curtain of smoke behind it stained red from a vast mound of burning sawdust. His headlights flashed across a field filled with the great tumbled bulk of felled trees, lying like stacked limbs, and then the darkness filled in around him, and he drove for another hour, a taste of smoke in his mouth, until he crossed an archaic-looking bridge above a dark river which tumbled and roared over rocks, and pulled slowly into a town where it wasn't supposed to be dark, where he had to search for the hotel by shining his flashlight out the window of the truck.

4

The Hôtel de la Prospérité et Tranquillité had been built during the days when the Belgians still controlled Terre Diamantée, or perhaps during the decade immediately after independence, when cocoa and coffee prices were high, and the diamonds were still flowing. The darkened, two-story structure still gave an impression of solidity, albeit a somewhat run-down solidity; there was an enclosed yard out front, and a broad terrace which opened to a sizable, if gloomy, restaurant with a black-and-white tile floor. A kerosene lantern suspended over the bar gave off a yellowish light. Two people sitting at another table—Africans who looked as if they might work there—paid him no attention when he walked in.

Behind the bar a short, broad, suspicious-looking European woman, wearing a shapeless sack of a dress, looked at him with a certain hostility, as if he'd walked into her living room.

It's hotter here than in the forest, he realized.

"*Qu'est-ce que tu veux?*" the woman said uncivilly.

"A cold beer," he said, "and something to eat. And a room with *climatisation*, if you think the electricity might come back on."

Some of the cottages, he'd noticed on the way in, had the square shapes of air conditioners in their windows.

The woman laughed. It was a short, bitter sound.

"Do you think you're in Paris?" she said.

Reaching beneath the bar, she brought up a beer, opened it, and brushed the cap onto the floor. As she pushed the bottle toward him a skinny cat leaped up onto the bar beside his elbow.

Two cat sightings in one day, he thought, looking it over. Not bad. Although this particular feline, with its chewed-up ears and crossed eyes, wasn't much of a specimen.

The beer was about the same temperature as the air.

"How long has the electricity been out?"

The woman stared at him a moment, then reached out and picked up the cat, cradling it in her arms.

"All day," she said, stroking the cat. "*Les nègres* are on strike again. It means nothing to me. Let them destroy their country if they like. There's nothing left here anyway. There's been nothing left since my husband died."

She looked past him at the two Africans with a tired glare. "They did it, you know. They made him crazy, because they don't know how to work, and they steal anything that isn't nailed down. It's no wonder his heart gave out. In any case, they're all dying of AIDS. I suppose it's God's revenge, *n'est-ce pas?*"

Trowbridge opened a menu lying on the bar.

"Don't bother," she said, stroking the cat steadily. "It's too late for dinner."

"What about an omelette?"

She dropped the cat unceremoniously and disappeared. A few minutes later she came back with a small omelette looking forlorn on a chipped orange plate beside some greasy french fries. Fortunately, there was also half a baguette, and some decent mustard. He ate standing at the bar while the woman stared out into the night. The cat hung limply in her arms, and looked hot.

"American?" she said finally.

He nodded.

"You must be with the timber company. Like the other one."

She'd probably been beautiful, he realized. A long time ago, when she was younger and not so bitter.

"I can't say I much like him, your friend. Something opportunistic there. Something cheap. You want to wash your hands after talking with him. But we never got a very good class of Belgians here—why should you Americans be any different?"

He said nothing.

She said, "Let me give you some advice. Watch out for the Lebanese if you're trying to make money in Terre Diamantée. They have their fingers into everything."

Trowbridge finished the omelette. He could feel her eyes on him. There was a faint sheen of sweat on her upper lip.

He said, "What about the air conditioning?"

Her face changed, and she cleared his plate away and dropped a large key onto the bar in front of him.

"This room has an air conditioner. But there won't be any electricity tonight, so it won't do you a lot of good."

She turned and disappeared into the kitchen, taking the cat. A moment later he heard footsteps going upstairs. He glanced behind himself and saw he was alone in the dim restaurant.

Well, it could be worse, he thought. Lord knows I've stayed in worse, and gone hungry doing it.

He went out to the truck, found some clean clothes and a flashlight, and began looking among the darkened cinderblock cottages for number five. Against the back wall of one cottage were silhouettes that looked almost like cages. When he aimed his flashlight at them he realized that was exactly what they were—and that three of the cages contained the shapes of animals.

His heart sank, but he resisted the urge simply to walk away. There was no changing it by not seeing what was there.

The animals were monkeys, and the wire cages were barely large enough for them to stand up in, particularly the two black-and-white colobus. In the wild, these were gorgeous, solidly muscled creatures given to acrobatic flights through the canopy, with black, spiky hair on their heads, and long tails tufted in white. These two lay on their sides, breathing quickly in the unaccustomed heat, barely opening their eyes as he came closer. The smaller of the two, a female, was sick; there was loose feces stuck to the wire of the cage bottom, and a bad smell.

The third monkey was a young diana, a male with a dark, ancient face. Dianas were among the most beautiful of all African monkeys, with lustrous, harlequin-patterned fur that was red, gray, white, and black. This animal's fur was dingy and colorless, its face marked with open sores. At Trowbridge's approach it grew tense and began thrashing about, screaming and baring its teeth. Then it flung itself against the cage front, clutching the wire, mashing its face into the wire, staring with eyes that could only be described as insane.

Behind him, with a sudden roar, a generator started up. He looked back at the main structure of the hotel. There was light in an upstairs room. Above the sound of the generator he heard an air conditioner go on. He stood a moment, then looked again at the monkeys, wondering how long they'd been there—how long, precisely, it took to reduce an animal to this condition—and turned away.

Number five, he discovered, was the cottage with the monkey cages against its back wall. He stood in the doorway, playing his flashlight over the interior, wondering whether it would be worth trying to get another room. He wasn't sure where the keys were kept, however—they hadn't been evident behind the bar—and he had no desire to climb the stairs to the Belgian woman's bedroom.

Anyway, he thought, the rooms are probably all just about this hot, filthy, and filled with mosquitoes.

He pulled down the blanket on the narrow bed, shined his light at the sheets, then pulled the cover back up and went back to the truck for his sleeping bag. When he returned he locked the door behind him, threw the truck keys onto a rickety table, and spread the sleeping bag on the bed. Then he went into the bathroom, which smelled of damp concrete and had water stains on the ceiling. Setting his flashlight on a dusty sink, he stripped to take a shower. It took a full minute for the water to begin its rusty dribble, and the rough concrete floor was black with scum, but he was able to soap himself, and rinse, and felt better for it.

Thankfully, the diana, which he guessed was directly under the single window above the sink, had stopped screaming.

When he lay down on the bed he felt sweat break out immediately. He considered opening a window, but decided it would only add to the mosquito population buzzing at his ears. Sleep eluded him, despite his exhaustion. He couldn't repress the simple, insistent thought that had been coming to him since this morning. You can't do it, it wasn't technically feasible, Jean Luc was right—there were good reasons why no one had studied leopards successfully in the forest, reasons why he'd failed the first time.

He wiped the sweat from his face and opened his eyes in the darkness. This failure of confidence was somewhat ironic, given the awe with which Guy had looked at him. He didn't much enjoy that sort of attention, and wasn't entirely used to it yet. A two-part newspaper profile last year in *The New York Times* had catapulted him from the ranks of the obscure to the ranks of the known; he'd found it embarrassing, although Gordon had been happy about it, because it was good publicity for the Society, and publicity brought in members and donations.

I preferred being promising and obscure, he thought, considering Gordon, who—after Goodall, and maybe Schaller—was probably the best-known field biologist in the world, and had been Trowbridge's role model and something of a father figure when he was at the university.

No, he thought, in theory, at least, there shouldn't be any problem with confidence. Gordon had paid him the highest compliment you could imagine. Only he didn't want what Gordon had offered.

⸻ ⸻ ⸻

After twenty years as director of the Society, Gordon was retiring. In part because his health was poor—years of working in the tropics had left him with a persistent and debilitating case of malaria—and in part because he was just plain tired of the administrative grind of running one of the three largest wildlife conservation bodies in the country. Like most groupings of scientists and conservationists, the Society was riven with conflicts. Things had been particularly difficult during the last couple of years; Gordon, at one point, had called an evening meeting at his home in Darien, a quiet, tree-filled town an hour from New York City. It had been Gordon's hope that getting the various antagonists out of the office, letting them hash things out in his big old comfortable house, would dilute some of the poison. The meeting, however, had been acrimonious, with ragged, repetitive arguments over the role of a wildlife society which had started, a hundred years ago, as a loose organization of geographers and hunters, and now had to make a series of difficult decisions on what role it would play in the modern world. Which causes to embrace, which political battles to fight, which issues to take unpopular stands on, even if it meant alienating some of the people who contributed money.

The only question which hadn't been discussed—and it was the question which would eventually decide most of the others—was the succession to the directorship. Gordon, looking thoughtful and unhappy, had raised an eyebrow at Trowbridge as the meeting ended and the others piled into cars and drove off into a chilly fall evening. The two of them had been left standing in Gordon's study, a place, with its piles of old books, maps on the wall, and African masks, that Trowbridge loved. Gordon was sipping port, which he was not supposed to do; his homely, weathered face was serious.

"David," he'd said unexpectedly, "I could lever you into the directorship. It would mean a hell of a fight with the board—they'll complain that you're too young—but I could do it. You'd have to stay on at least three years, though—*at least* three years—to make it worth the damage I'd have to do."

Trowbridge had stared at him in disbelief.

"What are you looking at?" Gordon had said crossly.

"I'm flattered, but I don't think I'd be good at it. I'm not sure I want it."

Gordon had stared back at him with the hard expression which surprised those who knew only his more genial exterior.

"You misunderstand. First, you *would* be good at it—you underestimate your ability to run an organization. Second, I'm not even considering what you want or don't want. I'm thinking about the Society. The next five years are going to be critical, and I can't do it. Give me that much, and then you can spend the rest of your life in the field. I understand that's your first love—believe me, I understand. But we can't always take the selfish course."

Gordon had given him six months to make up his mind. Six months for a study he was suddenly convinced he couldn't pull off. A mosquito dived at his ear; he waved at it, and wiped the sweat from his face again, and thought of his father, an administrator for most of his working life. A man who probably shouldn't, by temperament, have been an administrator, and had died too young; a man who'd enjoyed being surrounded by friends and family, and had died alone.

The thin sleeping bag beneath him was damp, already, with sweat. He visualized the station, the relatively cool air, the absence of mosquitoes. He ought to be excited at the beginning of a new study—particularly one he'd been thinking about for years—not scared. It's just been too long, he told himself, since you've been alone, hard at work, and of a single mind. That's all.

Gordon, he decided, was not going to get what he wanted. The hell with the Society. He'd been dragged into enough administrative work during the last two years to last him a lifetime. On the brief and doubtful momentum provided by that decision, he drifted, finally, into a fitful sleep, which lasted until he was wakened by the sound of the screeching diana.

5

The screaming seemed to fill the room. Reluctantly, he came fully awake and opened his eyes. The moon must have risen; there was a silver outline around the curtained window. His body was drenched in sweat, and his head throbbed, and the generator from the main part of the hotel was still roaring, making a nice background to the relentless shrieks of the diana.

Okay, Claire, he thought wearily, you're right—this is one of the all-time shitholes I've ever stayed in. He got out of bed and closed the door to the bathroom. This muffled the high-pitched screams, but not much.

Maybe another guest, arriving late, had set off the monkey. He looked at the luminous dial of his watch.

Almost five in the morning. Seemed unlikely.

He slipped into pants and tennis shoes, picked up his flashlight, and went to the door. Might as well have a look; he wouldn't get back to sleep any time soon, and it was probably cooler outside. He put his hand on the doorknob, then paused, realizing the diana might be screaming because there was someone outside his room. Someone who'd seen him, a conspicuous white face driving through Sandoukou, and—knowing this was the only hotel—decided to rob him.

No, he thought. Don't be paranoid. It's just a monkey screaming in a cage.

At that moment the doorknob moved. He pulled his hand back, startled, then touched the knob again, lightly, to be sure.

Tiny movements, back and forth, as if someone were trying to determine, without waking him, if the door were locked.

He considered yelling for help. Unfortunately, the only person certain to be nearby was the Belgian woman, who was unlikely to hear him above the roar of the generator. He did a quick mental survey of the room. The door, and the barred window beside it, were the only ways in or out. No, there was the window in the bathroom. Large enough to squeeze through, if he remembered correctly. But it was barred as well. Unless someone actually tried to beat the door down— or had a duplicate key—he ought to be safe in here.

The doorknob stopped moving.

Maybe they'll go away, he thought.

A heavy slamming rocked the door, bouncing it in its frame. He stood a moment in disbelief, heart pounding furiously. A second blow, then a third. This was crazy—were they trying to kick it in? Could they, if they went on kicking long enough? Half-frightened and half-furious, he looked down at the gap at the bottom of the door, drew a deep breath, and yelled, *"Arrête!"* The pounding stopped. He pulled his wallet from the back pocket of his pants, took out a wad of *befa* amounting to about thirty dollars, and said, in a loud voice, *"J'ai cinq cent befa ici! Prends-le, et va t'en!"*

He leaned down and shoved the money under the door.

There was a silence. Then the money disappeared, and someone laughed, and said, "Very nice, friend. Nicer if you give us what we want."

It took him a moment to realize it had been English spoken, not French. He stepped to the window and peered between the curtain and frame, hoping to see someone walking away. Instead he saw a pair of dark shapes, so close he could have reached out and touched them. He had a quick view of the nearer man's face—one temple marked with three neat scars, the other temple, strangely, without scarification—before he saw the rifle.

The next thing he knew the man had swung the rifle up and pointed it at his chest.

He jumped back in panic, and heard laughter. The rifle went off with a hard crack, sending a flush of adrenaline through him that was physically painful. No shattering of glass; the rifle hadn't been aimed at the window. Another crack, and the doorknob bounced in the door, tilting at an odd angle. They were shooting the lock out. He looked desperately around the room, hesitated, then picked up the wooden chair beside the table, held it sideways in the darkness, and swung it hard in a tight circle against the curtained window.

The ensuing explosion of glass would have gone directly into the face of anyone standing there.

He dropped the chair, grabbed his flashlight, and ran into the bathroom, pulling the door shut behind him and throwing the dead bolt. There was more firing, someone speaking a language he didn't recognize, a voice that was angry now. He aimed the flashlight at the bathroom window, the beam shaking slightly in his hand. Three solid bars, just as he remembered. He played the flashlight around the small room and saw an "S"-shaped catchment pipe lying on the floor beneath the sink. Scooping it up, he went to the window.

The first bar, loose in its frame, pulled out almost immediately in a small shower of plaster. The second, after a few blows, wobbled like a loose tooth. He grabbed it with both hands, worked it back and forth, then used the piece of pipe to knock it out into the darkness.

All three monkeys were screaming now. The last bar, dead center in the window before him, refused to budge. He bashed at it with the pipe, then gouged at the plaster around its base, hitting it again and again, hearing himself sobbing with the effort. A sound of splintering wood came from the bedroom. He redoubled his efforts and felt something in the recalcitrant steel bar give a little. He hit it once more with everything he had, and sent it flying with a neat clink out the window. More splintering behind him, the sound of a door slamming open, a brief deafening round of gunfire inside the room. He boosted himself up into the narrow opening, wriggled through, and rolled down into darkness, landing painfully atop one of the monkey cages, bouncing down onto dirt. The generator went silent, suddenly, leaving only the berserk chorus of monkeys and a wild thrashing in the cages.

A moment later he was up and sprinting between a pair of cottages toward an open field and a shadowy line of trees.

When he reached the trees he dove beneath the foliage, rolled onto his belly, and watched two dim figures come around the cottage, walking easily, the one with the rifle carrying it over his shoulder. Above the incessant screaming of the monkeys, he heard a low boom, and looked up. The Belgian woman was standing at an upstairs balcony. She cocked a shotgun and fired again. Not the right weapon, he thought, not at this distance. The men by the cottage laughed as she stepped back into the bedroom. One of the men raised the rifle, and Trowbridge put his head down.

The firing began. A window near the upstairs balcony exploded, followed by another in one of the cottages. Then the chorus of animal screams diminished abruptly, and diminished again, until there was only one frantic voice left in the darkness—unmistakably the crazed diana, with the dingy fur and the wild eyes—and then that ceased as well. When he put his head up he saw the two men trotting between the individual cottages toward the parking area. He heard another burst of firing, then the sound of an engine and someone driving away, and finally just the sound of insects, and birds, as the sky above him felt its way slowly toward a pale dawn.

6

He waited until he was sure no one was coming back, then walked out from beneath the trees and across the field to the restaurant, where there was a telephone on the wall. He found change in his pocket and called the number for *Gendarmes* written on a yellowed piece of paper tacked beside the phone. When he got no answer he tried calling the operator, and got no answer there.

A small town, and barely six in the morning. He put the phone down, went behind the bar, and tried the door into the kitchen, which had been blocked by something heavy. He stood a moment, then walked out onto the terrace and sat in a wicker chair, waiting until the morning sun—and then a decrepit-looking police car—made an appearance.

Two policemen in tan uniforms got out of the car. One of them was tall, one short. They stared at him a minute without speaking, then walked over to the cottage and looked in through the open door. When they walked around back he got up and went over to where they were standing by the monkey cages, looking down at the still shapes.

"Vous êtes l'Américain?" the tall policeman asked.

No, he thought, I'm Shirley Fucking Temple, just down from an Austrian mountaintop. He was bug-bitten, exhausted, and had several nasty welts on his chest from having squeezed out the narrow window. But he only nodded.

"Ça va?"

"Oui," Trowbridge said. *"Ça va."*

"Vous n'êtes pas blessé?"

Trowbridge shook his head.

"Pourquoi ils ont tué les singes?" the short policeman wondered aloud, looking down at the cages.

The diana's body had been hit by seven or eight bullets, but its head was untouched, its expression oddly calm. There was a pool of blood around its mouth.

"I don't know," he said. "Maybe they were disappointed at not getting me. What happens now?"

"Nous attendons le préfet."

"Can I get my things out of the room?"

The tall policeman shook his head. *"Ça, c'est la preuve."*

The short policeman was still looking down at the monkey cages with a perplexed face.

"I don't understand it," he said finally. "Bullets are expensive. And so many bullets ruins the meat."

Trowbridge walked between the cottages to the dirt parking area. A smoke-blue mist hung above the river to the east, curling through the high trees beyond; the air smelled of morning cook fires and fresh fruit. Even from a distance he could see that his truck was lower to the ground than it should be. When he walked closer he saw that all four tires had been shot out. He moved to the back of the truck, knelt, and looked beneath the rear bumper.

The spare, suspended in its rack, looked all right. That was something. But where was he going to get four new tires in a town like this?

He went back to number five. The doorknob had been blown entirely through the hardwood door, leaving a hand-sized hole. Shards of glass sparkled in the morning sun beneath the broken-out window, and there were drops of blood on the concrete. That would be the man with the rifle, the man with scarification on only one temple. He wasn't sorry, although it had upped the ante last night. When he looked in through the open door he saw with a somewhat hollow feeling that his sleeping bag and duffel bag had been perforated by gunfire.

He walked back to the main hotel building. The Belgian woman was standing on the terrace, wearing the same shapeless dress, as if she'd slept in it. She was looking at him as if this were his fault.

"You see?" she said bitterly. "It's a fine country in which to do business. Really, it's too much. They never attacked my hotel before."

Trowbridge stared at her in disbelief, then saw that the large fan above the dining room was turning slowly. The electricity must be back on. He cleaned up as best he could in the restaurant bathroom, and found himself, a few minutes later, sitting shirtless on the terrace, drinking very good *café au lait* and eating toasted baguette with butter and apricot preserves. He was midway through his second coffee when a dusty blue Peugeot sedan pulled up and a man in a red track suit got out. The man stood a moment, taking in the truck with flat tires and Trowbridge sitting on the terrace. Then he slouched rapidly, hands in pockets, over to Trowbridge's hotel room. He studied its interior, then walked around the outside of the cottage, where the two *flics* saluted him with a sudden display of energy and bodily right angles. Returning the salutes casually, he disappeared behind the cottage for a couple of minutes, then came across the courtyard and up the terrace steps. He looked to be in his late thirties; he had intensely black skin, and skeptical eyes behind horn-rimmed glasses.

"You're the American," he said, speaking English—American English—with only a hint of a West African accent.

"Yes."

"Douli ba," the man said, extending a hand.

His palm was pale compared with the rest of him; his grip, when they shook hands, was firmer than that of most West Africans.

"I'm the *sous-préfet*—acting *préfet* for the area. You know what a *préfet* is, right?"

Trowbridge nodded. *Préfets* were the equivalent of district governors; they reported directly to the capital, and in this very centralized system had a good deal more power than local elected officials such as mayors.

Douli ba, unexpectedly, grinned. In Trowbridge's experience West African officials didn't make that expression very often. They either repressed the feeling, or smiled cautiously.

"You're wondering if someone in a track suit can really be a *sous-préfet*, aren't you?"

Douli ba pulled out a wallet and showed him a badge with a little insignia of a bull elephant beneath a pair of crossed palm trees. Then he tipped his head toward the cottage where Trowbridge had spent most of the night.

"Do you always bust up a hotel room like this?" he asked.

❊ ❊ ❊

"I understand," Douli ba said, "given the rifle, how you might feel they were trying to kill you. But it's more likely they just wanted to rob you."

"They didn't seem very interested in my money."

"You didn't offer them very much—and they probably wanted the keys to your truck as well. You said they spoke English, right?"

"Yes."

"I hate to say this, because we have a tendency to blame everything on the country next door, but that suggests it was someone from Denkyara. The border's only about fifteen kilometers from here—and it's pretty much chaos on the other side. No, not chaos, exactly. More like anarchy, which is a different thing. A lot of people with guns and ambition and not much else, trying to impose their own particular kind of order."

"Does this kind of thing happen often?"

"Not often. But when it does, it's usually for straightforward reasons—money, car keys, and girlfriends."

"Good thing I only had the first two in the room. They might have been really difficult."

Douli ba looked at him questioningly a moment. Then a smile crossed his face.

"I'm glad to see you've kept your sense of humor. Most Westerners seem to lose that when they come to Africa—and it's precisely when they need it most."

"I got a look at one of them. He had scarification on one side of his face, but not the other."

Douli ba looked doubtful. "It's understandable if you got that wrong, given that it was dark, and you must have been a little scared. An African doesn't do that to just one side of his face."

"Three short lines on the temple."

"That's Ebrio. Which means they could have been from either Denkyara or Terre Diamantée. But the scarring would have been on both sides."

Trowbridge didn't think he was wrong about this, but there was no point pushing it.

"The border divides the Ebrio, I take it."

"Right down the center. Ebrio on both sides. Not a terribly logical arrangement."

Trowbridge braced himself for a lecture on the ineptness of colonial border makers. Instead, Douli ba said, "On the other hand, it's hard to say what *would* have been a logical border. You can't have a separate country for every tribe in Africa—there are over a thousand."

Douli ba sipped his *café au lait*, looking at it appreciatively. "For such an unpleasant woman," he said, "she makes very good coffee."

"You don't strike me as a typical civil servant."

"I'm not. They made a big mistake with me—allowed me to go to the United States for a year of military training instead of sending me off to Paris or Brussels with the rest of my colleagues. I loved your country, but I tell you, it was damn cold there—I went in December and thought I was going to die. My only complaint about the program was that they shouldn't send Africans to Fort Drum in the winter. Your Defense Department will never counter Francophone influence in West Africa by sending back frostbite victims."

"Why would a *préfet* get military training?"

"I came up through the gendarmes," Douli ba explained.

The gendarmes were the national police force. Trowbridge remembered reading somewhere that they were subordinate, here, to the *préfets*; it wasn't as illogical as it might sound for Douli ba to have shifted services.

Douli ba leaned back in his chair, raised his hands above his head, and stretched. There was an oddly reassuring intelligence in his eyes, but there was something else there, something hidden that Trowbridge didn't entirely understand. He noticed that Douli ba had a crosshatching of fine scars on each cheek.

"You're not Ebrio," he said.

"I'm from a small tribe in the west, on the border with Côte d'Ivoire. One of my country's more enlightened policies is to avoid stationing officials above a certain rank in their own tribal areas."

"I'd intended to come register with you at some point."

"Now's your chance."

He pulled his passport and study permit from his wallet and handed them across the table.

Douli ba glanced at the passport, then studied the permit.

"You work with Dr. Juvigny," he said, making it more a statement than a question.

"Not with him, precisely. He's studying chimps. I'll be looking at leopards. There's no overlap between our areas of study."

Not unless I can establish one, he thought.

"Juvigny isn't terribly popular here," Douli ba said. "There are people who think him arrogant and inflexible."

Seeing Trowbridge's hesitation, Douli ba added, "It's just something you should know."

"Jean Luc cares deeply about the park."

"That's clear—that, and the fact that you're a bit more diplomatic than he is. Personally, I'm proud of the park, but I wish Juvigny knew how to smooth the locals a little more. A lot of people see the park boundary as an artifice which keeps them from making money or building a home or growing crops. When you have a white foreigner who himself *lives* in the park, pursuing an apparently useless activity, and telling everyone else, often rather rudely, that they should stay out . . ."

Douli ba shrugged. "Well, I've made my point. And no doubt Juvigny won't change, since he's one of those people who seems to have received his difficult temperament directly from God. I'm sure he's a good scientist."

"Is it possible that what happened to me last night is related to Jean Luc—to Dr. Juvigny—somehow?"

Douli ba considered this a moment, then shook his head. "I can't think of a reason why someone from Denkyara would be angry with your colleague. His enemies, to the extent he has them, would probably be local."

Trowbridge finished his coffee. The air was getting hot already. He had a feeling it was going to be a long day.

"Will I be able to find tires here?"

"Maybe one or two, and they'd be old and patched. Never four. I'm afraid you'll have to go to the capital for that. In the meantime, you and I have a report to write."

⸱⸱⸱ ⸱⸱ ⸱⸱⸱

Douli ba's office was a large, high-ceilinged room in a single-story white building. An open window looked out on a schoolyard where kids in tan uniforms were kicking a soccer ball. On the wall across from Douli ba's desk—which was surprisingly neat, given his informality—was a map of West Africa on which someone had outlined Terre Diamantée in green felt pen. The roughly rectangular shape sat squarely in the center of the Guinea Coast, a thousand miles of south-facing beach along Africa's great western bulge. To the west lay Côte d'Ivoire, then Liberia, Sierra Leone, and Guinea; to the east were Denkyara, Ghana, Togo, Benin, and Nigeria. The colonial powers, sharing out tracts of land in a splintered refraction of European politics, had created ten countries whose national languages alternated regularly between English and French, setting them along the coast-line like irregular slats in a fence.

Douli ba returned, placed a sizable stack of paper beside a large manual typewriter, and rolled his eyes. The number of people waiting for him in the outside foyer had been increasing steadily all morning.

"That's a minimum of paperwork?" Trowbridge said.

"Blame the Belgians," Douli ba said tartly. "Anyway, the French are worse, I promise you. Now, before we start all this, we should talk practical details. I assume you still want to go to the capital."

Trowbridge nodded.

"My monthly gas ration, unfortunately, is only sixty liters, with which I'm supposed to cover an area of seven thousand square kilometers. I can't offer you the use of a vehicle."

"I'll take a bush taxi."

"Are you serious? Whites don't usually take bush taxis. Maybe it would be better if we called your embassy."

Trowbridge shook his head. "I hate dealing with the embassy, and I need to be in the capital tomorrow morning. Maybe you could help me find out where the bush taxi stops. I've ridden them before."

Douli ba's expression suggested he'd done what he could.

"It comes by about six this evening. I'll take you to the station my-self."

⁂

The "station" turned out to be a corrugated tin roof, supported by four crooked posts, set into a stretch of hard-packed dirt by the side of the road. Around it, in an informal market, a dozen or so women gos-siped behind wooden tables which bore pyramids of mangoes, green oranges, and papayas. The two of them were sitting in Douli ba's car; Douli ba had one foot up on the dashboard, and was drinking a beer.

"Are you sure you won't change your mind? I'm not exactly well paid, but there are benefits to being a bureaucrat in my country. The house is decent, and no one, I promise you, will attack the residence of the *sous-préfet*."

Trowbridge wondered if Douli ba might be a little bit bored in Sandoukou.

"Thanks anyway."

They were silent a minute. Trowbridge watched a pied crow tearing at the orange flesh of a mango squashed by the side of the road.

Douli ba said, "You know what they used to call this part of Africa?"

"White Man's Grave."

"Have you considered the implications of that? Even a practical-minded scientist like yourself, who can climb out a hotel window when he needs to, might need some kind of protection."

Douli ba set his beer on the dashboard, reached up to a thin cord around his neck—from which, Trowbridge now saw, a small cloth bag hung—and lifted it over his head. He held the bag in his palm, and said, "You think I'm kidding, don't you?"

"I'm not sure."

Douli ba flipped him the bag in a quick movement. Trowbridge caught it and held it, rubbing his thumb across the soft fabric. There was something small and heavy inside that might be iron. Something sharp—perhaps a bit of bone—and some small round objects like beads.

"Would this have helped me last night?"

"This is my *juju*, not yours. *Juju* is personal."

Trowbridge handed the bag back. His first thought had been that Douli ba was testing him to see if he would dismiss this, dismiss Douli ba himself as a superstitious African. Then he realized, seeing the easy confidence in Douli ba's eyes, that it was something more complex—that Douli ba, rather, was curious to know if Trowbridge was open to a different way of knowing, something beyond logic and scientific reason. He had no idea how to react to this, so he said nothing.

Douli ba seemed content to let the subject drop. The light in the sky grew thinner and less intense; the shape of the mango tree darkened, and one of the market women began packing up her things.

"Ah," Douli ba said, "here's your bus. Looks like one of the older ones—are you sure you want to do this?"

"I'm sure."

"It's your funeral," Douli ba said, and Trowbridge had a moment in which he wondered why that sounded familiar.

7

The bush taxi hurtled up a long slope through the green twilight. As they neared the top of the hill the driver pulled out to pass a flatbed buried beneath bags of home-made charcoal; the two vehicles crested the blind hilltop side by side, entirely filling the narrow road. Trowbridge gripped the seat ahead of him as they shot forward without meeting an oncoming timber truck and drifted back into their own lane. He looked around at the twenty-five or so other passengers of this rickety, top-heavy vehicle the size of a small schoolbus. No one else seemed concerned, or even to have noticed. He leaned back in his seat, letting himself slip into a useful African fatalism, and looked out the window.

The sky was filled with with turbulent gray clouds; beneath it, the landscape was an unbroken, violent green, the scrubby aftermath of what had once been rain forest. This thick, characterless vegetation, known as secondary growth, covered most of the country. Here and there individual emergents towered like sentinels left over from a grander age, their massive trunks looming in isolation. Up the road, a young man stood hopefully at the approach of the bush taxi, lifting a cane rat—a heavy-bodied rodent that looked like a small possum— by its skinny tail. Cane rat, known locally as *agouti*, was considered a delicacy, and thrived in this landscape. Unfortunately, not much else did, aside from a few adaptable species of birds. The soil beneath this riot of vegetation was nutrient poor, and eroding; rivers which had once run clear through the forest, even during the rainy season, now ran thick with mud, and every year the land produced a little less.

They curved down into a shadowy *bafon* where rice was planted, then soared up toward a town distinguished by a mosque with red clay domes and a pair of narrow minarets. They were north of the park now, into a predominantly Muslim area populated by Djoula, a prosperous merchant tribe whose trading networks extended throughout West Africa. As they passed the town a woman in full-length crimson robes turned to look at the bus. He saw a flash of dark eyes in a dark face, and felt a sudden desolation, a powerful sense of the gulf which separated him from this woman. Then she was gone, and there was only the pleasant smell of smoke as they left the town behind, a smell rich with associations of cooking, of home, of light—and, of course, of the end of the forest.

The park directly south of them, four thousand square kilometers of nearly unbroken trees, was the last sizable piece of forest remaining in a country which had once been covered with it. During the days of the great Islamic savannah kingdoms, the tribes living in what was now Terre Diamantée had sent a steady stream of slaves, gold, and kola nuts to the north in exchange for salt and cloth. Trade had shifted to the south when the Europeans arrived in Columbus's time; the newcomers had little desire to push up into the forest—enough of them were dying already, in their coastal forts, of malaria and various fevers—but the local chiefs and Arab traders were more than willing to bring ivory and slaves to them. Trade went on around the forest, and through it, but there was little reason to exploit it, except for what it provided in the way of kola nuts.

Terre Diamantée, lacking natural anchorages, and with a wicked set of currents along its coast, was largely ignored until the late eighteen hundreds, when it was carved out of neighboring French and British territories and given to Belgium, which came away with a lesser but not insignificant piece of real estate, a stretch of coast where the forest came right down to the sand, and where leopards had been sighted on the beach by unlucky mariners whose ships were about to break up in the surf. The new colony had the good fortune to escape personal ownership by King Leopold—the sorry fate of the Belgian Congo—and was administered more sensibly, along the lines of the French and English colonies, by the Belgian parliament. In practice this meant there was only forced labor, not outright slavery; that the locals were whipped when they failed to fulfill their rubber quotas, but rarely whipped to death; that the severing of hands as a punishment—the infamous *fembi* of the Congo—was unknown. A fair number of roads, administrative buildings, and even schools were built as the Belgians, in their practical, bourgeois way, turned Terre Diamantée into a profitable investment, dredging a small port and building a breakwater in Granville, then repeating the process on a larger scale in Pont Noir, where diamonds were discovered in the muck at the mouth of the country's largest river. Between the diamonds and the plantations of rubber, coffee, palm oil, and cocoa, Terre Diamantée became a lucrative if obscure little colony.

When independence fever swept Africa after World War II the Diamantiens negotiated a peaceful transition to independence, electing as their first president a rich coffee grower who had served as an honorary member of the Belgian parliament. The new president resisted calls to change the country's name—promising that through peace and commerce Terre Diamantée would become *le vrai diamant* of the coast—and he resisted the second and more virulent fever which swept Africa in the fifties and sixties, Marxism, which virtually destroyed Denkyara and Ghana, the larger and richer British colonies to the east. Belgian technical advisors stayed on, and there were no coups; the president successfully corrupted, and when necessary eliminated, his rivals; profits were good, and the country paid its debts. Terre Diamantée's economic future seemed guaranteed, for when the diamonds began to tail off they were replaced by a greater, and apparently inexhaustible, source of wealth—the forest, which had stood largely untouched throughout this turbulent history, except by the handful of people who lived on its edges practicing small-scale slash-and-burn farming. Timber companies built roads to haul out the most valuable trees; behind them, trickling in on the roads, came the immigrants, many from Sahelian countries to the north whose economies had fallen victim not only to Marxism but to drought. These immigrants arrived like troops mopping up after tanks, burning and clearing and settling, then moving and burning and clearing again. In the space of thirty years an underpopulated country became crowded, and a landscape which had been almost wholly covered by high trees was taken down and replaced by the monotonous view outside the window of the bus.

The park had been carved out shortly after independence, when the President had been prevailed upon by a farsighted member of the Belgian royal family to draw up its boundaries and do what was necessary to protect it. Thirty years later the President still kept his promise, despite being a farmer at heart, with no more interest in exploring or preserving *la forêt dense humide* than most of his fellow Diamantiens, for whom the forest was a frightening, inhospitable place, filled with spirits, ghosts, and a terrifying array of wild animals.

Maybe not such an array any more, Trowbridge thought, considering the total absence of leopard sign he'd seen around the station.

He leaned back in his seat and stretched his legs into the aisle. The bus wasn't all that uncomfortable, despite what Douli ba had said. If they didn't end up spilled across the highway it wouldn't be such a bad night. He closed his eyes and dozed, his forehead bumping against the window glass.

⸭ ⸭ ⸭

He was wakened by a squeal of brakes. The bus was easing to a stop at a little outdoor stand roofed with palm thatch and lit by a pair of kerosene lamps. Bottles of beer and Fanta lined the walls behind the counter; he could see pots hanging above charcoal fires, and realized he was hungry. Following the others down into the warm evening, he took a place on one of the high wooden stools. There was no menu— dinner was vegetables and *attieke*, a kind of couscous made from manioc, with a pleasantly bitter taste—but the *attieke* was good, and the *piment* sauce was hot and tasty. He drank a bottle of beer while he ate, listening to the crackle of wood and people talking quietly around him.

When he was finished he pushed the plate and the beer bottle across the rough plank counter, walked a few minutes down the road, and looked back at the small spot of life and color in the darkness. He was a long way from the place most people thought of when they thought of Africa. There were no open plains here, no vast animal herds or endless translucent skies as there were in eastern and southern Africa. This was smaller, older, more peopled, and more claustrophobic—definitely not tourist-poster Africa, and in fact not many tourists came here, with the exception of the Belgians and French, who stayed safely on the coast in big resorts, away from everything that was interesting and difficult about West Africa, the section of continent with the cruelest and most complicated history, the wildest art, the most highly developed belief systems, and the darkest and most intoxicating tribal tapestry in the world.

⸘ ⸘ ⸘

A solid Djoula woman in white robes heaved a bale of *pagne* cloth onto the luggage rack above Trowbridge's head, then slid in next to him, amply filling her seat. She smelled strongly of smoke and soap and sweat; there was a good deal of gold jewelry around her neck, and her robes were expensive and clean. After surveying him curiously a moment, she said, *"Ça va?"*

"Oui, ça va. Et toi?"

"Un peu," she said. "You're traveling light."

"Someone took my things," he said, which seemed easier than saying someone had shot bullet holes in his duffel bag and spare clothes.

The woman clucked her tongue disapprovingly. "It gets worse all the time—pretty soon it will be like Denkyara here. And the soldiers are the worst of the lot. They'll probably leave you alone, since you're European, although you don't exactly look like someone who could complain and get them in trouble."

He remembered he hadn't shaved in a couple of days. Not holding his appearance against him, the woman fished out a round kola nut, sliced it open with a knife, and offered him half. When he declined, she popped half into her mouth, sucking on the bitter red fruit.

"Can you sleep when you eat kola?" he asked.

"Eh! You get used to it. When you travel like I do, you get used to everything."

⸘ ⸘ ⸘

He was wakened again by the sound of brakes. Ahead of them in the darkness a flashlight waved. By dim moonlight he made out a thatched shelter and several figures by the side of the road. Stretched across the road was a long board with nails pounded through it.

"Time to feed the crocodiles," the Djoula woman said resignedly.

A soldier in fatigues and black boots boarded the bus. After a quiet discussion, the driver handed him something; then, reluctantly, after the soldier shone the light in his eyes for a long moment, something more. The soldier worked his way down the aisle, taking money from every passenger, occasionally making it clear the sum proffered wasn't enough. When he reached the two of them, he took the bills offered by the woman, and looked at Trowbridge.

"Tourist?"

"He's American," the woman interjected, "and doesn't speak French. Why don't you leave him alone? You should be out chasing criminals, not bothering innocent people like us. Listen to me, you! I'm like your mother—I'm telling the truth."

Trowbridge worried the soldier would take offense; instead, smiling in embarrassment, he said, "This is how it works. You know that."

"I know how it works," the woman said, "better than you. But you're asking too much these days. Now go away and let us get some sleep."

The soldier finished with the people behind them, walked back down the aisle, and climbed off the bus. Kicking the board aside, he waved the driver through.

"This happens often?" he asked.

"They're strangling us," she said bitterly. "We'll be lucky if it only happens two or three times this trip. How can I make a profit like this?"

"It was worse in Zaire."

"Yes? Well, it's getting worse here."

"How did you know I was American?"

"I made that up to keep him from bothering you."

"It's true," he said.

The woman made a little cry of pleased surprise. This time when she offered him half a kola nut he accepted, sucking the bitter juice as the bus rushed through the darkness toward the capital.

8

The passengers moved sleepily up the center aisle and stepped down into a predawn darkness that smelled of ocean and diesel and urine on wet asphalt. Trowbridge stood a moment, sweaty from sleep, cool air on his skin, then walked past the line of dark buses toward the street. This was the only time of the day in Pont Noir—an hour before the sun rose—when the air was relatively pleasant. A black Mercedes pulled up behind a taxi which had stopped in the street. At the wheel, dimly lit by reflected street light, was a startlingly beautiful Lebanese woman. She pressed on her horn, then leaned out the window and swore in specific and personal terms at the taxi driver, who was taking on a passenger. When the taxi driver ignored her—something that didn't seem to surprise her greatly—she glanced at Trowbridge; as their eyes met and held for a moment, her look of arrogance turned to curiosity.

She probably wonders, Trowbridge thought, what a European—the term was used for anyone neither African nor Lebanese—is doing getting out of a bush taxi at five in the morning.

It wasn't a bad question; he was conscious, suddenly, of how rumpled he must look. Resisting the urge to run his hand through his hair, he watched the Mercedes disappear after the taxi, then struck out into the narrow streets, heading down toward the water and his hotel. A sleepy desk clerk gave him the key to 210, the same room he'd had a few days earlier. He went up and took a much-appreciated shower, set his watch alarm for eight o'clock, and fell asleep on the soft, musty-smelling bed, the sound of traffic rising outside his window.

When he woke up he drank coffee and ate croissants in Le Deauville's run-down restaurant, which looked out across an empty terrace at the port. Beyond the dull shine of water, on a high point of land, was an enormous slave fort, a reminder of the country's first and most profitable export. Closer in, rust-stained freighters took on loads of coffee and cocoa. The waterfront was lined with colonial buildings whose pastel colors had long since faded; high palm trees leaned away from the prevailing wind, smoke rose from morning cook fires, and the bright yellow sign above a Shell gas station looked new and out of place. He left a few *befa* on the table, then walked through the down-at-the-heels lobby of what had once been the best hotel in town and went out onto the sidewalk. To his right, the concrete bridge which joined the two halves of Pont Noir—the original version of which, made of hardwood pilings blackened with creosote, had given the city its name—streamed with cars and people. Beyond it, a small island of skyscrapers looked anomalous in the ancient light.

He preferred it here, *en bas*, in what had once been called the native quarter. He raised his hand to a green taxi which knifed through traffic, picked him up, and took him across the bridge through the newer part of the city to Alain's building, where the electricity was out, forcing him to walk up nine flights to Alain's office in the Ministry of Waters and Forests.

☷ ☵ ☷

Alain was a broad-faced young man in his early thirties, with skin the color of milk chocolate, a sprinkling of dark freckles across his cheeks, and a perpetually sad expression, punctuated, on occasion, by a good if somewhat rueful smile. He'd been studying at the university during Trowbridge's brief sojourn teaching; Trowbridge remembered him as a decent student, if not an outstanding one, serious and filled with earnest plans to return home and transform the management of his country's national parks.

The connection had paid off in a way he couldn't have foreseen. As Assistant Director of Parks, Alain had been invaluable during the last few months, corresponding faithfully by fax and phone, guiding Trowbridge through the labyrinthine Diamantien bureaucracy to obtain study permits and import licenses. Throughout the process, he'd been unfailingly positive about the study, unfailingly helpful—which made it difficult to understand why he now seemed ill at ease. Almost as if he were unhappy to have Trowbridge sitting in his office.

"Tires," Alain said. He hadn't met Trowbridge's eyes since Trowbridge had walked in, and had seemed more distracted than sympathetic when told about the attack on the hotel room. "That won't be a problem. I know a Lebanese place."

"I'm hoping to get them in a hurry."

"If you have the cash, it'll happen in a hurry. People get annoyed with the Lebanese, but they know how to get things done."

Alain was holding a pencil between his hands, studying it as if it were of great interest. Trowbridge realized he hadn't been offered coffee, a fairly serious breach of politesse in Terre Diamantée.

"I had a couple of questions about the park."

Alain looked almost panic-stricken, and glanced at his watch. "Sorry, I have a meeting to prepare for."

Grabbing a note pad, he wrote out the address of the tire store and handed it to Trowbridge. Trowbridge glanced at the address, then looked up, feeling at a loss.

Alain flipped the pencil in the air, caught it, and flipped it in the air again.

"Alain—" he started.

Alain caught the pencil, then looked at Trowbridge with a flash of unhappiness, an appeal in his eyes. "David, can we have lunch together?"

"I'd like that. Where?"

"Maquis de Paris. Just around the corner."

"Twelve-thirty?"

"I'll meet you there."

⁖ 8⫶ ⁖

He took a taxi back across the bridge to the auto parts store, which turned out to be located a few blocks from his hotel on a potholed side street across from a soccer stadium. The store's display window was filled with cases of oil and stacks of air filters. He pushed through a glass door smudged with greasy fingerprints into an interior where parts books were laid out on an otherwise bare counter, and a foot-high plastic Michelin man stood atop a stack of receipts.

A young Lebanese man behind the counter—dark hair slicked back, a gold chain visible beneath a shirt open to the chest—expressed no surprise that someone had shot out his tires. Yes, they had the proper tires in stock; yes, they could send someone up this afternoon to have the tires mounted; yes, they could have the truck in Pont Noir by tomorrow morning. Cash transaction, up front. As the young man began filling out a receipt someone emerged from an office behind the counter. It took him only a moment to recognize her. Middle Eastern features, dark eyelashes, enormous dark eyes. Maybe a little older than he would have guessed; late thirties, or early forties.

She stood a moment, making sure he was being helped properly, then turned away.

"Where were you going this morning?" he said, surprising himself.

She turned. *"Excusez-moi?"*

"At dawn. By the bus station."

She stared at him a moment, managing to look both detached and mildly intrigued.

"Flying," she said finally, and walked back into the office.

"Is she the owner?"

"I'm afraid so," the young Lebanese man said. "I'll need your keys."

He pushed them across the counter, put the receipt in his pocket, and went back out into the heat and humidity. Someone was kicking a soccer ball in the stadium across the street; the sound echoed hollowly against the concrete bleachers. He glanced through a steel-barred gate beside the parts store into a courtyard where half-disassembled cars sat amid engine blocks and transmissions. At the far end of the courtyard, by the base of an outdoor staircase, was the black Mercedes he'd seen at the bus station. Straightening up from an engine compartment, a muscular, shirtless African, crescent wrench in his hand, glared at him, and he kept walking.

9

The Maquis de Paris served plates of rice and fish on long split-bamboo tables, and was open to the street. Its Belgian owner leaned on the bar, red-faced and apparently drunk, and a pair of waitresses made periodic forays from the kitchen, looking sleepy as they passed between the tables. It was hot, and there was street noise; the fans turning overhead didn't push the air around all that much. Someone leaned in from the sidewalk and tried to sell Trowbridge a hand-carved model of the Sabena airplane on which he'd flown in. When he said no he was offered a coconut shell carved into the shape of the African continent, then a village scene with little wooden models of villagers and animals, and finally some bootleg cassette tapes.

He and Alain moved to a table farther from the sidewalk to avoid the attention. Trowbridge could feel sweat running down his sides. Their waitress wore a T-shirt from Texas A&M, and had a memorable rear end Alain could not stop looking at.

"Six, now," he said, looking back at Trowbridge with a bemused smile. "Six in ten years. Not very Western of us, is it? And I think she's pregnant again—maybe we should give it a rest after this. But everyone's healthy, so that's good."

Alain had studied in Ghana before going to the States to do graduate work, and spoke fluent, natural English.

"You're in a better mood," Trowbridge said.

Alain nodded cautiously, acknowledging the reference to their morning meeting but not commenting on it.

"How'd it go with the tires?"

"They tell me I'll have the truck tomorrow morning."

"You'll have it," Alain said confidently. "Listen, I'm sorry I missed you last week."

Alain had been in Ghana with his wife's family when Trowbridge came through the capital three days ago.

"No problem."

"See anything out at the park?"

"Two poachers. No leopards."

Alain grimaced. "The poaching's getting worse. Ten years ago there was so much untouched forest out there you couldn't tell where the park ended and the buffer zone around it began. Now people are beginning to clear fields in the zone. Pretty soon they'll start building homes there, at which point the poaching will get out of control."

"Can't you stop that from happening?"

"Not till we get approval for the management plan. You've seen a map of the park, right? It's shaped like an hour glass, and especially vulnerable at the narrow part. It *needs* a decent buffer zone around it. The management plan would increase habitat area by a third, mostly around the middle section. Some extractive activity would be allowed—hunting, nondestructive plant gathering, maybe some artisanal logging, performed by local people and with profits going directly to them. The villagers would begin to see the buffer zone as something positive, something they would have an interest in protecting—"

"Because they'd be making a living from it."

"Exactly. We've even worked out an educational program to show how the park can be an inexhaustible cashbox, which if properly cared for will continue spilling animals into the buffer zone, where they can be legally hunted, not just now but for generations to come. That appeals to people who care about their children, which the villagers do."

"And?"

"And the plan's stalled somewhere in the bureaucracy, and I can't figure out why. Nothing's the way I imagined it in school, David. This isn't a government; it's a set of interlocking fiefdoms. The people in power skim off money for themselves and their friends, and they protect each other so they can go on doing it. I can't tell you how often I've tried to fire some of the worst guards in the park and been blocked because they have a relative somewhere. My boss has no scientific background—knows nothing about parks or animals, and cares less—but he has a protector, so he can't be gotten rid of. Of course that's how I survive when he tries to get rid of me, so I guess I'm no better."

"You are better. And keep pushing—it sounds like a good plan. Jean Luc spoke highly of you, by the way."

This wasn't precisely true, but Alain seemed as if he could use a little encouragement.

Alain looked skeptical. "That must have been painful for him. No, I shouldn't say that. He's a good scientist, and we've done some good work together on the management plan, but he's difficult. I get tired of covering for him."

"Why couldn't we talk about any of this in your office?"

Alain hesitated, and glanced around. Then he said, "I think my office is bugged."

He'd spoken so quietly Trowbridge wasn't sure he'd heard him right.

"Bugged?"

"Yes."

"Why would someone do that?"

"I don't know. But people around me seem to know things they shouldn't. Unless they'd been listening in."

Trowbridge wasn't sure how to respond to this. He recalled an incident at the university when Alain had come to him claiming a fellow student was plagiarizing his ideas in a paper. He remembered thinking at the time that Alain was being a little paranoid.

"Alain—"

"Never mind," Alain said. His face had gone slightly sullen. "I shouldn't have mentioned it." He waved at the waitress. "I have to get back to the office—anything else I can do for you?"

"You've done a lot already. But I'm having trouble getting the computer and radio collars through Customs."

"That's not good—I don't have any relatives in that office. But I'll send an expeditor with you, for what it's worth. He'll be in the lobby of my building at four o'clock."

"Thanks."

Trowbridge watched a cop in a faded tan uniform and white belt directing traffic in the street. A woman on the sidewalk holding a basin of mangoes caught his eye and raised the basin with a hopeful expression. He looked away, noticing a pair of portraits on the wall behind the bar. One of them was the President, the other a younger man he didn't recognize.

"Who's the other face?"

Alain looked blank, then glanced behind himself.

"The one on the left is the President, sometimes referred to as the Old Man—*Le Vieux*—which in my culture is a term of respect. The other one is the Justice Minister, sometimes called the Big Man—*Le Beeg Mahn*—also a term of respect, albeit one imported from our English-speaking neighbor, and with a somewhat different connotation. It's widely believed that the Justice Minister has been anointed by *Le Vieux* as his heir apparent. Try not to confuse the two if you meet them at a diplomatic reception."

"I'll remember that," Trowbridge said.

Across the street, on a high metal light stanchion, a row of bats hung like withered grapes. The woman with the mangoes was still trying to catch his eye. He shook his head at her. She looked disappointed and lowered the basin. The waitress came with the bill; he paid for Alain's lunch, and they stood and shook hands, then walked away in opposite directions.

1 0

Alain's expeditor was a roly-poly, cheerful little man in a green double-knit safari suit. His name ended in "ba," and he was thrilled that Trowbridge knew one of his tribesmen, particularly one so eminent as a *sous-préfet*. He asked immediately if Trowbridge could help him get an American visa; when Trowbridge said no, that he had no contacts at the embassy, Gueri ba said that was fine, asked who his favorite country music singer might be, expressed surprise when Trowbridge said he didn't have one, and plugged a tape into the dashboard of his Citroën. To the sound of the Judds, they drove over the bridge and down along the docks, past the warehouses and fish freezers and lines of trucks. The air this close to the water was incredibly hot and humid; the breeze off the lagoon was a wave of salt, sewage, and mud. When they went into the over-air-conditioned *Douane* building Trowbridge's damp shirt clung to him like a sheet of ice.

The expeditor's cocky demeanor altered the minute they entered the office. Clearing his throat, he smiled apologetically and told the secretary they hoped to be able to talk with *Le Directeur*. Without looking up from her French movie magazine, the secretary said *Le Directeur* was in a meeting. The expeditor apologized further, and noted that the matter was urgent and involved a European and some important scientific equipment. The woman looked at Trowbridge, unimpressed, then stood and strutted into the office behind her. A moment later she re-emerged, informing them that if they wanted to wait, *Le Directeur* might be able to see them, although it wasn't clear when.

Half an hour later they were called into his office. The director smiled and shook their hands, then settled back into his chair with a reasonable look. Maybe he just drew a lousy secretary, Trowbridge thought. The expeditor began explaining the situation. The director listened a moment, then cut him off.

"I've had a look at the equipment. It looks quite unusual. Quite specialized."

"Not really," Trowbridge said. "It's all commercial application, and commercially available. You could buy it in a Radio Shack."

The software was custom, and not commercially available, but this official didn't need to know that.

"Radio Shack?"

"An electronics store."

"Nevertheless, I'm afraid it's going to cost you a good deal in supplementary customs duties."

Trowbridge had intended to let the expeditor do most of the talking, but found himself saying, "No, that's not right. I paid customs on this in advance. I have the paperwork from your embassy in Washington."

He pushed the documents across the desk. The director scanned them with an unruffled expression.

"Well," he said finally. "It does look as if you've paid some portion of the necessary duties."

Trowbridge began to feel a heat in his temples, something he knew from past experience was not a good sign.

He made a conscious effort to keep his voice calm. "Your colleague in Washington told me I could simply present this paperwork and walk away with the equipment."

"Ah."

The director glanced at the expeditor as if Trowbridge had just embarrassed himself. Then he said, "Let me explain something to you. No doubt you saw the ships in our harbor. When a purser from one of those ships comes to my office to pay customs duties, he writes out a check. This check is for a good deal of money, because customs duties in my country are high. The purser, if he is wise, adds something in cash as a friendly gesture. A sweetener, if you will—usually about ten percent of the amount of the check. I sign the authorization, we shake hands, and the cargo begins to move."

The director reached down and pulled open a file drawer.

"The checks go here, and go to sleep, which makes the ship owners happy."

He lifted a multicolored handful of loose checks and let them flutter back down into the drawer.

"And the sweetener goes here, which makes me happy."

He indicated the vest pocket of an expensive suit.

"At the end of the day, everyone is happy. Now, you strike me as an intelligent person who won't try to impose Western values on a system that works so well in my country. Let's dispense with the check writing, and agree on, say, five hundred dollars."

Trowbridge didn't really care if the Diamantien government got stiffed, even though this was why the clinics upcountry had no medicine, and school teachers made ten dollars a month, and the Waters and Forests guards were underpaid and undermotivated. But he'd just spent several hundred dollars on new tires, putting him well over budget, and the bribe he'd anticipated having to pay in this office had been more like seventy-five dollars, maybe a hundred. Nothing like five.

The heat in his temples was not going away.

"Do we have an understanding?"

"No, we don't. Your system might make ship owners happy, but it doesn't do much for me. I'll give you a check for the full amount of the customs duties. But I'd like a signed receipt, and I'll send that receipt with a letter—several letters, actually, with the necessary level of detail—requesting a refund from your embassy in Washington."

The director was still smiling, but barely.

"If that's your preference, the full amount of the duties comes to something over three thousand dollars. I should have the exact figure next week."

"That's impossible," Trowbridge said flatly.

The expeditor, looking alarmed, started to speak. The director cut him off as if he didn't exist.

"Of course we won't be able to release the equipment until we have confirmation your check has cleared, and during that time you'll be liable for daily storage fees. And I feel bound to mention that despite my best efforts there's a certain amount of spoilage in the warehouses. I would hate for anything to be damaged or lost."

There was a silence. Trowbridge took a deep breath and looked out the window, considering how difficult it was to stay even a little bit clean when the system was wholly dirty.

"Now do we have an understanding?"

Before Trowbridge could reply, the expeditor said quickly, "Four hundred."

"Four hundred, then," the director said. He was looking at Trowbridge curiously.

"Is this your first time working in Africa?"

"No," Trowbridge said, looking back, not hiding what he felt. "But there are a few things I have trouble getting used to."

The director paused, as if examining what Trowbridge had said for possible insult. Then he smiled.

"These things take time. And you're lucky you dealt with me. Some of my colleagues might have taken offense at your attitude."

⁙ ⁙ ⁙

They stowed the equipment in the trunk of the Citroën, saying little as they drove away from the port. The expeditor wanted to give Trowbridge something, so they stopped off where he lived before going to the hotel. Trowbridge waited in the car outside a shabby apartment block. Slant lines of dingy laundry hung in the stairwells; children played in a dirt lot between a pair of rusting car bodies and a high mound of smoldering trash. This was the new Africa, where the urban almost-middle-class struggled to make a life. The expeditor came back with a small roll of *pagne* cloth from his part of the country and a pair of ripe avocados.

"It isn't much," he apologized.

"It's a lot," Trowbridge said. "And it isn't necessary. But thanks."

The expeditor pulled out into traffic. "It wasn't always this bad. It wasn't so much in the open, before—people were a little ashamed of it. That business with the checks . . . you begin to feel dirty, like you're part of it. But a man has to make a living, right? Especially if he has a family. Anyway, it could be worse. In Denkyara, he would have put a gun to your head, and the sweetener would have been twice as much, and your gear would have been damaged when you got it. No, we're a civilized and peace-loving people in Terre Diamantée. It's something to be proud of."

It was hard to tell how much irony was in the expeditor's voice. He parked in front of the Deauville and helped Trowbridge move the equipment up to his room. Then they shook hands and he waved dispiritedly and drove away.

Trowbridge ate one of the avocados for dinner, standing at the window of his room. Nigerian dance music drifted up from a bar in the alley below, sweet high guitar riffs and a steady beat. An image came to him of his father, sitting alone in the family pickup on a dirt road behind the ranch, staring out at the Beartooth Mountains. The night and the city around him seemed soft and beautiful, and the same time immensely lonely.

⠿ ⠿ ⠿

In the morning he laid out his gear on the bed and examined it, piece by piece. The core of the system was something that looked like an aluminum suitcase with a pair of sturdy clips on one end. Popping the clips, he pulled down the end panel, revealing a keyboard and computer screen—a modified Macintosh powerful enough to drive some fairly complicated software and versatile enough to run off anything from eight volts to two-twenty. Bracketing the computer was a pair of hefty, rechargeable gel-cell batteries; wired in behind it was a satellite transceiver.

Next to the computer was something the technical people with whom he'd worked had called "the football"; its size, and stubby conical shape, inspired an impulse, looking at it, to tuck it under your arm. This freestanding Thrane and Thrane antenna/low noise ampli-fier, or LNA, looked nothing like a traditional antenna, but was very effective—either hanging from a tree branch or standing on its own short tripod—at sending and receiving satellite messages. There was a pair of flexible solar panels, looking like rolled bath mats; six custom-built radio collars with battery packs and bulb antennas; various wires and connectors; spare batteries, triple-wrapped in plastic; spare com-puter disks; a tool kit; and a quantity of plastic bags to keep things from rotting in the humidity. Finally, a bulky Yagi antenna he hoped he wouldn't have to use.

It was an intimidating array of equipment, especially for someone who liked to keep things simple. Unfortunately, simple didn't get you very far in the forest. He knew a very good biologist who'd done groundbreaking work on ocelots in Central America. After trapping and collaring three study animals, she'd followed them with the Yagi all night, every night, for almost a year, stumbling along through the darkness behind them, mapping their movements, getting tangled re-peatedly in the thick brush. It had been the kind of study he'd at-tempted in the Ituri, carried out with more success—but in almost a year of work she'd only *seen* her ocelots once, when she trapped and collared them. Plus she'd only been able to track one animal at a time, and that only when she was physically pursuing it through the forest.

"The environment," Emmons had told him wryly, as they sat in her cramped, dusty office in the Smithsonian, "favors the study ani-mal pretty severely."

He didn't want to use traps, which were too heavy to be practical in the forest, and caused injuries. One of Rabinowitz's jaguars in Be-lize had broken a tooth trying to escape a box trap, exposed a nerve in the process, and died of infection after several days of agony. The sys-tem laid out before him, by contrast, should allow him to capture and collar his animals without using traps, and enable him to monitor their every movement, twenty-four hours a day, for months on end.

He picked up the smallest piece of electronic gear on the bed, touched the power button, and watched a readout panel come to life with a cheerful green question mark. The GPS, short for Global Posi-tioning System, looked like a pocket calculator with fewer keys and a rectangular, swivel-bar antenna on its side. He punched *Position*, waited a minute, then went to the window to give the unit a better view of the satellites it was seeking.

The coordinates came up: 004°58.05′N, 002°35.41′W. His first bit of hard data. For what it was worth, he now knew, within about ten meters, where he was on the face of the earth.

He turned off the GPS and set it back down. There were six leopards out there, going about their private lives in the forest, who were scheduled, although they didn't know it yet, to participate in his study. He thought about why he cared about leopards in the first place—their utter self-containedness, the sense of absolute and inhuman *other* in their gaze. Someone came down the hall and knocked at the door. He opened it to the young Lebanese from the auto shop, who handed him his keys, told him the truck was parked on the street, and walked away.

He carried his gear down the stairs and put it into the truck, lashing a tarp over what wouldn't fit in the cab, then drove over what had once been a black bridge past skyscrapers into the wall of green vegetation behind the city.

11

Claire's comment that Alberto lived behind the sawmill had led Trowbridge to visualize a small walkup apartment hanging off the back of the mill itself, with sawdust on the windowsills and pictures vibrating slightly on the walls; he was unprepared, after driving past the cavernous mill building, for the world which opened up on the far side of a small hill. Beyond a white gate were five or six pleasant, bungalow-style houses, with green lawns rolling smoothly between them, raked white-gravel walks, and orange bougainvillea growing up around their shutters. There was a pond and a swimming pool, a greenhouse with its sides winged open, and a little fenced enclosure where duiker browsed. At the center of the compound, sitting alone reading beneath a high *paillote*, was a smallish man dressed in tan trousers and a pressed white shirt.

Trowbridge parked and stood beside his truck, feeling out of place in the luxurious surroundings.

"Bonjour," the man said, looking up from his book. *"Vous êtes Trowbridge, sans doute."*

News traveled fast.

"Oui. Et vous êtes Alberto."

"I'm afraid so," Alberto said, switching from Italian-accented French to similarly accented English.

Motioning Trowbridge to the chair across from him, Alberto looked toward the nearest bungalow and raised his hand. A minute later a young and very attractive African woman in a tank top and shorts and plastic flip-flops came out with a bottle of white wine and two glasses. Alberto thanked her with a gentle smile, then poured the wine, and handed Trowbridge a glass.

"You're the one who's here to study leopards. I hate to be discouraging, but in twenty years of tramping through the park, I've never seen one."

"At the moment I'm more concerned with elephants."

Alberto looked interested. "Why?"

"Elephants are the largest animals in the forest, which means they have a fair amount of trouble moving around in it. They smash corridors between fruit trees and mineral licks and any other place they visit regularly. These corridors are called elephant lanes, and every other sizable animal in the forest uses them."

"Leopards included, I take it."

"Leopards especially, because they're opportunistic hunters. Searchers, as opposed to stalkers like cheetah or lion. They cruise the forest at a steady pace and charge anything that moves. Since the duiker they hunt also use the lanes—"

"The lanes improve the leopard's chance of a kill. And presumably, the chances of a biologist looking for leopards. Yes, I see. In that case, you've set yourself two impossible tasks. Finding leopards and elephants both."

"I don't need to find elephants. I'm just hoping they're still there."

"Ever seen one?"

"Not in the forest."

"I have. It's like watching the back end of a large creature in baggy gray pajamas disappear into a bamboo thicket. I've seen them from the air, as well. I used to fly over them so often they weren't afraid of the plane. Now—"

Alberto shrugged.

"What does that mean?" Trowbridge said.

"It means I'm no longer able to find them from the air, and haven't looked recently, because I find it depressing. It's been a while since I tried, though. What do you say we go up and see?"

"Today?"

"Why not?" Alberto said.

⠿ ⠿ ⠿

They drove south on the *piste* in Alberto's air-conditioned Land Rover. Occasionally, through the irregular secondary growth, Trowbridge caught glimpses of higher, untouched canopy where the park came close to the road. They drove past the turnoff to the station, and past another dirt road on the left which Alberto told him led to the border.

"It's quite close here," he said, nodding at a group of young men wearing cast-off Western clothing and sunglasses and looking generally more cocky and nervous than most of the people walking down the road.

"They're from Denkyara?"

"That's right. Same ethnic group, very different attitude toward life."

"Is it hard to cross the border?"

"There's a bridge down that road, and a border point which theoretically controls the traffic. But the river isn't much. There are a hundred places you could cross. A hundred places where people *do* cross, to visit one another or sell things."

They passed a group of women walking toward a water-filled ditch where other women were washing clothes. One of the more well-off in the group wore a white lacy bra above her wrap skirt and carried a yellow parasol. She smiled at them as they went by.

"I heard you had some trouble. Any idea who it was?"

"They spoke English. Douli ba thinks they were probably from Denkyara."

"If this country didn't have Denkyara as a neighbor they'd have to invent it. Douli ba's all right, though, in case you're wondering."

They turned off the main *piste* and drove along a narrow track through dense vegetation, emerging a few minutes later at one end of a long grassy airstrip. At the far end of the strip was a small hangar which sheltered a single-engine plane. Alberto went through his flight check carefully, then Trowbridge helped him kick the chocks away and push the plane out onto the grass. They bumped along the runway, gathered speed, and floated up into the sky. Alberto made a lazy spiral to gain altitude, then headed southwest toward the park.

Three distinct lines broke up the sea of trees beneath them: the sluggish brown river which formed the border with Denkyara; the *piste*, closer in, tracing a reddish, gently curving line; finally, the bulldozed boundary of the park, soft with pale green growback. There were cleared fields in what was probably buffer zone, the sort of thing that was causing Alain to feel a sense of urgency about his management plan. They flew deeper into the park, and soon there was nothing beneath them but treetops in bright sunlight, making up a brilliant, seemingly infinite expanse of green. He stared at this a while, enjoying the physical luxury of so much untouched vegetation; then he studied the forest surface more carefully, hoping elephant lanes might somehow show from above. There was no evidence they did. Either that, or there were no elephant lanes down there, which would be bad news.

"We're getting close to the center of the park," Alberto said, raising his voice above the engine noise.

"What's that?" Trowbridge asked, pointing.

"You didn't know about the inselberg?"

"The map showed some kind of rock formation, but that's all."

"It's more than just a rock formation. They call it *le dent d'ivoire*— the ivory tooth. It's almost six hundred meters high."

The inselberg rose from the forest like an ancient, weathered watchtower. Its lower reaches were covered with trees; higher up, on the steep places, granite showed through, mostly gray and black, but some a pale pink. No doubt that was how it had gotten its name; the tusks of forest elephants, shorter and straighter than those of their savannah counterparts, had a pinkish cast. Alberto steered the plane at the heavy stone pillar until they were barely a hundred meters away, then sheared off. Trowbridge saw a faint trail leading up the western face; it occurred to him there would be no better place in the forest to send or receive satellite transmissions.

"Ever climbed it?"

"Ten years ago. I collect orchids, and was looking for new species.

I found one, actually, not far from here. Nothing special, but it's named after my daughter. I'll show it to you in the greenhouse."

They turned south, passing down through the hourglass center of the park toward the coast. A thin line of smoke rose above the trees.

"Poachers," Alberto said, "smoking meat. Or gold miners—you get little gold deposits around the roots of some varieties of trees. They set up camp, spend two or three weeks, then pack out the meat and whatever gold they've found. Unfortunately, the tree comes down in the next storm."

"That sounds suspiciously like an environmental point of view."

"Maybe I just consider it a waste."

⠿ ⠿ ⠿

The shadow of the plane skimmed like a dark cross over the forest beneath them. The treetops were beautiful from above, rich and consistent, a luxurious explosion of green, but they made up an inhospitable surface; if the single engine of Alberto's plane failed there would be no place to land. From time to time a dead tree was evident, its naked white branches reaching up like splintered bone. Trowbridge was relieved when a blue line appeared on the horizon. The blue grew broader and nearer, and they shot out over a sand beach and the ocean. Alberto turned west, descending until they were only a few meters above the surf, a short band of white between the blue and the steeply sloping sand. Swells moved in from the horizon like ruled lines.

Up ahead, there were buildings.

"Granville," Alberto said simply.

Granville was protected in front by a long breakwater, and backed by groves of rubber trees and thick forest; it had a small port with cranes and warehouses, a handful of two- and three-story buildings, and a jumble of informal housing and winding alleys that showed dull glints of standing water and corrugated metal. Dockworkers shaded their eyes, looking upward as the plane passed overhead.

Alberto touched Trowbridge's shoulder and pointed forward. On the far side of a couple of kilometers of open water—laid out neatly along a narrow sandbar that paralleled the coast—was a line of palm trees and a row of buildings. As they grew closer he saw that the buildings were crumbling, and that some had collapsed into the surf.

"The old town of Granville," Alberto said. "Supposed to become the capital at independence until some engineer noticed the sand bar was disappearing. And then of course they found diamonds in Pont Noir."

Alberto throttled back the engine until it was barely turning over, and they looked down through the collapsed roofs. Behind one house was the symmetrical shape of what had been an elaborate garden, a fountain in its center; in another house, a tree had grown up through the stairwell, bursting into flower in the open second story.

"No one lives there now?" Trowbridge said, watching the surf pound away at the collapsing foundations.

"No. You'd have to take a boat from Granville even to get here. This is as close as I've ever been."

::: :: :::

When Alberto turned north there were thunderheads building before them, rain clouds they couldn't avoid. Trowbridge flinched as the first drops smacked the windshield with a sound of gravel.

"The moisture from the forest builds up during the heat of the day," Alberto said absently, concentrating on keeping control of the bouncing plane. "This isn't out of the ordinary, but it's a bit unfortunate—I wanted to show you something, and it may not be possible."

A few minutes later they emerged into sunlight. Alberto banked around an explosion of white cloud that looked solid enough to climb around on, then sent the plane slanting down toward the forest.

"Ah," he said. "There."

Trowbridge saw an open area in the trees, the first sizeable clear space he'd seen away from the coast. There was a muddy patch in the center, and some of the soil was oddly yellow. A mineral pan.

Alberto was diving toward the clearing as if it were a target he intended to hit. Making an effort to keep his voice calm, Trowbridge said, "This is where you saw elephants?"

"Here, and in the mangrove swamps by the coast. Let's have a closer look."

Trowbridge resisted the urge to say, *No, let's not.* When Alberto reached the edge of the clearing he expected him to pull up. Instead, Alberto set the plane down over the last of the trees and skimmed along a couple of meters above the dirt surface. For a disbelieving moment Trowbridge thought he was going to attempt a landing. The green wall of trees ahead of them was coming up so fast he almost didn't see the round depressions in the yellow dirt beneath them. At the last possible moment Alberto pulled back hard on the wheel, and the plane reared up, just clearing the advancing canopy.

Trowbridge's mouth was dry, not a common experience in the tropics. He could have counted individual leaves on the treetops racing by beneath them.

Alberto said, "Until a few years ago they felt safe enough to come here during the day. They may still come at night, I don't know. But somehow I doubt it. You can imagine how exposed they would be, standing in the open like that."

"Someone's been hunting them?"

"If you consider going after an animal with an automatic weapon to be hunting, yes."

The plane drifted higher, and Alberto banked east, steering them back toward the air strip.

"You wonder," Alberto said, "why elephants migrated into the forest in the first place. It seems like such a difficult environment."

"This *is* the first place. This is where they came from."

"I'd assumed they migrated here from the savannah."

"That's what most biologists assumed. The latest data suggest they originated in the forest, and only moved onto the savannah during the ice ages, when the forests shrank."

Alberto looked pleased. "Really? What about leopards?"

"Leopards too," he said, looking down on treetops encircled by mist. The rain had started again, and the sky around them was an enormous dark vault, and the plane felt small and vulnerable floating within it.

1 2

It was dusk when he pulled into the station, parked the truck, and carried a box of gear toward the *paillote*. The shower was running. That would be Claire, or Jean Luc, since the only person in evidence was Guy, sitting on the edge of the *paillote*, still wearing his forest greens and looking thoroughly dispirited.

"How's it going?"

Guy shook his head.

"We lost the chimps twice. Nearly didn't find them the second time. Jean Luc says this group is more difficult, but I wonder if he's just forgotten how hard it was the first time around."

Guy hadn't seen Jean Luc emerge from his hut at the beginning of this unfortunate monologue.

"It strikes me, Guy, that if we're not habituating a second group, I don't need a second assistant. You can write up your thoughts on how I've forgotten chimp habituation on the plane and work them into a thesis when you get back to Belgium."

Guy looked stricken. "Jean Luc—"

"Never mind," Jean Luc said, stepping up beneath the *paillote*.

Trowbridge went back to the truck for another box of gear. When he returned, Jean Luc, standing in the kitchen, said, "So how was your trip to the capital? Pick up all your electronic toys?"

"I had a little trouble, but yes, I got my stuff."

"That's good, isn't it? Now you can go find your study animals and collect your data and hurry back to civilization."

When Trowbridge made no immediate reply, Jean Luc stopped what he was doing and looked at him. The forest around them was darkening rapidly. Jean Luc had a knife in one hand and an eggplant in the other, and he looked slightly ridiculous that way, but it was clear he took this seriously and was waiting for a response.

Trowbridge said, "What's that supposed to mean?"

"Nothing special. Just a reference to people who blow in, collect their data, move their careers up a notch, and then leave, and the hell with the place, the hell with the animals and people that live there."

Jean Luc set the eggplant onto the cutting board and began slicing it with quick movements.

"No comment?" he said. "You're probably thinking Jean Luc is the same old asshole he always was. But the fact is, places like this won't go on supplying study animals forever. Not if no one studies them but smash-and-grab scientists like yourself."

This accusation stung a little, because it was at least partly true. He *didn't* want any part of the problems Jean Luc and Alain faced trying to run a park. He was a scientist, not an administrator—despite what Gordon had in mind for him.

Guy, wisely, had chosen not to involve himself in this one-sided conversation. He was standing in his underpants and T-shirt pumping the lantern. Trowbridge could see him moving his lips as he counted to himself. When he reached some chosen number he stopped, turned the valve, put a match to the mantle, and the station became a lighted place.

⁂

At dinner Claire told him she'd be going out tomorrow morning at four thirty if he still wanted to join her, which prompted Jean Luc to deliver the chimp lecture. It wasn't something Trowbridge felt he needed, since he'd read everything Jean Luc had published, and knew his methods by heart—he wondered how long it would take to get to the "moving tree" part—but that didn't stop Jean Luc from giving him the long version. He was instructed never to point at a chimp, and never to make eye contact. He was always to stand at an angle, one shoulder slightly lower than the other, because facing a chimp squarely—particularly an adult male—would be taken as a challenge, and he emphatically did not want a male chimp to feel challenged by his presence.

"No sudden gestures, or loud noises," Jean Luc continued. "The main thing is to avoid interaction—"

"Because interaction alters behavior, and altered behavior results in tainted research," Trowbridge said.

"That's correct," Jean Luc said. "Basically, behave like a moving tree. If there's a machete or a flashlight in your pack, leave it there. Other intruders in the forest will dress differently than we do, and act differently, and carry machetes or weapons. We carry notebooks and canteens and tape recorders, and that's all. The chimps need to know the difference. Do you have the right clothes?"

"I have forest clothes, but they're lighter in color than what you wear."

"They have to be identical. We'll lend you some."

Trowbridge bit back the impulse to remind Jean Luc that he'd written several months ago asking what clothes he should bring, and been informed, in a curt response, that since the joint study wasn't going to happen, he didn't need to know what kind of clothes the primatologists wore. Never mind. He cared more about seeing the chimps tomorrow than he did about having the last word with Jean Luc tonight.

While the others prepared for bed, Trowbridge, working by flashlight, moved the balance of his equipment from the bed of the truck into a storeroom behind the *paillote*. By the time he was finished the lantern had been turned off and the *paillote* was dark. The door to Jean Luc's hut was shut, as was the door to Claire's room; Guy was snoring quietly on his cot.

When he lay down, the cool forest air drifting across his face was pleasant, but sleep eluded him. After a while he stood, pulled on pants and tennis shoes, stepped down from the *paillote*, and walked across the clearing to where the trees began. Standing in darkness, he listened to the endless night sounds, thinking about how the forest had looked from above during daylight. How it would look now, a wide dark ocean, deceptively still, no surface evidence of the abundant life going on around him. He still felt strangely *apart* from this place, which bothered him. Was there some way to get inside the soul of this forest without being overwhelmed by it? He looked up at a few fuzzy stars in the tropical sky, then over at the *paillote*, a high dark shape in a light-well of starlight, and became aware that someone was standing in front of Jean Luc's hut. Two someones, in fact—and he was quite sure Guy was still lying on his cot. He stayed motionless, reasonably certain they hadn't seen him. The two figures merged for a second, then separated, Jean Luc going into his hut, Claire moving toward her room, stopping to look toward Guy's cot, then his own, which he realized was sufficiently rumpled in the darkness to give her the impression someone was there.

Claire opened the door to her room and slipped inside, and the *paillote* was still again.

Well, he thought. It shouldn't be a surprise. She was single, attractive, and basically alone out here. And Jean Luc, for all his faults, was charismatic, an authority in a field they shared, and equally alone—at least when his wife and children were in the capital, which was a good deal of the time. He moved quietly back to the *paillote* and sat down on his cot, amused at discovering in himself a tiny element of disappointment.

13

They went out before sunrise, plunging into the pure darkness beneath the trees. Claire kept up a brisk pace, and seemed to know precisely where she was going, despite the absence of a discernible trail. The tangled, sopping undergrowth tore at his clothes, and he tripped regularly, swearing silently as he went down. Before long he was convinced she was forcing the pace deliberately because she hadn't wanted him along in the first place.

His mood was not improved when she looked back, her face serious in the earliest light, and said, "If we don't move more quickly, we'll miss them coming down from their nests. I assume you want to see that."

"You assume right," he grunted, redoubling his efforts, considering how much he would rather be in the mountains. Some rocky slope in the Himalayas, where it was cold and one's mind stayed sharp, where the landscape was clean and barren. That led him to thinking about Nima, and then to Claire and Jean Luc. He found that he disliked the too-obvious parallel—younger assistant, inevitable attraction, and eventual failure—and pushed it out of his mind.

A thread-thin vine with tiny thorns slid like broken glass across his cheek. He stopped a moment, wiping blood and sweat from his face, then plunged on after Claire, determined not to give her a chance to chide him again.

Half an hour later she held a finger to her lips, and began moving more quietly. Then she stopped, indicating a dark blot of leaves high above them. There were more of the dark shapes scattered through the treetops.

A spectacular shriek cut the forest silence, and she tipped her head back.

"They're coming down," she said, and he could hear the happiness in her voice.

☷ ☷ ☷

Forty meters above them a dark figure appeared above one of the nests, grasped a pair of branches, and began shaking them furiously, emitting a bloodcurdling shriek that split the morning. Other shapes appeared, each erupting into the same mad display of energy and screams. Soon there were nearly twenty; the canopy roiled as if disturbed by a small storm, leaves scattered down in a steady shower, and the forest reverberated with the incredible, raucous sound of a band of forest chimpanzees greeting the dawn.

Jesus, he thought. Not an animal that survives by stealth.

The first chimp began a rapid descent, crashing in a kind of controlled fall down through the branches of a *makore* tree. When it reached a low limb, it scanned the forest floor, then dropped with a solid thump and raced about the tree's base, vocalizing excitedly. Chimps were shorter than humans, barely four feet tall, but had several times the physical strength. As the male chimp moved by barely two meters away, Trowbridge kept his head down, watching in wonder, well aware that this animal, if it were so inclined, was capable of tearing his arm off at the shoulder. He forgave Jean Luc, at least partially, for the didactic lecture last night. It had taken two full years in the forest before Jean Luc was able to get within fifty meters of a chimp, another three before he could accomplish what they were doing today. This was such an overwhelming experience it would be easy to forget the rules if they hadn't been drilled in thoroughly.

"One thing Jean Luc didn't mention last night," Claire said quietly. "It's all right to talk, even when we're close to them. As long as we keep our voices down, and don't make any abrupt noises."

Another sizable male crashed down onto the forest floor, setting off a display of aggression that included mock charges, hurled vegetation, and a cacophony of howls and shrieking. Eventually the females filtered down, and the band settled into a relatively peaceable chimpanzee morning, eating the shoots of young plants, grooming one another, and looking after the infants. The first male who'd come down, Lucifer, after copulating with one of the two females in the band who were fertile—a condition advertised by red and very swollen rear ends—ran along a fallen log a meter above their heads, stopped at a point almost directly over them, and lay on his back, feet lolling comfortably in the air, one arm hanging down. Trowbridge could have reached up and taken his hand. He had a full view of Lucifer's face, and saw consciousness in the dark arched eyes. Volition, calculation, and thought—undercut, at the moment, by a feeling of laziness and contentment.

Lucifer yawned, revealing a mouth filled with impressive yellow teeth.

Not beautiful, he thought to himself. Not beautiful the way big cats are. But more complex, and infinitely more human. Which was precisely why they were so interesting, not only to biologists, but to anthropologists, behaviorists, and a whole range of individuals who used information compiled on chimps to support their particular theories of human nature and development. And precisely why the chimp-leopard study would have been something worth attempting.

"They're obviously comfortable with you," Claire said in a low voice. "You have a good presence."

Her approval, he noticed, was like her disapproval, clean and without ambivalence.

After a moment she said, "Are you still angry with me for this morning? Honestly, I wasn't trying to run you into the ground."

"No problem," he said, watching Lucifer stare up through the trees at the blue morning sky. "This is terrific stuff."

⁝⁝ ⁚⁝ ⁝⁝

Two hours later the chimps were up and moving, and he and Claire were moving with them. There were something like thirty in the band, counting the infants, and they spread out between the trees as they traveled, until only five or six were visible from any given point. It was a strange feeling to travel as part of the group; he had a sense of prehistory, of what it must have been like to be a member of a hunter-gatherer group fifty thousand years ago.

A hollow drumming echoed in the distance, the sound of a hand slapping a hollow tree root.

"Lucifer's found a nut tree," Claire said.

A few minutes later they emerged into a clearing at the base of a tall *Panda oleosa* tree and sat against a downed log, surrounded by chimps who ignored them as if they didn't exist. The nearest, a gray-faced female, was holding an infant in one arm. Using her free hand to set a *panda* nut into a rounded depression, she smacked it with a piece of granite Claire referred to as a hammer. After several blows the nut cracked open. A young chimp wandered over, watching solemnly as the female made soft hooting noises and placed another nut on the anvil.

Claire was setting up a tape recorder.

Trowbridge said, "You're studying vocalization?"

"As it relates to learning. It's my dissertation."

"That kind of research would have been useful to the study I was thinking about doing."

"The one Jean Luc turned down?"

"Yes."

"What was it, exactly?"

"Well, it wasn't moving tree stuff. It would have entailed simulating a leopard attack and recording the chimps' alarm call, which I would guess is distinctive. Then collaring a couple of chimps with special audial sensors that would let me know when a real leopard showed up."

She looked cautiously interested. "It's a long shot. And pretty invasive."

"A very long shot. But it might have produced some interesting results."

They watched the gray-faced female, who had put down her hammer and was nursing her infant.

"What are your plans when the dissertation's done?"

"I've applied for a post-doc, a year of behavioral work in Tanzania. But what I really want is a permanent job in the field somewhere."

"Bouncing around for a few years isn't a bad way to get experience."

"Maybe for some people. I need something stable, and I need it soon."

He looked at her, made curious by her emphatic tone. She had to know that finding a stable job right out of school was virtually impossible. Competition in this business was fierce, and funds were perennially tight; there simply weren't that many full-time field positions around. Most field biologists lived from grant to grant until they couldn't take that life any more, and were driven to desk jobs at zoos or universities—or driven out of the profession altogether. It got harder, as one grew older, never to have a regular paycheck, never to accumulate possessions, never to buy a house or have insurance.

Trowbridge was one of the lucky few to have some kind of job security, and a normal, if unspectacular, salary.

Some of the younger chimps were scattering up a small tree, playing roughly, attempting to push each other off. One of them fell several meters, landing with a thud in the leaf litter.

Claire said, "The BBC is coming out to film a special, did you know that? One of their producers has been interested in Jean Luc's work for a long time. Jean Luc has finally agreed."

"That's terrific," he said. "It'll be great for the chimps, and for Jean Luc's career. But it seems out of character. He used to complain to me in the Ituri that Jane Goodall was a media hound."

"He's changing," she said simply. "He realizes he can't protect the park by himself, not forever. The reason he's habituating the second group is so we can bring in tourists, people willing to pay for the experience of seeing wild chimps. The money would go to the park, and to the people who live around it, which might help protect the park after we're gone."

"When's the BBC coming?"

"I'm not sure. His wife, Pascale, is handling the details."

He glanced at her to see if anything showed in her face, but nothing did.

She switched on the tape recorder. Sunlight filtered down through a gap in the canopy, making the clearing—with the chimps vocalizing quietly, and the irregular, hollow knocking of the nut hammers—a sleepy, peaceful place. He leaned his head back and saw a thrust of gray parrots, fifty or sixty at least, pour from the crown of an enormous tree, veering upward in a smooth arc, then disappearing down into another treetop. The bright scarlet of their tails lingered against the blue and white sky like the stroke of a paintbrush. Higher up, well above the canopy, a crowned hawk eagle, the largest raptor in the forest, drifted on solitary patrol.

Late that afternoon the chimps left the nut tree and began moving purposefully through the deepening shadows. Claire was off to one side and slightly behind him as they followed; he glanced back at one point, and saw that she'd stopped and pulled her pant leg out of her boot to remove some bit of vegetation. He saw a flash of pale skin, and something else, a set of purple welts running diagonally down her calf.

Claire tucked her pant leg back into her boot, glancing at him as she did so. Then they moved more quickly to catch up with the chimps, whose progress through the forest was steady.

"They're looking for a tree to roost in," she said, which was something they both knew.

"When did it happen?"

"What?"

"Your leg."

"*Merde.* You weren't supposed to see that."

"From the claw spacing I'd say it was a less-than-full-grown leopard."

There was a silence broken only by the steady, prehuman sound of bodies pushing through the forest. Finally she said, "I don't know whether it was full grown or not. It looked pretty big to me."

"What happened?"

She shook her head. "You'll have to ask Jean Luc. I think it's a little ridiculous, but it's his choice how much to tell you, and I have to respect that."

14

Shortly before dusk the following afternoon Trowbridge slung his hammock between a pair of high trees, putting a ring of Vaseline on the guy lines against driver ants and other crawly visitors, and raising the insect netting, protection not so much against mosquitoes, which were rare in the forest, but against a range of other night-flying creatures which might or might not bite, but would certainly wake and disconcert when colliding with one's face; there were forest moths, for example, with bodies the size of sparrows. He'd spent the day walking long diagonal transects down the eastern side of the park, moving closer to, then farther from, the Denkyara border. He'd seen birds and monkeys, a banded duiker dead in a wire snare, and seemingly endless amounts of green forest. But no elephant lanes, and no sign of leopard.

He made dinner, fell asleep, and woke at dawn with a hammock backache and a black-and-white face staring down at him from the canopy. Pushing back the netting, he fished in his bag for the binoculars and focused on a gorgeous, healthy, black-and-white colobus, the same species that had been caged—and killed—behind the hotel in Sandoukou.

The colobus, known locally as a *magistrat* for the white beard which ringed its dark face, was staring at him disapprovingly.

"Seen any leopards lately?" he asked.

The colobus failed to answer. He rolled out of the hammock, boiled water on his camp stove for coffee, ate bread and jam, then checked his position on the GPS. Today he would move west, into the center of the park; tomorrow, north again; on the fourth day, east, back through the elephant pan toward the station. Four days of walking, roughly a box shape around the center of the park. He hefted his pack and began moving west beneath the high ceiling of a vast green cathedral, where he still felt out of place, and where no other human being had come to worship.

⁂

At some point during the morning he realized he was becoming more accustomed to the forest. He was fighting it less—spotting and stepping over lines of driver ants, holding his elbows forward against creepers and thorns, ducking and slipping sideways without a break in his pace. It became an act of faith simply to walk, and to trust, not to think too much. In the absence of large mammals he looked carefully at trees. There were hundreds of different species, but they could be divided into three basic models—those whose heavy-columned trunks went straight down into the forest floor, those whose trunks were supported, five meters or more above the ground, by an intricate latticework of roots, and those with high flange-roots wandering like slender walls around their bases, forming a kind of protective labyrinth. The forest looked luxurious, but was set atop an austere foundation; a thin layer of soil, often only a few inches deep, covered the granite shield which underpinned most of West Africa. With so little soil to burrow into, the trees relied on above-ground support—the exposed root systems around him, and the interlocking chains of creepers and vines above his head—to keep from being blown over in a storm.

Occasionally he stopped and simply stood, listening and watching, feeling his heart rate slow and the sweat roll down his temples, letting the forest fill in around him. No matter how gloomy it was, how green and close—no matter how color seemed to disappear into a dark green sameness—there was usually some splash of illumination, some bit of yellow light pouring down through a gap in the canopy, scattering like mist on the vegetation and making the forest a more liveable place.

It was a good sign that he could see this, and see other details. He was differentiating; the forest was no longer just a mass of hostile vegetation. He walked until it was nearly dark, ate quickly, slung his hammock, and slept.

The next day he turned north and walked hard until the light began to die and the GPS told him he was near the center of the park. Throwing his hammock onto the forest floor, he looked at the coiled guy lines, feeling exhausted, then lay down on the hammock without bothering to sling it or to raise the netting. His legs trembled as he fell asleep, and he was wakened twice in the night by cramps. In the morning he made bouillon, realizing he had a salt deficit, and ate sardines on salty crackers, and drank deeply from a little stream. His clothes were clammy, and smelled of sweat and the forest and his own body, which had taken on a rich, identifiably African smell. A different crop of micro-organisms, in a different climate. Tonight he would stop earlier and take a bath, even if he had no choice but to put on the same clammy clothes afterward.

Act of faith, he told himself. Do the work, and eventually the data will start coming in.

On the following day he walked east, no longer bothering to move in diagonal transects. When he reached the mineral pan at sunset he walked out into its barren center, which felt holy and lonely, a place abandoned, and stood in the translucent light beneath a sky going orange and peach. The dirt around him was packed hard and marked by mineral deposits. He felt a moment of vertigo—the forest seemed to be revolving around this naked place at its center—and then the vertigo went away and he was left with a pure and bitter disappointment.

There were elephant footprints around him—what he'd seen from the air had not been an illusion—but they were indistinct, softened by age, and would probably disappear after the coming rainy season.

He moved into the trees and found a pair of elephant lanes, so overgrown as to be almost invisible. Then he found the picked-clean skeletons of the last animals to use those lanes. The bones were small, even for forest elephants; this had been a remnant band of adolescents, scared and probably leaderless when they'd finally been taken. He played his flashlight over the skeletons—black and white death sketches, with green vegetation growing up through their ribs, and machete marks in the smallish skulls where the tusks had been hacked out—then went back into the pan and crossed into the trees on its far side and kept going. He'd intended to sling his hammock here, but the silence was too depressing; if there were elephants still alive in this forest, it wasn't at the mineral pan.

He walked a long time in darkness, following the beam of his flashlight, considering what he would do if there were no elephants left anywhere in the forest. The north end of the park was reportedly riddled with poaching activity; the south, near the coast, was mainly mangrove swamps. The only area he hadn't yet seen was around the inselberg, in the north center. If he failed to find elephant lanes there, a study that was high-risk to begin with would become even more so. Elephant lanes, by funneling the movements of his study animals down into one or two percent of their territory, would make the difference between success and failure.

Was there an alternative? He could move the study to another country, but he wasn't sure where. Zaire, even if he'd been willing to go back to the Ituri, was collapsing beyond its usual state of anarchy; Liberia, Denkyara, and Sierra Leone were even worse. There were other countries which had once been covered with forest—places like Nigeria and Benin—but the forest there was simply gone.

No, it was this place or no place.

He thought about what he'd learned the day he went out with Claire. There was one leopard in this forest, at least. And Jean Luc's secretiveness about Claire's experience could mean only one thing—

that he was on to something about leopards. Something good enough to keep to himself, but not good enough to publish. No wonder he'd turned down the proposal for a joint study.

Is it science we're working on, or just our own careers?

Shut up, he told himself, as he spread out his hammock and lay down on it. Shut up and go to sleep. There's nothing you can do that you aren't already doing. Maybe you'll find elephants tomorrow at the inselberg. He flicked an ant off his neck and closed his eyes.

Early the following afternoon he dropped his pack at the edge of a little clearing where a stream turned beneath the roots of a massive tree, wiped the sweat from his face, and stretched. All this ducking and crouching had caused him to feel like some kind of forest gnome. He unclipped the GPS from his belt and checked his position. Three more kilometers to the south face of the inselberg. He squinted up at the mosaic chips of blue sky visible through the canopy, then poured out the last of the tepid water in his canteen and knelt beside the narrow stream to refill it. Despite the vast numbers of crawling and flying beasties in the forest, the water itself, filtered by vegetation and running silently over white sand, was clean, if slightly tea colored from the tannin in the forest leaves. He held the canteen below the surface, listening to its steady gurgling, the pitch rising steadily as it filled, then capped it and set it aside. Beneath the flowing water a patch of granite showed through. He put his hand below the surface and touched his fingers to the rough stone, watching the water moil around his wrist, and thought of mountains. Then he put his face down and drank deeply.

When he sat up he saw what looked like a shadowy corridor running away through the trees. After a moment of perfect disbelief, he stood, hopped the stream, and walked fully upright down an open passage that seemed to have been cleared for him alone.

Three hours later, exhausted and happy, he sat listening to the hissing of the stove. He'd gone three hundred meters down that shadowy lane before remembering his pack and canteen; after hurrying to retrieve them, he'd spent the afternoon wandering elephant lanes, feeling a growing euphoria at the seemingly endless pattern they wove around the inselberg. The lanes were fresh, marked by great swathes of torn bark and ripped vegetation, and they were *everywhere*, open passages with more light and more space—even more air, it seemed—than the surrounding forest. Young trees were knocked down whole, and veils of creepers torn away, opening gaps where light streamed in to ignite an explosion of new growth. At one point he'd stood at the base of an enormous *makore* tree, surrounded by dozens of what looked like yellow cannon balls on the forest floor—*Strychnos aculeata,* a rock-hard fruit only elephants could break open and digest—and seen five separate lanes coming in from the surrounding forest, making a wavery star shape around him.

He contemplated a nearby pile of scat, a thing of beauty which had drawn him to make camp precisely here. Not the copious, bulky dung of an elephant, but something more austere—carnivore scat, and because it was fresh and nutrient rich, butterflies had been drawn to it. He'd found it lying squarely in the trail, a deliberate marker laid down to announce that this territory was claimed by the only large predator in the forest, *Panthera pardus,* an animal that killed to live. The butterflies had softened the message, burying it in a fluttering mass of yellow, violet, and cobalt blue. Now, in the near darkness, the butterflies began to flit away through the trees.

15

He dumped his gear at the station and made some lunch, taking it to the rough plank table and eating hungrily. When he carried his plate back to the kitchen he noticed the door to Claire's small room was open and looked in. The narrow room was neat and oddly peaceful, with books arranged on a small writing table, a battery-operated fan on a crate beside the bed, and an unlit candle in a carved wooden holder. The only decoration was a pair of masks mounted on the wall, life-sized faces gazing back at him, one slightly larger than the other, with stylized, serene eyes, blue hair, and high foreheads marked with diamond scarification. Gordon had a similar pair, funeral masks from Gabon.

Setting his plate in the sink, Trowbridge decided to postpone his shower—there were only a couple hours of daylight left—and took the truck to Kisanga, clumping over the bridges which led away from the station, turning right when he reached the *piste*, and taking it south toward the ocean. He rolled the window down and put the close sweaty work of the last few days behind him, enjoying the feel of air and open space, of going somewhere new. The light was hazy and rainy, and it shone on the bright vegetation crowding against the road. He drove past a tall man with very black skin and dark clothes and a white skull cap walking down the road carrying a green plastic pail, and past a clutch of schoolgirls in blue cotton dresses who pointed at him and waved, laughing, all but the oldest, who looked serious and had a bruised expression. There was an open-sided coffee warehouse where men climbed about on ten-meter-high stacks of filled burlap bags; one of them wore pink pants, smudged and dirty from the work, and had one leg shorter than the other and a face slick with sweat. Then the forest opened up; he slowed to avoid the children and goats and dogs that gusted across the *piste*, and drove into Kisanga, the largest town between Granville, on the coast, and Sandoukou at the northern corner of the park.

Kisanga was a welter of thatched huts, a handful of more sub-stantial wooden houses, a police station joined to the mayor's office, and—most importantly to Trowbridge—a two-story covered market made of water-stained concrete.

He parked the Toyota, walked past a line of women squatting be-side cookpots selling food, and went inside, sifting slowly through the open stalls and the smells and dark faces. Beyond heavy slabs of meat, slick with blood and darkened by flies, were heaps of small fish laid out on broad *marantaceae* leaves. Larger fish, dried and salted, were formed into hoops, tails thrust into sharp-toothed mouths, and stacked in pyramids. He bought a square block of soap, bigger than his fist and wrapped in paper, and onions and sardines and palm oil and rice, then carried it all out to the truck and locked it in the cab, hiring an eager ten-year-old to keep an eye on things. He went back for or-anges and peppers and a bag of yellow squash; then sunflower seeds, a pineapple, several baguettes, and a sack of tomatoes green enough to survive transport in a backpack. By the time he hauled out a case of beer it was nearly dusk. He stood by the truck a moment, pleased with his colorful haul, then went back into the market, climbing a rough concrete stairway to the second story, where electric lights were coming on over bright tables of *pagne* cloth.

Pagne, for Diamantiens, was a way of life. Every year new patterns came out, and every year it was essential for a woman of any substance to have outfits made from the latest and most stylish design. Men wore *pagne* made into matching short pants and shirts; individual tribal groups had their own *pagne*, as did women's associations, church groups, and labor unions. Most of the rolls of cloth around him, stacked like multicolored loaves of bread on wooden tables, were bold geometric prints, but Trowbridge saw one with the President's face on it, a celebration of his eightieth birthday. Dozens of presidential cameos—the aging, elfin little face in dark glasses and a leopard skin topi—stared at him as he walked by.

Beyond the *pagne* stalls was a bead table. Among the garish plastic beads were older beads made of glass, darker and more lustrous in tone, some on long strings, others in loose piles. These trade beads, produced by Venice glassmakers in the seventeenth and eighteenth centuries, had helped slavers and explorers buy their way through the African continent, and the Hudson Bay Company buy its way through North America. He saw an individual design he remembered from the Ituri and picked it up. Nearly as large as the knuckle of his little finger, it was glossy black, and decorated with white dots shaded with pale colors. It seemed remarkable that the dark history of European expansion through Africa—all that suffering and destruction and brutality—had left behind a trail of beautiful little art objects, some of which had found their way here, to a local market in a small town in the forest, shining on an open table beneath a bare bulb, offered for sale by a man whose ancestors, not that long ago, had been pursued by slave traders.

He paid a few *befa* for the bead, then moved on until he found the fetish table, which stood alone in a darkened corner with no sign of a proprietor. Along its back edge was a line of old gin bottles filled with powdered blue potter's clay; there were heaps of ten-penny nails, and crudely made iron rings, and roots and seed pods and cowrie shells, once used as money. But the bulk of the table was covered by animal parts, the reason he was here; in its own way, the fetish table was a census of the local animal population. There were enormous snail shells, brown and translucent; dried snakeskins, bird beaks, and duiker horns; the skin of a flying squirrel, and another skin he couldn't identify; monkey skulls and teeth; civet tails, claws, and whiskers; a cluster of dried eyeballs that looked like shriveled peas; a tortoise shell, and tortoise leg bones; other bones which looked to be either chimp, or human.

And here, near the front of the table, the perfect white skull of a leopard.

A shape materialized out of the darkness, startling him. An old man, sunken-chested, peering at him with a strangely dolphinlike smile. Trowbridge glanced past him, made out a chair in the shadows, and wondered why he would choose to sit in darkness. Then he saw that the man's eyes were still, and milky in color. River blindness. A million Africans a year lost their eyesight to this disease, which progressively thickened the eye cover, turning it white and opaque, and was imparted by a particularly nasty worm—carried by the female black fly, *Simulium damnosum*—which nested and bred in human eye tissue.

A fetish couldn't protect you from that, he thought.

Quietly, in slurred melodious French, the fetish seller said, *"Les Européens ne s'intéressent pas, normalement, aux fétiches."*

"How did you know I was European?"

"Europeans have a different smell."

"I just spent six days in the forest. It's hard to believe I still smell like an outsider."

The fetish seller didn't answer directly. His stare was as fixed as his smile. His hands moved over the table, touching his things.

"Why did you spend six days in the forest? Are you a hunter?"

"Sort of. More a scientist."

"I thought scientists worked in *les laboratoires.*"

"Not all of us. Aren't you afraid someone will steal your things?"

"Because I am blind?"

"Yes."

The dolphin smile widened slightly.

"No one ever has."

"May I hold the leopard skull?"

As the man held the skull across the table, Trowbridge saw that his wrists were marked by neat little scars in groups of five, vaccinations against witchcraft. He took the skull and held it carefully, running his hand over the delicate cheek bones. Some part of him wanted to have it. But buying it would make a hole in the old man's collection which would soon, by market economics, be filled with the skull of another animal.

"If I wanted protection from this animal," he said, "in the forest, what would you sell me?"

The fetish seller lifted his hands, as if to separate himself from something.

"I am not a fetish doctor," he said. "Only a fetish *seller.*"

Within this belief system, a pharmacist, not a physician.

"I'll be honest with you—I don't intend to buy anything. But I would pay something for your knowledge. Not as a fetish doctor, simply as a *spécialiste.*"

The man considered this. "For protection against leopards—speaking as a specialist—I would sell you a gun."

The smile widened again.

"Would that help me at night?"

"At night is different. For that I would sell you something to make you invisible and let you see in the dark. These are a leopard's great advantages, and you must counter them."

Trowbridge saw something that had been obscured by the leopard skull, a severed chimp hand with pale shrunken fingers. When he picked it up it felt light and cool, like the hand of an old person. He could feel the bones inside the skin.

He said, "Do chimpanzees need protection from leopards?"

The fetish seller considered this a moment. Then he came around one side of the table, hands moving like dark crabs over his merchandise. Loosening the top on a small glass bottle, he poured a green organic material, something that looked like crushed leaves, onto his palm.

"Chimpanzees can protect themselves during the day, so long as they are not caught alone. For protection at night I would give a chimpanzee this."

Trowbridge set down the chimp hand, took a pinch, and smelled it.

"What plant is this?"

"It is not a plant—it is from the top leaves of a very tall tree. And if I sold this to a chimpanzee, I would ask for his hand in payment, because the advice would save the rest of him."

The fetish seller smiled in a way that made Trowbridge know why no one had ever stolen any of his things. Then he cupped his hand to pour the leaves back into the bottle. As he did so, the lights went out in the market, and it was dark, suddenly, darker than any darkness he'd experienced, even in the forest. He felt panic rise, something to do with being a white person alone in a strange place filled with Africans, and something more practical—how would he find his way out through this maze of little stalls? A rough hand grasped his wrist; his heart leaped, and he nearly jerked his hand back before realizing it was the fetish seller.

The grip was strong, but not threatening.

"*Ça va.* It is only the electricity."

Trowbridge forced himself to relax, and took a deep breath. The man was in his element, and had simply wanted to reassure him.

"How did you know the lights went out?"

"Listen."

Trowbridge listened, hearing a murmur throughout the market that hadn't been there before. Soft cries of disgust and exasperation; a clink of metal on glass as people fumbled for lanterns; the scratch and flare of a match.

The hand was removed from his wrist.

"My nephew will be here in a minute."

Soft halos of light appeared in some of the stalls as flashlights came on and candles and lanterns were lit. Somebody was laughing now. A kerosene lantern approached, carried by a young man whom Trowbridge remembered from one of the *pagne* stalls.

"*Oncle,*" the young man said. "*Je suis là.*"

"*Je sais.*"

"*Ça va?*" the young man said cheerfully to Trowbridge.

"*Un peu,*" Trowbridge said. "*Merci pour la lumière.*"

He paid the fetish seller something and followed the nephew down the stairs and out between the stalls, buying candles—which he would otherwise have forgotten—along the way. When he reached the Toyota he paid the ten-year-old car guard, who had begun to look worried, and was no doubt overdue at home, and drove slowly back through town.

As he drove he remembered, in a sudden rush of feeling, what he loved, and had forgotten he loved, about Africa. Lanterns and candles glowed in the darkness; people stood talking to one another in small groups, holding each other's hands, smiling, laughing softly. Children's faces looked solemn, and there was music coming from a bar somewhere, and smells of cooking food. He felt intensely alive and encouraged. *I found leopard sign today,* he thought. *Leopard sign, and elephant lanes.* When he passed an open-front restaurant and saw Alberto sitting alone at a table, he U-turned and pulled in next to the Land Rover and walked up onto the terrace.

⠿ ⠃⠆ ⠿

"Timber rights?" Alberto said. His reproving look suggested that reasonable people ought not to talk business after hours, especially over a half empty bottle of wine.

"I'm curious."

"A short explanation, if you insist—and only if we can talk about something more agreeable afterward."

"Deal."

"The President grants the rights to individual timber tracts to members of his family, and to various hangers-on and sycophants who convince him they're more loyal than the rest. They sell the rights to people like me, who cut the roads, take out the commercial trees, mill them, and ship the timber. Once in a while someone complains, pointing out that too much of the forest has come down—"

"How much?"

Alberto refilled their wineglasses. "About three percent of the forest which covered this country at the turn of the century is still standing. Most of that is in the park. The people who sell their loyalty to the President have expensive tastes, and now their children have expensive tastes as well—it costs a lot of money to maintain a house in Monaco or Paris. I'd like to forestall your probable comment at this point and admit it hasn't worked out the way one might have hoped."

"No comment."

"Good," Alberto said.

They sat in silence a moment. Then Trowbridge said, "How did you get into this business?"

"Through my father. Indirectly, anyway. He was a furniture builder—just a small shop, nothing special. My earliest memories are of tools hanging on the wall, the smells of freshly cut wood and linseed oil. The way sanded wood feels against the palm of your hand. I thought I might design furniture for a living, discovered I wasn't much good at it, and went into the timber business. In those days you didn't have to worry so much. You could take pleasure in a particular kind of tree for the beautiful piece of furniture it would make. Even just for the piece of lumber it would be milled into, straight and strong."

Alberto shrugged. "When I came here I told myself that I was—in addition to earning a good living, and keeping the company happy—helping develop this country. I thought that eventually Terre Diamantée would become more European, with a middle class that would demand limits to the corruption, and would visit its parks, and maintain them. A balance, somewhere, would be struck."

Moths fluttered in drunken arcs through the darkness above their heads.

"As it turned out, Terre Diamantée didn't become more European, except in the most superficial of senses, and no balance was struck. It all just came down, and most people are poorer than ever, except for the elite, whose children come back from expensive European schools ready to carry on a tradition of looting the country for their personal benefit. And the trees I loved, there aren't many left, not outside the park, anyway. I haven't seen an elephant in years, and my daughter, who lives in Milano—and who, in a nice touch of irony, is a leftist and a Green—lectures me every time I see her. Which is not all that often since my wife died."

Alberto sipped from his glass. "I'm afraid I strayed a bit from your question."

"That's all right."

"What about you? How did you get into your line of work?"

"I grew up on a ranch in Montana. Never much cared for domestic animals, but I was camping alone in the mountains one day when I was fifteen, and saw a lynx take down a young deer, and felt something. I realized that what I appreciated in animals wasn't their company, or their practical use, but what was wild in them, what was different."

It was an answer Trowbridge had given before. But it occurred to him now that he, like Alberto, had found his profession indirectly through his father. Russel Trowbridge had been a civil engineer, good at what he did, promoted further and faster than he ever expected until one day he found himself running the Montana State Traffic Department. A gentle man who disliked conflict and wanted people to like him, but whose professionalism and conservationist views—and a stubborn sense of right and wrong—often put him at odds with powerful ranchers and developers. A man who worked long hours, because he didn't think it fair to burden his employees, and who bottled up stress rather than yelling and kicking a desk and forgetting about it. A first heart attack when Trowbridge was fourteen; a second, followed by open-heart surgery, three years later. His father eventually having to leave his job, deeply, clinically depressed, feeling betrayed by the organization to which he'd given his life.

Trowbridge's mother, in the years after the first heart attack, had been deeply wrapped up in her husband's needs; later, she'd needed more than anything to get out and take care of herself. Trowbridge, through most of his adolescence, had been left to his own devices, and in many ways had thrived on the solitude. By the time he turned eighteen and left for college, he'd resolved never to become the boss, never to be the poor bastard sitting behind a desk trying to solve other people's problems. Never to become his father. Resolved, instead, to find some kind of profession where he could work alone, rely on himself alone.

Alberto was looking at him curiously. He shrugged and said, "I watched a lot of open country get fenced off, and a lot of wild animals disappear. And the clarity of science appeals to me."

"You've come to the wrong place for clarity."

"What about the park? Is it in any kind of danger?"

"If there's good news, that's it. The money from timber and diamonds and cocoa wasn't enough—the country ran up huge debts even beyond that prodigious income—and now can't meet its payroll without help from the World Bank and the IMF. These institutions have been so beaten up recently by environmentalists like my daughter that they've become sensitive about their image. They'd be forced to cut Terre Diamantée off totally if the park came down."

Trowbridge remembered something the Belgian woman had said.

"I heard there was an American timber operator working here. Know anything about him?"

A look of disapproval crossed Alberto's face. "His name is Randy Foote, and he's not a timber operator. He's got one rig and a pickup truck and a few people working for him, at least two of whom I fired from the mill. He drives around giving village chiefs whiskey and a little money and persuading them to let him cut down the last trees remaining within the limits of their villages. I also suspect he poaches trees from the buffer zone, and maybe even the park itself, although he's never been caught. No, people like Foote can nibble away at the margins, but the main body of the park is safe. It's hostage to the country's foreign debt."

1 6

"Six weeks from today," Pascale said. "A photographer and two support people."

"Firm?" Jean Luc said.

"Firm. They'll buy plane tickets as soon as the permits come through. They're wondering about refrigerated storage for their film, and how much food they should bring."

Pascale was about Jean Luc's age, Trowbridge guessed, and pretty, but looked a few years older. She was fair-complexioned, and—in contrast to his indestructibly hard features—the skin around her eyes showed the years and the tropical sun. He remembered that she was a biologist too, that the early papers to come out of the forest had borne both their names. This wasn't an uncommon pattern in the profession; often only another biologist could understand and put up with the hardships of living and working in the field. But if you wanted children, someone had to step back from the research and take that on.

He could hear the two children, a boy, nine, and a little girl of five, playing behind the *paillote*.

"How long will they stay?"

"Ten weeks—through the beginning of the rainy season. They want to set up a blind near the station. Choose a tree and put nuts around it."

Jean Luc frowned.

Unfazed, Pascale said, "I told them it might not be acceptable. It's just another decision we have to make, that's all."

There was sudden wailing behind the *paillote* as the little girl protested some transgression on her brother's part. Pascale called their names and they came running, each talking at once, while a hornbill, invisible above the *paillote*, made a chuffing sound so loud it seemed to fill the clearing.

When Claire came in from the forest she greeted Pascale with what struck Trowbridge as a surprising naturalness. This can't be easy for her, he thought. She may have been alone with Jean Luc a few nights ago—whatever that adventure meant, whatever it was worth to her—but Pascale was the working partner, the one who'd be sleeping tonight with Jean Luc in the hut they'd built together to house a family.

He wondered if Pascale knew what was going on between her husband and his research assistant. He heard her ask Claire casually how her work was going, and imagined there might be an unspoken question there: When are you going to be finished, and when will you go away?

The talk over dinner was all about the BBC, and weather and work plans and accommodations. Afterward Trowbridge helped Guy and Claire do the dishes, then moved to the couch and sat working on his notes. Pascale began a card game with the children. Jean Luc played a few hands of the game—a noisy thing with shouts and slapping cards—then stood, went to the edge of the *paillote* not far from where Trowbridge was sitting, and leaned against a post, ignoring the children's complaints that the game required a fourth player.

He looked distracted and unhappy, no doubt contemplating the upcoming invasion of his privacy and disruption of his study methods. Trowbridge's satisfaction at seeing Jean Luc faced with a situation he wouldn't be able entirely to control was mingled with an unexpected sympathy.

"Mixed feelings?" he said.

Jean Luc looked at him, holding his gaze as if assessing his sincerity. Then he said, "I don't like the idea of setting out nuts, like this was some kind of bird-feeding station. And I'm not sure I want my face on a bunch of television screens all over Europe."

"They show these things in the States, too."

"*Merde.*"

"It'll be good for the chimps. In the long run, anyway. And it'll be good for the park."

"That's why I'm doing it."

The children gave up on their father and drafted a willing Guy into the game; the sound of slapping cards began again.

Trowbridge said, "Who's the photographer?"

"Some Brit. Malcolm Ridland, I think."

"Malcolm Riddick. I worked with him in Nepal. He's good."

Trowbridge saw Pascale glance over with a slight frown. This probably wasn't the way she'd imagined the family reunion, Jean Luc talking with a strange scientist while she and Guy and the children played cards.

Jean Luc said, "Does he speak French?"

"Passably, although you won't enjoy the accent. And he's better company in the evenings if he has a couple of gin and tonics with dinner."

"We'll lay in some gin, then."

Trowbridge waited a moment, then said, "I saw the scar on Claire's leg."

"She told me," Jean Luc said evenly.

"Did it happen when she was out with the chimps?"

"It did."

"There's more data on leopard-chimp predation, then."

"Not enough to write a paper on, but yes, there's more."

"If I knew what you'd seen, I'd be able to keep my eyes open for supporting data."

Jean Luc's expression was difficult to read. Finally he said, "If you find supporting data, we'll talk."

⸭ ⸭ ⸭

He lay with his hands behind his head, wide awake, feeling the cool air drift across his face. When a slender shape moved through the darkness, he sensed more than saw who it was.

"Hi," Claire said shyly, sitting beside him on the cot.

"Hello," he said. He tried to make out her features, but it was too dark. In the moment of silence that followed he realized she was not here on any errand that had to do with chimps, or leopards, or with helping him find someone to bring him supplies in the forest, which she'd said she was willing to do, and he was filled with a strange mixture of emotions. Surprising exultation; an immediate erotic response when she put her hand on his arm and stroked it lightly; pleasure that at thirty-eight he was attractive to someone ten years younger.

Well, he and at least one other person.

Some of the exultation went away, replaced by a sense of how immensely complicated this was. The last thing he needed was to get involved in some kind of triangle—quadrangle, for God's sake—with the others at the station. And there was something else. If Claire was here just because she felt unhappy that Pascale had supplanted her, that Jean Luc was suddenly ignoring her . . . something prideful in him resisted this, and caused him to wonder if it made much difference whether it was him lying here or someone else.

His fingers, belying every reason why this was a bad idea, had entwined with Claire's. The feeling was pleasant. She was leaning down to kiss him.

"No," he said quietly.

She froze.

"Why?"

"It's just—"

He stopped, unable to complete his sentence. Claire started to speak, then stopped as well.

He said, "What about Jean Luc?"

He sensed her staring at him in the darkness.

"What *about* him? He doesn't have to know. It's none of his business."

She was disentangling her fingers. "I'd forgotten how puritan you Americans are. How complicated you make everything."

"Claire—"

"It's all right, don't explain. I liked you, and I thought you were sexy, that's all. And I was feeling lonely. Never mind. Go to sleep."

She was already standing up. There was nothing to say. He could see her profile for just a moment before she was swallowed by the darkness beneath the *paillote*.

17

The cry of a wounded duiker filled the night. Silence, then the thin nasal cry came again, a sound which seemed to beg for an end to the pain, a sound, he hoped, that would be irresistible to a predator. He'd been listening to these cries for nearly an hour this evening, and six hours last night, and still found them distressing, despite knowing they'd been recorded months ago in a different forest by another biologist, and rerecorded, at some effort, onto a loop cassette now being played on a tape player protected by a wooden box in a hole beneath a heavy log.

Trowbridge leaned back in the harness, allowing himself to move for the first time in almost an hour. Somewhere up there a full moon was shining, although you would hardly know it beneath the canopy. He'd seen it rising over the forest, yellow and huge, three hours ago when he left his inselberg base camp and plunged down into the trees.

Just enough moonlight filtered through to differentiate the strips of pale liana vine he'd scattered along the trail. The leopard, if and when it came, would make a dark shape crossing those markings.

He shifted his legs in the harness, and went still again. Leopards had an unearthly ability to spot the tiniest movement, even in near total darkness, but they weren't nearly so good—in fact, less able than humans—at discerning a motionless shape against a background. He took a deep breath and let it out slowly, feeling a sense of well-being after the brief stretch. It would be a few minutes before the ache came back. For the moment, he was more or less comfortable, suspended five meters off the ground, with a good line of sight between him and the log, a loaded, full-sized crossbow across his thighs, and a smaller, pistol-grip crossbow, also loaded, resting loosely in his right hand.

Now all he needed was a customer.

☷ ☵ ☷

Black Leopard

The dark shape came down the trail an hour later, blotting out the individual strips of liana like a figure moving along a ladder. He'd been on the verge of allowing himself another stretch—two nearly motionless hours in the harness had brought on leg cramps—but as the shape drew nearer he forgot the pain and concentrated on stillness, on keeping the sound of his breathing infinitesimal and regular. The liana beneath him faded, then reappeared; the shape, moving off the trail into the clearing, had its back to him. He flipped down the night scope, turning it on in a single movement. The world beneath him opened out in pale yellow, and through that world, moving like a creature across the ocean floor, was a lithe, heavy-tailed leopard, magnificent in outline and extremely cautious in its demeanor. Not large; perhaps three-quarter size. That meant a female, or a subadult male; he wouldn't be able to say for sure until he was able to employ the old-fashioned technique of lifting its tail.

The leopard moved toward the log, clearly intrigued by the cries of the duiker, but uneasy. He wondered if, despite his elaborate precautions—which included soaking his gloves and the cassette player in duiker musk he'd gotten from the Bronx Zoo—there might be some lingering human smell. Maybe he'd touched something when he wasn't wearing the gloves, or maybe he'd touched a gloved finger to his bare skin. In the motionless forest air, at this height, it was unlikely the leopard could smell him; this, and the fact that an aggressive leopard wouldn't be able to leap this high, had been the reason for the climbing gear. For a moment he was afraid the animal's natural wariness would cause it to leave. But curiosity, and no doubt hunger, overcame its uneasiness, and it moved two steps nearer, tipping its head toward the log. He could see the tufted ears, one higher than the other, with perfect clarity. Raising the crossbow pistol, he aimed and squeezed the trigger.

There was no distinguishable sound against the background noise of the forest, and the leopard made no reaction. But he was almost certain he had a hit.

Got you, he thought, silently exultant. At least for as long as that dart stays in, and the battery keeps transmitting. This first dart was too light to penetrate the pelt, but its small barbs would hook it securely in the fur.

The leopard, in a melting bound, disappeared over the log. He held his breath—had it heard something, felt something, after all? A moment later it stalked back into view, losing all wariness under the influence of the insistent cries. He raised the rifle-crossbow. This part was trickier. He needed to put the second, more substantial dart into a fairly precise area of this animal's hind leg, where, on impact, a pressurized chamber would erupt to drive a syringe through the fur and into the thigh muscle, pumping in a dose of Kezol.

He had no idea how the leopard would react to this—hence the first dart, not much heavier than a trout fly, which would allow him to track it with the Yagi antenna if it bolted.

The leopard leaned forward, putting its muzzle close to the log. He would never have a clearer shot. He adjusted his aim slightly and squeezed the trigger. This time he heard the hiss of the dart leaving the bow. The leopard heard it too, swiveling its ears back. He saw a twitch in its thigh, and worried it would bolt; instead, it began digging furiously at the leaves and dirt beneath the log. He lowered the crossbow and looked at his watch, luminescent green in the darkness. Watched the digital numbers pulse steadily. Three minutes after the darting his first study animal remained fully active, digging away with such good effect he was afraid he might lose his cassette player. At six minutes it stopped, stepped back, and looked around itself, as if it had heard something a long distance off. At seven minutes it began to sway slightly on its feet; at eight minutes forty-two seconds its back legs folded and it was down.

☷ ☵ ☷

"Shit!" he said out loud. "Shit, shit, shit."

He sat back and rested his hands on his knees, looking down at the animal lying before him. He should have known it was all going too smoothly.

The unconscious leopard, stretched full length and illuminated by the warm light of the lantern, was beautiful—long-bodied and spotted, with lithe, satisfying muscles beneath the pelt, one slightly torn ear, and a dark necklace of rosettes at the throat. The delicate throat markings were now partially obscured by the collar, an inch-wide belt of nylon webbing wrapped in a soft sleeve. Attached to the webbing, at the top of the collar, was a small transceiver that looked like a quail's egg; beneath the egg, extending out to one side, was a slender, foot-long whip antenna; at the base of the animal's throat was a battery the size of a cigarette pack. After adjusting for tightness, he'd slipped a pair of inch-long stainless-steel bolts through a set of pre-drilled holes and screwed a pair of nuts onto each, locking them tightly against one another. The leopard was now properly collared—with a battery which ought to be good for at least six months, and a tiny backup transmitter still firmly snagged in its fur—and ought to wake up in three to four hours feeling groggy and slightly encumbered, but otherwise no worse for this strange experience.

Unless there was a problem with the Kezol.

He crouched beside his first study animal, running his hand through the ruff behind the collar. The fur was luxuriously thick, a bit oily. As he felt for the pulse he found a hard-bodied tick swollen with blood, and resisted the impulse to remove it. This was a wild animal that had lived with ticks its entire life; he wasn't here to make it into a pet.

He put his hand on the belly and palpated gently, once again, to be sure.

"Shit," he said again. He supposed it was good news and bad news. There had to be at least one other leopard around somewhere, and it had to be a male—because the leopard which lay before him was female, and she was pregnant.

⸪ ⸬ ⸪

There was nothing intrinsically problematic about a pregnant leopard. But he was using a new drug, and had no idea—nor did the manufacturer—how it might affect a pregnant animal. More precisely, how it might affect the cubs. He swabbed the Telinjekt syringe dart with alcohol and packed it away in its case. There was no point rereading the accompanying literature, which he knew by heart. Kezol, a new drug on the market, was easier to handle than Tagamine; a powder instead of a liquid, Kezol mixed easily with water, and was essentially benign—an overdose simply meant the animal in question would sleep longer, whereas too much Tagamine could be fatal. Moreover, an inadvertent needle-stick, working with Tagamine, was an extremely serious business; even a small amount of the older drug had a spectacular range of undesirable effects on human beings, including what an otherwise dry brochure described as "violent paranoid hallucination, to include self-mutilation." Trowbridge knew of a team of Forest Service biologists in Alaska who had gone in by chopper to collar a Kodiak bear; one of them had slipped, and put the syringe filled with

Tagamine into his own arm instead of into the bear; before his partner could stop him, he'd climbed up into the chopper blades.

On the other hand, Tagamine, for all these well-known disadvantages, had never been reported to have a deleterious effect on a feline fetus.

I guess we'll find out, he thought, pulling the wrench out and giving a final cinch to the lock nuts. He'd brought along a few doses of Tagamine for precisely this eventuality. Unfortunately, unless a female leopard was in a very advanced state of pregnancy—sometimes even then—it was difficult to know whether she was pregnant, or had simply eaten a large meal in the last few hours.

He retrieved his backpack from where it hung in a tree fifty meters away, prepared the climbing line and ascenders so he would be ready for a quick ascent, and sat down to wait. Until the sedated animal recovered, it had to be watched. A whole range of creatures which would normally avoid the top predator in the forest would have an entirely different reaction finding it unconscious. Leaning over his first leopard, henceforth to be known as *L1* for notetaking simplicity, he loosened the masking tape and cloth which covered her eyes—when drugged, an animal's eyes remained open and dilated, and might be scratched or damaged by dryness—then sat back against his pack.

Three hours later the leopard raised her head, blinking away the cloth over her eyes. Trowbridge slipped into the ascenders and giant-stepped up into the darkness. The leopard was too groggy to pay any attention; she sat awkwardly, then stood, making a vague effort at cleaning her chest before wobbling off. Trowbridge watched her disappear, feeling like a happy—albeit worried—parent. The study was launched. He had a successful collar, and proof the new technique was effective. On only his second night in the harness, he'd accomplished something that had taken him six difficult weeks in the Ituri.

He would just have to wait and see about the cubs.

18

Trowbridge stood at the edge of the world, with granite at his back and a pale blue sky, wide open and flawless, before him. The forest horizon was a broad green curve, broken at its most distant point by an upthrusting of white cloud; nearer in, at about his elevation, a crowned hawk eagle floated above the canopy. He felt a breeze, the soft breath of the equator, touch his face, and looked down between the tips of his tennis shoes. Fifty meters of empty space, ending in a green carpet of treetops. Beneath that, another forty meters or so to the forest floor. A bad place for a fall—and the narrow trail up the side of the inselberg was a stiff workout. But satellite reception would be immaculate, and the abundance of sunlight meant he would get the most out of his solar panel, reducing the need for fresh batteries.

The platform on which he was standing had been formed when a kapok tree atop the inselberg had toppled in a storm, rolled down the inselberg's steep face, and wedged against a pair of smaller trees in such a way that one of its broad-flanged buttresses was roughly level. After a month spent mostly beneath the canopy, home base for the next five months would be a tree house above it, a perch on the side of a stone pillar.

He stepped away from the edge of the platform, tightened the line which anchored one corner of the tarp, and tied it off on a protruding root at the platform corner. There was a good deal of Robinson Crusoe work yet to be done, but it could wait until his next trip, when he would bring in a cot, a second tarp and solar panel, and a host of other useful items.

The breeze came again, stronger and cooler this time. He looked back toward the horizon. The distant pillar of innocent white cloud had built rapidly into a high, roiling thunderhead, and was sweeping toward the inselberg, trailing an opaque wall of rain. He saw lightning flash within that wall and realized it would be better not to use the computer for a while. He checked the knots on the tarp, then retreated beneath it, sitting on his rolled sleeping bag, leaning back against his camping pad. The squall hit the inselberg with a gust of wind, enveloping it wholly; the first heavy drops came down, and the world contracted into an unrecognizable place, windy and charcoal gray, filled with flying water. He listened to the rain beat on the tarp above his head. The bare granite of the steep inselberg surface was mostly black and gray, like the sky, but it had a scattering of pink lichen, and had begun to run with a flat sheen of water, as if it were encased in ice.

He reached out and touched the blue plastic housing of the Thrane and Thrane antenna hanging from the guy line of his tarp. This and the computer were two of the three main elements of his system. The third was the collar he'd placed on *L1* last night, a custom-built piece of equipment which incorporated a GPS, a transmitter, and an interface microchip to call the electronic shots. Since the moment he'd put a narrow screwdriver blade into a recessed point on the collar and switched it on, the microchip had been coming alive once an hour to interrogate the GPS for a position fix. It then transmitted the information—at a frequency of 1.6 gigahertz, with a collar-specific ID number—up through the canopy. Thirty miles up, *Atlantic East*, one of four commercial INMARSAT satellites moving in a geo-synchronous parade above the earth's surface, picked up the transmission, processed it—billing the Society by the information bit—and beamed it back down here, where it was picked up by the Thrane and Thrane, fed into the computer, and plotted on a geographical grid.

That was how it was supposed to work, anyway. He'd done everything he could to simulate field conditions, going so far as to collar five grad students and have them wander, the length of a hot summer day, through Central Park. But you couldn't know whether a system like this would work in the field until you tried it.

Flickers of silent lightning appeared over the forest; the water came down in torrents. It was nearly dark beneath the tarp, and a mist rose into the air as raindrops pounded the platform. He took off his jacket, covered the computer, and found himself thinking about what had happened with Claire. She couldn't know he'd seen her with Jean Luc, so she couldn't know that had been part of his reaction. He felt a tinge of regret, an awareness that he would be spending most of the next few months alone.

It had been the right decision, though. That kind of complication wasn't something he was looking for. He watched the rain make little water craters in the wood, and wondered what, or whom, he *was* looking for. Someone like Pascale would be the practical partner. Someone willing to step back and let him be what he was and make the necessary adjustments.

The problem was that he wasn't attracted to women like Pascale, no matter how sensible such a relationship might turn out to be. He was attracted, instead, to women as single-minded and independent as himself. Nima, for example, who had left him after a difficult year together in New York, and who was now studying wolves in Alaska.

He shrugged off this line of thought and reminded himself that what he was looking for, in fact, was a successful outcome to his study. The rest would take care of itself. It occurred to him that he might end up saying that forever, and he wrapped his arms around himself, shivering a little in the rare coolness.

▦ � ▦

Water dripped quietly onto the platform. The sky was gray with departing cloud, but the thunderstorm was over. He flicked the power switch on the laptop and watched the blue screen swim into being. A dark grid was superimposed upon it, the inselberg at its center. He plugged the antenna cord into the computer, making the system fully operational for the first time, then checked his watch, ducked out from under the tarp, and went to the edge of the platform, moving carefully on the water-slick wood.

A smell of wet vegetation rose from the treetops below him. Beneath that opaque surface were elephant lanes, slender scrawlings in a vast dark manuscript, an illuminated network through the forest. Leopards were down there, moving along those lanes at this very moment.

His leopard was down there somewhere.

He made himself wait until five minutes past the hour, then ducked back under the tarp and touched a key, waking the computer from its self-imposed, energy-conserving sleep. Once again, the grid came up, anchored by the inselberg. Nothing else, at first. Then a single dot, small but unmistakable, in the quadrant to the southeast of the inselberg.

He sat back and released a deep breath.

Data. In a world where truth so often seemed elusive, debatable, and endlessly relative, he now had an unarguable fact. There would be another dot in an hour, and then another. Soon they would form a line, and eventually a pattern.

He punched in a quick command. Along the bottom of the grid the coordinates of the fix appeared, complete with a compass heading to take him there if he wished to go. He stared at the screen, letting the implications of what he was seeing sink in slowly. The dot told him the location at twelve noon—seven minutes ago—of a leopard he hadn't seen since last night. That information was a small miracle, data that had long resisted scientists, and before scientists, hunters. He'd cracked the code of the forest, found a way to look down through its opaque surface and see what lay beneath.

He realized he was staring at the screen to no good purpose, wasting precious battery time; he turned the computer off and looked at his watch. If he left for the station now he would get something for dinner besides the pathetic contents of his food bag—broken saltine crackers and bouillon. No, he would try for another collar tonight, even if it meant walking hungry tomorrow. At the station he would arrange for someone to begin bringing him provisions on a regular basis—with Claire's help, assuming she wasn't terminally annoyed with him—then return with a load of food and gear and get down to some serious work.

In the meantime, if he was going out again tonight, he'd better get some rest. He rolled out his camping pad and lay down, pulling a handkerchief from his pocket to cover his eyes against the sun, which had emerged with a sudden tropical brilliance, causing the wet wood of the platform to send off steam.

19

Late in the afternoon on the following day he walked into the clearing before the station, which seemed strangely quiet. His first thought, even before he emerged from beneath the trees, was that a predator was in the area; the insects seemed to have gone still. He felt nervous and alert, sensing some kind of trouble even before he saw the figure draped over the edge of the platform. The body lay in an unnatural position, as if it had fallen backward, neck bent forward and face pushed down into the chest. The shirt had ridden up, and a stretch of generous white belly, dark-haired, was visible. It was Guy, and it had not been a simple fall; there was blood, a vivid darkening red, in the sunlight. He felt a sense of disbelief as he moved toward the *paillote*, a voice telling him this wasn't possible, that Guy would get up and it would be a joke.

He slipped out of his pack, realizing this wasn't a joke of any kind. He began to kneel, then stopped. There was no point; Guy was beyond help, thoroughly dead. Three bullet wounds stitched his chest, a tattooing of small holes across his camouflage green shirt. *Executed* was the word which came to Trowbridge's mind; it looked as if Guy had been shot from fairly close range, flung backward by the impact, and left where he'd fallen. A casual, indifferent killing.

He heard blood rushing in his ears, and looked past the *paillote* to where the trucks were parked. Two were there, his and Jean Luc's, both turned on their sides and riddled with bullet holes. He felt a sense of doom permeate him, an unfolding tragedy. Some part of him noted that bullets made neater holes in metal than they did in flesh. The truck windows had been shot out; a wet patch beside his truck made a shimmering rainbow where gasoline had run from the perforated tank. Only two trucks . . . When had Pascale said she was taking the children back to the capital? Today was Monday, which meant they had school to return for; they would have left yesterday. He stepped past Guy's motionless figure up onto the platform. His eyes adjusted slowly to the shaded light, so that it was a moment before he saw Gregoire.

Gregoire had died differently, perhaps because he was African. His hands had been tied behind his back; there were no bullet wounds in his muscular body, but his head had been nearly severed from his shoulders, and turned, so that while his body lay chest-down, his face—Gregoire's gentle, handsome face—stared upward, eyes open and expressionless. There was more blood this time, diagonal hack marks across his neck and collarbone, bruising around the wrists where the cord had damaged the skin. Gregoire's killing had involved real physical work, not the simple pressing of a trigger. He realized suddenly that whoever did this might still be around. That he might be in danger.

No, if the people who did this were still here he would know it already.

Where were Claire and Jean Luc?

He looked into Claire's room. No one; nothing. Just the pair of masks looking back at him. With an unhappy sense of inevitability he went to Jean Luc's hut and stood in the doorway. Only one body, Jean Luc's, lay on the floor in the near darkness of the interior. Face up, one arm flung to the side, as if he were reaching for something, or trying to ward something off. A series of gaping wounds opened his chest. Exit wounds, jagged, fist-sized craters that exposed muscle and bone. Jean Luc had been shot in the back, presumably as he turned to run, and continued turning as he fell.

In the enclosed space and the tropical heat the hut smelled of death, a sweet close odor that Trowbridge felt, with sudden panic, attaching like cobwebs to his skin.

He stepped out into the sunlight and stood a moment, staring at his silent surroundings. When he felt himself beginning to shake he forced himself to carry out a systematic search of the station and the area around it. Then he looked at the bodies again, one by one, trying to learn what he could. This concrete task allowed him to fend off the sickness, the roaring in his ears, the disbelief.

It must have happened this morning. The bodies hadn't been disturbed by animals, as they would have been if it had happened last night. All three men were dressed for the forest, but their clothes were clean, and there were breakfast things on the table—mango skins, scraps of toasted baguette, nearly finished cups of coffee. He looked in the sink and found a single rinsed coffee cup, then went back to Claire's room and saw that her forest gear was gone. Either she had already departed on her morning trek to the chimps' roosting tree, or she'd been taken away by whoever did this. His first thought was that kidnaping wasn't something in which these people appeared to have any interest; his second was that Claire had been the only female at the station.

Eventually there was nothing more to be learned, and he found himself sitting on a low stump in the clearing, incapable, suddenly, of further effort. He should do something about the bodies. He should probably go for help. What if Claire didn't come back? If she did, he ought to be here. The complexity and contradictory nature of these tasks overwhelmed him and he was unable to move. As long as he was here animals would not disturb the bodies; that was something, anyway—it was more than he could do, at the moment, to disturb them himself. A while later Claire appeared at the edge of the clearing. Her clothes were wet from the forest; her hair was damp and slicked back from her pale forehead, and she smiled when she saw him, a generous, questioning smile that wondered why he was sitting in the middle of the clearing like that. Then she saw his face, and looked immediately toward the *paillote*, as if somehow she knew.

⠿ ⡇ ⠿

Headlights from half a dozen pickup trucks speared the station and the clearing around it, dividing the scene into a confusion of darkness and light; the lantern had run out of fuel and no one had bothered to refill it. Police officers in coffee-colored uniforms milled about. One had a Polaroid camera and was making little white explosions which went off painfully in the darkness.

He and Claire had gone together to Gregoire's hut in the forest—Gregoire's wife and children had been away visiting relatives—and sent a *petit frère* on a bicycle for help. A while later people had begun to show up, one of them Douli ba, wearing a uniform and looking serious, alert, and very much in charge; the investigation, after his arrival, had become more coherent. Twenty minutes later a Land Rover had pulled into the station and a man had gotten out wearing a uniform with braid on the shoulders. Douli ba, standing stock still for a moment, had gone to the man and saluted crisply, and was now giving him some kind of report with a deferential expression. Deference seemed out of character for Douli ba; it struck Trowbridge that this must be someone from the capital.

He was standing alone for the first time in a while, and felt light-headed and sick, and remembered he'd eaten nothing since last night and drunk no water since this afternoon. He stepped up beneath the *paillote*, moving through areas of shadow and glare into the kitchen. A policeman made a motion to stop him—perhaps worried he would disturb *la preuve*—then saw his face and looked away, not interfering.

He drank deeply from what had been the communal plastic bottle beside the sink, closing his eyes as the water went down his throat. When he opened his eyes he saw Claire walk through a headlight beam toward the man with braid on his shoulders, and talk to him urgently, pointing behind herself.

Trowbridge turned to the policeman and asked who the man was. *"Le Chef des Gendarmes,"* the policeman said.

The *Chef* turned away from Claire, ignoring her. She looked around and saw Trowbridge and came up under the *paillote*. Her face was strained, but no longer as numb as it had been. She said, "David, come here," and he picked up a flashlight and followed her back to the parking area behind the station. They knelt, and she took the flashlight and pointed it at a set of tire tracks in the soft red soil.

"None of our trucks had this kind of tread," she said. "I know; I've changed tires on all of them. And look at this."

She aimed the flashlight beam at a distinctive scarring on one of the tread marks. This tire had been punctured and repaired with a plug. She swung the beam a meter or so farther along, where the scar repeated.

They looked at each other. He nodded and stood in time to be accosted by one of the coffee-colored uniforms and asked yet again to produce his passport and study permit. By the time he disentangled himself from this interrogation Claire was being questioned again as well. He looked around for Douli ba, who was kneeling over Gregoire's body. He saw someone sewing burlap coffee bags together, and wondered why until one was laid across Guy's body to see if it was long enough. He walked over to the *Chef des Gendarmes* and said, "You should have a look at these tire tracks."

The man turned. Trowbridge sensed a coldness, and disliked him immediately. There was a hard cynical glitter in his eyes which belied the softness around his mouth.

"Du calme. We have professionals working here."

"Your professionals missed something. There's a tire tread with a scar on it that doesn't belong to any of the vehicles at the station."

The *Chef des Gendarmes* stared at him. Then he caught the attention of one of the men in uniform and tipped his head in the direction of the open area.

"Have a look at those tire tracks," he said indifferently.

The man glanced at Trowbridge with a puzzled expression, then wandered off, shining a flashlight randomly across the ground. Trowbridge saw Jean Luc's body being loaded into the bed of a pickup.

"Do you know why someone would want to kill him?" the *Chef des Gendarmes* asked.

Guy's body was being loaded in next to Jean Luc's.

"No," Trowbridge said.

"Then you're the only one who doesn't. We have our own Dian Fossey now. It was predictable."

The pickup truck with the two bodies backed into the open area of dirt where the policeman with the flashlight was standing, then turned and moved off. Trowbridge met Claire's gaze and lifted his hands helplessly. She shrugged as a policemen took her by the shoulder and led her toward one of the trucks. She was carrying a duffel bag with some of her things, and got into the truck and held the bag on her lap, leaning away from the passenger side door as it closed on her. He walked over to the truck and put his hand on the rolled-down window. Her duffel bag was partially open. He could see notebooks and cassettes and the candle holder which had sat by her bed. Not the masks, he noted irrelevantly. He had a sudden image of the masks being danced at a village funeral, the swirl of raffia in flickering firelight.

"I'll tell Pascale," she said. "I'll have to."

He tried to think of a way to let her know he understood how hard that would be, how complicated, but he couldn't, and simply nodded. The truck door slammed on the other side, and the engine started, and then the door handle moved in his hand and he let it go and stood dully a moment in the darkness. When he looked back toward the *paillote* he saw that Douli ba was still bent over Gregoire, and that he was holding something in his hand that had been around Gregoire's neck, holding it up away from Gregoire's severed head, and then someone came for him too, and he was driven away into darkness.

20

"What a terrible thing," the Justice Minister said, sorting through a sheaf of papers on the desk in front of him.

They were sitting in the largest office Trowbridge had ever been in. It was carpeted with an expanse of thick, cream-colored berber, and air-conditioned to a very livable temperature. There were art pieces from Africa and Europe, and windows which looked out on a courtyard several stories down where people in uniform stood at attention in the sun.

"I'm concerned about Gregoire's family."

When the Justice Minister looked up Trowbridge realized why he looked so familiar. This was the Big Man, whose picture had been hanging with that of the President in the Maquis de Paris.

"The African? His family will be taken care of, I promise you."

"What about Jean Luc's wife and children?"

"They are already gone. The Belgian ambassador took charge immediately. He even sent someone out to collect the personal belongings, and the books and papers. The other scientist, the Swiss woman, is gone as well."

It hadn't occurred to him he might not see Claire again. He was feeling exhausted after the all-night ride in the truck, and a little bit stunned, and not entirely certain why the second most powerful man in the country felt it was worth talking to him.

The Justice Minister said, "Your French is immaculate. Very impressive, especially for an American."

"Not immaculate, I'm afraid."

The Justice Minister shook his head, brushing Trowbridge's self-deprecation aside. He was a big man, solidly built, with features that were heavy and handsome, and long eyelashes, frosted an amazingly pure white, which gave his eyes a luminescent quality. His hair was closely cropped and silver at the temples, and he wore an expensive suit that must have come from somewhere in Western Europe.

It was all very calm, and civilized, and not very West African.

"You're a biologist as well, I understand."

"Yes. I'm studying leopards."

"Leopards," the Justice Minister said. "Now *there* is an animal worthy of study. More so than chimpanzees, if I may say so without disrespect to your colleague. Did you know the Ebrio believe our kings—our precolonial kings—to have been descended from leopards? Our word for leopard, in fact, means both 'holy child' and 'holy ancestor.'"

If Trowbridge hadn't been so tired, he would have been interested in this.

"I wouldn't have known you were Ebrio."

"Because I don't have the scarification."

"Yes."

"My father was a surgeon, educated in Brussels. He saw scarification as something barbaric, and refused to let me undergo the ceremonies. My mother, by contrast, was unhappy at the break with tradition. Now, of course, we're moving past our tribal heritage; it isn't the issue it once was."

The Justice Minister selected a single sheet from the papers in front of him and set the others aside. Trowbridge found himself watching his hands. Strong, graceful fingers, with pale half-moons on perfectly manicured fingernails.

"I understand the BBC intended to make a film about Dr. Juvigny's work with the chimpanzees. I suppose his death means they won't be coming after all?"

"No, the BBC won't be coming now."

"It isn't something you could handle in his place?"

"I'm not a primatologist."

"But couldn't you help the photographers? Show them where to go, and so on?"

"They'd need someone who understands chimps, someone who could tell them what they're seeing. Anyway, I'm not based near the station—I work deep in the forest."

"What a shame. The film would have been a credit to Dr. Juvigny's work, and to my country."

Trowbridge said nothing. The Justice Minister, after a thoughtful moment, said, "I suppose it must be gloomy, deep in the forest."

"I have a view, actually."

"Yes?"

He was about to mention the inselberg when a voice inside told him not to say anything more than he needed to, even to someone as apparently reasonable and sympathetic as this.

The Justice Minister looked back at the papers on his desk. "My investigators have a suspect for the murders, if you're interested."

"I am."

"Dr. Juvigny captured a poacher a few weeks ago and turned him over to the police. The man subsequently fell sick and died. The family apparently believes your colleague was responsible—specifically, that Juvigny used witchcraft to bring about the man's death. We think the family may have hired someone to take revenge, probably someone from Denkyara, where weapons are easy to come by, and people are more than willing to use them for money. Of course, this is just a working hypothesis—we have no direct evidence, and we may have trouble finding any, given the circumstances."

"There were tire tracks at the station that weren't from any truck that should have been there. A recognizable scar on one of the treads. I brought it to the attention of the official in charge. He wasn't very interested—and then someone drove over the tracks."

The Justice Minister frowned. "That's unfortunate. I'll certainly look into it."

He made a note on the report, then said, "What are your plans now, Mr. Trowbridge? I suppose you'll be returning home?"

"I want to go back out to the park."

"Do you think that's a good idea?"

It occurred to him that the Justice Minister might be the one to decide whether he was allowed to stay on in Terre Diamantée. He had almost mentioned the attack in the hotel room in Sandoukou—the possibility that someone in the area might have a grudge against Europeans. Now he was glad he hadn't.

"I have too much invested in the study to pull out now. And I work deep in the forest, as I said. It would be hard for anyone to find me, even assuming they wanted to."

"It does seem as if this was an isolated incident," the Justice Minister allowed. "And you strike me as someone less likely to make enemies than your colleague. If you'll promise to exercise caution—"

"I do, and I will."

"That's settled, then," the Justice Minister said. He pushed the sheaf of papers to one side of his desk and glanced at his watch.

Trowbridge assumed the interview was over, but the Justice Minister leaned back in his chair, brought his palms together before his throat, and said, "Maybe you can explain something I've always wondered about. Leopards strike me as vastly more cunning, capable, and deadly than lions, for example. With so many people crowding into the places they live, why don't they attack human beings more often? It seems as if they could, if they were so inclined."

"A human being isn't a normal prey image for a leopard."

"'Prey image'?"

"A predator will attack an animal that conforms to its prey image, and ignore one that doesn't. Some predators have a narrow range of prey images. Cheetah, for example. Leopards have a much broader range—but that range doesn't normally include human beings."

"What you're telling me is that it isn't in a leopard's *nature* to attack people, at least under normal circumstances. You haven't explained why."

"We establish behavior first. Then we work backward toward motivation."

The Justice Minister smiled. "The opposite of a police investigator."

"I guess so."

"Are there animals for whom human beings *are* a natural prey image?"

"Just one I can think of."

The Justice Minister smiled again. His teeth were very white, and he looked astoundingly healthy and rested.

"*Homo sapiens,*" the Justice Minister said.

"In your line of work," Trowbridge said, "you ought to know better than me."

21

The lobby of the Deauville was filled with a group of cosmetics sales-men from India who smelled like their products and were busily booking every room. He walked back out into the hazy sunlight and flagged down a taxi and had it drive him along the broad boulevard that lined the port, past the Belgian embassy, and past a half-sunken ferry boat from which an old man was casting a hand net, around the bay toward the dark bulk of the slave fort on the point. He took a room in a small hotel set back from the boulevard, drew the curtains, and turned on an air conditioner that put out more noise than cold air.

When he lay on the bed he found himself thinking about the con-versation he'd just had with the Justice Minister.

It wasn't that the Minister had lied to him, and he hadn't been rude or dismissive, like the *Chef des Gendarmes*. What was troubling was the neatness of the explanation he'd put forward for Jean Luc's death. It was thoroughly plausible, and at the same time thoroughly unverifiable. All theory, no evidence. Less than thirty-six hours after the murders the authorities had chosen a suspect, or suspects, and seemed to be ready to give up on getting a conviction. Blame, in the main, had been deflected onto another country, and onto the persis-tence of old beliefs in witchcraft. You could almost hear people talk-ing about it. *Terrible, but it's the sort of thing that happens in Africa, at least once in a while.*

Jean Luc might have been difficult, but he'd given an enormous amount to this place. He'd committed himself wholly to the park, done his best to try to protect it, and treated at least some of the peo-ple here reasonably well. It seemed as if the place owed him some-thing in return, even if it was only a decently vigorous investigation of his murder. Trowbridge went to the sink and splashed water on his face, then locked the door behind him and walked back along the boulevard toward the Belgian embassy.

☷ ☷ ☷

"Look," he said, "I'm an American, and Jean Luc and Guy were Belgian, so in some ways this is none of my business. But I was there—and for what it's worth, I don't think they're doing a very thorough job investigating what happened."

A Diamantien woman in the next room—one of the vice-consul's assistants—was conducting visa interviews behind bulletproof glass, and had lost her temper and was shouting. The atmosphere seemed tense both inside and outside the building; he'd had a fair amount of difficulty simply getting in. His white skin, and the fact that he wasn't seeking a Belgian visa, had helped him jump the long line of Djoula *commerçants* and prospective Brussels taxi drivers waiting in a crooked line outside the front gate, but it had been difficult to convince the guard at the front door that he did, in fact, have a good reason to speak to the Belgian consul, given the misfortune of his American citizenship.

In the end, he had been ushered into the office of the vice-consul, who was young, with thin blond hair plastered straight back on his head, wire-rimmed glasses he peered through like portholes, and a harassed look which was probably related to a desk covered with paperwork. His phone rang intermittently; so far, in deference to Trowbridge's presence, he had ignored it.

"Well, it's a terrible thing," the vice-consul said, echoing the statement of the Justice Minister. "And it's generated no end of difficult paperwork—you can't imagine what it's like to get a pair of bodies shipped out of this country. But we're handling that, and it seems to me that the Diamantiens are handling their end as well. I understand that both the acting *préfet* from the region and the *Chef des Gendarmes* were on the scene almost immediately. And you've just come from the office of the Justice Minister, who happens to be an extremely busy man, because he's handling both the Justice and Interior portfolios. What more, exactly, do you expect the Diamantiens to do?"

"The Justice Minister handles both Justice and Interior?"

That meant one individual—the individual he'd spoken with barely an hour ago—was in charge not only of the court system, but of the police and the civilian *préfets*, the district governors like Douliba. He wondered why the President would allow such a concentration of power, then remembered Alain saying the Justice Minister had been anointed as the President's successor. If the President had decided to abandon the classic strategy for longevity at the top—dividing power among rival successors—and given the nod to someone loyal enough and patient enough to wait for the Presidential funeral, it made sense. Control over the entire security apparatus would allow the Justice Minister to ensure that no rivals to his successor status emerged, thus protecting not only himself, but the President.

"I grant you, it's not ideal," the vice-consul admitted. "But we're in Africa, after all. And we have a very high opinion of the Justice Minister. The ambassador does, anyway."

Trowbridge saw the vice-consul's eyes flick toward the paperwork on his desk. He said, "Look, it isn't that they're *not* doing anything specific—it's just that it all seems too neat. Too easy a way to sweep what happened under the rug. Also, there was a strange set of tire tracks at the station. No one paid them much attention, and I'm afraid they've been destroyed by now."

"Did you say something to the *Chef des Gendarmes*?"

"Yes."

"And what happened?"

"One of his men looked at the tracks."

"And?"

"And nothing. It seems like, I don't know, they should have taken a plaster cast, made a sketch or something."

The vice-consul gave him a weary look which suggested nothing in the way of inefficiency or botched procedure could surprise him or outrage him any longer. He lifted his glasses, rubbed his eyes, and said, "I grant you they have an interest in resolving this as quickly and cleanly as possible. They're in the middle of very difficult negotiations with the World Bank and their creditors in Paris, and they don't need embarrassments, even of this kind. But it doesn't necessarily follow—"

Something behind Trowbridge caught the vice-consul's attention, and he frowned. Trowbridge followed his gaze.

"Kwame," the vice-consul said sharply, "I've told you before to announce yourself, not just stand in the doorway like that. What is it?"

"*Des actes notariés, monsieur,*" said the man, holding up a sheaf of papers. He was thin and balding, and had a goatee and three neat lines of scarification on each temple.

"Deux minutes," the vice-consul said, then looked back at Trowbridge with an expression that suggested the interview was drawing to a close. "Are you staying in town? I'll contact you if I hear anything."

"At the Petit Griot. But I'll be going back out to the forest soon."

The vice-consul nodded distractedly.

Trowbridge made one last attempt. "Maybe you could try pushing them a little harder. I think the families deserve that, at least."

"I'll see what I can do," the vice-consul said, and then the phone rang, and he answered it with a harried *"Oui!"* and Trowbridge left.

It occurred to him as he walked back along the boulevard that he ought to call Alain, but he didn't feel up to it. Then he remembered he'd had almost nothing to eat in two days. He walked past his hotel and crossed a crumbling bridge over the lagoon, the water beneath him turning gray blue as the sun disappeared behind clouds. He went up beneath the massive walls of the fort, and down a sandy slope to a little restaurant under some mango trees with a view out over the ocean. It was early for lunch, and he was the only customer. He ordered fish with green peppercorn sauce, and green beans and french fries. While he sat waiting for his food a storm came in over the ocean, trailing high translucent curtains of rain. Celestial light poured down between the dark clouds, making the water silver. After a while the storm overwhelmed these shafts of light and became a heavy charcoal shape, sweeping toward the beach in a breathtaking, catastrophic rush. The rain pocked the water surface, and tamped down the beach sand like a million individual finger stabs. Then it hit the restaurant, pounding down onto the thatched roof and the white plastic chairs and tables on the terrace. The waiter stood at the terrace edge looking out.

"In another week or so we'll have the *harmattan*," he said, "and there'll be no rain for a while. No rain, and fewer tourists, because tourists don't enjoy lying on the beach when the sky is hazy. Did you hear someone killed a European scientist upcountry? That won't bring in the tour groups."

The waiter shrugged and left Trowbridge alone. The rain was making a tremendous washing noise. He saw movement and looked toward the fort, where people had come out from under the walls and stripped to their underwear to bathe, standing in the rain amid waist-high heaps of bleached clam shells. He realized these people lived in the recesses in the walls of the fort, that they must make their living gathering clams in the lagoon. He closed his eyes and considered the different experiences available to a human life. Listening to the water come down, letting the cool rainy air bathe his face, he began, for the first time in thirty-six hours, to feel something like a sense of peace. The waiter brought his meal, then a *crème caramel* which he said was on the house.

By the time Trowbridge finished and paid his bill the rain had stopped. He walked back up the wet sandy slope, feeling as if he would be able to sleep now, lousy air conditioner or no. When he reached the hotel there was a police car with four men in it dressed in civilian clothes and wearing guns. One of the men got out of the car and informed him he was being deported, that he had five minutes to pack before they left for the airport. He wasted three of those minutes arguing, then grabbed his things, and found himself, something less than an hour later, pressed back into his seat as the Sabena Airbus angled up off the runway into leaden clouds. He was wondering if the plastic bag which enclosed his computer was sufficiently watertight, and how long the battery would last, and if the chimps had noticed they were no longer shadowed by moving trees.

22

Pinwheels of dry brown leaves swirled down the sidewalk, making a scratching noise; above him, in the winter blue sky of the northern hemisphere, white clouds sailed distinctly. He stood on the hospital steps and looked up at the red brick building, shivering. It was cold, and he'd come directly from the airport wearing the only sweater he'd taken to Africa.

Hospitals. Between the ages of fourteen and nineteen—from the time of his father's first heart attack, to when he died—Trowbridge had seen enough of hospitals to last him a lifetime. He was looking forward to seeing Gordon, but he didn't much like the idea of Gordon lying in a hospital bed, despite the fact that they had told him, when he called the Society from the airport, that the worst of the attack was over, and that Gordon would probably be released in a couple of days.

He hesitated a minute longer, then went up the steps and pushed his way through the high doors, feeling his skin prickle unpleasantly at the smell.

Gordon was sitting up in bed drinking grapefruit juice through a straw. He wore pajamas and had a tan, although beneath the tan his color wasn't good, and he looked tired, which wasn't surprising, given that he was coming off a debilitating bout of malaria—several straight days of a raging fever that peaked, at some point, in delirium, combined with a headache that surpassed belief in the capacity of one's skull to generate and contain pain. Trowbridge knew the symptoms; he'd had them himself in the Ituri. The difference was that when he left Africa he'd been able to take Primaquine, a drug which was very effective at killing off the malaria bugs in one's system. Gordon, because of a quirk in his chemical makeup—he was G6PD deficient—couldn't take Primaquine, for which there was no effective alternative; Gordon's malaria bugs had been comfortably established in his liver for two decades, emerging once or twice a year to seed his blood and bring on an attack.

Trowbridge closed the door behind himself. "Looks like we both just got back from Africa."

Gordon, who referred to his malaria bouts as "return trips to Africa," looked at Trowbridge with an amused expression that only partially masked his surprise.

"You came all the way from Terre Diamantée to make jokes?"

Trowbridge dropped his bag and sat in a straight-backed chair beside the bed.

"It's good to see you."

"I *think* it's good to see you," Gordon said. "What are you doing here?"

There must not have been anything in the New York papers. It made sense; Jean Luc was Belgian, after all, and hadn't been a public figure—although, ironically, he might have become one after the BBC film.

Three moving trees, falling in the forest, making no sound, he thought. Just how somebody wanted it. He took a deep breath and told Gordon briefly about the study, and then what had happened at the station.

When he finished there was a long silence. Then Gordon said, "Jesus, we lost a good biologist—that's a tragedy. Are you all right? In a personal sense, I mean."

"I'm all right."

"You could have been there when this happened, couldn't you?"

"Yes."

Gordon's expression was searching. Trowbridge sensed he was being looked over both as a friend who'd gone through something difficult, and as a piece of valuable machinery that might have sustained damage in an accident. Gordon was the closest thing he'd had to a father since his own father had died; the expression unlocked something vulnerable in him, and he felt oddly close to tears, something that didn't happen often.

Perhaps sensing this, Gordon said briskly, "Why did they kick you out?"

"I have no idea."

"What are you going to do?"

"Let things cool down for a couple of weeks, then apply for a new visa. The computer's running on solar power. If I get back within a month or so I shouldn't lose any data."

"That's a terrible plan."

"It is?"

"Let me see your passport."

He took his passport from his chest pocket and handed it to Gordon, who flipped through it quickly until he found what he was looking for.

"Just as I thought. They didn't bother canceling your visa."

"They were too busy hustling me through Customs. But the visa runs out in five days, and the next Sabena flight—"

"—isn't for a week, I know. This happened on Friday, and you were thrown out of Terre Diamantée on Saturday evening, right? What are the chances their embassy here knows what's happened? Get down to Washington tonight and apply for a new visa first thing in the morning. Tell them you had to come to Washington unexpectedly because I was sick, tell them anything—just get the visa now, and go back. The longer you wait, the worse your chances of getting back in will become."

"What if they recognize me at the airport?"

"A week from now the people at the airport will have forgotten all about you. But if the Diamantien consul gets a telex tomorrow afternoon telling him not to issue you a visa, he *won't* forget that, not for a long time. If you don't go back immediately you may not get back in at all."

Trowbridge hesitated. Gordon had spent twenty years in Africa. And yet . . .

He said, "Somehow I expected you to tell me that it was too dangerous. That I should stay on here and take the directorship."

"Honestly, both things occurred to me. Particularly in light of what happened to me in the Congo."

Gordon had been the last biologist out of Katanga in 1961. More precisely, the last one to make it out, after spending three days in a jail cell being beaten every couple of hours.

"I was sorry at the time I stayed on," Gordon said, "but I'm not sorry now, because those final data I collected were important. You have a breakthrough study going, David, and frankly I'm jealous. In your position, I wouldn't give it up for anything. Get back in there, take care of yourself—take your damned malaria medicine; I know how you feel about hospitals—and get it done. This doesn't change our deal, by the way. I still want you back here to take the directorship."

"Gordon, I'm not sure—"

"The deal was, if I recall correctly, that you would decide at the end of six months. Go finish your work, and we'll talk. In the meantime, you might want to consider what you've received from the Society—the opportunity to do this study, for example—and whether you have an obligation to give something back. Now get the hell down to Washington before the embassy receives a telex from Pont Noir."

⸙ ⸙ ⸙

It was raining on Monday morning on Massachusetts Avenue. The row of embassy mansions looked hooded and gloomy, like birds of prey. He waited in a darkened outer office, running his hand nervously through rain-soaked hair. When he was finally ushered in, the Diamantien consul—a small man in a suit that seemed too large for him—was sitting behind the cone of light from his desk lamp, hands folded neatly before him. He was oddly polite, more so than Trowbridge remembered him being on the first visit.

After listening attentively to Trowbridge's request, the consul said, "May I see your passport?"

Trowbridge started to push the passport across the desk, then stopped.

"You haven't said whether my visa will be renewed."

"I need to see your passport before making that decision."

"Why?"

"I need to know how long your current visa runs."

"It expires in four days."

"I have to see it," the consul said, extending his hand.

Again, Trowbridge started to push the passport across the desk. Then something in the man's face struck him, and he hesitated. There was an ink pad and rubber stamp at the consul's elbow.

"I can tell you what it says."

"I doubt it. It's in French."

"I read French."

There was a silence. Then the consul withdrew his hand and shrugged elaborately.

"I've been instructed not to give you a new visa. If you try to enter on this one before it expires you'll be detained and sent out on the next flight."

"Would you mind telling me why?"

"We're concerned about your safety in my country. Another scientist was killed there recently."

"My situation is very different than the scientist who was killed. The Justice Minister himself agreed it was safe for me to stay."

"I'm afraid that's not his decision. My instructions come directly from the Ministry of Foreign Affairs. If you like, I'll request a formal explanation for the denial, but the decision won't change."

Trowbridge considered this a moment, then stood, slipping his passport into his pocket.

"Do whatever you feel like," he said. "I have no intention of going back to Terre Diamantée."

In a phone booth across the street he looked up an address and wrote it down, then called a travel agent and booked a flight out of Washington that evening. He put the phone down and walked out to the curb and hailed a taxi. The rain had stopped. Pale sunlight shone on the wet street, and the cars going by made a tearing sound. Gordon had been wrong, as it turned out. Someone felt strongly enough that he not return to Terre Diamantée that they'd contacted the embassy on a weekend. But there were still four days remaining on his visa—and there wouldn't have been if he'd followed his original plan to let things cool off for a couple of weeks before reapplying. Something else he owed Gordon. He climbed into the taxi and gave the driver the address of the embassy of the Democratic People's Republic of Denkyara.

23

The sweltering heat was relieved only somewhat by the salty breeze off the blue ocean beneath him, as he sat in the shade of the Don't Mind Your Wife chop bar, with its rusty tin roof and its hand-carved wooden chairs and a group of old men playing dominoes quietly in the corner. The proprietor set a plate of scrambled eggs and a beer in front of him. Food would be more difficult to come by once he left the capital; he needed to stock up any way he could, beginning by having a big meal.

He was waiting for someone, and he knew it would be a while before that someone showed up.

At the far end of the square, dividing his view of the ocean, was an enormous silk cotton tree almost three hundred years old; wisps of seed drifted like off-white snow across the paving stones. Beneath the tree was a high wooden platform, worn with use, from which slaves had been auctioned until the British had renounced the trade. From then on, as in Freetown, slaves recaptured from slaving vessels had been brought here and given their freedom. The local chiefs, deeply involved in the profitable slaving commerce, had not fully appreciated the humanitarian merits of this change in policy, and several pitched battles had been fought—one of them in this square—before the Brits had finally convinced the locals that the slave business which had once been right was now wrong.

An outlaw state, Trowbridge thought, right from the beginning. To his surprise, particularly after all the stories he'd heard in Terre Diamantée, he liked the place. In particular, he liked the people he'd run into since getting off the ferry this morning. The citizens of Terre Diamantée had inherited some of the reserve and formality of their Belgian colonial rulers; here, by contrast, there was something loose in the atmosphere, a refreshing lack of caution. The people were aggressive, blunt, and funny. You could feel the danger beneath—probably not far beneath—but there was a good-natured quality to human interactions, a quality which the danger, somehow, did not contradict.

A crowded and very decrepit ferry had brought him across the wide bay from the airport. Customs, when the ferry docked, had been a chaos of yelling and shoving; he'd waded into the fray, using his elbows and swinging two oversized duffel bags, until he reached the head of the line, where he showed his visa and paid a healthy bribe to a customs official who took his money with a grin. Then he threaded his way between a pair of rusting tanks—gun turrets aimed at the port, presumably to protect the city from a sea-borne coup—and hiked up through the narrow streets, past decaying buildings with faded gingerbread trim, past an open fish market where mounds of fish gleamed in the sun, until he reached the Don't Mind Your Wife, where he propped his feet on his duffel bags, ordered breakfast, and began asking questions.

Denkyara City was set against a pair of hills which formed a natural amphitheater above the port. Atop one hill was the university, which produced a small but steady stream of intellectuals and political dissidents whom President for Life Akrudju regularly had arrested or exiled. Atop the other hill was a prison which had once been a slave fort, controlled in succession by the Portuguese, Dutch, Danish, and finally British. The joke in town was that the university produced graduates with "leftist tendencies," since they tended to move from the university on the right-hand hill to less comfortable accommodations on the left.

At independence in 1959 Denkyara had thrown out every Brit in the country, taken the name of a powerful pre-Asante forest kingdom from the seventeenth century, and pronounced itself a Marxist paradise, only to collapse twelve years later under the weight of its economic failures. A group of young army officers had mounted a coup and installed Akrudju, who had guided the country from Marxist inefficiency toward the purest form of West African corruption, known locally as "help yourself" government—those who governed helped themselves. A decade of this finished off what was left of the civil service bequeathed by the British, and chased out the few large companies which hadn't been nationalized by the Marxists. The last election had been held eight years ago, shortly before the President had decided to move the capital to his hometown, a village of fewer than a thousand people near the eastern border. Some members of the army, reluctant to comply with this latest whim, had rebelled, briefly encircling the presidential mansion; this attempted coup, known as the "Little Rebellion," was put down firmly. Those who'd stayed loyal— and thus avoided being shot on the beach—now raced back and forth in their Mercedes, on the only good road in the country, between the new capital, Akrudjutown, where a facade of government was carried on in a half-finished set of grandiose buildings, and the old capital, where they installed one or more mistresses in comfortable houses with a view similar to that which Trowbridge had from the chop bar, and where the real business of the country, the making of black market money, took place. Denkyara was an economic basket case—but it was a basket case through which sluiced a good deal of profitable smuggled goods. Cigarettes, liquor, and bales of used clothing were the chief imports; in exchange, there were phosphates and groundnuts in the north, cocoa and gold in the south, and to the west, toward Terre Diamantée, endless tracts of forest.

For better or worse, the country had been so mismanaged that this last resource hadn't been exploited with anything like the efficiency of Terre Diamantée; after the timber companies had been nationalized, the machinery had rusted and the roads had melted back into forest. Outside investors were sufficiently put off by Akrudju's unpredictability, and his bloodthirsty style—there were rumors that young children were sacrificed in the basement of the presidential mansion, while Akrudju looked on in Mickey Mouse pajamas, drinking beer and smoking marijuana—that little exploitation had taken place since then.

Timber people weren't the only ones to have avoided Denkyara; it had been seven years since any biologist had worked in the country. While passing through London, Trowbridge had called the last one to do so, and had been given Thomas Fulton's name.

He scanned the quiet square. The proprietor, who wore flowered shorts and a Madonna T-shirt, caught his eye, reached down into a chest full of ice—there was no electricity—and pulled out a bottle, flipping it confidently across the bar. Trowbridge caught the beer, used the opener tied to the table leg, and leaned back in his chair. The bottle was cold, beaded with moisture, a pleasure. Two beers would have to be the limit if he wanted to keep his head clear. He felt good, felt the sense of freedom and optimism which came at the beginning of a new venture—in most cases, he remembered, shortly before the problems began.

☷ ☵ ☷

BabySitter strolled across the square. She picked up a beer from behind the bar—pointing to Trowbridge as the person who would pay—and seated herself across from him.

"He'll be here in a while."

"Okay," Trowbridge said.

The young woman sitting across from him wore a red tube top, a mini skirt, and plastic sandals. Her features were broad and pretty, her eyes a deep brown, her hair woven into cornrows with bright beads. It wasn't immediately obvious to Trowbridge where she'd gotten her nickname. According to the bar owner, who called himself Chevy-Man, she had a hair salon around the corner. Everyone in Denkyara seemed to be called something other than his or her real name. When he'd asked BabySitter about Thomas Fulton, she'd looked blank until he added, "I think he's called Utopia."

A smile had broken across her face. "Oh, I can find Utopia for you."

Now she was looking at him with a thoughtful expression. "How much time do you have here?" she asked finally.

Her teeth were amazingly white.

"Not much."

"Can you help me get an American visa?"

"I'm not very good at getting visas."

"How about a baby instead?"

He looked at her.

"We could make a baby. If I get a copy of your passport to prove you're the father, they have to give me a visa. I want to go to New York. I'm a hairdresser."

"Business isn't so good here?"

"Take a look."

He looked around. The square was empty, and had been that way for a full ten minutes. The most recent sign of life had been a jeep full of soldiers which had careened through a few minutes ago, siren blaring.

"We have enough time. Utopia isn't gonna be here for a while. My place is just over there."

She motioned around the corner.

"Thanks. But I have some thinking to do before I talk to Utopia."

She looked disappointed.

"Can I have another beer?"

"Sure. Why don't you get something to eat."

Music started up from another bar across the square. BabySitter went over and picked up a beer and came back, dancing slightly to the music. She sat back down and looked at him again. It was clear she was trying to find some use for his presence in her life. Her gaze focused somewhere above his eyes.

"I could do something to your hair," she said doubtfully. "But I haven't had much practice on white people."

⠿ ⠰ ⠿

When Utopia arrived he shook Trowbridge's hand enthusiastically and declared he was overjoyed to have a scientist as a client again; scientists, he said, were infinitely more reasonable than the cigarette smugglers and gun runners who'd been using his services in recent years. Utopia was a fixer, a man who could get things done in the freewheeling Denkyara environment. He'd graduated from the university with a degree in French literature, but had a more practical bent—"and better instincts," he said—than his politically minded colleagues, and had managed to avoid imprisonment or exile. Utopia asked about Perkins-Swayne, the Brit whom Trowbridge had contacted in Lon-

don, a forest ecologist who'd been beaten senseless by Denkyaran soldiers and left for dead during the Little Rebellion. Utopia noted regretfully that those circumstances had been beyond his control, but
that very little else in Denkyara was. With Trowbridge's cash, he said
confidently, and his—Utopia's—connections, anything could be done.

Some of his enthusiasm wilted when he learned what Trowbridge
had in mind.

"The western border?"

Trowbridge nodded.

"That's Ebrio country. Real different from here. You gotta go
through a lot of checkpoints. They'll want money—and they aren't
nice people, these smallboys."

"'Small boys'?"

Utopia grimaced. "It's not a term you'd use to their face—there's
some irony involved. You sure you want to go there? You're a biologist, right? Maybe we could find you some animals around here."

Trowbridge convinced him, eventually, that he did want to go to
the western border. They worked out an estimate of what the checkpoints would cost, and discussed Utopia's fee, settling on a figure that
would allow him to take out an insurance policy on his truck from a
Syrian money man downtown. Trowbridge asked if they ought to obtain some kind of permit authorizing their travel. Utopia thought this
would be a good idea, and said he would have the Syrian get one—although its usefulness, the farther they went from the city, would diminish.

"The Ebrio don't care much about paper issued by the government. It would be better if we could get something from the Big Man."

They have one here too, Trowbridge thought. Seems to be a West
African phenomenon.

"Can we do that?"

Utopia snorted.

"That's pretty funny," he said.

⸭ ⸭ ⸭

They left that afternoon. "If we wait till tomorrow," Utopia said
glumly, "I'll come to my senses." Utopia's little brother—Trowbridge
wasn't sure if he was really a brother, or perhaps a cousin—rode between them in Utopia's pickup. He was appallingly shy and said nothing, staring back at the trail of red dust behind them as if he would

rather be going back to the capital. They passed a bush taxi with its roof buried in bananas and the words *Fight the Good Fight* painted on the front, and *Suffering Is Truth* on the back. The road grew steadily worse, and their progress slowed. Shortly before sunset Utopia pulled off into a small grouping of huts that turned out to be his home village. They were received with great happiness by his mother, who rushed to prepare mounds of orange-colored *foutou*, and a pot of cane rat *kedjenou*, the village specialty. Trowbridge choked down the cane rat with a grim smile, killing the taste with palm wine; after dinner he was escorted to the hut reserved for distinguished visitors, and lay awake most of the night, marveling at the fact that the local mosquitoes, diving noisily against his skin, were willing to brave the smoky interior. In the morning, for the first time, he began taking malaria medicine.

They reached the first checkpoint shortly before noon. Utopia did not look worried as they slowed to a stop. There were a dozen or so soldiers, most of them playing soccer in a cleared field beside the road. They were cheerful, aggressive, curious, and happy to receive the three ten-dollar bills Utopia recommended Trowbridge hand over as a "gesture of cooperation and support." They lost half an hour while the truck was refueled with a hand pump from a fifty-gallon barrel raised on stilts; then Utopia accelerated into the forest.

"So far so good," Trowbridge said.

Utopia shook his head. "Bad luck talking like that."

"Two more checkpoints?"

"If we're lucky, only two," Utopia said. "You won't be able to afford any more."

☷ ䷂ ☷

An hour later they stopped beside a disreputable-looking structure built of cinderblock and woven palm fronds.

"Last bar before the border," Utopia said, climbing out and lifting the hood of the truck. "Bad place to eat, but the beer's all right. Go on in. I'll check the oil and join you."

Trowbridge ducked in through the low door. It was dark inside, and he had trouble seeing in the gloom. Someone emerged from a corner, a slovenly-looking woman with Medusa-like coils of dark hair and high heels. Her hands were on her hips, and she was smiling as if she knew him, but it wasn't a very pleasant smile. He looked past her at the bartender, who nodded, reached behind himself, pulled down a bottle, and poured a drink. The friendliness in both faces was false and sycophantic; he had a momentary feeling he was someone else, and didn't much like whoever that person was. The woman said, "Honey, you still owe me—" Then she stopped, wavering slightly on her heels, and looked at the bartender, saying something in a dialect Trowbridge didn't recognize. The bartender studied him a moment, then poured the drink carefully back into the bottle and put it away.

"What do I owe you?" he asked the woman.

This time when she smiled there was no falsehood in the expression; just a weary, and minimal, level of interest.

"Why don't you give me an hour of your time? Then we can talk about what you owe me."

He moved past her to the bar. "Two beers," he said.

The bartender nodded. The emptied glass was still sitting on the bar, and the smell hit his nostrils. He wondered how anyone could drink whiskey on a hot day. Apparently someone could—someone who must look something like him. A figure materialized at his elbow, the woman in high heels.

"What about half an hour," she said. "I don't have a lot else going on today."

⁂

The atmosphere at the second checkpoint was noticeably less pleasant than at the first. Soldiers scanned the permit presented by Utopia suspiciously, finding a number of inadequacies. In all likelihood, they were told, they would have to turn back. Utopia nodded, enduring these necessary preliminaries. Trowbridge's statement that he planned to do research in the forest was received skeptically; he was forced to empty the contents of his duffel bags and watch in silence as a pair of soldiers, ostensibly looking for "contraband," sifted avariciously through his belongings. A set of flashlight batteries disappeared into a soldier's pockets; the soldier looked up at him with flat eyes, daring him to say anything. Utopia was still negotiating their "fine" with the leader of the group, who postured angrily for his subordinates, slamming his hand repeatedly on the hood of Utopia's truck. Eventually they settled on seventy-five dollars—after an initial demand of three hundred—and were allowed to drive on.

The dirt road became asphalt, suddenly, although this wasn't an improvement; the asphalt was opened by deep potholes which forced them to drive more slowly. White-trunked rubber trees rose about them in regular rows—an abandoned plantation, which explained the road. The groves gave way to a factory falling down in places, and Trowbridge looked up at the most sky he'd seen in a while. Then the asphalt and potholes and rubber trees ended, and they were in deep forest again.

"Like a museum exhibit," Utopia said. "From when we used to have an economy."

Occasionally they passed small villages set among the trees. The people here stopped what they were doing, and stared; they looked poorer than those near the capital, and were dressed more shabbily, in ragged, cast-off Western clothing instead of the more expensive *pagne*. Trowbridge was forced into making the obvious comparison with Terre Diamantée. The government there might be corrupt, but at least *some* money went for roads and schools and wells and village warehouses. Here, there was no human prosperity, little human activity. He saw handprints in white paint decorating the brown clay exteriors of some of the round, palm-thatched huts.

"Ebrio?" he said.

"Yeah. We're not in Denkyara any more."

Trowbridge looked at him.

"I'm joking you. Technically, we're still in Denkyara. But we're a long way from the capital. In the bush, people think about themselves, their family, and their tribe. You'd have to remind some of these people what country they live in."

Something Utopia said yesterday came back to him. "Why do they call them small boys?"

"If you're going to say it, say it right. One word, emphasis on the first syllable."

"Smallboys."

"Better," Utopia said. "As to where the term came from, I have no idea. Maybe because of the size of their brains, or because they fight small wars. Or because they hang around someone bigger who tells them where to point their guns."

"The Big Man you referred to yesterday. Is that one of the ministers, like in Terre Diamantée?"

Utopia looked at him with a puzzled face. "What do you mean?"

"I mean—" He stopped. Then he said, "When you told me a permit from the Big Man would be more helpful—"

"I *meant* the Big Man in Terre Diamantée. I told you, this is Ebrio country."

☶ ☵ ☶

They slept sitting up in the cab. It would have been more comfortable to stretch out in the bed of the truck, but Utopia said it wasn't safe, and Trowbridge was inclined to believe him. The forest looked uninhabited, but he knew that even here, in the extreme west of the country, there were villages, and supposedly armed bands that moved between those villages. Drops of condensed moisture fell onto the truck from the trees above them, making a random, metallic tapping all night; at dawn, with birdcalls echoing through the forest, they began driving again.

Trowbridge had trouble waking up. He felt groggy and headachy and stared without interest at the forest flowing by in a green wall. After a while he closed his eyes and dozed. He had a dream in which Jean Luc was alive and showing him a notebook of some kind. Then he was jounced awake by the lurching of the truck, and opened his eyes, and remembered that wasn't going to happen, that Jean Luc was dead. He grasped that reality slowly, and a debilitating unhappiness welled up in him as he stared at the forest going by, disliking this place, feeling low and at the same time jumpy and anxious.

The malaria medicine, he told himself.

Or maybe, he thought, as Utopia negotiated a particularly bad section of road, it was the prospect of what he was driving toward. Assuming he made it over the border, his plan entailed weeks, perhaps months, of working in almost total solitude. He was capable of working alone, and often preferred it, but this kind of utter isolation would be something new.

He took a deep breath. The anxiety wasn't going away. If this was what malaria medicine did to a person, he would take his chances with getting sick. He looked over at Utopia, who, oddly enough, looked uneasy as well. Then he realized they were slowing down, and looked forward to where a heavy branch lay across the road. Behind the branch a clot of figures was beginning to assemble.

Utopia shook his head. He looked—there was no other word for it—scared.

"This is the checkpoint," Utopia said, "I would have liked to skip."

⸭ ⸭ ⸭

When they rolled to a stop an automatic weapon was jammed in his window so that the barrel was close to his head. There were more weapons pointed at them from both sides of the truck. Utopia got out with a nervous smile and looked around for someone with whom to begin negotiations. The people pointing guns were dressed in a motley combination of military fatigues and Western clothes; one man, weirdly, wore a woman's red wig and a white housecoat, and some kind of strange white makeup around his eyes. Several of the soldiers were young, fifteen at most; one looked more like twelve, and had a child's doll in one hand and an AK-47 in the other. Off to the left in a clearing were several poorly constructed huts. A thin woman with a listless face squatted beside a fire. Someone else lay sprawled in the dirt wearing only a pair of underpants. At first Trowbridge thought the man was sleeping, then saw that his hands were handcuffed behind his back, and his face was bruised and swollen.

Something banged against the side of the truck, sending a jolt of adrenaline through him. One of the soldiers was motioning at him to get out. As he did so he noticed that all of the men had Ebrio scarification on their temples.

Utopia was talking to a man who appeared to be the ranking military officer, addressing him as "Colonel," which seemed unlikely. The man's fly was open, and he wore reflective glasses and a cluster of charms and fetishes around his neck, and had a prominent pot belly and appeared to be drunk. He studied Trowbridge's passport contemptuously while the contents of Trowbridge's duffel bags were dumped into the back of the truck. Soldiers began picking eagerly through his things, taking what they wanted. The food went immediately. Then a couple of shirts, more batteries, a tarp. A young soldier with an automatic rifle slung over his shoulder picked up one of Trowbridge's two camp stoves—the newer of the two, still in the box—and

looked at it admiringly, and tucked it beneath his arm. He began to
walk away. Then he looked back at the other stove, which was
chipped and stained with use, and shrugged, and scooped it up as
well.

"Hey, smallboy," Trowbridge said. "How about leaving me *one.*"

It grew very quiet. Utopia looked at him as if he'd lost his mind.
The young man stopped and turned. The others watched with interested, amoral expressions as he set both stoves down and walked over
to Trowbridge. Slipping the rifle from his shoulder, he set the muzzle
against Trowbridge's chest. Trowbridge felt the pressure, like a finger
poking him. The soldier pursed his lips, and Trowbridge saw his finger
tighten. Then the soldier blew a quick puff of air—a small explosion—
at Trowbridge's eyes. Trowbridge blinked involuntarily, making the
others laugh. The young soldier laughed with them, then picked up
the newer stove and walked away.

The colonel, who had watched this with no change of expression,
closed Trowbridge's passport and shouted an order. Reluctantly, the
soldiers stepped away from the truck, leaving Trowbridge about half
of what he owned. The colonel looked at Utopia from behind the
glasses.

"Five hundred dollars," he said.

Utopia protested that this was impossible. The colonel looked over
at someone who appeared to be his second-in-command, a stocky
man with heavy blunt cheekbones that nearly obscured his eyes. The
man unbuckled his webbed belt, wrapped one end around his fist, and
swung it in a quick motion. There was a smack as the webbed material hit Utopia's face.

"Stop," Trowbridge said.

"What's the matter, *smallboy,*" someone said. "Afraid he's going to
hit you too?"

Utopia had his hand to his face. Blood was running down his
wrist. The second-in-command held the webbed belt loosely, looking
expectantly at the colonel, who looked at Trowbridge. Trowbridge
took out his wallet and counted out five fifty-dollar bills.

"This is all I can afford. Please ask your men to let us go."

The colonel considered this a moment. Then he took the money,
put three of the bills into his pocket, and handed the remaining two
to his second-in-command with a gesture toward the others. Then he
turned and walked toward one of the huts. Trowbridge, moving

slowly and deliberately, put what remained of his belongings back into the duffel bags. One of the things which had not been stolen was the first-aid kit. He opened it and took out alcohol and cotton wool and swabbed Utopia's temple. Utopia's ear, sliced through at the lobe, was bleeding as well. He opened a paper-wrapped bandage and pressed it to the side of Utopia's face.

"Gonna have your own little Ebrio scar," he said quietly.

"I'm okay," Utopia said, taking a deep breath. "Let's go."

Someone dragged the log from across the road. The soldiers moved away from them and stood watching. Trowbridge had an uncomfortable feeling this might not be over yet; the colonel should have shared more of the money with his men. He climbed into the driver's seat. As he started the engine and put the truck into gear the second-in-command walked to the passenger door, told Utopia to move over, and climbed in.

"I'll escort you to the border."

Utopia was holding the bandage against his face. Trowbridge could see his expression, and what he saw confirmed that having an escort was not a development Utopia had hoped for.

They drove slowly away from the checkpoint.

"How far is the border?" Trowbridge asked, keeping his voice normal. It seemed better to say something, to get the man talking.

The man said nothing for a moment. Then, "A couple of kilometers."

His voice was neutral; his rifle, an AK-47 with a forward curving magazine, rested in his lap. The checkpoint behind them seemed suddenly like a place of relative safety. They went over a low rise and kept going until an open area appeared before them. There was a small, ramshackle building with a shed next door which had been mostly burned down. Beyond the building was a bridge over a narrow river.

"Stop the truck," the soldier said.

Trowbridge slowed to a stop. Utopia was staring forward, as if he were thinking about something. The soldier got out and pointed his rifle at Trowbridge.

"Get out," he said.

Trowbridge got out of the truck, noticing a bad smell. He looked over and saw a partially decomposed body lying in a shallow depression beside the burnt shed. The soldier followed his gaze.

"Do you like that?" he said. "Give me your wallet."

Trowbridge pulled his wallet from his pocket and handed it over. The soldier emptied it of what money remained, then looked up.

"There's only a hundred dollars here."

"You weren't the first to get to us."

The soldier looked angry and raised the rifle so that it was pointed at Trowbridge's face. Then his expression changed, and he looked amused, and threw Trowbridge's empty wallet at his feet.

"Next time bring more money," he said, "or you'll go where that smell comes from."

☷ ䷜ ☷

Trowbridge stopped the truck at the near end of the bridge. The building said "Customs" over it, but there was no one around.

Utopia said, "What are you going to do without money?"

"I'll be all right. I'm sorry they hit you."

"It's okay."

"Will you make it back all right?"

"I think so. They know there's nothing left. They might as well let me through in hopes I'll be stupid enough to do this again."

"I didn't know it would be this bad."

"It didn't used to be. Things have not improved in my country. I guess things never improve in my country."

Utopia shrugged, forcing a grin. "Anyway, it's just business. Welcome to Denkyara, David—I think I forgot to tell you that before."

Trowbridge watched him drive away, one hand on the wheel, the other holding the bandage to his face. It was very quiet as he walked across the bridge. The water beneath him was slow-moving, an oily green. When he reached the far side he saw a white-painted customs hut set a hundred yards back from the river. It looked neater and better kept than any structure he'd seen in Denkyara outside the capital. Two Diamantien customs officials were in evidence, one asleep on a cot on the porch, the other, in his shorts, taking a bath in the yard, using a towel and a red plastic tub. The bather yelled at the sleeper, who sat up and squinted at Trowbridge, then said, "Ça va?"

"Oui," Trowbridge said. "Ça va."

"You came through Denkyara?"

"Yes."

"You'll like it better here."

"I think so," Trowbridge said.

Black Leopard

The official thumbed through Trowbridge's passport until he found the visa. He studied it a moment, then stamped it, recording its number and Trowbridge's name in a ledger, and handed it back.

That was all. Trowbridge thanked him and picked up his duffel bags and walked up the *piste*. He didn't stop until the customs hut was at least a kilometer behind him. Then he stepped off the *piste* and set his bags down. Unzipping one, he took out the old camp stove and unscrewed the fuel chamber and tipped it upside down, shaking it. There was a hollow rattling; then a tight roll of bills, wrapped in a rubber band, dropped into his palm. He peeled off some of the bills and put them into his wallet. Then he put the rest back into the stove and screwed the two pieces together and put it back in his duffel bag.

He wiped the sweat from his forehead and drank some water from the canteen. It was early afternoon, but the sky was shaded with dust, and strangely ominous. The *harmattan*, a dry wind that came down each year from the Sahara, was beginning; he could feel desert in the air, and smell smoke from burning fields. He looked at his passport. The visa expired at midnight tonight, something the border official either hadn't noticed, or hadn't cared about. What was more important was the length of stay he'd stamped beside the entry date: *"Six mois—Tourist."*

Six months. More than enough time to finish the study, unless someone found out he was here who thought he shouldn't be. He looked around. There was nothing, and no one; just him and the forest and this red dirt road and the ominous sky. It was unlikely that his name, recorded in that water-stained ledger, would come to the attention of anyone in authority any time soon.

He felt a strange, bitter happiness. This time if they kicked him out he would have data to take with him. That would have made Jean Luc happy. And if he was never allowed to come back here, that would be fine—he would take what he needed from this place, and go back to the mountains where he belonged, and try and forget most of what had happened here. He was a smash-and-grab scientist after all. In the meantime he had work to do. He coughed, and picked up his bags, and walked up the red-dirt *piste* through the logged-out forest.

24

A rust-colored dove bobbed its head, looking for seeds, or perhaps insects of some kind, in the clearing before the station. From where Trowbridge stood concealed by trees it all looked very peaceful. You wouldn't know anything had happened here.

He waited a while to be sure he was alone, then went up beneath the *paillote* and dropped his bags beside the sofa. Someone had washed the concrete in the place where Gregoire had lain, but the blood stain wasn't entirely gone. In the open kitchen, familiar coffee mugs hung neatly on hooks, and utensils were arranged in a basket on the wooden counter. Gregoire's relatives, he decided, must be looking after the place in hopes another researcher would come and provide another source of income. It made the place feel like a museum.

He looked into Claire's room, empty but for the watchful pair of masks. Then he went to Jean Luc's hut, pausing at the door before ducking in and moving through the sleeping area to the room which had served Jean Luc as a study.

In contrast to the *paillote*, the study had been thoroughly cleaned out. Whoever had come out from the Belgian embassy had done a good job. The drawers of Jean Luc's desk, and the bookshelves, were empty.

What he'd hoped to find wasn't going to be here.

He stepped back out into the smoky sunlight and stood a minute. His legs were tired from the walk; his skin, suddenly, felt sticky with several days of hard traveling. It occurred to him that if there were utensils in the kitchen there might be water in the fifty-gallon drum which served the shower. He walked behind the *paillote* to the little shower enclosure, began to strip, looked down, and saw that the concrete beneath him was damp.

It was such a simple detail it took him a moment to realize what it meant. A glance told him the rusty shower head wasn't leaking. Someone had used this shower within the last couple of hours. He turned quickly, scanned what he could see of the forest, then went up beneath the *paillote* and picked up his bags and moved across the clearing. He was about to disappear beneath the trees when he heard someone call his name.

⁂ ⁑ ⁂

"It seems dangerous," he said. "Whoever killed Jean Luc and the others could still be around."

"You came back," Claire pointed out.

She was sitting cross-legged on the couch across from him, hair still wet from the shower she'd taken shortly before his arrival. Beside her was a net bag with an onion and pasta and a can of tuna. She'd been holding the bag when he turned and saw her standing beneath the trees.

The dove had disappeared; around them, the clearing darkened peacefully.

He said, "Yes, but I won't be spending time at the station."

"I'm not here all that much. I've got a tarp and a cot set up about a kilometer into the forest, and I'll move someplace new every few days. I cook here when I need more than a one-burner stove, and I take showers here. I don't see a practical alternative, since I'd rather not live without a shower."

She looked at him with a bleak smile. She seemed almost too collected, given what had happened to people she knew much better than he, and given that she was living almost totally alone in the forest.

"You didn't have any trouble getting back in?"

"No. I got off the plane in Zurich, walked to the Swissair counter, bought a return ticket, and flew back three hours later. I don't think it occurred to them I might try to return."

"It didn't occur to me."

"No? I should have thought it would be obvious. How'd you get back in?"

"Through Denkyara. The consul in Washington told me I'd be turned back at the airport if I tried to fly in."

"Denkyara," she repeated. "Any trouble?"

"I wouldn't do it again."

"I saw Alberto. He told me he asked Douli ba what had happened to us. Douli ba checked with the capital and was told the 'other scientists' had been sent out of the country for their own safety, and weren't coming back."

"I guess we're keeping a low profile, then."

She nodded.

"I'm glad to see you," he said. "I expected to be entirely alone."

In the silence that followed, she surprised him by crying. Quietly, holding herself rigid, but crying.

"Sorry," she said, her voice breaking as she looked around at the station. "I hadn't planned on seeing someone I knew here either."

☲ ☷ ☲

"I have use of a car, if you need one."

She was standing in the kitchen with her back to him, her voice level, in control once again.

"It belongs to a friend in Granville—she's gone to study for a year in the Netherlands. I've got another friend in one of the villages who's keeping it for me, and who'll bring me food. He could do the same for you."

"You think that's a good idea?"

"Nobila's pretty discreet—and the locals don't talk to the police much if they can help it. Anyway, I don't think Douli ba would throw me out unless he was forced to."

"How much more time do you need here?"

"In three months I'll have enough data to finish the dissertation. In the meantime, I can keep the chimps habituated—the main group, anyway—and keep an eye on the park. If Jean Luc's university can get organized and send out another researcher, all this work won't go down the drain."

Above them a fruit bat skittered silently between the beams of the *paillote*. It occurred to him that Claire was more than capable of taking over both Jean Luc's study and the management of the park. She would probably be better than Jean Luc, in fact, at the administrative end of things, at dealing with people. But the university wasn't likely to hire her in that capacity—they'd be looking for a name, to attract funding—and the Diamantien government wouldn't take her seriously without a Ph.D.

He considered the unfairness of that.

"You're pretty stubborn," he said.

She reached into her shirt pocket for a pack of cigarettes, and lit one. "That makes two of us."

There was a shaking in the trees at the edge of the clearing. A group of red colobus, sixty feet up, leaped from branch to branch in a great thrashing, then went still suddenly, as if they knew they were being watched. Their bodies made dark substantial shapes against the pattern of trees and the failing light. He remembered a local belief from the Ituri that when monkeys gathered on trees around a grave-yard it meant they were possessed by the spirits of those who had died.

There was more thrashing, and then the colobus were gone, with a single long shriek to mark their passage.

❖ ❖ ❖

He took a cot from the storeroom and followed her through the forest to where she'd established a camp beside a narrow stream. After setting up the cot, working by candlelight to save flashlight batteries, he set his watch for five a.m. The chimps had nested in a part of their territory roughly in the direction of the inselberg; he and Claire would be able to walk together for the first half hour or so. He felt like talking to her more, felt like asking her, suddenly, about whatever life she had outside the forest, but when he stepped nearer to her hammock and held up the candle she was already asleep.

25

When he reached the platform the sun had lofted to its highest point in the sky, and hung shimmering above the inselberg like a vague mask. The smoke and dust of the *harmattan* had changed his view out over the forest; the trees filtered out some of the *harmattan's* influence, but even here, near the center of the park, enough of that alien wind penetrated to give a gritty, hazy look to things. He stepped back from the edge of the platform, sat on the camp chair he'd brought from the station, and pulled the plastic housing off the computer.

"Here we go," he said quietly.

He touched a key. There was a pause which seemed, for a heart-stopping second, to be too long. Then the screen came up and the grid appeared, the inselberg at its center. He punched in *L1/last(1)* and saw a dot appear, a tiny star blooming in space. A surge of excitement went through him; then he reminded himself this only meant the collar was transmitting, not that it was necessarily around the neck of his study animal, or that she was alive and well. He punched in *L1/all,* and waited. He'd collared *L1* on the fourth of January, and it was now the fifteenth. Eleven days—something over two hundred fifty dots—if the system was working properly.

Here it came. A constellation of points, making up a roughly pentagonal shape. He counted grid squares quickly. About two kilometers on each side; a home range, then, of four square kilometers, smaller than that of savannah leopards. A dark cluster of points in the lower right corner of the screen caught his attention. Was this a core area within the larger home range? Rabinowitz had found a pattern like this in the hills of Thailand, but those core areas had been centered on water, which was scarce in that habitat. Here, there was water everywhere, even during the *harmattan.*

He punched in *L1/one,two, three . . . /10sec.* The screen went blank, reconfiguring the data, and began serving up sequential, single-day segments, twenty-four dots at a time—a day-to-day narrative, rather than a cumulative portrait, of his leopard's movements. A quick spray of points hit the screen like a frozen meteor shower; ten seconds later, a second spray, then a third, filling in the pentagonal shape. Three more sets of points repeated the shape, darkening it. The pattern began to repeat on day seven, and then, on day eight, *L1* stopped moving. On the ninth and tenth days, movement again, but in a restricted area.

The darker area wasn't a core area to which the leopard returned repeatedly, it was a discreet event—something particular which had happened during the last three days. He sat back from the screen. There was only one reason—barring sickness or injury—for the leopard to restrict her movements like this.

As he watched, a new dot appeared with a silent pulse. He looked at his watch—twelve noon—and moved the cursor to the top of the screen. Pulling down a menu, he clicked on *Batt* and saw that the batteries were down to thirty percent of capacity. That wasn't good, after only eleven days; the *harmattan* was doing an effective job of blocking out sunlight. He would have to set up the other solar panel first thing.

He shut down the computer and sat thinking. Somewhere down there—no, not somewhere, he knew precisely where—his study animal was operating on less sleep than she was accustomed to, and hunting with more urgency in a smaller area, torn between the need to feed herself and her cubs, and her reluctance to stray too far from where they were hidden. The cubs would be three days old, blind and utterly helpless—but at least he knew they were alive; if they'd been stillborn, or badly deformed, *L1* wouldn't be staying in one place.

Whether or not they would develop properly was an open question.

He would give them a few days—until their eyes were open and they were tumbling about in whatever enclosed space their mother had found for them—and have a look. In the meantime, he would hope she was the only pregnant female in his study area, and get on with collaring five more animals.

Six days later, carrying an empty backpack through a darkening forest, he neared Claire's camp. He was feeling low and discouraged, and had surprisingly little to show for a week's work. He'd gone out every night intent on darting another leopard, and watched, instead, a parade of forest hog and ratel move through several clearings beneath him. The taped duiker cry, apparently, was as attractive to lesser predators as it was to leopards. He tried chasing these intruders away, shouting at them and pelting them with small branches, to no effect. This wasn't a problem he'd foreseen, and he had no idea how to deal with it; he hypothesized that when leopards realized there was another predator on hand, they simply sheared off and looked for prey they wouldn't have to fight for. They would win a given conflict, but even a minor wound in this environment carried the risk of a fatal infection, and a more serious wound—one that meant the leopard couldn't hunt—would mean slow starvation, since leopards were solitary predators, and didn't have the kind of support system that lions had, for example.

That, or he was just having a spectacular string of bad luck. Either way, the study was going nowhere.

He whistled the warning they'd agreed upon, and walked in. Claire was sitting on the edge of her cot, staring into the forest. It didn't look as if she were doing terribly well herself.

"Hey," she said quietly, standing and handing him a bottle of water. She lit a second candle, sat back down, and said, "How was your week?"

"Don't ask. The chimps?"

"The chimps are fine. Lucifer's still holding off Odysseus as alpha male."

Her tone was flat. There was an unsettling echo in their conversation of the way she and Jean Luc had talked at the end of a day, and they both heard it.

He wasn't sure she would want to talk about what had happened, but had a feeling that silence might only make it worse.

"This must be tough on you. Working so close to the station, still not knowing who killed them, or why."

"It's hard not to think about it—although it's a line of thought that doesn't get me very far. It's better when I'm working."

"You can't work all the time, though."

"No," she said.

A moth wavered past the pair of candle flames, making strange shadows on the trees.

"The police have a suspect. I met with the Justice Minister before I was thrown out."

"The Justice Minister?" She looked at him. "It sounds like they're taking this seriously."

"I'm not so sure they are. Apparently Jean Luc captured a poacher a while back and turned him over to the police. He got sick and died, and the police are saying the family blamed Jean Luc, and hired gunmen from Denkyara to take revenge. I guess it's plausible—but I can't help wondering if they made the whole thing up so they wouldn't have to bother with a real investigation."

"They didn't make it up. At least not all of it. I was there when he caught the poacher. I heard the man had gotten sick, but I didn't know he'd died."

"The family supposedly claims Jean Luc killed him with witchcraft. I find it hard to imagine someone as relentlessly scientific as Jean Luc being taken for a witch."

She was looking at him strangely.

"What," he said.

"Someone *did* take him for a witch." Her face was unhappy, almost apprehensive. "We came in from the forest at dusk one day, not long before the murders, and found a stick with a bloody hen's wing in the cleft jammed into the ground before Jean Luc's hut. You know what that means?"

He nodded. A hen's wing left like that was an accusation of witchcraft. An accusation, specifically, that a witch was leaving its body at night and flying through the sky to eat the heart life of its victim.

"What did Jean Luc do?"

"Got angry, and flung the stick into the forest. Said we should forget it ever happened."

He saw that she was beating herself up for not having tried to make Jean Luc take this more seriously. Another line of thought that wouldn't get her very far.

"If the family really believed Jean Luc killed the poacher with magic," he said, "wouldn't they use the same method? Go after him with vengeance magic, rather than guns?"

"Maybe they tried that and it didn't work."

"Would it make a difference if we knew what really happened?"

She stared into the darkened forest, as if the answer might be there.

"I don't know," she said finally.

26

Claire was gone when he woke the next morning. He lay in his cot, listening to the twittering cry of a red colobus, searching for it in the canopy above. An image came to him of how he would look from up there, a diminished human shape against the forest floor. Then another image came to him, something he'd seen by night scope his first night in the forest, and he felt sick, suddenly, felt some kind of emotional ground go out from beneath him.

A practice target, bristling with darts, and a pair of poachers staring in wary fascination. If those two men had talked about stumbling onto this dark and hostile *juju*—in a forest with which Jean Luc was indelibly associated—it would have been damning evidence for anyone who suspected Jean Luc of being a witch.

He'd assumed himself, without consciously thinking it, to be a bystander to the deaths at the station. Horrible as they were, no direct connection to him.

But maybe there was a connection.

What do I do with this? he thought. *What if I'm partly responsible, no matter how unwittingly, for these three deaths?*

The next image that came to him was of Guy lying on his back beside the *paillote*, which caused him to get up, and make tea, and go to work resolutely on his notes.

Late that afternoon he heard someone approach and looked up, expecting to see Claire coming in through the trees. Instead he saw a gawky scarecrow figure, well over six feet tall, dressed in an appalling collection of clothes with more holes than whole places. The man's face, beneath a bowl cap that announced he was Muslim, was a jigsaw mosaic of black and white. Something, at first glance, out of a nightmare.

Lowering a filled burlap bag, the man smiled shyly, stepped forward, and put out his hand. Trowbridge had seen cases of dispigmentation in Zaire, but nothing this extreme.

"*Ça va?*" he said, remembering his manners.

"*Ça va un peu.*"

The mottled skin of the man's hands was strangely soft.

"*Sans doute, tu es Nobila.*"

"*Oui.*"

"*Je suis Trowbridge.*"

Nobila nodded gravely.

"*Madame est là?*"

"*Plus tard.*"

Nobila knelt beside the bag and began pulling out provisions. One of his sharp elbows—a study in black and white—protruded from a hole in his shirt. Batteries appeared, which Trowbridge hoped might be intended for him.

Nobila looked up. *"Tout ça, c'est à toi,"* he said, pointing, and Trowbridge realized he was making two separate piles; Claire, with characteristic efficiency, had already put in an order for him.

A few minutes later Claire walked in, forgetting the warning whistle they'd agreed upon. She greeted Nobila warmly, put on tea to boil, and began grilling him on recent events in his village. With a bemused smile, Nobila told her that two babies had been born during the last week; that one of Nobila's relatives, an aged aunt, had died; and that someone's husband had created a scandal by running off to Granville. This was the third time the husband had abandoned his wife; the births, and the death, were considered more significant.

Nobila's digital watch went off in midconversation. He glanced up through the canopy at the sky, then took a small rug from his bag and walked off through the trees. Trowbridge could see his gaunt shape folding and unfolding as he knelt repeatedly, pressing his forehead to the rug laid out before him. It was a strange image, a gust of the Muslim north, penetrating, like the *harmattan,* deep into the forest. When he finished his prayers, Nobila returned, put the rug in his bag, and said to Trowbridge, gesturing at the pile of things, *"Tu es content?"*

"Très content."

Trowbridge gave him some money and several specific provisioning requests, and Claire gave him a letter to mail; then Nobila extended his hand for a pair of soft, patterned handshakes, and walked back into the trees the way he'd come.

Claire disappeared to the station for a shower. When she came back a few minutes later in jeans and a white oxford shirt, skin shining and clean, he felt a jolt of physical pleasure, felt the heavy mood he'd been battling all day lift some. She seemed to be in a better mood as well; she collapsed into a chair, took a cigarette from a blue Gauloises pack, lit it, and said lazily, "You on dinner patrol tonight?"

"Sure. Who was the letter to?"

She hesitated.

"Someone in Switzerland."

Apparently realizing how evasive that had sounded, she added lamely, "My mother."

If she doesn't want to tell me who she's writing to in Switzerland, he thought, she doesn't have to lie about it.

"Aren't you worried someone in the Kisanga post office will notice a letter addressed to Switzerland?"

"Nobila's brother is going to Granville. He'll post the letter there."

"Ah," he said. Then, "Granville. I was thinking of going there, before—"

He stopped. It was impossible not to stumble over what had happened at the station. Everything was defined by having taken place before, or after, that event.

She said, "Before Jean Luc and the others were killed."

"Yeah. Granville was going to be a reward after spending a few months in the forest."

"Maybe we can still go. After we've both gathered enough data it doesn't matter any more if we're kicked out."

"Deal," he said.

They sat in silence a moment. Then she said, "I'm trying to decide if I have a right to tell you about my encounter with the leopard."

"They're your data now, not Jean Luc's."

"I guess so," she said. "And I don't much like being the only one who knows about all this. It isn't my area of expertise."

"So tell me."

"It happened pretty fast. I was sitting with the chimps about noon one day, feeling sleepy, which I think is why I reacted so instinctively. The chimps erupted, suddenly, into this incredible screaming, like nothing I'd ever heard before, and there was a leopard among them, its jaws sunk in a young chimp's shoulder, coming in my direction. I just stood up and yelled and ran toward it—if I'd had time to think I wouldn't have done it. The leopard dropped the chimp, reared back, and slashed my leg. By then the male chimps had rallied, and came in as a group, and chased the leopard away. That's it, except for the fact that Jean Luc was furious. Almost sent me home. Told me that what I'd done was sentimental, false heroics, that I could have screwed up the observer status he'd worked so hard to achieve. Fortunately, the whole thing was so traumatic for the band I don't think they noticed one of their moving trees stepped forward and got involved in their lives."

"That's some story."

"There's something else that may interest you. I had the tape recorder going."

He was silent a second, then said, "No."

"Yes."

"A good-quality recording?"

"Decent."

Neither of them spoke for a moment. Then she said, "There's more information in Jean Luc's notes. A lot more. If you like, I'll contact Pascale and ask her to go through his papers for leopard data and make you a copy. I don't think she'll mind. She's a scientist, after all—she'd probably like to see it come to something."

"I'd appreciate that."

She stubbed out her cigarette, drew up her legs, and wrapped her arms around her knees, as if she felt vulnerable.

"You're not really going to try to habituate one of your leopards, are you?"

"If I can," he said. "*L1* would be a good candidate, assuming her cubs are healthy. She'd be more likely to stay in one place, more predictable in her movements."

"I'm afraid of them. I love this forest, but I'm terrified when I have to walk through it in the dark. It's stupid, I know."

"Not all that stupid. In theory, leopards ought to be the most dangerous of the big cats. They're smaller than lions, but they're stealthier, and—"

He stopped, remembering his conversation with the Justice Minister.

"What," she said.

"I was going to say leopards were more intelligent, but I don't know that. They're certainly more adaptable, which strikes me as a form of intelligence. Anyway, for whatever reason, human beings aren't a prey image for most leopards."

"'Prey image' is precisely how I imagine myself."

"You can make that less likely. Stand up straight, wave your arms, don't turn your back on the animal. Most of all, don't bend over or crouch. That seems to trigger the attack mechanism. Most leopard victims have been villagers who left their huts at night to go out and use a nearby field as a toilet."

"That's inglorious. So all I have to do is stand up straight, wave my arms, maybe sing a little—and never have a shit or a piss in the forest."

"Do it standing up. Probably wouldn't hurt to smoke a cigarette, either. I would imagine the smell of burning tobacco bothers them."

"Does it bother you?"

He listened for an element of flirtation, but couldn't find it—or if it was there, it was so well disguised it might as well not have been.

"No, not usually. If we had to ride an elevator together it might be different."

"I'll keep that in mind."

⸪ ⸪ ⸪

They cleaned up the dinner things, blew out the candle, and climbed into their respective cots. He lay a while, not feeling sleepy. Then he heard a rustle from her direction. She appeared beside him in the darkness and climbed in wordlessly and put her arms around him.

"Can I just—"

"Sure."

"Not—"

"I know."

They lay like that a while, him holding her cautiously. He felt her breathing relax, felt her fall asleep, and lay a long time with her in his arms, feeling hidden and watchful in the darkness, listening to a range of animal and insect noises, but hearing no sound at all of chimp or colobus, mammal species that were prey animals at night and knew enough to stay high in the trees and keep silence.

27

Shortly after sunrise three mornings later Trowbridge watched a pair of handsome leopard cubs emerge from a tangle of roots at the base of a straight-trunked ironwood tree. He'd identified the den by GPS the previous evening, waited till *L1* went off to hunt, then hurried to the spot, put up a line, climbed up off the forest floor, and waited for her return.

He was holding very still, and watching them through a screen of foliage. The cubs looked well proportioned and full weight for their age. Their mother, who had apparently been successful in her quest for food, was full bellied and tolerant; as the morning wore on she allowed them to range farther from their root-protected den, giving him a better view from his vantage point twelve meters off and five meters up. The larger and more aggressive of the cubs made persistent, stiff-legged charges at his mother's head until she put out a great paw and pinned him to the ground. He squirmed, complaining in a high cracked voice; she put her face down to his, rubbing him gently with her cheek, and he went limp, staring into the distance. Her eyes were contented slits, his eyes round and passive, and his tail curled up in a perfect question mark around his mother's muzzle.

Unfortunately, that moment was the high point of the week. He continued to battle forest hogs and ratel, and was increasingly concerned that his first collar had been a fluke. After two weeks of work he hadn't even sighted a second leopard. Once, just before dawn, he glimpsed a large cat shape at the edge of a clearing, but it slipped away before he got a decent look, and was so sizable he doubted what he'd seen.

He was in danger of having a one-animal study, which was no kind of study at all.

A fox kestrel dove at the cliff beside the platform, taking insects on the fly, making shrill *ke-ke-ke* calls in the twilight. Its dark-red body twisted through the sky in precise, accomplished movements, veering so close he could count the narrow black bars on its tail. The sky was a dusky, indistinct shroud, still fully in the *harmattan*'s grip; the tops of individual trees, isolated by smoky red mist, rose like green atolls in a sunset ocean. He wondered again about the quality of the chimp alarm calls Claire had recorded, whether the acoustical pattern would be good enough, distinctive enough, to be identified by a radio collar listening for precisely that sound. Then he began his preparations to go out into the darkness and try again.

"Here," she said, leaning down, one hand on the steering wheel, feeling around in a dirty cloth bag on the floor of the Peugeot as they jounced away from the station. "I brought you a present."

The Peugeot, temporarily unpiloted, veered toward a huge *acajou* tree.

"Jesus," he said, "whatever it is, let me get it."

She straightened up, and he reached down into the bag and pulled out a Y-shaped piece of wood—a slingshot, about the size of his hand, smooth with years of use and showing a comfortable, lustrous patina. Beneath the fork, carved into the wood, was a perfect, bas-relief leopard head no larger than his thumbnail, eyes and ears dabbed white.

"This is beautiful," he said appreciatively.

She looked amused.

"Keep digging."

He reached into the bag and pulled out a rubber sling, then a plastic Ziploc bag filled with something heavy.

"Ball bearings," she said. "There were a couple of old truck wheels at the station."

"Thanks. But—"

"You're wondering what you're supposed to do with a slingshot and bearings."

"Yes."

"Think you might be able to hit a forest hog with one of those bearings? If you practiced some?"

Comprehension dawned. He opened the Ziploc, took out one of the bearings, about the size of a small marble, and held it between his fingers.

"We can get more," she said. "This is all I had time for before you showed up. I'll let you clean the next batch, though—they're pretty greasy."

When he'd walked into camp an hour earlier, she'd told him she had the Peugeot, the one her friend had left. Nobila had brought it to her yesterday, and she'd used it last night to drive into Kisanga to make phone calls; Nobila would be back for it tomorrow, but tonight she was feeling claustrophobic and they were going to take the car and go to a party. He'd been about to point out how unwise it would be for the two of them to be seen outside the park, when she'd said, "Trust me on this, we aren't going to get into trouble." He'd been feeling discouraged and a little claustrophobic himself, and had simply dropped his things and walked with her to where the car was hidden near the station.

They coasted up to the T-intersection. Yellow headlights loomed, and a big log truck rolled by, heading south toward Granville, riding low through the smoky darkness beneath the burden of a single enormous *iroko*.

Claire frowned. "I wonder where they're getting that stuff. There aren't many trees of that size outside the park."

"Good question," he said.

Letting the dust settle, she followed the truck south until they came to an open-air bar roofed with palm fronds and lit by a pair of kerosene lanterns. She parked a little distance away in the darkness against a high stand of bamboo and got out of the car. When she came back she had a bottle of rum, a carton of pineapple juice, and a bag of shelled groundnuts.

"Cups are in the glove box."

He took out a pair of plastic cups and poured drinks. They tapped the plastic in a wordless toast, and drank. He closed his eyes, tasting rum and dust and sweet juice. Music came from the bar, faintly. Claire released a long breath.

"What did I tell you."

"It's a good party. Better than I expected."

"A little ice wouldn't hurt."

"No. But it's all right."

"It is."

Another log truck rumbled by. Someone was laughing, and a couple was dancing in the red dirt before the bar. The woman was barefoot.

"I talked to Pascale," she said. "It isn't good news."

"She's not willing to let me look at the leopard notes?"

"She can't find them."

"Does she know his filing system?"

"She created it for him."

He digested this a moment, then said, "That's strange."

"Yeah. Sorry."

They sat looking out the windshield at the hazy light cast by the kerosene lamps at the bar.

After a while, she said, "Nobila found out which village the poacher was from. Apparently he died about a week before the murders."

"What do people think he died from?"

"Guess."

"Witchcraft?"

She nodded. "I still don't know whether it would make a difference. Knowing what really happened, I mean. But Nobila said he would go with us to the village, if that's what we want to do."

"When?"

"Tomorrow night."

She held up her empty cup. He poured her another drink, rum first, then pineapple juice, then did the same for himself. He could feel the rum already and didn't mind it.

"So," he said, "is there someone in Switzerland?"

"Because of the letter?"

"Just because."

"There was, but it's over now. His name is Didier."

"Were you married?"

"No," she said. "What about you, were you married, ever?"

"Almost. About a year ago."

"Let me guess. Another biologist, an American with whom you had a lot in common professionally, but who was too ambitious to follow you around the world."

"She was Nepali, actually."

"Nepali. That sounds exotic."

He looked at her, eyebrows raised.

"Sorry," she said. "That didn't come out quite right."

"It's all right. It was exotic. Where's Didier?"

"In India."

"A scientist?"

"A physician. Or he was until he decided his own spiritual quest was more important than me, or..." She hesitated, then said, "...than anything. He lives in some kind of ashram now. Maybe the two of them ought to get together, Didier and this person you almost married. Is she in Nepal?"

"Alaska. Studying wolves and working on her master's thesis."

"Sorry if I'm being flip. Rum goes to my head pretty quickly."

"It's okay. It isn't a big issue any more."

"You sure?"

"No. Are you sure about Didier?"

"Pretty sure."

He set his drink on the dashboard, picked up the slingshot, and slipped the ends of the rubber sling over the prongs. Pinching a ball bearing in the leather pad, he leaned out the window and took aim at a tree trunk twenty meters away. There was a hard crack when the bearing hit the wood.

"Nice," he said.

"Very high-tech."

He set the slingshot down. He knew he wouldn't be asking this next question if it weren't for the rum.

"What about Jean Luc?"

She looked at him.

He said, "I saw you standing by his hut one night."

"Ah," she said. Then, with a touch of defiance in her voice, "I was in love with him, if that's what you're asking. I know he was an asshole, but sometimes that doesn't have much to do with it."

He considered this.

"Was he an asshole to you?"

"He was when Pascale came out. He had a way of looking at me behind her back that said, 'You knew the rules when we started.' Which was true, of course."

She took a long drink and stared out the windshield. He had a sense he'd touched on something deeper than he knew.

"Pascale and the children left the day before the murders," she said finally. "Jean Luc and I had an argument that night. I was still angry when I woke up, which is why I left early. It's why I'm alive. I walked away from the station wishing with all my heart he would just disappear, just go away, somehow."

She looked at him. "I wished he was *gone*. And then it happened. Just like that. Do you understand?"

"Claire—"

"Don't tell me it didn't make a difference. Maybe somewhere else it wouldn't. Here I don't believe it. Not when it's dark out."

He didn't tell her it meant nothing, because he wasn't sure. In the silence he felt some connection to the scientist in him loosen, and wondered if this internal alteration might be something dangerous.

He put another bearing into the slingshot pad and leaned out the window, shooting it across the *piste* into the forest beyond.

He listened for a sound, but there was nothing.

"I think we should go to the village," he said.

28

Early the next morning he stood in Jean Luc's study in dim, first-dawn light, eyes closed, trying to put himself into Jean Luc's head. Outside the hut, the cry of a cicada shimmered. He fought down a faint impression that there was a lingering smell of death here—a literal smell, not a memory—and opened his eyes and began looking around. He reached up beneath a low wooden cot, running his fingers along the wire mesh that supported the mattress, but found nothing. He got down on his knees and felt beneath the desk, exploring, and found nothing at first. Then he found something which surprised him, but was not what he was looking for—the handle of a machete, jammed in beneath the desk. He left it where it was, pulled the desk out from against the wall, and looked behind it. Then he looked on the underside of some low shelves.

Claire stood in the doorway watching doubtfully.

"I don't think even Jean Luc was this paranoid," she said.

He pushed the chair over to the desk and stood on it and reached up above his head to where a beam went into the palm thatch roof. He felt droppings and spider webs, and was about to give up when he felt something else. Something like stiff cardboard. He stood on his toes, supporting himself with one hand on the beam, then pulled out a manila envelope, brushing off cobwebs and termite dust as he stepped down.

They stood outside the hut, looking at the several dozen sheets of unbound paper covered with notes that the envelope had contained.

"This is it," she said. "Everything he had on leopard-chimp predation. These are his notes from the day I was clawed."

"Why would he go to such lengths to hide this?"

"I don't know. Maybe he was afraid you would come into his study and look around while he was gone. Maybe it's what he would have done if your positions were reversed."

⸎ ⸎ ⸎

He sat alone at Claire's camp, reading the notes carefully, page by page. When he was finished he went back to the beginning and read them again. Then he put his head back, and squinted up into the sun-flickered canopy.

The notes, in Jean Luc's small, precise hand, covered a period of almost nine years, during which time there had been six unexplained nighttime disappearances from the band of chimps. Jean Luc would leave them at dusk, apparently safe and sound in their nesting tree, and return in the morning to find them nervous and agitated and one fewer in number. After the second disappearance he began sleeping at the base of the roosting tree. He was wakened one evening, shortly before midnight, by a whimpering, then a thrashing and wild screams above him. Frustrated at his inability to see, he'd violated his own rules and turned on a flashlight. In the sudden silence, a pair of yellow-green, distinctly nonchimpanzee eyes, twenty meters up, had stared down at him, then disappeared around the trunk.

Over the next few years Jean Luc tried repeatedly, and failed repeatedly, to confirm that the animal he'd seen had been a leopard, and that it was responsible for the disappearances. An alternative explanation, he observed, was that some heretofore unknown disease was causing the chimps to go off and die on their own. The notes were largely emotionless recordings of data; at one point, however, Jean Luc expressed unmistakable frustration that after eight years working on this problem he had six disappearances, one brief sighting of what might—or might not—have been a leopard, and no witnessed predation event.

A more recent entry described Claire's experience, which Jean Luc dismissed as an interesting aberration, probably carried out by an inexperienced adolescent leopard that didn't know enough to avoid attacking chimpanzees in daylight. Then, on July 20 of the previous year—shortly, Trowbridge noted, before he'd written Jean Luc to say he wanted to come work in the park—Jean Luc had discovered a chimp carcass, mauled and partially consumed by a leopard, at the base of a roosting tree. His exultation at finally coming across what seemed to be hard evidence of leopard predation had been undercut when a brief autopsy revealed that the chimp had been sick, which raised the possibility it might have fallen on its own, and simply been discovered, already dead or dying, by the leopard in question.

Trowbridge looked back down at the notes. It was clear now why Jean Luc hadn't gone to print with any of this. The notes raised all kinds of interesting possibilities, but weren't really publishable as a full paper—there was very little hard data here beyond the disappearances themselves.

Was there a way to fill in the blanks? It seemed improbable; he would be here only five more months, and there had been gaps longer than that between disappearances.

Something in him resisted giving up on this, not making an effort to find out.

A bird warbled sweetly, invisibly, in the trees. He put the notes aside, and considered the machete he'd found in Jean Luc's hut. Its presence explained something that had bothered him. It had seemed out of character for Jean Luc to be running away from what had been happening at the station—and yet he'd clearly been shot in the back.

He hadn't been running away at all. He'd been running toward something he had hidden under his desk.

⚏ ䷁ ⚏

Claire came in from the forest in the late afternoon. He cooked while she read the notes, and then he gave her a few minutes to think about what she'd read, and made her the following proposal: her taped alarm call would be sent to a bioacoustician at the State University of New York at Stony Brook, someone who owed Trowbridge a favor, knew a lot about radio collars and audial detection, and would be willing to take on a fairly difficult technical problem if he was given credit in any published papers. Hassan was an Afghani who'd been doing graduate work at Stony Brook when the Soviets went into his country; he'd woken up one morning to find himself a refugee, and stayed on, retooling his Soviet training into a wizardly expertise with the manipulation and detection of sound. He would build audial detectors per Trowbridge's specifications into a pair of radio collars designed for chimps, and key those detectors, through a complicated set of software instructions, to ignore a broad range of chimp vocalizations—

including the various screeches and howls and screaming that took place during dominance interaction—but to *recognize* the specific pitch and audial characteristics on Claire's tape, the peculiar call the chimps used to tell one another that danger was near.

The next challenge would be getting the collars into the country. But once that was done, the rest was straightforward fieldwork, sedating and collaring a pair of chimps, then sitting back to wait. If a predation event took place, and if the real call activated the radio collar the way the taped call had done in the laboratory, a message and position fix would go up to *Atlantic East*, which would pass the information back down to Trowbridge's computer; then, if he reached the nesting tree in time, he would see the dark shape—the pair of yellow-green eyes—that had been moving about above a blind and frustrated Jean Luc. And he would have night vision equipment when he got there.

"God," Claire said, putting her head in her hands. "I'm having trouble with this. We're talking about breaking every single rule Jean Luc lived by, every rule that made his work unique. It seems disloyal, at best—and in practical terms, it could endanger habituation status and ruin my own work."

"Not if we use the second group. They were only partially habituated anyway. I assume they're losing that without Jean Luc and Guy around."

Claire frowned. "I hadn't thought of that. How close would we have to get to dart them properly?"

"Ten meters. Twelve, maybe."

"Without saying yes or no," she said slowly, "I'd say it's feasible. Technically, anyway."

"Jean Luc wanted to solve this problem. If we pull it off—and that's a very big if—we'll make it a three-author paper, you, me, and him. That would make Pascale happy, and cap Jean Luc's career—and it wouldn't do yours any harm. It's exactly the kind of thing that would help you stand out from the hundreds of other promising young Ph.D.'s in the field. Help you find a stable job somewhere, if that's what you really want."

She looked at him a little resentfully for throwing her own words back at her; he worried that something stubborn and perversely ethical in her might say no to this precisely because it was in her own interest to say yes.

"Jean Luc would have said no."

"Probably. But—"

"But he was changing, and the circumstances have definitely changed. And you're right, we're losing habituation on the second group anyway."

She took a deep breath. "Okay. On the condition that I do the immobilization. If the rules are going to be broken I want it to be done by a primatologist. And there's one more thing."

"Yes?"

"I want to go out and see a leopard with you. Not now, necessarily. Sometime."

29

They drove with Nobila to the village, parked the truck in the Burkinabe section, and waited while Nobila spoke quietly with the Burkinabe chief, a small man in a cream-colored skullcap and a flowing *boubou*. Then they walked into the Lagoon *quartier*, where the huts were smaller and the passageways narrower. Threading through firelight and moonlight and darkness, they caught glimpses of hut interiors that seemed crowded and hot. They reached a small stream which ran through the village, the dividing line with the Ebrio section, and crossed a bridge made of narrow tree trunks lashed together, entering a neighborhood with an older, more established feel. Some of the houses were built of cinderblock; all had white handprint decorations. The men they saw had three-slash scarification on their temples, and both men and women stared with expressions that were less gracious and more suspicious than in the Burkinabe or Lagoon *quartiers*. Trowbridge realized that these were people who believed outsiders had rarely brought them anything good, and that the three of them—a white man and woman, and a solemn, lanky Burkinabe with advanced dispigmentation—made up an outlandish tableau.

At the far end of the village they stopped before a small hut set off by itself. A young woman sat on a stool before the hut, rocking a plump, sleepy little girl who was naked but for a string of colored beads around her waist. At their approach the woman stood and held the girl protectively. Nobila asked politely, speaking French, if they might talk for a few minutes. Without replying, she made a low noise in her throat and took a step backward. An older woman wearing only a wrap skirt appeared in the doorway, surveyed the scene, and said something sharp in Ebrio. The young woman picked up the stool and backed into the hut, stepping, as she did so, over a small earthenware pot in which something smoldered. He caught a glimpse of animal skulls hanging from the ceiling of the hut; then a woven panel made of thatch was placed over the doorway from inside.

"They're afraid," Nobila said.

"Was that his wife?" Claire asked.

"His wife, and his mother. There are no brothers or uncles."

"She's much younger than him," Claire said, looking troubled, as if it hadn't occurred to her the poacher might have a young wife and child.

The hut wasn't much, compared to some of the others they'd seen; poaching, in general, was poor people's work, not lucrative or respectable, even on a village level. Nobila walked to one side of the hut and stood staring behind it. They followed him and saw something which appeared, in the partial moonlight, to be a shoulder-high misshapen tree. As they moved closer Trowbridge realized it wasn't a tree at all, but a crudely carved wooden stand covered with animal skulls, bones, and clay figurines.

He shone his flashlight across the stand, spotting the intact bones of a leopard's paw. Nestled in the paw was a hen's egg, making a perfect white oval. There were more eggs tucked away in various places.

Nobila said quietly, "The Ebrio believe the spirit of an animal, its *bei*, does not die when its body is killed by a hunter—but rather floats freely for a while, without a home. This is a dangerous time for the hunter who killed the animal, because the *bei* is uncomfortable, and may become angry before it finds another animal body."

Nobila gestured at the egg nestled in the bones of the leopard's paw. "To keep the *bei* from becoming angry, a hunter builds a stand like this and makes consolation offerings."

"So when the poacher got sick," Claire said, "he and his family would have believed, at first, that it was the *bei* of some animal he killed."

"Yes."

"But when they made these offerings, and he didn't get better—"

"They might have believed he had an enemy," Nobila said. "And they would have begun to wonder who, and why."

Claire and Nobila turned away. Trowbridge saw movement in the darkness and pointed his flashlight toward the trees, where a purple-white, iridescent worm, nearly a foot long, squirmed slowly on a pile of human shit. He felt his skin crawl, and wondered at the reaction—he wasn't usually that squeamish. The darkness around him seemed palpable and stifling—the moon had gone behind clouds—and he had a sudden uncharacteristic feeling that he would be afraid to walk into the high brush that surrounded the village.

He looked once more at the egg in the leopard's paw, then returned to the front of the hut. Claire and Nobila were studying a peculiarly decorated bark cloth hanging beside the door.

"A sign of mourning," Nobila said.

Trowbridge said, "And the symbols?"

"The symbols express gratitude that vengeance was achieved."

⁂

They retraced their steps through the village. Trowbridge assumed they were heading back to the Peugeot, but Nobila turned right at what looked like a nonfunctional well—some development project gone wrong—and led them into a different part of the Ebrio *quartier*. When they stopped before a hut that was larger than that of the poacher's family, Trowbridge saw reluctance on Nobila's grave features.

"The fetish doctor lives here."

Trowbridge said, "Are you sure this is the one they would have gone to?"

"There's only one among the Ebrio in this village."

Nobila went to the low doorway, stood in the kerosene yellow glow which came through it, and spoke in a low voice, saying there were three visitors who had heard of the fetish doctor's reputation and would like to talk with him. A backlit figure appeared, examined Nobila a moment, then looked past him at Trowbridge and Claire before stepping aside without a word. Trowbridge followed Nobila and Claire through the doorway. As he did so he smelled something burning, and saw a wisp of smoke coming from a clay pot on the floor. Like in the hut of the poacher's family.

Gum copal, protection against witches. The smell was nauseatingly intense in this enclosed space.

The fetish doctor had narrow shoulders and a forward-thrust head, giving him a vulturish appearance; he wore orange *pagne* wrapped loosely around thin hips, and a ripped plaid shirt which hung open to reveal a dirty-looking fetish bag and a wooden whistle. Moving toward a dark corner of his hut, he brought three stools forward, one at a time, setting them in the packed dirt; then he fetched a fourth stool for himself. Behind him, against the mud-and-wattle wall of the hut, was a Western-style wooden dresser covered with fetishes and roots and plastic bags filled with herbs. Amid this, a bottle of liquor with flakes of ivory in the bottom, and a pharmacy pill bottle; above the dresser, hanging from a cross beam of the hut, was a crucifix.

Nobila expressed appreciation for the opportunity to talk with a fetish doctor known to have considerable powers. The fetish doctor listened carefully, his features a mask. Trowbridge, watching him, felt a sudden sense of alienation that bordered on vertigo. I will never know these people, he thought, never understand them, never be one with them in the most rudimentary sense. Even Nobila, who smiles when he sees me, and with whom I have an ongoing business relationship, is like someone from another planet—and Nobila is like my twin brother compared to this character.

"I don't have a personal interest here," Nobila said. "But these two people are friends of the white scientist who was killed in the forest. I'm sure you have heard of this."

"Everyone has heard of this," the fetish doctor said.

His voice was raspy, and his hand had gone to the fetish bag at his throat; he hadn't looked at Trowbridge or Claire since they came in. He's *afraid*, Trowbridge realized. He's too proud simply to shut the door on us the way the poacher's family did, but he's no less frightened. Is it because he thinks we'll get him in trouble with the police? Or is he afraid that we're witches too?

Trowbridge noticed a small pedestal in the corner of the hut. On it was a hunched, malevolent little figurine, perhaps a foot tall, leaning on a chicken-bone cane. The figure had a cowrie-shell humpback, white feathers stuck to its base, and stains that were probably chicken blood. Looking at it made him feel itchy, and as if he were falling from a great height.

The sense of the irrational here was so strong it felt like an attack. He felt another small connection to the scientist in him begin to loosen, and this time he resisted it. Data, he thought. Data, and daylight, and you'll be out of here in a few months.

Nobila said gravely, "If you've heard of this death, then surely you know what people are saying."

There was a flicker of indecision on the fetish doctor's face. Nobila, Trowbridge realized, had him neatly trapped. If he nodded, Nobila wouldn't tell him what it was that people were saying, which might be of interest. On the other hand, it would be awkward for an accomplished fetish doctor to admit ignorance.

Finally, he said, "I know what people are saying here."

Nobila nodded, as if this had been a wise response. "Some people say that the white scientist practiced witchcraft against the hunter from this village who died. That later, when the scientist died in turn, it was vengeance magic that killed him."

This was getting close to the bone. What Nobila had just said bordered on an accusation that the fetish doctor had initiated vengeance magic—and the practice of any form of magic which resulted in injury or death was illegal under Diamantien law.

The fetish doctor said cautiously, "Such things cannot be talked about by a practitioner. But it is true that a man died in this village, and it is true that his heart life was stolen by a witch."

"Speaking in general," Nobila said, "and so that we may learn something, what would be the role of a fetish doctor in such a case?"

"First, to identify the witch who caused the death. Then to strike back by calling up vengeance magic. This requires great skill, because the medicine is honorable and will not kill an innocent person. If it is created out of spite, or for personal gain, it will return upon the fetish doctor and destroy him."

Nobila considered this. Then, "Other people say the white scientist did not die of vengeance magic. They say the family hired a fetish doctor, but that this fetish doctor failed because his power was less than that of the white scientist. They say the family grew impatient, finally, and hired people with guns."

The fetish doctor looked at Nobila angrily. It was the first flash of unguarded emotion on his face, the first moment Trowbridge had felt he understood the man. Nobila had wounded him in his professional pride.

"Count the days," the fetish doctor said harshly. "Count the days between when the hunter died and the scientist died. No one would become impatient in such a short time. No, if I were the one to create this vengeance magic—and I am not saying it was me—then you can be sure my magic would have found the witch, and slain him fairly. If bullets were involved that only means the magic was strong enough to choose its own weapons."

⸬ ⸬ ⸬

The Peugeot's yellow headlights splashed against the darkness on either side of the *piste* as they drove away from the village. Trowbridge was glad to be back in the car, surrounded by engine noises which were reassuringly mechanical and logical.

He and Claire had glanced at one another as they left the hut, sharing a moment of unspoken communication. Someone might have hired people with guns to carry out the killings at the station. But it hadn't been the family, which was too poor and too poorly connected. And it hadn't been this fetish doctor, who had almost certainly launched vengeance magic against Jean Luc, but who believed so utterly in the effectiveness of his own magic that he would never have deigned to pay someone to back him up with bullets.

⸬ ⸬ ⸬

He had a dream that night in which the fetish doctor's disembodied head came closer and closer. He was unable to move, unable even to turn his head away. When the narrow face was only inches from his own, the low-lidded eyes glanced down, and the head dipped down and passed out of his vision. He felt something rough against his chin, and realized the fetish doctor was lapping at the sweat at the base of his throat. He woke with a cry that caused Claire to sit up and ask him if he were all right, a cry that seemed to echo in the night around them.

3 0

The first three forest hogs came in twenty-eight minutes after he turned on the duiker recording, and departed between two and three minutes later, evidencing a strongly negative reaction to being whacked from above by truck wheel bearings, especially those aimed at their hairless and relatively tender snout, anus, and testicles. Several more forest hogs appeared, then a civet, and two ratel, and then shortly before midnight a leopard came in, a more slender animal than *L1*, with dark tail spots like rings and a line of distinct rosettes along its backbone. As it paced nearer the log, then froze, head low, making a perfect shape against a riot of branches behind, Trowbridge was struck by its utter, watchful stillness, and by how physically perfect this animal's proportions were—particularly in comparison to the gangly, apple-headed cheetah, or the larger, clumsier lion. Lions were big-bodied family creatures, electrifying when they hunted, but comical and clunky most of the rest of the time; they were social, lazy, full of bluff, and prone to vanity and showing off, especially the males. Lions were familiar creatures to which human beings could relate.

The animal beneath him, by contrast, was so self-possessed and solitary—so stripped down and fine in its nature—as to be from a different world. He was overwhelmed, suddenly, by a strange sense of love for this slender, deadly animal out hunting alone in the darkness, unaware of what was about to happen. The feeling was unexpected—particularly at this fairly crucial technical moment—and had to spring from his own loneliness, but was no less real or intense for being so. He waited a moment, then raised the bow and sighted. There was a small hiss, and *L2* was part of the study.

⠿   ⠿   ⠿

He looked up from the claw marks he'd been examining on a tree trunk and listened a moment, frowning. There it was again. A high, sustained whine, faint but unmistakable, cutting through the irregular trill and chatter of the forest. He consulted the GPS at his belt, then looked at the topo map. He was in the southeastern corner of the park, an area he hadn't visited before—but he was at least two kilometers from the park boundary. There was no way sound would carry this far in dense forest. Whoever was operating that chain saw was doing so inside the park.

The sound was clear, but the direction, baffled by trees, was not. Looking around, he chose the highest emergent he could find, put a line over a lower branch, maybe thirty meters off the ground, snaked up a climbing rope, then attached his harness and ascenders and went up. When he reached the branch he hung beneath it a while, not looking down, letting his breathing return to normal. Then he inspected the branch to make sure it was ant free, stepped carefully out of the ascenders, and free-climbed another ten meters or so until he emerged into sunlight and breeze.

A butterfly floated beside a yellow orchid, near enough to touch. He breathed deeply, enjoying the air and the openness. It was late February, the *harmattan* was over, and they were into the pleasant weather gap between the *harmattan* haze and the steady downpour of the rainy season.

He remembered why he'd climbed up here and looked east, across an uneven sea of treetops, in time to see the crown of a huge emergent a kilometer away shudder as if it had taken a blow. The crown shuddered again, this time with a piercing crack, and began to shift and go over. There was a vast tearing as it fell from sight, taking down the dense network which connected it to its neighbors. Then a deep thump—he could feel it in the wood supporting him—when the tree met the earth.

Silence reigned for a few seconds, and the high whine began again.

The butterfly had disappeared. He took a compass reading on the gap where the tree had gone over, and began his descent. A few minutes later he stood on the forest floor, coiling the climbing line, trying to decide what to do. This was none of his business—and yet it bothered him to see a tree go over like that and do nothing; he had four leopards collared now, was making steady progress habituating *L1* and the cubs, and was beginning to feel proprietary about this forest. He stowed his gear and began walking in the direction of the fallen tree. If nothing else, he could find out what was going on.

Long before he saw the tree itself, he smelled ripped vegetation and opened earth, and began moving more cautiously, watching where he put his feet; there had been no rain in days, and the leaf litter was prone to crackle when stepped on. A massive, uptorn tangle of roots became visible through the vegetation, brilliant light cascading upon it. He heard voices, and the loud whine of a pair of chain saws, working irregularly now as the crew cut away lianas and lopped off branches and roots and began sawing the trunk into sections. The tree was rough and dull on the outside, but a rich, buttery red inside—a *sapele*, one of the more valuable trees in the West African forest.

Valuable enough to tempt someone into the park itself, not merely the buffer zone, to cut it down and drag it out.

A thick chain was hauled up over the top part of the tree. Someone yelled, and a section of *sapele* began snaking east. He followed a few meters behind as the *sapele* ripped a broad, irregular gash through the forest. When it reached the park boundary—an open lane that marked the beginning of the buffer zone—he waited a moment, then followed again, moving more quickly to catch up.

A few minutes later the section of trunk stopped moving. He heard the sound of a single stroke engine—the skidder—die with a sputter, and continued forward cautiously until he made out an open clearing bathed in sunlight. In the center of the clearing was a pair of crude shelters made of saplings and roofed with plastic; at its far side sat an empty log truck and a battered Toyota pickup. One of the shelters was for the loggers, who were taking a lunch break; beneath the other shelter hung dozens of animal carcasses. He'd stumbled upon a camp where not only trees were being poached.

He inventoried the carcasses. Half a dozen flying squirrels spread-eagle on a rack, several tortoises, a pair of slender-snouted crocodiles, already skinned, and a good deal of unidentifiable meat that was probably duiker. Monkeys, ten at least, some that had been skinned and smoked and were thus barely recognizable, others, including a pair of diana and several bewhiskered mona, that had been hung up whole. He smelled food cooking, and heard laughter and the sound of a scratchy radio. The quantity of meat, and the fact that some of it hadn't been smoked, suggested the animal poachers would be breaking camp soon; the logging truck, and the road which had been cut for it, would allow them to take out a vastly greater amount of game than would otherwise have been possible. No doubt they provided meat to the loggers in return for the favor of transportation.

He hesitated a moment, then decided there was nothing more he could learn by standing here. He would tell Alain about this at some point, and that would be all; it wasn't as if it would be a revelation to anyone. He was about to move away when he saw a pair of banded duiker lying in the dirt in odd positions. They weren't dead—he could see their open eyes—and they weren't tied up, but neither were they running away. One, an adolescent, thrashed and made a bleating noise, its back legs twisting helplessly.

He felt the heat begin to rise in his temples. He'd forgotten about this practice, an old African technique for keeping meat fresh while it was being transported, but preventing escape. Something crashed through the bushes beside him and he crouched instinctively, heart slamming as a ragged-looking man with a shotgun and a bag stepped past almost near enough to touch. The man knelt in the clearing, took the bag by its end, and dumped out a pair of trussed animals. One was a young diana, a female, which had been shot—he could see the blood. The other animal, a royal antelope, had been caught in a wire snare and looked more or less intact. He could see its terrified eyes, trembling body, and slender legs, barely as thick as a finger, ending in dark, perfect little hooves. A fully grown adult, weighing barely two pounds, the smallest grazing animal in the forest.

Crouching over the antelope, the man looked up and called out casually to his companions, *"On part demain, oui?"*

Someone called out, *"Oui,"* and the man took one of the antelope's back legs between his fingers and thumbs and snapped it like a pencil. He did the other leg, then threw the antelope toward the pair of duikers, where it made little flopping movements, and turned his attention to the diana monkey. Slitting the diana's tail from base to tip, he pulled the skin apart with a tearing sound, then grasped the diana's throat, forced its head back, and pushed its head through the opening in its tail. Then he stood, lifting the diana by the loop of tail flesh so that it hung like some grotesque article of clothing on a hanger. Trowbridge had been wrong; it wasn't dead. He heard it expel a tiny breath, a nearly inaudible gasp. Saw it shake its head slightly, in a strangely human movement, and found himself rising and stepping into the clearing.

"Tuez-le," he said to the poacher, who stood staring at him as if he were an apparition. "Kill it now."

There was a frozen moment as the poacher, clearly uncertain whether Trowbridge was a forest spirit or flesh and blood, stared at him in disbelief.

"Pourquoi?" he asked finally, looking down at the diana, then back up at Trowbridge. Trowbridge stepped forward, shoved him in the chest, took his shotgun, and pointed it at the diana. When he squeezed the trigger, the shotgun jumped in his hand and the forest echoed. He turned and went to the royal antelope and shot that as well. Then he picked up a rifle leaning against the curing shed, checked to see it had shells, and shot the two duiker. He was breathing hard, and felt sick to his stomach, and threw the weapon down on the ground.

The poacher from whom he'd taken the shotgun had disappeared. The three loggers, all Africans, stood in a cluster by the logging truck, watching him in stupefaction. Out of the corner of his eye he saw another figure standing at the edge of the clearing holding a shotgun. A voice inside told him he was doing something dangerous, but it was too late to stop now. He walked up to the three loggers.

"Who owns this rig?"

The men looked at one another nervously.

"If you don't tell me, I'll have you put in jail."

"The *patron* told us we had to get least two *sapele* this week, or we wouldn't get our wages," one of them blurted out.

"Who's your *patron?*"

"Monsieur Foote."

"Give me the keys to the pickup."

The man who had spoken looked panic-stricken. "But the truck belongs to the *patron.*"

"Don't worry," Trowbridge said. "I'm going to take it to him."

He shoved past them and opened the truck door. The keys, as he had guessed, were in the ignition. He climbed in and shut the door and started the engine.

"Where is he?" he asked.

The man looked agitated. "At Le Leopold, near Granville. But you must tell him you took the keys by force."

Trowbridge backed the truck, spun the wheel, and turned toward the dirt track which led away from the clearing. As he did so, his eyes met those of the poacher holding the shotgun. The man did not look afraid, the way the other poacher and the three loggers had; he was staring at Trowbridge as if to be sure he could identify him for some future encounter.

⠿ ⠿ ⠿

He drove too fast on the narrow track, but it was freshly cut and relatively straight and it wasn't his truck so he didn't much care. He half noticed that it *felt* like his truck—a couple of years older, maybe, but otherwise identical to the one he'd lost, a white Toyota with a winch and cable mounted on the front bumper. On either side of the dirt track were freshly cleared fields, the work of villagers who'd taken advantage of the illegal road to penetrate the buffer zone. Behind him in the truck bed a chain saw bounced back and forth in a tangle of wire snares until a particularly hard bump sent it flying out.

When he reached the north-south *piste* he had a moment of doubt, a rational voice inside telling him this wasn't exactly keeping a low profile. Then he turned right, south toward the ocean, driving fast for an hour and a half until he reached Le Leopold, a ramshackle, colonial-style hotel set back a full kilometer from the road and surrounded by miles of white-trunked rubber trees. From where he parked the truck he could see down toward Granville. Blue-green ocean was visible, and a lighthouse, sitting at the end of a breakwater like a toy structure at the end of a line of gravel. To the right, on a long sandbar, was the abandoned city he'd seen from Alberto's plane. He'd hoped his first trip to Granville would be a pleasure, something to do with Claire. Nothing was what it should be.

He walked past the hotel entrance and stepped up onto the terrace. There was only one white person there, sitting alone at a table with a glass and a bottle of whiskey before him. Trowbridge could see the side of his face, nothing more, but what he saw gave him enough of a shock to stop him in his tracks.

The squareness of the man's shoulders, the color of the hair, were virtually identical to his own. From the back or the side the two of them might be mistaken for brothers.

He glanced back at the white pickup, remembering what the Belgian woman had said in Sandoukou—"You must be with the timber company. Like the other one"—and remembering the bar in Denk-yara, where they'd poured him a glass of whiskey. This explained a hell of a lot. He walked across the terrace, pulled a chair out from Foote's table, and sat down.

Face on, the resemblance was less striking. Foote's eyes were small and close-set, his hair thinning on top.

"What sort of shit are you pulling, that makes people want to shoot at you in a hotel room?"

For the second time that day someone stared back at him as if he were a bad dream come to life.

"Is this some kind of joke?" Foote said.

"What they did to my hotel room in Sandoukou, thinking you were in it, wasn't a joke. What happened later to Jean Luc Juvigny and two other people wasn't any kind of joke at all. I'm trying to fig-ure out the connection."

Foote, suddenly, looked nervous and drunk, instead of merely drunk.

"I had nothing to do with what happened to that monkey scien-tist. Nothing. And I worked out my differences with those guys, so everything's fine."

"You gave them what they wanted."

"That's right."

Foote lifted his glass and tossed off a fairly significant portion of what was in it. Then he wiped the sweat from his face with the palm of his hand and rubbed the hand on his pants.

"Who the fuck are you, man? Are you some kind of international spook? 'Cause I haven't done anything illegal. I'm working *with* the government here."

Trowbridge, deliberately, said nothing. The silence seemed to un-nerve Foote, and he plunged on.

"Look," he said, "I got the import license, like they wanted me to. I signed where they wanted me to sign. I get some trees down the line, lots of 'em. I scratch their backs, they scratch mine."

"What kind of import license?"

"None of your business. Like I said, it's all legal."

"You've got a logging crew taking trees in the park—and they've got poachers with them killing protected animals. That's illegal. Twice."

Foote looked at him incredulously, as if wondering how he knew all this. Then he said, "My crew has *strict* instructions not to take trees illegally."

Trowbridge remembered the broken-legged antelope lying in the dirt, and then he remembered the bodies at the station, and he felt violence rising in him. He pushed his chair back abruptly, stood, and walked back across the terrace and down the steps toward the parking area.

"Hey," Foote called out from behind him, "that's my truck!"

Trowbridge stopped, fished the keys from his pocket, and flung them into the chest-high scrub at the side of the parking lot.

"Chop that down," he said, "if you want your keys."

31

He put his eye to the crossbow sight, taking aim at the substantial hind leg of the darkened cat shape beneath him, feeling uneasy, somehow. He'd collared five leopards now, and was relatively experienced; this ought to be routine. But there was something unusual about the animal which had slipped directly out of the undergrowth rather than coming down the trail, and was now partially obscured by the log which covered the cassette player. It was big, the largest he'd seen in the forest—a male, by definition—and seemed to be physically denser, darker somehow, than his other study animals. He couldn't make out individual spots and rosettes, and wondered if the batteries in the scope were getting weak.

Never mind. There would be time to look more closely at its coat when it had a dose of Kezol in its system.

There, it had stopped moving. He released a slow breath and squeezed the trigger. There was an audible, off-key twang; the dart wavered weakly out of the pistol crossbow and fell beneath him. He dropped the bow, swearing, feeling its cord tug at his harness, and pushed the scope up onto his forehead as he reached into his bag for the flashlight.

A busted bowstring. The leopard would be miles away by now, and thoroughly spooked; the best he could hope for was to avoid losing the transmitter dart. He shone the flashlight beneath him, passing the beam slowly over the leaf litter, recalling with some annoyance how the crossbow company had assured him that tropical humidity would have no effect on the integrity of their equipment.

No sign of the dart. He would have to wait until the sun came up in an hour or so.

Dimly, in the periphery of the flashlight beam, something shifted. He swung the beam up and found himself staring at a solid, unfrightened ghost, the largest leopard he'd ever seen, and the first he'd ever seen in the wild without spots. *L6* was *black*—utterly, spectacularly black, a melanistic anomaly rare in Latin America and practically unheard of in West Africa. Its heavy, blunt-nosed head was tipped to one side; its eyes, green in the flashlight beam, seemed intrigued instead of worried by this less than angelic figure wielding a shaft of light from above.

Wondering at the coloration, at the heavily muscled chest and thick forelegs, Trowbridge reached slowly into his bag for another bowstring. At the movement *L6* vanished in a bound, leaving him staring after it, the false cry of the duiker ringing in his ears.

⠿ ⠿ ⠿

Trowbridge looked up, frowning, from the telegram Nobila had handed him.

"*C'est pas une bonne nouvelle?*" Nobila asked.

"No, it's good news," he said. "Mostly good news, anyway."

"*Bon,*" Nobila said, looking satisfied, as if he were responsible for the telegram's contents.

In a way, he was, since the telegram was a response to a package he'd taken to Granville three weeks earlier and sent FedEx to New York. The package had contained a cassette tape, a letter to Hassan, and a letter to Gordon; the return telegram which had arrived yesterday had been addressed, per Trowbridge's instructions, to Nobila.

Dear Nobila (?), The collars work—in the lab, anyway. Pouched them to a little patch of American soil near you. Bring your passport. Good luck. G.

He folded the telegram and put it in his pocket. Sending the collars through the diplomatic pouch was a perfect way to bypass Customs; Gordon, resourceful as ever, must have pulled some interesting strings to get this done. On the other hand, going to the embassy meant a trip to the capital, which wasn't exactly keeping a low profile, and forced a decision on him he wasn't sure he was ready to make.

It had been a week since he confronted Foote on the terrace at Le Leopold, and made the long, dispiriting bush taxi ride back to the park. A full, productive week, alone at the inselberg with his leopards and notes and computer—pure, straightforward science, exactly what he'd told himself he wanted. Only there was a whole range of questions and implications and responsibilities that wouldn't leave him alone. He *wasn't* just a scientist here, not any more, no matter how much he might prefer it to be that way. He was linked to what had happened to Jean Luc and the others, and he cared about what was going on with the park—whatever the hell that might be.

He looked at his watch. Claire wouldn't be in for at least an hour. He wrote a quick note of explanation, walked with Nobila to the station where the Peugeot was hidden behind a screen of trees, then dropped him at his village and headed north on the *piste*.

⁙ 𝕭⁝ ⁙

A vast orange sunset was dying slowly above the peaceful compound; he could see Alberto's dim shape in the greenhouse. Stepping into the moist air, closing the door behind himself, was like stepping into another season; there was a peculiar smell, pleasant and yet slightly unearthly, like the flowers themselves. Rows of orchids stood in pots along either wall of the greenhouse and down a long center table. A series of fans at the far end of the greenhouse turned with a steady noise.

Alberto was bending over a flower spike which stood up stiffly from shiny green leaves; a series of miniature orchid blooms ran up the spike like graceful little helicopters. He straightened, studied Trowbridge with raised eyebrows, then set down his tweezers and wiped his hands on his gardening apron.

"Well," he said, "we seem to have two forbidden scientists in the country. Assuming Claire is still here."

"She is," Trowbridge said.

"How many people know you're back?"

"Claire, a friend of hers in the village, and now you." He tipped his head at the orchids. "I didn't know they had a smell."

"Some do," Alberto said, "some don't. Actually, the potting soil has its own smell—it's made from the bark of Douglas fir, did you know that? Some people mistake that for the smell of flowers."

Alberto took Trowbridge's arm in a very Italian form of physical intimacy and steered him toward the greenhouse door.

"Given your interesting circumstances," he said, "why don't we continue this conversation in somewhat less visible surroundings?"

⠿ ⠃⠆ ⠿

Alberto made them omelettes and a green salad, and they sat at the kitchen table rather than on the terrace. A little spiral of smoke rose from the mosquito coil beside the kitchen sink.

"Someone put pressure on Foote to sign papers and get an import license—for what, I don't know," Trowbridge said. "Now he's talking about being given trees, lots of them. I'm worried there's some scheme to get access to the park. Wholesale access, not just a tree here and there."

"The President wouldn't allow it. And the Justice Minister—who stands to inherit the President's job if he can avoid making any big mistakes—wouldn't allow it either. He headed the debt negotiating team which cut the most recent deal with the World Bank and the IMF, which means he knows better than anyone how quickly this country would be cut off, ruined financially, if the park were opened up to logging."

"What if they told the World Bank and the IMF to go to hell? Opened the park, and started selling off timber to repay their creditors?"

Alberto shook his head. "David, this country owes almost *twelve billion dollars* to its creditors. There aren't enough trees in the park."

"Maybe Foote's going to try logging in Denkyara."

"Aside from the political chaos, there's only one decent bridge. I don't think it would take the weight of a loaded truck."

"I walked across that bridge."

"You came back through Denkyara?"

"Yes."

"My God," Alberto said. "You must have been crazy. Is it as bad as they say?"

"It isn't good."

Alberto leaned back from the table, and sighed. "Frankly, I don't know what to tell you with regard to Foote. You're hardly in a position to go knocking on official doors in the capital. But I suppose you might try knocking on an unofficial door."

"Meaning—"

"Meaning someone in the Lebanese community. They're big in shipping and banking, and very good when it comes to tracing money—and money, I assume, is at the root of all this. It usually is."

"Who would I talk to?"

"I had better contacts in the old days, when it was mostly Sunni Muslims. The generation that moved in when Beirut went up is mainly Shi'ite, and I don't know that group as well. But I can put you in touch with one of my old Sunni friends and let him know you're coming. Yes?"

"Yes."

Alberto jotted down an address, then poured them sambuca, dropping a coffee bean into the bottom of each fluted glass. He turned off the terrace lights and they went and sat outside in comfortable wicker chairs, surrounded by a darkness filled with insect noises.

"I've realized, finally," Alberto said meditatively, "that people here live in two places at once, and we only live in one. There's another world going on that we don't have access to. Some place of darkness that I still don't understand. I'm not talking about the generic darkness of the human soul—that's a Western invention which is actually rather demeaning to Africa, the idea that you come here and find a darkness within yourself, as if Africa were just a vehicle. No, this is something different. The young woman you met the first time you came by—do you remember her?"

Trowbridge nodded.

"Her name is Therese. She keeps house for me, and cooks for me sometimes, and sometimes we sleep together. She's good for me, and she seems happy with the arrangement—I don't ask her what she's doing when she isn't here, and on the whole she's very honest, very fair with me. I woke up one morning at first light and saw her standing at the window looking out. I asked her what she was doing. She said she was watching a kob antelope, an animal which doesn't live in the forest—only in the savannah to the north, where she came from. When I pointed that out she said the antelope she was watching was *in* her home village, not here."

Trowbridge had a sudden vision of one of his leopards moving through the darkness. The steady, watchful pacing, the dark rosettes and the pale coat, the collar about its neck. A pure, compelling image—as if he had perfect night vision—not something seen through the yellow tones of the scope.

"I think I understand."

"I'm not sure I do. I asked her if she meant she was remembering an antelope from her village. She said no, that she was watching it at this very moment, that it was feeding on shoots of new grass beside the canal. She did this sort of thing once in a while to keep from feeling homesick. We're talking about a woman who went to a very good *lycée*, where she read Proust, and who can decipher an airline schedule better than I."

Alberto was silent a moment. "When you and I look at darkness, darkness is all we see. When Therese looks at darkness, she sees something. It doesn't mean she isn't afraid of what she sees—she may even be more so—but there's something there, and it changes everything for her. I'll say one more thing, and then shut up. The Africans I know believe that an individual, alone, is *lost*. Utterly. That he or she only finds identity and protection and discipline as part of a group. An individual alone will disappear into that darkness, have no defense against everything out there. Think about it. If you really believe that, right and wrong as we know it—in the abstract sense, in the sense that there will be some ultimate accounting of one's individual sins—go out the window, and are replaced by family and tribe."

"Who you can touch in the darkness."

"Exactly. For independent agents like you and me—people who believe in logic and abstract principles and the scientific method—that's a frightening idea."

3 2

He slept in Alberto's guest room and left early, driving the now-familiar route to the capital. As he neared Pont Noir he felt increas-

ingly uneasy, and had to remind himself that there were enough foreign businessmen, diplomats, and aid workers living in the city that a
white face wouldn't stand out. His passport contained a valid visa and
entry stamp, and as a biologist, it was plausible he might have entered
through Denkyara to see the forest there; that ought to be good
enough for any Diamantien policeman who asked to see his papers.

On the other hand, he still had no idea who'd had him thrown out
of the country, and he emphatically did not want that to happen
again. Not yet, not with a successful study taking shape in the park.

He drove through the slums on the outskirts of the city and into
the center. The embassy was a three-story building with a welter of
complicated antennas on the roof, a row of heavy concrete planters
out front, and a familiar flag hanging limply from a pole. He showed
his passport to an African guard in a blue uniform, who scrutinized it
carefully, then ushered him through a heavy glass door marked *American Citizens Only*.

He found himself standing in a narrow room with a teller-style
window at one end. An older woman with a no-nonsense expression
appeared at the window. She wore a high-necked navy blue dress,
which seemed impractical for Africa.

"Passport, please."

He pushed his passport through the window slot. The consul examined it, and said, "Registered with the embassy, Mr. Trowbridge?"

When he said no, his passport was returned to him with a registration form and a ballpoint pen.

"Mind filling this out?"

The tone suggested it would be better if he didn't mind. He filled
it out, giving an accurate date of arrival, leaving the port of entry
blank, and showing as his address *Poste Restante* in a small savannah
town on the northern border. He pushed the registration form back
through the teller slot. The consul scanned it, and said, "You came in
at the airport, I suppose."

"Mmm," Trowbridge said.

The consul made a note on the form. Then she looked up and said,
"You are now registered, which is good. If you aren't registered, we
don't know you're here, much less how to find you if you get into
trouble or your relatives need to contact you. That leads to accusations
we're incompetent bureaucrats, something we're familiar with, but
don't particularly enjoy. Are you a missionary?"

"No."

"They're the worst."

"I believe it," Trowbridge said. "I was told there might be a package here for me."

The consul looked more closely at the registration form. "I thought the name looked familiar."

She disappeared, returning a moment later with a battered cardboard box and a disapproving expression. Setting it on the shelf behind the window, she peered at a small green label beside the address, then looked up.

"Designer pet collars?"

"Yes," Trowbridge said.

"You realize we're not a post office, and you're not a government employee, which means this is illegal and I should send it back where it came from—and I would if the ambassador hadn't leaned on me. I hate it when people break the rules. You must have some kind of contacts in Washington."

The consul unlocked a latch on the window, swung it open, and pushed the box through.

"For all intents and purposes, this never happened, do you understand?"

"Perfect," Trowbridge said.

He drove into the older part of town, feeling a welcome anonymity amid the narrow streets and open sewers and little bars and shops. He found a small hotel, put the collars under the bed, and drove back across the bridge and up a gently curving road to a sloping plateau with a view of the lagoon. This was the best neighborhood in Pont Noir, the place where those who could afford it had their homes.

He drove slowly between houses that were large and solid looking and set back from the street. Most were surrounded by high concrete walls with spikes and broken glass set into their tops; there were mango trees and banana trees and green lawns marked by white-gravel walks and sprays of *citronnelle*. Guards stood in the driveways, looking bored, watching him go by. When he found the address he parked the car, walked up to a steel gate, and rang the bell. The front door opened and a heavy man with a vigorous black mustache came out the front door and down the walk.

Monsieur Barakat, it turned out, was in Beirut on business, and was not expected back for at least a week. Trowbridge considered this, then said, "Perhaps you could help me."

The man smiled opaquely.

"I'm afraid not," he said, and walked back to the house.

☵ ☷ ☵

Trowbridge sat a moment in the car, looking down the long, tree-lined street. Then he drove back to the old part of the city, through air that was sultry with ocean smell and traffic fumes, until he found the stadium and then the auto parts store. When he went inside the same Michelin man stood atop what looked like the same pile of receipts. The young Lebanese man recognized him and asked how the truck was running. He said about as well as could be expected, then asked if he could talk to the boss, the woman with whom he'd spoken on his previous visit. The young man said the boss had gone home for the day. If Trowbridge wanted to see her, he should come back tomorrow.

He stepped back out into the street and walked next door and looked in through the bars of the high gate. The black Mercedes was parked by the stairs, surrounded, as before, by an entourage of half-disassembled cars. When he pushed the buzzer the mechanic with the crescent wrench appeared from a small structure at one side of the courtyard, stripped to the waist and covered with grease, and gave him an unfriendly look through the bars. He said he had business with *Madame*, and was asked if he had an appointment. No, he said, but it has to do with airplanes—*Madame* will be unhappy if she doesn't see me. The mechanic walked back to what served as an office and picked up a phone. A few moments later a face appeared at the edge of the second-story rooftop, studied him, and disappeared. Crescent Wrench put down the phone, returned to the gate, and opened it wordlessly.

Trowbridge threaded his way between the cars to the outdoor staircase, and went up.

The rooftop terrace made a pleasant contrast to the courtyard below; it was solid and established, with worn, colored tiles, modern patio furniture, and potted plants sitting on the low wall which ran around its perimeter. Sitting in one of the patio chairs was the woman he'd seen briefly at dawn at the wheel of a Mercedes, and equally briefly in the auto shop next door. He had sudden doubts about what he was doing, doubts which were not relieved when she spoke.

"I don't need an airplane, I have a very good mechanic, and if you're a pilot, I don't need that kind of help either—I fly my own plane."

She had a mass of dark hair tied back loosely, and a skeptical expression. She hadn't asked him to sit down.

"I'm not here about an airplane."

"Then why are you here?"

He took a deep breath. "This is a little difficult. I'm a biologist, working in a national park in the eastern part of the country. There's something going on there I thought you might be able to help me understand."

It sounded ridiculous, even to his own ears. Feeling increasingly as if this had been a bad idea, he kept talking.

"There's an American taking trees illegally in the park. That's a problem in itself, but I'm worried that he's bringing in more logging equipment, and might be planning to expand his operation."

A set of carefully plucked eyebrows came together; she studied him with a critical expression.

"I'm a businesswoman," she said, "and I've never been to this park you're talking about, and frankly, I'm not much of a nature lover. Why—"

She stopped, then said, "It's because I'm Lebanese, isn't it? Someone told you the Lebanese know everything that goes on here, and you decided to presume upon the fact that we had this slight connection—the fact that you bought tires at my store."

"Roughly," he said, "yes."

There was a silence. He said, "Maybe you know a friend of mine who's a pilot. Alberto Fignoli. He lives near the park."

"I know Alberto. I wouldn't say we're friends. I landed at his airstrip once."

Another silence lengthened. Fine, he thought. I give up. This had been a lousy idea.

"I'm sorry," he said. "It wasn't my intention to waste your time."

She made no move to stand up.

"How long have you been here? In Terre Diamantée, I mean."

"About ten weeks."

Minus the six days when I was deported, he thought.

"It must be lonely in the forest."

He found this assumption annoying.

"Not really. I have friends there. Anyway, to the extent it's lonely, that's part of the job."

"What makes you think this timber operator plans to bring in more logging equipment?"

"I talked to him. He probably wouldn't have admitted this if he hadn't been drunk, but he told me he'd just obtained some sort of import license."

"Ah," she said. Then, "You aren't doing too badly, for being an American, and for having been here such a short time."

"Which is the worse liability? Being American, or only having been here ten weeks?"

When she got up from her chair he noticed she had a very nice body beneath the jeans and a sleeveless T-shirt.

"They both leave you pretty innocent," she said. Then she walked him to where the stairs began at the edge of the roof, shaking his hand briefly before he started down.

⚏ ☶ ⚏

He found a bar with a phone booth, and spoke French when he got Alain's secretary, and didn't give his name.

"Alain," he said, when Alain's voice came on. "This is an old friend. A former teacher. We haven't spoken in a while."

There was a lengthy pause. Then, "Are you calling long distance?"

"No."

Another pause. Then, "I don't have time to talk to every researcher who comes through Pont Noir. Why don't you send me your report?"

"Alain," he said, *"écoute—"*

The line went dead. He held the receiver a moment, considering whether to try again, then set it on the hook and walked back to the car.

⚏ ☶ ⚏

It was too late to start back to the park, so he slept for an hour on a fairly lousy bed, then took a shower and put on clean clothes and went out and sat at a table beneath a faded umbrella in the hotel courtyard. It had rained briefly; the darkening sky was the same color as the wet concrete beneath the tables. Bats flew and dipped like starlings. A slender *métis* with straightened hair and skin the color of *café au lait* sat at the next table arranging the contents of what looked like a sales case. At another table, a *marabout* holy man in white robes sat staring impassively at nothing. The lights came on, making islands of yellow illumination. He had just opened the menu when someone from the front desk came out and gave him the message that he was invited to dinner by an individual named Najla, who was waiting for him at her house on Rue Delacroix, near the stadium. He folded the menu and went through the lobby and found a taxi, leaving the Peugeot where it would be watched over by the hotel guard. It wasn't until he gave the taxi driver directions that he remembered he hadn't told Najla where he was staying.

33

By the time he climbed the stairs and emerged onto the rooftop it was dark. Najla was standing in the doorway, looking transformed from her afternoon self, and drop-dead gorgeous. Her hair was up in a dark, wild riot; she had on long earrings, high heels, and a tight dress; one wrist jangled with slender bracelets. Locking the door behind herself, she handed him a sport coat.

"We're going out. You'll need this."

"I didn't think there was any place in Terre Diamantée you needed a coat for dinner."

"Then you have something to learn about Terre Diamantée," she said.

The mechanic rolled back the gate, and she drove them through dark streets down around the port, past a row of warehouses and a sizable military compound ringed with a high barbed-wire fence. They passed a restaurant built on stilts over the lagoon, and a string of nightclubs. This strip along the water, despite being on the wrong side of the bridge, was clearly expensive real estate. She parked the Mercedes in front of a small restaurant with frosted glass windows, and they went into an elegant interior where people were speaking quietly, and most of those people were European or Lebanese, and there was a pleasant sense of stillness and refinement, of being a long way from everything that was ugly and difficult and frustrating about Terre Diamantée.

The maître d' greeted Najla by name and led them to a table set with white linen. She brushed against Trowbridge slightly as she sat down. Her scent lingered in his nostrils, lending a slight sense of unreality to the situation.

She picked up the menu and studied it. "Do you know what endive is?"

"Yes, I do. How did you find out where I was staying?"

"What difference does it make?"

"It makes a difference."

"I had someone follow you. The man in the courtyard."

"Why?"

"I'd rather talk about endive."

He said nothing.

"All right," she said, setting down the menu, "if you think it's important. When you walked down the stairs this afternoon I noticed that the prospect of going to my sports club, then spending the evening at home, sounded boring. I had a feeling I might be throwing away something nice. For what it's worth, I did remember you from the other morning at the bus station, and from when you came into my store. Maybe it's just that I'm not a teenager any more, but I'm aware that men might stop noticing me back one of these days."

"Not any time soon," he said, appreciating the fact that there had been no self-pity in her voice.

"It's also true," she said evenly, "that I was intrigued by what you told me about the park, and this other American. I might be able to help you. But the person who can get the information we need won't have it until tomorrow morning, so you're having dinner with me tonight. Satisfied?"

He nodded. The waiter materialized. Najla ordered two endive salads and a reasonably expensive white Bordeaux, then put her chin on her hand and looked at him thoughtfully.

"Why would an American biologist bother to learn French? I would expect you to know more exotic languages."

"French is useful in Africa. But I speak some exotic languages too."

"You must have been a very single-minded student. Learning both biology and languages. I'm impressed by people who work that hard."

The waiter set down plates of endive, slender, pale green flutes dressed with walnuts and blue-veined Roquefort, then hesitated discreetly with the bottle of wine. Trowbridge nodded at Najla, who escorted the waiter through the ritual of tasting and pouring.

She raised her glass, and said, "To freedom. And to making money."

They clinked glasses, and he said, "Whose jacket is this?"

"My brother's," she said. "Don't worry."

When they left the restaurant and climbed into the Mercedes she started the engine, but left it in neutral. He could just see her face in the dark interior of the car. The engine hummed quietly; it was a strangely peaceful moment.

"I intended to pay," he said. "Or at least to split it with you. I'm the one who came to you asking for help."

"But I was the one who invited you to dinner. Anyway, Emil sends me a bill at the end of the month; it's easier this way."

She put the car in gear and drove them back past the string of nightclubs, and then the military base, surrounded by white-painted lines of stone and sandbag bunkers. He saw a machine gun in a tower at a corner of the compound, and watched a camouflage-green Renault truck pull up and stop at a barricaded entrance. A white face was driving, and a white face waved the truck through. The truck, he noticed, had narrow tires, and wasn't *quatre-quatre*—four-wheel drive.

"The Old Man's insurance policy," she said. "Eight hundred Belgian marines, fifteen minutes, by good road, from the Presidency."

"That truck wouldn't be much good upcountry."

"Coups don't happen upcountry."

She accelerated smoothly through a yellow light, leaving the base behind them. "Do you want to go to a club? They don't open until eleven, but we could sit in a bar somewhere and wait."

"Not really."

She took one hand off the wheel and entwined her fingers with his. He abandoned all thoughts of asking her to drop him at his hotel, and let her drive, without saying much more, back to her apartment.

⁂ ⁑ ⁂

The first thing he saw when he walked in was an enormous pair of elephant tusks forming an archway against one wall. They must have been imported—no forest elephant had ever carried tusks of that size. There were shelves filled with books and vases, brass mirrors on the wall, low couches, and a number of photographs of what must have been family members. Most seemed to be voluptuous, dark-haired women like Najla, or men with a good deal of mustache and eyebrow but very little hair on their heads. Everything about her apartment suggested not merely wealth, but the spending of it—and yet everything was kept carefully on the inside, not for the scrutiny of strangers. It seemed very Lebanese, to the extent he was beginning to understand what that meant.

He looked through a hallway door and saw a leopard skin against a wall.

"I thought you said you weren't a nature lover."

She sat down on the couch and looked at him steadily.

"Are you angry at me for those things?"

"There isn't a lot of point getting angry. If you'd seen the animals alive, you might have a different feeling about them."

"I believe that."

He was still standing.

She said, "Do you want something to drink?"

"No."

"What do I have to do to get you to sit down?"

He sat down across from her. She looked pleased, and lit a cigarette.

He said, "Do you live alone?"

She nodded. "My little sister spends a lot of time here, but she lives with my mother."

"And the rest of your family?"

"Spread out across West Africa. Accra, Abidjan, Dakar. Plus I have a sister in Paris, and two brothers still in Beirut."

"Things are calming down there."

"Some. But there are still a lot of surface-to-air missiles on apartment building roofs, which, being a pilot, makes me nervous. Anyway, it's better for me here. I can do what I like."

"That's where the freedom part comes in."

"And the making money part."

She put out her cigarette, carefully, in the ashtray, and then she looked up and asked him if he would like to sleep with her, and he found that the answer overwhelmingly was yes.

❖ ❖ ❖

The bedroom lights were off, but light came in from the living room, making a pleasant twilight. Her bed was so large and soft he felt as if he were falling into powder snow. When she emerged from the bathroom he thought she might have taken her clothes off, but only the heels were missing.

"I took off my makeup. I can't stand to wake up in it. Do I still look all right?"

She climbed onto the bed, on her hands and knees above him. They kissed, and he put one hand around her neck. She pulled away and straightened, her body in shadow above him. She took one shoulder of her dress and pulled it down, then pulled down the other shoulder and slid the dress down to her waist. Touching her breasts was the purest pleasure he could remember experiencing in a long time.

"You didn't answer me. About how I look without makeup."

"I didn't think you needed it in the first place."

"Ah," she said. "You're nice."

She reached down and began unbuttoning his shirt.

"Listen—" he started.

"I told you not to worry," she said, leaning to one side and opening a drawer in the night table and pulling out a condom. "When it rains, you put up an umbrella. We're in West Africa, after all."

❖ ❖ ❖

He slept late, waking with a clear memory of physical pleasure, a drowning in flesh that left him calm and peaceful and ready to accept whatever came next. He lay a moment in the big bed, enjoying the silence and the smell of bodies and the feel of the sheets. Then he remembered he'd driven out from the park in a borrowed car. He felt a quick moment of guilt before reminding himself that Claire had shown no sign of wanting them to be anything more than friends and co-workers. No betrayal here—even if he might have wished it to be so.

He got up and pulled on pants and went out to the dining room. There were coffee and croissants, a pitcher of pineapple juice, a mango sliced in a diamond pattern and opened like a flower. Beside the coffee cup was a note from Najla—jotted in fountain pen on expensive card stock—telling him she'd be back soon.

He glanced again at the photos of what seemed to be innumerable family members scattered about the apartment. There was something reassuring about being surrounded by all this company. He owned an apartment in New York—purchased in college days with money his father left him—but he had more photos of animals there than of people. A snapshot of his sister, with whom he had little in common, cutting cattle on one of her quarter horses; another of his parents before his father had gotten sick; a third of his mother graduating from college at age fifty-one. The photo of him and Nima, standing in front of a prayer *chorten* in the Himalayas, had stayed on the living room bookshelf for six months after she'd moved out; then he'd packed it away.

A while later he heard a key in the lock. Najla opened the door, smiled when she saw him, and said, "Breakfast all right?"

"Breakfast was great."

She took a sheet of paper from her purse, dropped the purse on the couch, and sat beside him. "This must seem excessive to you. My apartment, I mean. I saw it through your eyes when I got up this morning."

"Actually, I'm very comfortable here. Leopard skin and tusks notwithstanding."

"You're beginning to surprise me. Most men wake up nervous."

"I don't do this often enough to know the rules."

A shadow crossed her face.

"I don't either," she said.

"Sorry. That's not what I meant."

She nodded, and took a sip of his coffee.

"Here's what I've got," she said.

She unfolded the piece of paper and set it in front of him. It looked like a photocopy of some sort of official document.

"This is a copy of the import license given to your friend Randy

Foote. It's for a good deal of heavy machinery. Enough that he's chartered a small freighter to bring it in."

"Logging equipment?"

"And trucks. The freighter—the *Tsar Simeon*—is Bulgarian registered, chartered out of Varna on the Black Sea."

"How did you get this?"

She looked at him askance.

"Never mind," he said.

"Foote transferred a lot of money to Cyprus last month. Several
million dollars. Presumably some of that went on to Bulgaria, although it's not clear how much. The *Tsar Simeon* is in Varna right now
taking on logging equipment. It's scheduled to stop in Cyprus for a
load of Toyota long-bed pickup trucks, then continue on through the
Med, and around to Terre Diamantée."

"How many trucks?"

"Fifty."

"That's crazy."

"Is it? I don't know the timber business."

She indicated a signature on the photocopy. "This is Foote's signature. You'll notice he writes like a child, and not a very intelligent
one. The signature beside it is that of a Deputy Minister in the Ministry of Trade. Not particularly hard to get—there's a set payoff of
about three thousand dollars. What's more interesting is the adden-
dum beneath it providing for duty-free import. That *is* hard to get."

Trowbridge pointed to an illegible scrawl at the bottom of the document. "And this?"

"That's the signature of the *Chef des Gendarmes.*"

The *Chef des Gendarmes*. He remembered the night of the murders,
the man's soft, contemptuous face lit by headlights, the cold eyes.
Now we have our own Dian Fossey, he'd said. Something didn't feel
right about the image, and he struggled to identify what it was—and
then he had it, and it was so simple and obvious he wondered why he
hadn't figured it out sooner.

The *Chef des Gendarmes* was stationed here, in the capital, a six-
hour drive from the station—and Douli ba had said he rarely *left* the
capital. Yet he'd arrived barely half an hour after Douli ba had.

How had he gotten there so fast?

Trowbridge stared at the photocopy, looking for answers he knew it wouldn't give him. What could Foote possibly plan to do with an entire shipload of logging equipment? Were Foote and the *Chef des Gendarmes* working together in some fashion—and was there a link, somehow, to the murders of Jean Luc and Guy and Gregoire? A new image came to him, the man outside the window in Sandoukou, scarification on one side of his face. What role did he play in all this, aside from having intimidated Foote into cooperating with the import scheme?

Random pieces of data, explaining nothing, suggesting no line of inquiry.

"Are you all right?" she asked.

"Yes. Why would the *Chef des Gendarmes* sign a customs document?"

She shrugged. "Granville's pretty close to the border with Denkyara. Maybe they justify it on the grounds of national security. Any excuse for a bribe."

She took another sip of coffee, and said matter-of-factly, "We're worried, a little. As a community, I mean. Things seem to be getting less and less stable as the Old Man gets older."

She didn't spell it out, but her meaning was clear. In the chaos which had enveloped Uganda under Idi Amin, thousands of Indians had been expelled, their businesses and homes seized and given to Amin's friends and promptly run into the ground. The Syrians in Denkyara had been chased out the same way, although they'd filtered back over time.

"The Justice Minister seems to be consolidating power," she said. "Buying some people, scaring others. It's happening quietly, but it's happening—and it's not clear what he wants."

"It seems obvious. He wants to be ready when the Old Man goes."

"He's moving awfully quickly for that. Unless he knows something about the Old Man's health that no one else does."

"So what does it all mean?"

"I don't know. But we have a good thing going here, and we'd hate to lose it. People are making money, and no one is killing each other. That's pretty good for this continent."

⠿ ⡃ ⠿

They made love on the white rug between the dining room table and the couch. She had one arm around his waist, and braced herself with her free hand by holding onto a table leg. He heard something rocking, and realized one of his feet was pushing against an end table on which a glass lamp was wobbling dangerously.

"Najla—"

"I know."

"But—"

"Don't stop."

He didn't, and the lamp quit making noise. When they sat up they saw the lamp had fallen off the end table harmlessly onto a throw pillow, and she laughed out loud. She reached up to the tabletop for a glass of pineapple juice, and leaned back against the couch.

"So. Now what."

"Now I go back out to the park."

She made a face. "Why?"

"I have work to do there."

"Work," she said dismissively. "Anyone can work, anywhere."

"You probably wouldn't enjoy working where I do."

"Probably not," she admitted.

He collected his clothes, dressed in front of her, then kissed her, closed the door behind himself, and went down the stairs and took a taxi back to the hotel.

As he packed his things in the hotel room he thought about the brief phone conversation he'd had with Alain. Alain had made it abundantly clear he didn't want any public contact with Trowbridge—and yet he now knew, at a minimum, that Trowbridge was in the country. There was nothing to lose by trying to contact him again, so long as it could be done discreetly.

He took a tattered address book from his duffel bag. Like many Diamantiens, Alain didn't have a home phone—he was on a twelve-year waiting list—but Trowbridge had a P.O. box address for him that was separate from the office. He tore a piece of paper from a notebook, wrote Alain a short letter, and posted it on the way out of the city.

34

He reached Kisanga in the early afternoon, parked the Peugeot outside the market, and climbed the concrete stairs to the second story.
The fetish seller's table was empty; there was no sign of its proprietor,
either in darkness or light. Grains of charcoal and a scattering of red
powder were just visible on the rough wood before him. He stood a
moment, feeling at a loss, then heard someone coming toward him,
and turned and saw the fetish seller's nephew.

"*Ça va?*" said the nephew.

"*Ça va un peu,*" Trowbridge said.

"My uncle is away on a buying trip. But he told me you would
come back. He asked me to give you this."

The nephew handed him a little cloth bag with a knotted draw-
string.

"How did he know I would come back?"

The nephew shrugged, as if such things were beyond him.

"Do you know what's in the bag?"

"Useful things. My uncle said it would be protection in the forest."

The bag was made of soft brown cloth, nothing remarkable, and
was lighter than the bag Douli ba had shown him.

"Do I owe him something for this?"

"For the magic to work properly, there must be some payment.
But it can be small."

Trowbridge gave him a few *befa* and put the fetish bag into his
chest pocket. "Tell him thanks. And that I'll come see him another
time."

The nephew nodded. Trowbridge noticed that his cheeks were
marked with small round scars, the scarification of the Poroufo, a savannah tribe.

"Tell me something," he said. "Do you know what it means when
someone has scarification on only one side of his face?"

He put a finger to his temple and drew three straight lines.

"Scarification is on both sides, *patron.*"

"But what if it's only on one?"

The nephew said, "I know of a man with a face like that. He's called Moneyboy. With such a name he can only be from Denkyara." He glanced uneasily around the market, and lowered his voice. "The Ebrio elders in Kisanga seem to think he's an important person—when he visits they have secret meetings, and afterward they act agitated and important themselves, although they won't say why."

"What else do you know about him?"

"The Ebrio wouldn't like it if they knew I had been talking about him. But are you going to Pont Noir?"

"I was just there."

"When you go back, talk to someone named Komo. At the Thai Girl Bar. She might be able to tell you something more."

"Who is she?"

The nephew looked unhappy, suddenly, as if he wished he'd said nothing.

"I hope the fetish bag is of use to you, *patron,*" he said, ending the conversation.

⌗ ⌗ ⌗

He and Claire sat on the forest floor at the far side of the clearing where she'd established her most recent camp. The late afternoon light was filtered and dim. He put his feet against the wings of the crossbow, took the string in the fingers of both hands, and pulled it back until it hooked over the release mechanism. Then he looked at Claire beside him.

"Got it?"

"Yes."

"The sights are adjusted already. It's just a matter of aiming and squeezing the trigger."

He put a practice dart into the slide and handed her the bow. The target was a plastic bag filled with leaves and placed against a tangle of roots fifteen meters away.

"The timing will be important," he said. "We have to be sure the drug kicks in before they start up. Otherwise—"

"Otherwise they could get partway up, then fall."

"Next week?"

"Next week is good. It might take a few days to find them."

Her voice was firm, and she seemed to have no more doubts about the darting. He was happy to be working with her, to be sitting here in the forest collaborating with someone in his own profession—a profession which had been, to this point in his life, mainly a solitary endeavor. He tried to think of a way to say that without sounding foolish, without ruining a good moment, and failed.

"Rest it on your knees," he said. "It's steadier that way."

She took a deep breath, shifted the bow on her knees so that it rested steadily, and aimed. When she squeezed the trigger the dart went singing across the clearing into the bag of leaves.

⠶ ⠿ ⠶

The forest darkened around them, and she methodically shot one dart after another. He told her what he'd learned in Pont Noir, keeping things vague when it came to whom he'd learned it from. As he described the import license something occurred to him, and he stopped, and said, "Logging would be totally prohibited under the management plan, right? Commercial logging, I mean."

She set the bow down and looked at him.

"We built in some provisions for artisanal logging, but yes, the big companies would be kept out. They have to build roads into the forest—even for a limited harvest—and that's the beginning of the end."

"If someone had unrestricted access to the buffer zone he could make a lot of money, couldn't he?"

"Sure. But—"

She stopped. "You think Foote and the *Chef des Gendarmes* have a plan to go after the buffer zone?"

"It would explain why the management plan has been blocked."

"But that would have a terrible effect on the park. It would—"

"It's the only thing that makes sense of what we know."

Claire raised the bow, then lowered it again. She looked like she was ready to cry.

"I worked hard on that plan. So did Jean Luc and Alain. It may sound naive, but I came here hoping to make a difference of some kind. I didn't see myself just hiding in the park, then sneaking out with my data. Is there anything we can do?"

"I don't know," he said. "Foote's got a piece of paper signed by the highest-ranking policeman in the country."

"But that's just an import license. Not a license to cut down trees in the buffer zone."

"Presumably he has some plan to get around that."

"So we just get on with our work, then?"

Her voice was bitter, and the words *smash and grab* hung between them, as if Jean Luc had spoken them out loud. He didn't feel all that happy any more, and he no longer felt as if the two of them were alone in the forest.

"I guess so," he said.

35

Hiking up the narrow trail to the platform was something he'd done dozens of times now, but it still required careful attention. He edged past a granite outcropping where the trail was barely a meter wide, then stopped to watch his favorite bird in the forest, the naked-faced barbet, a dumpy, quarrelsome creature, entirely drab brown but for a featherless, blackish head and short bristles at its chin and nostrils. A colony of fifty or so lived in a *musana* tree which grew out from the steep side of the inselberg; he watched one of these good barbet citizens jump restlessly from branch to branch, balancing improbably and making rasping *shreep-shreep* noises at its neighbors. The naked, prehistoric face, impossibly ugly, and the industriously social behavior always made him cheerful.

When he reached the platform he pulled the cover off the computer, touched a key, and watched the screen come to life. It had been eight weeks since he walked across the border from Denkyara. In addition to *L1* and *L2*, he had a young male, an older male, and another adult female, all moving through their home ranges, hunting and resting and keeping track of one another by means of scent marks and vocalizations. His regular visits to *L1* and the cubs—staying on the ground instead of hanging in the harness, inching almost imperceptibly nearer each time—were beginning to pay off; the three leopards looked almost bored now when he arrived. And he'd identified a pronounced home-range overlap between *L2* and *L5*, the adult female; the two even met on occasion and spent short periods of time together. Leopards, in the main, were solitary animals; a meeting between two females suggested a mother-daughter relationship.

At the center of all this activity, a blank area, the home range of the black leopard. He stood, took the sixth and last collar from a bag, twirled it in his hand, and looked back at the computer screen. Even from across the platform you could see the hole in the middle of his study.

⠿ ⠓ ⠿

Claire hired one of Nobila's innumerable *petits frères,* a young man named Seydou, to help her find the second band of chimps. The two went out each morning to the primary band for a session of *petit frère* training and note taking; then Claire would leave for the second group's territory, where she walked steady transects, listening and watching. When Trowbridge came out from the inselberg she'd been doing this for four days without success, and was worried that poachers had taken the band, or that they'd moved for some reason. She decided Seydou was doing well enough to go out with the habituated chimps, and she and Trowbridge began searching together for the second group.

Two days later, shortly before noon, they heard distant booming, a male drumming on a flanged tree root, and found them alive and well in a far corner of their range.

They sat beside one another, watching the animals which had been Jean Luc and Guy's last project. These chimps hadn't lost habituation entirely, but grew agitated if he and Claire moved closer than about five meters, so they kept their distance. Most of the adults were peaceful and full-bellied, lolling sleepily, like scattered raisins, in various outrageous positions on a downed tree. One or two of the females managed an occasional hoot of admonition at a pair of adolescent chimps wrestling their way up and down a strangler fig.

Beneath Claire's controlled exterior, the practiced attitude she maintained in the forest, he sensed both professional excitement and a degree of personal reluctance at what they were about to do. She watched the chimps intently, trying to gauge how close they were to going up into the nesting tree.

"I think it's time," she said finally. "I think we should do it."

He handed her the crossbow. She braced the wings against her feet, pulled the string back, then rested the bow on her knees. He took the syringe dart from the case and handed it to her.

She said, "You double-checked the dosage?"

"Triple-checked."

She took a deep breath.

"Routine," he said, knowing better than to offer to do it himself. "Who's first?"

"The female with the gray patch on her rump. She looks healthy, isn't pregnant, and doesn't have offspring to be traumatized. Number two will be that young male over there, the one who was harassing his little sister."

"There's a chance," he said, "that they'll react negatively to having something pointed at them. Once you bring the bow around, aim and shoot. Don't wait."

"There's also a chance they'll react negatively to being darted," she said coolly. "If so, roll in a ball and cover your head."

"Not my private parts?"

"Your private parts may not be all that useful if your face and scalp have been removed."

"I'll remember that."

She took another deep breath, and said softly, "Routine."

He saw that her hands were steady, and felt reassured. She was watching Gray Patch carefully. Swinging the bow around, she aimed with a serious expression and pulled the trigger.

☷ ䷗ ☷

"Give it another twist. It has to be more than finger tight. Fingers will be working at these bolts."

She gave a final turn to the last locknut on the collar, then sat back with a satisfied expression. There had been a screech when the dart hit the female's gray rump, but she'd only batted at it angrily and gone on nibbling at a bit of plant. Thirty seconds later, the young male had reacted with similar unconcern. One of the advantages of working in this environment was that chimps, like leopards, were accustomed to having their hides pierced by driver ants and other crawling-biting creatures. Nine minutes after being darted, Gray Patch and the young male had lain down, suddenly possessed by the idea of taking a nap; twenty minutes after that, the other chimps—after some evidence of distress, and various efforts to wake the two sleepers—went up the tree. He and Claire had moved in, covered the chimps' eyes, swabbed the wounds with alcohol, and given them each a shot of penicillin.

He put the tip of a small-bladed screwdriver into the recessed hole in the collar, found the slot, and gave it a twist, activating the battery.

"That's it."

Gray Patch was lying on her side with her head resting on Trowbridge's rolled shirt. Her position was strikingly human, her formidable chimpanzee muscles, for the moment, totally relaxed.

"Their breathing seems good," Claire said.

"It does."

"Now we wait, right?"

"Now we wait."

They looked up through the dim light at the canopy above them. Branches cracked and leaves rustled as the chimps made their nests. Some of the chimps stopped what they were doing, occasionally, and bent their heads down, dark curious faces looking down at him and Claire in the dusk.

 ⸭ ⸭ ⸭

It was a long walk back to Claire's camp, sweaty, buggy work in the darkness. When they got there she declared she couldn't go to bed like this, and they picked up clean clothes and soap and walked to the station. He showered quickly, then toweled off and put on shorts and a T-shirt and sat on the edge of the *paillote*. Claire disappeared into the shower enclosure, pulling off her clothes. A full moon, ringed with a fuzzy orange halo, came over the edge of the treetops, flooding the clearing with light. The shower water stopped. He could hear her toweling her hair, and pulling on clothes, and then she came out wearing jeans and a tank top, smiling and running her hands through her hair. Her jeans weren't buttoned yet, and her shirt was pulled up, and the thin scar that ran across her belly above the top of her bikini underpants was unmistakable.

"Another leopard scratch?" he asked.

She looked at him blankly, then glanced down at her belly.

"Damn," she said ruefully, buttoning her jeans. "That's twice."

☷ ䷀ 　☷

"Why didn't you try to bring her with you? Other people have done that sort of thing. Pascale had two children here."

Claire was sitting next to him on the edge of the *paillote,* looking out at the clearing. She snorted in quiet disbelief. "Jean Luc picked me from about seventy-five applicants. Can you imagine if my letter of application had included a request to bring a ten-month-old baby? In his place, would you have accepted me?"

"I guess I wouldn't have."

"I *know* you wouldn't have."

She was silent a moment, then said, "My mother's looking after her, and doing a good job of it. Being a better mother to Isabelle, in fact, than she was to me."

"Didier's not interested in being a father?"

"Didier's interested in Didier. Although I guess I'm in no position to criticize him for that."

"Do you want to have her with you?"

"Very much. That's why if I'm going to stay in this business, I have to make a reputation fast, and find some kind of steady position."

It occurred to him that if he took the directorship he would have a good deal of decision-making control over which projects the Society supported. A rain-forest project in Terre Diamantée, for example, run by someone who was unquestionably the most qualified primatologist available.

"The predator-prey study would help. Assuming we get something."

"That's part of why I'm doing it."

She took a deep breath, and released it slowly. "It's funny, I never resented it that much, being shuttled all over when I was growing up. California with my dad, Lucerne with my mom, boarding school in England. Vacations all over the world with one or the other. I took a stubborn pride in being at home in so many places—or more than that, really, in having no home at all. I told myself it was an advantage, that it made me tough. I still see my upbringing in a positive light—it helped me move as far as I have in this field—but I'm changing, somehow. I want Isabelle to have more security than I did, and I want some kind of home for both of us."

　　▦　▦　▦

He had trouble going to sleep that night, and found himself thinking about the parallels between Claire's rootlessness and his own solitude. The way they had each developed a stubborn acceptance—maybe rationalization—of something forced on them when they were too young to have a say. He thought about Nima, and how the failure of that relationship had changed his perception of being on his own. Before Nima, when he felt lonely, it had been a badge of honor somehow, proof that he was living up to his resolution to work alone, gather data on his own, avoid becoming dependent on other people. Proof that he was nothing like his father. Now when loneliness struck he was less convinced of this, and it occurred to him, lying in the darkness, that in trying so hard to avoid becoming the man his father had been before the heart attacks—to avoid becoming entangled in a professional web of dependence and vulnerability—he was in danger of becoming his father *after* the heart attacks, toward the end of his life, isolated and without connection to the human world.

36

He shut down the computer and glanced at the amber disk of the sun floating slowly down toward the horizon. Three hours till darkness. An hour for his preparations, an hour to reach the site—in the center of *L6's* territory—and an hour to put a line over a branch and get ready to go up. He went to his bag of tricks and laid out the contents on his cot, checking each item methodically. He made sure the collar was working, and that he had his crescent wrench and nuts and bolts. He checked the strings on the two crossbows, and lubricated the trigger mechanisms. He made sure there was a backup dose of Kezol, and ophthalmic gel and penicillin, and he put in the slingshot and ball bearings, and checked to see there were spare batteries for the cassette player. Then he ran his fingers over the harness and ascenders to be sure everything was working properly. He needed this leopard before the rainy season started, which meant he only had about four weeks.

☷ ⚏ ☷

Something over twelve hours later, at four a.m., the only animals he'd seen had been a group of forest hogs who'd been spanked smartly with ball bearings for their interest in the duiker tape. Ironically, for all his care in preparation, he'd made a mistake. The batteries in the scope were weak, and he had no spares. When he turned on the scope he had close to normal visibility for about a minute; then the yellow light would begin to dim, until soon he could see only the ghostly columns of tree trunks, then nothing at all. He'd considered writing the evening off, then decided that if the leopard came in, a minute's worth of scope visibility would be enough. Once it was darted and down, he could work by flashlight.

Of course this required the presence of the leopard, which was looking unlikely. Most of his collars had taken place between nine and three; only one had been as late as four. He stretched and took a deep breath, tempted again to give up on tonight as a bad job, and go back early.

No, he told himself. Another half-hour. You don't deserve this animal if you don't do the work to get him.

A few minutes later one of the pale strips of liana beneath him disappeared. He stopped breathing as a second strip disappeared, and a third. Now the first was visible once again. Too big for a civet, or golden; too big for anything but a leopard. He waited a few seconds, giving it time to reach the log and the cassette player, considering the problem with the scope. Maybe he ought not to fire the insurance dart, go directly with the Kezol. No, he would stay with the system that had worked before. He raised his hand, flipped down the scope, and brought up the pistol crossbow, seeing the dark bulk of what was, unquestionably, a full-grown male leopard.

He squeezed the trigger, and felt the slight ease of tension as the tiny dart flew free.

The light from the scope was going fast; the leopard, and the trail, faded into darkness. He turned off the scope and waited, holding the rifle crossbow loosely in his right hand, counting to a hundred to let the battery recover. He touched the syringe dart with his free hand to make sure it was properly in the slide, then flipped down the scope and raised the bow. The leopard was there, dimly, in partial profile, one muscular shoulder high, massive head down as it investigated the duiker noise. He felt a sudden reluctance to do this, even as he was struck by the strength and sheer size of this animal—by far the largest he'd ever seen in the wild. It would go at least a hundred and twenty pounds. He adjusted his aim slightly—the scope was fading fast—and fired, and saw the syringe dart bloom from the powerful thigh. The leopard's head came up sharply; its jaws opened in a snarl, and it swatted with a broad paw at the place the dart had struck. There was another angry snarl as it gathered its hind legs beneath it to spring away, and then the light was gone, and he could see nothing at all.

⁜ ⁜ ⁜

He played the flashlight beam over the forest floor beneath him. Nothing, and no movement in the surrounding vegetation. He glanced at his watch. A minute and a half since the dart had plunged a dose of Kezol into *L6*'s flank. Why had it reacted that way? He'd darted five animals—seven, if you counted the chimps—without any of them taking more than passing notice.

He visualized the dart going in. Had it had been a bit high, perhaps because of the failing light? Had he hit a nerve?

Whatever the explanation, he now had a problem. Descending quickly to the forest floor, he stepped out of the harness and reached into his bag for the Yagi antenna he'd hoped he would never have to use. He unfolded its elements—roughly doubling its size, so that it was a meter square—then plugged the cord from the battery unit into the back of the antenna, clipped the unit to his belt, and put on the headphones.

Three minutes and forty seconds since he'd darted the black leopard. Now he had to go find it.

⁜ ⁜ ⁜

The antenna was a smaller version of what he'd had in the Ituri, and was thus easier to use in dense forest; nonetheless, walking with it held before him—pushing and tearing his way through the vegetation, trying not to advertise his presence to every living creature within ten kilometers—was slow, difficult work. Worse, the antenna was an imprecise tool. It had a range of barely five hundred meters, and gave direction, not position; only the relative strength of the signal provided a rough indication of whether the animal was ten meters distant, or five hundred. He stopped, holding the antenna at arm's length in his right hand, swinging it in a slow circle. There, a faint beeping. With his left hand he aimed the flashlight down a narrow elephant lane. Five minutes and twenty seconds. The prudent thing would be to wait, give this animal a full ten minutes and be sure it was unconscious. And yet if it were spooked and moving quickly, it might pass beyond the range of his antenna before it went down. In that case he would never find it, and it would lie there, vulnerable to anything that came along, for several hours. Vulnerable, for example, to driver ants.

No, he wouldn't take a chance of that happening. Not to this animal, not if he were responsible. He moved down the elephant lane, playing the flashlight beam before him. At seven minutes he stopped and raised the antenna. The beeping was there, in roughly the same direction. At eight minutes the beeping held steady before him, although it seemed fainter. He pushed on more quickly, not stopping until his watch said it had been a full ten minutes.

No leopard had gone more than eight and a half. It had to be down by now. He raised the antenna and made a slow sweep before him. Nothing. Damn, he thought, it's out of range. He lowered the antenna and started forward, then stopped, listening to a quiet voice inside him, and raised the antenna again, moving it in a slow circle until he faced back the way he'd come. Nothing in the headphones but a faint hissing of background noise. He continued the sweep, until, three quarters of the way around the circle, he heard a beeping. He stood very still, considering this. Then he lowered the antenna and began walking at a deliberate pace back the way he'd come, playing the flashlight beam off to what was now the right side of the trail. At fourteen minutes he stopped and raised the antenna again. The beeping was still there, off to his right, at the same ninety degree angle.

Something was wrong. He wasn't dealing with a drugged animal, as he had supposed. Nor was he, any longer, the one in pursuit.

⁘ ⁛ ⁘

A few meters farther on, the elephant lane ended in a head-high tangle of tree roots. It seemed to him he would remember this if he'd passed this way. He shone his flashlight on the roots, realizing he'd made yet another mistake. The GPS was in a bag with the rest of his gear, hidden near the darting site—and it looked as if he'd blundered off the trail.

He moved the antenna until he found the beeping, directly behind him now. He felt a prickling at his neck, a rise of gooseflesh, and forced himself to think rationally. What appeared to be movement on the part of the leopard—stalking movements, to be precise—might be simply a reflection of his own twists and turns as he followed the path.

On the other hand, he was alone and possibly lost in a dark tangled forest, with a predator, apparently unsedated, which had been born to live and hunt in dark tangled forests. He needed to get back to the harness and up off the forest floor, where he could wait safely until daylight.

The site couldn't be far. He closed his eyes, listening for the taped duiker cry. Was that it, off to the right? He heard the beating of his own heart, a distant thudding in his chest. He shone the flashlight across the vegetation behind him, then turned and bent down to duck through the tangle of roots. As he did so, he realized he'd been moving with instinctive quiet, and heard his own advice to Claire: Stay upright, make noise, never bend over so that you resemble a four-legged animal. Never conform to a leopard's prey image.

He gathered sound in his throat, sensed movement behind him, and turned, straightening and putting his arm up as a physical darkness rose before him. The flashlight was knocked from his hand and he was flung back into the root system, banging his head, barely managing to stay upright. A heavy body was hard against him; stiff forelegs pinned him, and a hot stink of breath was in his face. Jaws closed on his raised forearm, once, twice, lunging for his throat. He fought back, pushing off with his arm, reaching up with his free hand for the leopard's face. He felt the broad nose and stiff whiskers, the crinkled skin above the jaw where the skin pulled away from the teeth. He reached higher, going desperately for the eyes. The jaws released fractionally, then came forward again, forcing his left arm into his throat. He was having trouble breathing now, and felt a click of tooth on bone—a small, precise sound—as the powerful jaws tightened. His head swam, and some part of him noted that a broken collarbone would be a serious problem. Then the jaws loosened, and the leopard grew heavier, and he was staggering, incredulous with the realization that he was supporting an unconscious animal. He let himself slide to a sitting position, bringing the leopard down with him, feeling its heart beat against his chest. Feeling that heartbeat grow slower.

He tipped his head back in disbelief. His breathing, slowly, returned to normal. With his right hand he disengaged the leopard's jaws, felt its head loll away. He touched his shoulder gingerly, then his left forearm. There was blood, but less than he'd feared; he'd been punctured rather than torn as he would have been if the leopard were fully conscious. Puncture wounds brought their own problems—the danger of infection was worse—but at least he wouldn't bleed to death on the forest floor.

The leopard lay half atop him, breathing in his face.

Jesus Christ, he thought irrelevantly. I didn't know any animal alive had such horrible breath. He must have had carrion for dinner.

He sat a few minutes, gathering his strength, then dragged himself out from beneath his sixth study animal, picked up his flashlight, and walked unsteadily back to the darting site and his gear, following the duiker cry. When he returned he injected first himself, then the leopard, with penicillin. By this time the strange grace period during which he'd felt almost no pain was ending; he had to force himself to concentrate, to work slowly and carefully, as he collared *L6*. Then he turned off his flashlight and sat back against the tree, holding on against the pain, waiting for sunrise with a black leopard, white tape over its eyes, lying beside him.

3 7

He rinsed his toothbrush in a pan of soapy water, raised the camp mirror, and began probing at the messy scrabble of puncture wounds across his shoulder. Leopards fed on their kills long after the meat was rotten and crawling with maggots; they had filthy mouths, and their claws were worse. He would soon be fighting a battle with infection, and was in no condition to walk out of the forest. The wounds had to be cleaned now, before the fever started.

He explored gently at first, then gritted his teeth and began scrubbing. By the time he set down the mirror and started on his left arm, which had sustained the worst damage, the pan of water was brilliant red, and a pale wash of blood was seeping down his chest and stomach. He'd injected himself with a local anesthetic when he arrived at the platform, and taken a pair of Vicodin, the pain-killer pills in his first-aid kit, but was very glad when he was able to lay down the toothbrush and declare the job finished. He spread half a tube of antiseptic cream across the wounds, taped on gauze bandages, then tipped the pan of water over and stood unsteadily.

When he put on water for bouillon he noticed his canteen was almost empty.

Bad luck, he thought vaguely. His thoughts were getting hazy already, courtesy of the pain-killers.

He picked up the syringe dart, which he'd found after the sun had come up, and the black leopard had roused itself and wobbled away, and he'd returned to the clearing for his climbing gear. The dart had a pinhole in the injection chamber; about a third of the Kezol, a clear liquid, remained in the syringe. It could have been worse. If all of the Kezol had been in the syringe, the leopard wouldn't have been groggy when it attacked.

He set the pill bottles of Vicodin and penicillin beside his cot and lay down, propelled by the Vicodin into an uneasy sleep. When he woke several hours later tiny flies buzzed against his shirt, which was sticky with blood, and his forehead felt hot. He lay passively, watching the horizon seethe with orange flame as the sun went down. There was nothing to be done now but to hang on, get through this.

The next day the fever was worse. The thermometer in the first-aid kit had been broken in some obscure backpack mishap, so he didn't know how much of a temperature he was running, but it was enough that the world was tinged red at its edges, enough to feel slightly hallucinogenic. He had difficulty remembering why it was so important to take those other pills. All he wanted—staring at his watch, waiting, as the pain took hold increasingly, for the end of the fourth hour—was to take more Vicodin. To lie there feeling the pain ebb, feeling sleep become possible.

It rained a little about noon. He realized the canteen was empty, that he wouldn't be able to choke down his next set of pills. He sat up, grimacing as his shirt pulled at the wounds, and started clumsily down the trail. When he bumped his shoulder against the granite outcropping he passed out, and woke sitting with a bit of rooted vegetation clenched in one hand and the forest beneath him moving in slow green circles. He crawled down the narrowest part of the trail, stood, and walked down to the forest floor and the little spring there, where he put his face down into the cool water.

The fever peaked that night. In the morning he woke from a deep sleep with a clearer head, wounds that were warm to the touch instead of hot, and an awareness that he'd already developed a thoroughgoing attachment to Vicodin. At noon he took one pill instead of two, and one pill again at four o'clock. The pain sharpened, but as the light failed his mind sharpened as well, and he remembered what he'd accomplished two nights ago. He turned on the computer and saw the first dark scribbling of *L6*'s movements through its home range, surrounded by the more complete biographies of its neighbors.

Six leopards. He'd made a bad mistake, but he'd survived it, and now there were no more gaps in the study. He could sit here for a month if he needed to, convalescing, while the study carried forward on its own.

Then he remembered something, and looked at his watch for the date. Claire expected him tomorrow. He'd asked her to have Nobila bring the Peugeot so he could drive to Sandoukou and receive a phone call from Pont Noir. Assuming the letter had reached Alain, and he was willing to make the call. She'd be worried if he didn't show up.

He turned off the computer, stood stiffly, and carried his camp chair to the edge of the platform, easing down into it with some relief. The last of the sunset floated on the horizon like a band of red cellophane. He felt a strange elation, and considered something that had happened well before he came to this forest, a bit of history that explained why the black leopard had been so wary, so difficult to dart. He reached into his chest pocket and took out a stiff black whisker nearly the length of his hand. He'd pulled the whisker from the flesh of his shoulder while sitting at dawn with the sedated leopard. On one of *L6*'s powerful forelegs, just above the paw, he'd seen a strange thickness, a nobbled ring of scar tissue which told him this leopard had been caught in a snare once, probably near the periphery of the park as a nomadic adolescent. Somehow he'd broken free, survived the snare, and made his way here, to the center of the park, where he had fought or perhaps lucked his way into a good territory, and lived undisturbed until Trowbridge turned up.

In a very unscientific way he loved this animal that had almost killed him. A literal blood brother, he told himself. No, that wasn't right. None of his blood was in the leopard's veins. But something of the leopard was likely in him, given the damage he'd sustained.

He lifted his right arm carefully. Felt a stretch of healing skin, a throbbing in his collarbone. Of the two of them, the leopard was relatively untouched, and he was more than willing for it to be so. *Good hunting*, he said quietly to the forest beneath him. *Good hunting, and health*. Then he coiled the whisker, tied it with a bit of string, and put it into the *juju* bag given to him by the fetish seller.

38

A thin electronic piercing split his dream, filling him, for a startled moment, with a sense of urgency he couldn't attach to anything meaningful. Then he rolled quickly off his cot, crouched before the computer, and tapped in a command. A set of coordinates appeared, unfamiliar numbers which described a location a good distance from the inselberg, roughly in the direction of the station.

He cancelled out of the tracking program, returned to the menu, and clicked the cursor on a file called *Maps*. A moment later a color map of Terre Diamantée sketched itself before him, glowing like a vision of another world. Blue ocean along the bottom of the screen; a dotted line down the screen's left side, demarcating the western border; on the right, another dotted line, the Denkyara border, entwined with a blue-green thread of river.

In the center, the park, a distinct green hourglass surrounded by slanting dark lines which indicated the buffer zone.

He punched in the coordinates and watched a tiny cross begin pulsing on the screen. About halfway to the station, something more than a two-hour walk in the darkness. He looked at his watch. It was barely one-thirty, which meant he would get there well before sunrise. He grabbed the scope and the GPS, pulled on clothes, and started down.

⊞   ⊟   ⊞

He covered the last half kilometer by night scope instead of flashlight, feeling exhausted and weak, holding his left arm above his head to lessen the throbbing. When he reached the place and looked up, studying the canopy, he saw nothing but the endless weight of branches and leaves. There was the usual panoply of trillings and hootings and buzzings, but no sign, or sound, of chimps.

He sat down, leaned back against a tree, and waited.

When it grew light he saw chimp nests, dark blots against the green canopy and the pale gray sky, but no predator. Either the collars had sent up a false alarm, or something had been there and slipped away before he arrived. He greeted the day with a feeling that he had almost, but not quite, learned something; it made him feel strange, as if he were walking in Jean Luc's footsteps, and they were unlucky.

⊞   ⊟   ⊞

Two hours later he reached the station, stepped up beneath the *pail-lote*, opened the kitchen cupboard, and found a note and set of keys beneath an agreed-upon frying pan. The note told him where the Peugeot was hidden, and how to find Claire's most recent campsite when he got back that evening. He put the keys in his pocket, went into her narrow room, closed the door, and collapsed onto the cot, sleeping soundly beneath the vigilant stare of the masks for five hours. Feeling stronger when he woke, he splashed water on his face, changed the bandages on his arm and shoulder, found the Peugeot, and left the park.

When he reached Sandoukou he drove past the Hôtel de la Prospérité et Tranquillité and on to the shabby PTT building. The single bored employee had some difficulty understanding he wanted to receive a call, not make one; eventually, however, he caught on, and Trowbridge was motioned toward one of the wooden booths.

He stepped inside, pulling the door shut behind himself.

At five-thirty precisely the phone rang.

"David?" Alain said when he picked up the receiver. "Is this you?"

"It's me," Trowbridge said, feeling a rush of relief and appreciation. He'd begun to feel very much alone with all of this. Now maybe he was going to get some help.

"Listen," he said, "I'm sorry for this complicated way of getting in touch, but—"

"It's all right, it's better this way. I'm calling from a bar, so there's no chance anyone's listening. What are you doing back in the country?"

His letter to Alain had been deliberately vague, to protect both of them in the event it was intercepted. Now he filled in the details. His blocked visa and return through Denkyara, Foote's duty-free permit, and the *Tsar Simeon*, en route with a load of logging equipment. The early arrival at the station of the *Chef des Gendarmes*, which suggested prior knowledge of the murders, and the *Chef des Gendarmes'* signature on Foote's permit, which suggested they might be working together. Finally, the ambiguous role of a Denkyaran named Moneyboy.

"My guess," he concluded, "is that the *Chef des Gendarmes* is the one who's blocking your buffer zone plan. Presumably he's working on some legal mechanism to let him eliminate the zone altogether. Cut it down wholesale."

Alain made an inarticulate, anguished noise. "Why doesn't anything work the way it should? This country *needs* the park—it's all we've got left—and the park needs a properly managed buffer zone. We should be sending school kids out there every day to see how beautiful it is. They'll be the ones to protect the park when the Old Man is gone. If only the BBC had been able to make that film before Jean Luc died—if only those permits hadn't been blocked—we could have shown that film in the schools. *Merde*, David, I don't know, sometimes it all seems so hopeless . . ."

Alain's voice trailed off.

Something struck Trowbridge, and he said, "Were you involved with the BBC thing?"

"Only to the extent of helping get their study permits—or trying, anyway. The permits were held up, like everything gets held up. Jean Luc called me in a rage, saying if I couldn't handle it he'd take care of it himself. He had a connection in Brussels, someone who'd be willing to make a phone call to the Presidency. It probably would have worked, although I guess it doesn't make any difference now."

Alain was silent, then, unexpectedly, blurted out, "David, do you think there's any chance of a job with the Society?"

It took him a moment to realize what Alain meant.

"I don't know," he said cautiously. "There's a lot of competition for a very small number of jobs. Anyway, I didn't think you wanted to live anywhere but in your own country."

In the silence, it sank in slowly that Alain had called not because he was willing to help Trowbridge, but because he hoped Trowbridge would help him. Alain was well-intentioned, intelligent, and concerned about his country—but he was also scared.

"I never *did* want to live anywhere else," Alain said finally. He paused, then said, "David, if I go away—I mean, if you try to contact me, and I'm not here, I'll be in Ghana with my wife's family."

"What do you mean, go away?"

"I mean if I leave the country you should probably do the same. There are some very strange things going on here. I'm no hero. I love my country but I'm not . . ." He stopped. "If I go on a regular vacation, I'll leave a message for you. But if there's no message, if I just leave, then you better leave as well."

"That's all you can tell me?"

"I shouldn't have told you that much."

⁙ ⁙ ⁙

He sat in the booth a moment, then returned to the desk and asked the PTT employee to place a call to London. He got lucky, and the call went through, and the person he wanted to talk to was there.

"David Trowbridge!" exclaimed the voice on the other end of the line.

Trowbridge, accustomed to Riddick's conversational style, held the receiver away from his ear.

"What the hell mountaintop are you calling from? This connection is terrible."

"I'm calling from Terre Diamantée."

"Terre Diamantée? You mean *West Africa* Terre Diamantée? I was supposed to make a film out there! A chimp researcher, Jean Luc Juvigny. Ended up getting himself killed just before we came out.

We had our rubber boots and plane tickets and a hundred cans of film, and it all got called off at the last minute. Were you working with him?"

"Sort of. Do you remember when you last talked to him? The exact date, I mean."

"Is it important?"

"It is."

"I only spoke with him once, right after the New Year. Hang on."

There was a clunk as the receiver went down onto some hard surface. A few seconds later Riddick came back on.

"I'm looking at my diary. We spoke the day after New Year, January second. A couple of days later I heard he'd been killed. I moped around here until they couldn't stand me any longer and sent me off to film Japanese cranes. What are you doing out there, anyway? Do you know anything about this?"

"A little. But before we lose this connection, what did the two of you talk about?"

A high-pitched, whinnying laugh, famous throughout the world of nature film makers and biologists, caused Trowbridge to retreat, once again, from the receiver. When he realized Riddick was talking again he brought it nearer.

"—mostly about the permits. There was some holdup, and he was in a perfect lather. Sounded a formidable chap, even on the phone. He carried on about the incompetence of the authorities, but said he would take care of it, that we should go ahead with our preparations. I encouraged him to do whatever it took. Told him I was going to make his park as famous as Gombe, and make him into a bloody Jane Goodall—I assumed he'd be pleased to hear that, most biologists are, although I'm not sure he was. Listen, we've still got funding approval—all we need is a biologist to stand in front of the camera. What about you?"

"I'm not a primatologist. And I'm not here."

"You're not there," Riddick repeated. "Mysteriouser and mysteriouser. Well, if you change your mind, I'm still the best wildlife photographer the BBC can scrape together in any given situation, and I'm available, so—"

The scratchy line went dead. Trowbridge held the receiver a moment, considering whether to call back. Then he put the receiver down and pushed his way out of the wooden enclosure. He went to the desk and paid a few hundred *befa* to the bored employee, then walked out beneath a sky filled with orange and pink and pale blue, and drove through Sandoukou, back past the Hôtel de la Prospérité et Tranquillité to the other side of town, where the *préfet*'s office was located.

☷ ䷁ ☷

Douli ba was alone in his office, as Trowbridge had hoped he would be. He was wearing a uniform instead of a track suit, and drumming his fingers on the desk beside a large and disheveled pile of paperwork. The drumming stopped when Trowbridge walked in, and there was an awkward silence in which Trowbridge was suddenly aware how different this was than talking to Alain. There was no bond of past friendship here; he might well find himself on a plane again with an incomplete study in his wake. But it was done, and couldn't be undone now if he turned around and walked out.

"If you're interested," he said, "I don't think the guys who shot up my hotel room just wanted my truck keys and a little more money."

Douli ba pushed his horn-rimmed glasses back up on his nose, and raised his hands in mock offense. "We're supposed to chat a minute before we start talking business. African traditions are very strict on this. We should discuss family, and crops, and the weather."

Douli ba was smiling, but seemed less than entirely comfortable.

Trowbridge sat down in a hard wooden chair. "I don't have a family, and the crops are no longer burning, and the weather, consequently, is less smoky than it was."

"What's that around your neck?"

"Someone gave me a *juju* bag."

"And you're wearing it. That's interesting." Douli ba nodded at the bandage on Trowbridge's left forearm. "Although I'd say you received it a little late."

"Or just in time. Enough small talk?"

"Okay. Although if we're done with small talk I have to ask if you're here legally. I understood you'd been told not to come back."

Trowbridge pushed his passport across the desk.

"I entered on the last day of my visa. They gave me a six-month stay. I'm legal."

This was true, as far as it went. There was no reason to burden Douli ba with the knowledge that the Diamantien consul in Washington had told him not to return.

Douli ba leafed through the passport, found the visa, and studied it. Then he pushed the passport back across the desk.

"If they didn't want your truck keys, what did they want?"

"They thought someone else was in the room. An American timber operator named Randy Foote. They were trying to encourage him to do something he was reluctant to do."

"Go on."

"Foote has chartered a freighter to bring a huge amount of logging equipment into Granville. He's transferred a lot of money to Cyprus to pay for this equipment, a surprising amount of money for a wildcat timber operator. At the same time, a management plan for the park has been blocked in the capital."

"Why are you coming to me with this?"

"Because it's happening in your jurisdiction, and it all seems to relate to the park. It also seems to relate to an Ebrio man from Denkyara with scarification on only one side of his face. Apparently he's called Moneyboy."

Douli ba's expression altered slightly.

Trowbridge said, "You may remember that's how I described the person who attacked me in the hotel room."

"I remember that. I also remember you saw this person by moonlight, for a split second, through a narrow gap in the curtain. Whites are notorious for being unable to tell Africans apart."

"But—"

Douli ba raised a forefinger. "Let me examine what you've told me, step by step, as a policeman might. With regard to the management plan, you know as well as I do that such things move slowly and inefficiently—there are a dozen reasons it might have been blocked. With regard to Foote, I'm not sure how you found out about his activities—and it's fairly impressive you did—but I haven't yet heard evidence of a crime. People *expect* timber operators to transfer money overseas, and to import equipment. It's what they do."

"What about the quantity of equipment?"

"That's something I can't explain. But once again, it's not illegal. Not yet, anyway."

Douli ba separated his hands in a brief gesture that suggested something had evaporated between them. Trowbridge wasn't sure what was going on behind those guarded, intelligent eyes. But there wasn't the same friendliness that had been there the last time they talked. Something had changed; something, for Douli ba, had gotten more complicated.

"So none of this means anything?"

"Oh, it means *something*. It's just that the meaning wouldn't be immediately apparent to a prosecutor, or to a judge. Not unless you can pull it together in a way that makes sense."

"I think I can, actually. I think it may all be related to the murders at the station. But I'm a little reluctant to spell it out for you. I don't want to put you in a position of divided loyalties."

"Meaning?"

"Meaning I think your boss, the *Chef des Gendarmes*, is involved. But I can get up and walk out right now if you don't want to hear that."

Douli ba sat perfectly still for a moment. Then he said, "Technically, this meeting is after hours, and informal. I could listen to what you tell me, and then erase it from my mind."

"My guess is that Randy Foote and the *Chef des Gendarmes* have a plan to open the buffer zone to logging. Large-scale, unrestricted logging. I don't know how they'll justify it, exactly—maybe they've got some expert who'll claim the buffer zone isn't essential to the park, or maybe they'll claim they're acting on behalf of local people who need land. Opening the buffer zone to logging would make both of them rich—and it would explain the quantity of equipment, and why the management plan has been blocked."

"And the death of your colleagues?"

"First, I don't believe the official explanation that the murders were a vengeance killing related to the death of a poacher. I went to that poacher's village, and talked to people there. Second, the BBC was about to come make a film that would have transformed Jean Luc from an obscure scientist into someone with an international reputation—someone who could have contacted the international press and made a nasty fuss if big chunks of forest started coming down. The simplest way to prevent that was to block the permits for the camera crew, which is what happened. But then Jean Luc got personally involved, and threatened to contact a friend in Belgium who had influence with the President. At that point someone realized their scheme was in trouble—that it would be better, from their perspective, to have a dead Dian Fossey than a live Jane Goodall."

"You haven't told me why you think the head of our gendarme service is involved."

Trowbridge hesitated. If he mentioned the signature on Foote's import license, it might implicate Najla somehow.

"Haven't you wondered how he got to the station so fast after the murders?"

Douli ba said simply, "Yes, I have."

"That suggests he knew what was going to happen."

"The *Chef des Gendarmes* has a radio in his Mercedes. He may just have been in the area and picked up the radio transmission. That's how they got me, in fact."

"You told me he hardly ever left the capital."

Douli ba was staring out the window into darkness. When he looked back at Trowbridge, his face, normally animated and skeptical, was tired.

"I did say that, didn't I? Still, my inclination would be to give him the benefit of the doubt. If it weren't for something else that happened. Something I'm not sure I should tell you about."

"Why not?"

"If I tell you, you're going to expect me to take some kind of concrete action, and I'm not sure I'm in a position to do that."

"Tell me."

Douli ba sighed. "The *Chef des Gendarmes* called me a couple of weeks ago. He told me someone named Moneyboy was in my area, and that he was very well connected, and that he was not, under any circumstances, to be touched."

39

With data coming in on all six leopards now, virtually independent of his own efforts, the core of his study was in place, and he began going farther afield. Predictably, it was more difficult to find leopards where there were no elephant lanes. In three weeks of steady searching he found nothing but an occasional claw mark and pile of scat. It wasn't until the last afternoon of a several-day swing through the northern part of the park that he found a seventh leopard. It was caught in a wire snare, dead when he found it, but hadn't died long before; the wire had cut to the bone, and the paw and foreleg beneath the wire were swollen like a balloon. Driver ants had gotten there first, starting their efficient work by going in at the eyes and nostrils, which explained why the ground around the snare was torn up. Most leopards caught in snares would hunker down and wait.

When he reached the inselberg at dusk that evening he opened the computer soberly and studied the movements of his leopards during his absence—leopards that had the good fortune to live a long way from the boundaries of the park, and were able to go about their lives without human interference. If he'd needed further evidence of how important the buffer zone was, he had it now. He made two backup copies of the data, put the disks in a plastic case with half a dozen others, and sat back from the screen. With a small jolt of comprehension, he realized he'd accomplished most of what he'd come here for. He knew how many hours a day his leopards spent hunting and resting, the size of their home ranges, the degree of overlap, and how they practiced avoidance. And he'd successfully habituated an adult leopard and two cubs to the point where he could stand within ten meters of the den, something that had never been done in the forest.

The fact that he had enough data to write several solid papers didn't mean there was no reason to stay on longer; it would be useful, for example, to know what kind of behavioral changes took place during the rainy season. But in the main, he'd achieved his goals. His only remaining grant obligation was to collect six very expensive collars before their batteries ran down, something he could do a year from now. The predator-prey study was still a question mark, but it hadn't been part of his original intention, and wasn't something he could use to justify staying on longer.

A damp breeze came up from the forest below, bringing a rank smell of vegetation rotting and regenerating. The rainy season was getting close; it had rained hard for an hour last night, and he'd noticed, when he left the inselberg four mornings ago, that his long-time companion, the fox kestrel—a migratory species which flew north to the savannah when the rains began—had disappeared.

He looked again at the case filled with disks. A successful study brought him closer to a decision on the directorship, a decision he thought he'd made on three separate occasions during the last few months, only to wake up a few days later and find it wasn't so, that the question was alive in him, still troublesome. A successful study also meant he was free, if he so desired, to try again to find out what was going on with Foote and the freighter and the *Chef des Gendarmes*. To find out if there was, in fact, some kind of threat to the park and buffer zone. And a successful study meant he was free to make one more attempt to find out why Jean Luc and the others had died, and who was responsible.

Free to risk being thrown out again, if that's what was entailed.

Like it or not, he was the only person in a position to try. Alain and Alberto had too much at stake in this country to risk making waves; Claire had not merely her dissertation to consider, but her entire career, and a child.

He looked out into the darkness above the forest. A successful study, and with it, a whole new set of problems. *Be careful what you ask for*, he thought.

⸪ ⸭ ⸪

Four nights later, when the alarm went off shortly after midnight, he knew precisely what it meant, and was crouched in front of the computer almost before he was awake. He plugged the coordinates into the *Maps* program, saw the little cross pulsing on the screen, and felt a quiet surge of excitement. Closer this time. He dressed and grabbed his gear and plunged down the trail, moving from a relative darkness in which there were fuzzy stars and a rising half-moon into a more profound darkness beneath the canopy.

An hour later he heard chimps screaming in the distance. He moved forward cautiously, wearing the night scope, until he found himself beneath an enormous ironwood tree, the upper reaches of which writhed in a chaos of thrashing branches and falling leaves. Thirty meters up, a sinuous, confident shape was taking its time as it hunted its way through a tree full of terrified, screeching chimps. The leopard—for it was a leopard, unmistakably—moved in an almost leisurely fashion, with no need for surprise. The dozen or so male chimps in the tree—males which in daylight, and on the ground, would have banded together to mob this intruder—were isolated in their individual nests, and as blind as Trowbridge would have been without the scope.

Visually, it was an uneven contest; the chimps saw only darkness and shadows, while the leopard could see exactly what it was doing.

What it was doing at the moment was moving out along an increasingly slender branch toward its intended prey. The chimp scrambled backward, screeching in terror as the limb grew less substantial and began to bend appallingly, so that both leopard and chimp swung in broad arcs through the darkness. Backing off, the leopard returned to the trunk, where it looked around, washed its chest for a minute, then scanned the trunk above it and went up. Trowbridge could see the muscles in its chest bunch powerfully as it scaled the straight side of the tree, claws hooking into wood. When it reached what looked like an insurmountable obstacle—a fluted extrusion on the trunk—it angled its upper body, put its front paws on either side of the extrusion, then swung its hindquarters nimbly across in a maneuver a rock climber would have been proud of.

A young animal, he realized. Relatively slender, better adapted to climbing than a heavier animal like *L6*. Could chimp predation be an adolescent phenomenon?

He put theory away and watched the reality unfolding above him. As the leopard moved in a low crouch toward a dark bundle backing toward the end of the branch, Trowbridge realized the retreating chimp wasn't just one animal, but two, a mother with an infant. When she reached the end of the branch, with barely two meters separating her and the oncoming leopard, she turned and flung herself, with a hopeless wail, into open space. The leopard rose, ears forward, watching and listening; the other chimps erupted in a chorus of screeches. There was a heavy crashing in the lower branches of a neighboring tree, then silence, and the sound of furtive movement. The mother chimp might have broken a bone or two—most adult chimps had broken bones from falls—but she, and presumably her infant, had survived.

The leopard stared down at the prey it had missed, then made a tight circle and returned to the trunk, moving as easily as a house cat along a fence. Once again it looked upward, choosing a route; once again, it went up, emerging onto another substantial branch, where a young chimp looked to have made a bad mistake in its choice of a nest. The branch was solid all the way to its end, where it had probably been broken off in a storm.

The leopard, in a sudden controlled rush, moved forward; the chimp, crouching before its nest, emitted a terrible scream, hair on end, and rushed its attacker. The leopard flattened, ears back and tail twitching, but gave no ground, and at the last second the chimp spun and skittered away, disappearing into its nest, taking what had to be illusory refuge.

Trowbridge stepped to the left for a better view, then froze. The leopard was looking down at him.

Don't stop, he pleaded. With all due apologies to your intended prey, this will be a hell of a lot more meaningful if I see a kill. He stood motionless, feeling individual drops of sweat trickle down his neck, until the leopard raised its gaze, stared a long moment at the nest before it, and moved forward in precise, flowing movements. Its shape blended with that of the nest. There was nothing to be seen for a moment. Then the nest erupted in a thrashing and scattering of leaves, and the two animals reared up as one. The chimp's head was bent forward onto its chest; one of the leopard's powerful forepaws was locked on the back of its neck, the other in its shoulder. For several precarious seconds, as the leopard stood on its hind legs, barely managing its prey, he feared both animals would fall. Then the leopard lunged forward, achieving a purchase with its jaws, and there was a final struggle, and a cessation of movement.

A few minutes later the leopard began to feed, oblivious to the continuing screams around it.

Shortly before sunrise, as the sky grew pale above the canopy, the leopard worked its way head-first down the ironwood tree. From where Trowbridge stood a few meters away he could see its full belly, hear the controlled scrabbling of claws as it accelerated downward. It jumped the last couple of meters, landing with a *whoof* of expelled breath, then froze, staring in Trowbridge's direction, probably having caught a whiff of his smell. There was chimp blood on the young leopard's jaws, and a red slash across his chest, the one evident price of the night's hunting. As it leaped away Trowbridge felt a sense of exultation and triumph that verged upon the bloodthirsty. Then exultation ebbed slowly, leaving him with a quiet happiness, an awareness of how unlikely it was to have witnessed this. Some kind of gift from the forest.

☷ ☵ ☷

"You're the first person ever to see this," Claire said wonderingly.

"How long has it been since we darted the chimps?"

"Four weeks."

She was smiling in disbelief, shaking her head at what they'd done. He pulled the cork from a bottle of wine, filled the cups she held out, and said, *"Nature* will take this paper for sure. And every biologist reading it will look at your name and file it away as someone who's been associated with a breakthrough. Someone who's not only a good biologist, but could help attract grant money."

"Even if she had some unusual requirements? Child care for a three-year-old, for example?"

"Even if. You're going to have to earn it, though—you're the logical one to write up Jean Luc's notes. I'll write up the methods and a section on the collaring technique, and we can work together on the discussion."

"I want Jean Luc to be first author."

"I do too."

They touched cups, and drank. The euphoria of what he'd seen two nights ago was still in him, mingled with a sense of loss that had to do with the deaths of people they both knew, and an awareness that their time together here was drawing to a close. In his pack, sealed in a Ziploc bag, was a set of disks that meant he was on the verge of doing something that might be foolhardy. Something he hadn't yet told Claire about. All of this gave a heightened quality to the moment. He felt a growing awareness that he was—slowly, quietly, and unexpectedly—falling in love with this woman. An awareness that she was right for him in a way no one else ever had been. He wanted to say that, but was painfully conscious that doing so would raise all kinds of practical considerations, so he set his glass down, leaned over, put his arms around her, and kissed her on the mouth. Her arms went around him instantly, one hand pressing against his back, pressing him against her, the other hand, practically, holding the glass of wine.

After a moment she pulled away and looked at him with a mixture of regret and amusement.

"There must be some mistake. You can't possibly want to make love to someone with a baby in Switzerland and a cesarean scar on her belly."

"That description exactly."

She laughed softly. Then her face grew serious, and she said, "David, I'm sorry, but I already have one complication in my personal life. I don't think I could handle another."

"It isn't just—"

"No, and that's the problem. We should have done it when it would have simply been fun, and nothing more. Now it would mean something, and I don't want that. I can't afford to want that."

⠿ ⠂ ⠿

In the morning he woke alone, feeling desolate in the empty camp. When he walked to the station for a shower he found something unexpected on the kitchen table. An orchid, a little pile of sawdust, and a note that said, "Phone call from a friend of yours in the capital. The freighter docks in six days."

He put the unsigned note into his shirt pocket and walked back to Claire's camp, where he spent the day sketching out his contribution to the predation paper.

⠿ ⠂ ⠿

"If I'm going to talk to someone," he said, "it has to be someone powerful enough to act on what I tell them."

Claire said, "You'll never get into the Presidency."

"I'm talking about the Justice Minister."

She looked incredulous. "David, for all you know, he may be involved in this."

"That's possible. If so, I'll be deported again, and you and Seydou will have to hike to the inselberg and retrieve my equipment. I brought out the GPS, and I'll leave you the coordinates. On the other hand, if the Justice Minister *isn't* involved, he might be able to stop whatever's going on. Before it creates a scandal that might endanger his succession to the Presidency. He still strikes me as one of the more reasonable people I've met in this country."

"And when he points out you aren't supposed to be here?"

"I came back on a valid visa, at a valid crossing point. If he says anything about my safety, I can tell him the fact that I'm sitting before him proves it wasn't dangerous."

"What about this woman the *fétichiste*'s nephew told you about?"

"I'll go see her first. It probably won't amount to much, but I'll give it a try."

"David, I hate everything about this. The Justice Minister may have been the one who had you thrown out in the first place."

"If so, why would he have gone through that lengthy charade in his office, deciding whether to let me come back to the forest? No, my guess is that the rot doesn't go any higher than the *Chef des Gendarmes*."

She looked doubtful.

"I grant you," he said, "that as a working assumption, it's risky."

"But you're still going to do it?"

"Unless you have a better idea."

"I'll go with you, then. Two scientists standing in his office will be more convincing than one."

"No. If I'm right, I don't need your help—and if I'm wrong, there's no sense both of us getting deported. You'll be more useful here."

"It seems dangerous."

"I'll be seeing him in his office, in broad daylight, not in an alley somewhere. He's the Justice Minister, after all."

He reached down into his bag and pulled out a Ziploc.

"Backup disks. Would you mind giving them to Nobila to mail? And if you still want to do something rash in my company, drive me out to the *piste* where I can get a bush taxi. That's enough."

40

They drove out early and sat waiting in the Peugeot at the side of the *piste*. The sky was filled with big, complicated cloud structures, shot through with dissipating orange remnants of the dawn; the white trunks of great trees gleamed like naked bodies in the silvery light.

When the bush taxi appeared he climbed out of the car. Claire got out as well, walked around the Peugeot, and hugged him unexpectedly, holding him fiercely a moment before pushing him away.

By the time the bush taxi lurched onto the paved highway at San-doukou raindrops were scattering down. The sky darkened, and the asphalt was a wet dark line beneath them. Their tires hissed as they passed a bus in which a video player was mounted above the driver's head; a kung fu movie made quick dark flickers on the blue screen. Atop another bus, amid the bundles and baskets, were seven or eight goats, all but one of whom had accepted their situation without com-plaint; the exception, a white ram with horns like spiral scimitars, stood stubbornly at the front edge of the roof, legs splayed to keep his balance, head lowered only slightly in deference to the rope around his neck, ragged white beard streaming as the bus hurtled beneath a charcoal purple sky through the wet green landscape.

⚏ ䷜ ⚏

He walked from the bus station to the post office and mailed a manila envelope of disks and notebooks to Gordon. A Ziploc with yet another set of disks was safely tucked away in the side pocket of his bag. He left the bag in a hotel room and took a cab to the Thai Girl, which turned out to be located in a not-very-good section of town. The first thing he noticed when he walked into the gloomy interior was the splay-legged outline of a woman above the bar, a blue star blinking between her red thighs. The second was that there didn't appear to be anyone from Thailand in sight; there were a handful of Asian women, but the two he heard talking seemed to be speaking Tagalog. It was late afternoon, and quiet; there were no other customers.

The only African woman in the bar was sitting alone. She was thin, and rested her head on her hand.

He sat down across from her. The bartender snapped a finger at him.

"I'll have a beer," Trowbridge told him. He glanced around the bar, then said to the woman, "They don't look like Thai girls to me."

"They're Filipino slaves," she said. "They think they're coming here to work as maids. I'm sick of their complaining."

The bartender set down a bottle of beer and walked away.

"What's your name?"

She gave him a worn, professional smile.

"What do you want my name to be?"

"Komo would be all right."

Her eyes widened.

"All right," she said slowly. "Then I'm Komo."

He noticed a doorway at the back which opened onto a dingy corridor. Komo saw his gaze, misinterpreted it, and stood wordlessly. He hesitated, then followed her down the corridor to a small room with an unmade bed. The only light came from a shutter propped partly open; he could hear someone washing dishes outside in a courtyard, and laughing.

"You're in a hurry," she commented in a listless voice, raising her arms to unzip her dress. By a shaft of light from the shutter, he saw boils in her armpit and felt his stomach tighten. No wonder she kept it gloomy in here.

"Listen," he said, still standing in the doorway, "I'd like to go someplace else."

She looked at him doubtfully.

"You want to do it someplace else?"

"I'd like to have you for the evening."

She stared at him a moment, saying nothing. Then she zipped her dress back up and they went back into the bar. He paid the bartender something and they went outside. In the back seat of the taxi she said, "It's been a while since someone paid for the whole evening. Do you have a hotel?"

"I'd like to have dinner first."

"You don't want to sleep with me?"

"We can talk about that later. Where would you like to go?"

She looked thoughtful. "I'd like to go home for a few minutes. Change my clothes and wash myself. After a while in the Thai Girl you don't care what you look like. Then maybe we can go to a place I know."

"Okay."

"That's all right?"

"Sure."

The taxi driver dropped them in front of a three-story apartment building with laundry hanging from the balconies and children running up and down the stained concrete stairwell. Several women leaned on the railing of the third floor balcony, looking down at him. One, very young and pretty, with close-cropped hair and slender arms

and a big jeering smile, laughed and beckoned him up, making a bob-
bing motion with her fist. Another pointed to the door Komo had
gone in and drew her finger across her throat. He pretended he didn't
understand what they meant.

☷ ☵ ☷

They went to a place with square-cut wooden tables set outside in the
dirt street, and wooden chairs painted bright colors. There were no
empty places, but the proprietress, a massive woman with an expressionless face, stood on a chair and reached up to a high stack of tables
and lifted one down. While she went to get chairs, they looked at the
fish in plastic tubs outside the kitchen. Komo chose two, and watched
to make sure those two went onto the grill.

A waitress brought them hot black tea, sugared, in little glasses
that burned their hands. People strolled and talked and laughed in the
street; reggae music started up next door.

"Why don't you want to sleep with me?"

"I didn't say that."

"Don't you think I'm attractive?"

"Yes, I do."

"You can wear a *préservatif* if you like."

"Do most of your clients wear *préservatifs*?"

"Not most. Some. When they're drunk, they usually don't bother.
How come you ask so many questions?"

"I'm doing a study. For the United Nations."

"A study of *poules?*" She looked amused.

"Yes."

"Then you have to sleep with me or your study won't be complete."

She smiled, wrinkling her nose. He realized she was pretty when
her face had a little animation.

"If you're really doing a study, why aren't you wearing a suit? And
why aren't you taking notes?"

"It's too hot to wear a suit. And I have a good memory."

"Well, I'm working as an independent now, so I can talk to you,
as long as you're paying. Before I would have had to ask the guild if it
would be all right."

"The guild?"

"We have a union, like other people. Not a government union, something we made up between ourselves. There are rules on how much to charge—if you charge less you get in trouble. I used to pay money to the guild every month in case I got sick, or I died and needed funeral money. Now too many people are sick and the guild doesn't have any more money. Do you want to know the differences in my clients? I have some observations."

He nodded.

"You're American, right?"

"Yes."

"You're my first American. Mostly my clients are Europeans—Belgians and French—and Lebanese, and Africans. How am I doing?"

"You're doing great."

"The Europeans," she said, putting a delicate finger to her lips, "prefer *la bouche*. The Lebanese prefer *les relations anales,* and the Africans are more straightforward—they put it where it's supposed to go. But they don't pay very well. Do you really work for the United Nations?"

"Yes."

The fish arrived; it was delicious, succulent and white, served with *piment* sauce and salad and slightly bitter *attieke*. He ordered them beers. Halfway though the meal he realized he was eating more than she was. He put down his fork and looked at her.

"Are you all right?"

"Sure," she said. She was leaning back in her chair, smiling a little. "This is fun. Like the old days."

"What were the old days like?"

"Wah," she exclaimed quietly. "The old days were a long party. Nice restaurants, and nice hotels. I worked at a better place, then, and a special man came for me once a week. I could tell you who he was, but it might get me into trouble. Let's just say he was someone important in the government."

He said, "It doesn't matter."

"Sometimes he took me on trips. We went to Switzerland once, and we went to Denkyara a lot of times."

"That's a hard place to get to."

"Not if you have a boat. This man had a speedboat in Granville, and a house on the beach in Denkyara."

Why, he wondered, would the *Chef de Gendarmes* have a place in Denkyara?

"Lots of people came to see us at the beach house. Even an American, like you. He used to get drunk and fall down in the surf."

"Denkyarans?"

"Lots of Denkyarans. My boyfriend's assistant was from Denkyara. I didn't like him at all."

"Why?"

"Because of the way he looked at me, sometimes, behind my boyfriend's back. My boyfriend would have killed him if he'd seen it. And because of his face. He had scarification on only one side. You know how they do it: When you're a boy, the elders of the village make cuts in your face and rub ashes in to make the scars. He claims he was given special scarification because he was the best hunter in his village—but I heard he was a coward, that he got scared and ran away after one side of his face had been done."

The waitress cleared their things away. He ordered *crème caramel* and coffee. Komo lifted her glass and smiled, looking relaxed and happy, and he felt a quick stab of guilt at what he was doing. She said, "Here's to the rainy season. May it make us rich and powerful."

"What does that mean?"

"I don't think it means anything. It was just something we used to say at the beach house."

☷ ☶ ☷

In the taxi he gave her some money and told her she ought to go to a hospital. She shook her head, and said that hospitals were places where people went to die, that it was better to die working than to die in a hospital, even if you could afford it. She waved at him as she walked up the stairs, walking a little carefully after the beers, and disappeared. By the light of an open doorway he could see the young woman who had jeered at him earlier in the evening. She was standing alone, looking down at him from three stories up, just staring now, not laughing. She drew her finger across her throat, once, and once again, and then she withdrew from the light.

41

"Alain's gone," the secretary said in a bored voice.

There was a strange hollowness to the line. That might mean someone was listening in, or it might just mean the phone system in Terre Diamantée was as bad as everyone knew it was.

"Gone where?"

"He took a leave of absence and went to Ghana. His wife is there. I think his whole family is there."

"Did he leave a message for me?"

"That would be difficult to say," the secretary said exasperatedly, "since you haven't given me your name."

When he made no reply, she added, "He didn't leave messages for anyone I don't know personally, if that's of any use."

"That's helpful. Any idea when he's coming back?"

"No. Would you like to leave a message for him?"

"That's all right."

"You're very mysterious," the secretary said, "and very annoying," and she hung up.

⁙ ⁙ ⁙

At the reception desk of the Ministry building he gave his name and showed his passport, lying his way upstairs by citing his previous visit and hinting that the Justice Minister would be unhappy if he were turned away. A glum-looking soldier accompanied him into the elevator and up to the top floor. The Justice Minister's personal secretary, an officious young man with mocha skin and narrow shoulders, remembered Trowbridge from his previous meeting, but pointed out this was not the same as having an appointment. Trowbridge said the subject of his visit had come up unexpectedly. The secretary eyed Trowbridge's rumpled clothing, clearly tempted to rudeness, but worried at the same time he might turn out to be someone important, and said simply, "The Minister is out."

"I'll wait."

The secretary looked irritated.

"He won't be back today."

"I understand," Trowbridge said, and sat down on an absurdly soft couch. If the Minister was in his office, he would spot him when he greeted or dismissed other visitors.

He picked up the local newspaper, *Le Diamant Quotidien*, from a coffee table made of glass and mahogany. At the top of the second page the Justice Minister's smooth, handsome face leaped out at him. In a signed commentary, he praised the evenhandedness of the President, who had preserved ethnic peace on a continent where so many countries had been torn by ethnic conflict. "Terre Diamantée," he concluded, "is a diamond of peace in a rough tapestry of war and privation. Every Diamantien, every waking moment, owes an incalculable debt to our guiding light, the President."

They must get tired of the *diamant* metaphors, he thought, putting down the newspaper. On the wall behind the secretary's desk was the usual pair of portraits. The President looked withered and frail beside his younger, more vigorous colleague.

The secretary was frowning at him. "I promise you he isn't here," he said, gesturing at a package on his desk. "Someone else is coming at ten-thirty. The Minister left this package for me to give them. Would he do that if he were here?"

Trowbridge looked at his watch. It was almost ten-thirty. What the secretary had just said had a certain ring of truth to it, although even if the Justice Minister wasn't in the office now, maybe he would return later. Might as well go find something to eat, maybe a book to read, if he was going to spend the day here.

When he salvaged himself from the soft couch, the secretary, looking vindicated, asked if he wanted to leave a phone number.

"The phone isn't working in my hotel. I'll come back in an hour."

"I can't promise—"

"I understand."

He rode the elevator, unescorted, down to the ground floor. The doors opened and he stepped out into the foyer. As he did so two people came in the front doors of the building. The man in front wore a dark, expensive-looking suit, and had features Trowbridge had come to recognize as Ebrio; he was clean shaven and powerfully built, and had one smooth temple unmarked by scarification, and another distinguished by three neat scars.

Trowbridge, feeling a quiet shock of recognition, kept his expression neutral as they neared one another.

Moneyboy stopped, frowned, and started to speak.

Trowbridge walked past him without meeting his eyes.

Foote, he realized, as he neared the doors. He thought I was Foote. Second time he's made that mistake. He pushed through the heavy glass doors of the Ministry, forcing himself not to look back, blinking in the heat and sunshine as he stepped into a taxi which he was very glad to find waiting by the curb beside an illegally parked white Land Rover.

⊞ ⽥ ⊞

"*A droite,*" Trowbridge said.

The taxi driver turned right. No one had yelled at him from behind. He leaned back in his seat, feeling shock and relief and a fair amount of disbelief at his own stupidity. If he'd stayed five minutes longer in the Justice Minister's outer office he would have been sitting there when Moneyboy and his friend walked in.

The taxi approached the corner and stopped at a red light. He leaned forward and told the taxi driver to turn right, then right again. Shortly before they reached the next cross street he told the driver to stop. He gave him a few *befa,* said, "Wait for me here," and climbed out and walked to the corner and looked down the street.

The Diamantien flag hung limply above the Ministry portico; the white Land Rover was still parked at the curb. He took a deep breath, gauging his reluctance to do this—identifying it as fear—and then walked down the street until he could look in through the high glass doors. The glass was tinted, but not opaque; he could see that neither Moneyboy nor his companion was in the foyer. He walked out to the curb, stepped into the street before the Land Rover, bent down, and looked at the front tires. Then he moved around the car on the street side—so he would be less obvious to the pair of bored soldiers who stood in little booths on either side of the Ministry entrance—and knelt and studied the front tires from behind. Moving to the rear tires, he scanned them from beneath the car, then stepped to the back of the car, and knelt there. When he stood he saw that one of the soldiers was watching him. He smiled, raised his arm, and tapped his watch, motioning to the top floor of the building as if he were waiting for someone.

How much more time did he have before Moneyboy and his friend came back down?

Reaching up beneath the vinyl cover on the rear-mounted spare tire, he unhooked the bungee cord which held the cover in place and lifted it off. The soldier was frowning now, saying something to his colleague on the other side of the doors. Trowbridge looked at the spare tire from the top and both sides. Then he knelt and looked at it from beneath, and saw a plug-shaped scar on the otherwise neat tread. A scar he remembered from what seemed like a long time ago in a different place. He stood and put the cover back on and walked away.

42

He packed quickly at the hotel and had the taxi take him to the bus station, where he spent three hours—feeling increasingly nervous— in a small bar on a side street waiting for the next bus to Sandoukou. At two o'clock he climbed aboard and took a seat. A few miles outside Pont Noir the slums which covered the surrounding hills gave way to palm groves and banana plantations. They passed a small village where some kind of festival appeared to be in the making—people were climbing down from buses, and a palm-frond archway was being raised at the village entrance—and then they passed through a larger town, Jacquesville, which he recalled vaguely had been the original capital under Belgian rule until an epidemic of some kind had wiped out most of the inhabitants. A few miles beyond this crumbling *ville* the bus pulled to a stop at a roadblock. He saw resigned looks on the faces around him, people digging in their pockets. A pair of uniformed men boarded the bus and began working their way down the aisle. He noticed they weren't taking money, only looking at documents. The man in the seat beside him looked puzzled.

"Soldats?" Trowbridge asked him.

"Gendarmes," his neighbor said. *"C'est pas normal."*

The relatively small gendarme force, he remembered, was controlled by the Ministry of Interior, not the Ministry of Defense. And the Minister of Justice was acting Minister of Interior. He glanced behind himself. There was no rear door to the bus. When he looked forward again one of the gendarmes was staring at him.

He glanced away. Maybe this was just a routine check of some kind; maybe they would check his passport, and go on. When the gendarmes reached him they looked at his passport, and motioned at him to get up. They led him off the bus and waved at the driver to go on. One of the gendarmes went to a car parked by the side of the road and sat in the front seat. Trowbridge could hear the crackle of a radio, and hear the man saying something, although he couldn't make out the words. The man got out and came over to where he and the other gendarme were standing in the shade of a tree. Trowbridge made an effort to talk to his companions, but they refused to be drawn into conversation. Half an hour later a black Mercedes pulled up—the biggest he'd seen in Terre Diamantée—and the rear door opened, and someone beckoned, and he climbed in.

The air inside the car was air-conditioned and pleasant, and the door locks clicked as he sank back into a soft and very new seat.

"I understand you wanted to see me."

The Justice Minister was studying him with a calm, interested expression. He looked as impressive and collected as he had at their last meeting, dressed in an immaculate gray suit, with a pink silk tie and leather shoes that gleamed. There was something compellingly reasonable in his voice and his expression. Something in those intelligent eyes with their frosty lashes made you want to tell the truth, in the confidence that whatever you had done, this man could make it right.

He realized he would have to tell a good deal of the truth—most of it—if his story were to be even remotely plausible.

"Yes," he said, "I did want to see you."

"About what?"

"I was worried about the park. There's a logging crew taking trees inside the boundaries, and an American timber operator who may be involved."

"Go on."

He took a deep breath. "I was told by someone at the port that this

American had chartered a small freighter. That he was bringing in a lot of timber machinery and trucks."

"And?"

"That's all. I remembered that when we talked you expressed interest in what I was doing, and in the park. I hoped you might be able to help."

"This all has to do with the park, then."

"Yes."

"Why, then, have you been talking to an old friend of mine?"

Trowbridge hesitated.

"Someone who works at the Thai Girl," the Justice Minister prompted gently.

The silence in the car was suddenly tense. The engine was still running; Trowbridge could feel cold air from the air conditioning pouring over the front seat.

"Look," he said, deliberately meeting the Justice Minister's gaze, "whatever's going on here is clearly bigger and more complicated than I realized. Bigger and more complicated than my concerns about the park. Someone told me this woman might know something useful, and I went and talked to her, that's all. If I made a mistake of some kind, it wasn't intentional."

"What did she tell you?"

"She wasn't very helpful. It's clear she's come down in the world, but she refused to talk about about her former life, and she had no interest in the park."

The Justice Minister considered this gravely for a moment. Then he reached over and took Trowbridge's passport from his chest pocket. Trowbridge disliked this casual assumption of power, but he glanced at the two men in the front seat, one of whom was watching them carefully in the rearview mirror, and saw he was in no position to complain.

"I see you re-entered Terre Diamantée through Denkyara. It's an unusual route."

"I wanted to have a look at the forest on the other side of the border. See what kind of leopard habitat was there."

"I also see that you returned the day your visa expired."

"That's not illegal."

"It is if you were told not to come back."

"The people who put me on the plane didn't tell me why they were doing it. No one said anything about not coming back."

"And our consul in Washington? Or had you forgotten that?"

The Justice Minister slipped the passport into the chest pocket of his suit, then pulled out a small pocket knife, opened it calmly, and leaned over, putting the knife to Trowbridge's throat. Trowbridge's heart leaped—it happened so fast he had no time to react—and he felt a sense of astonishment that he would allow someone to slit his throat without a struggle. There was a sharp tug against the back of his neck, and then his fetish bag was sitting in the Justice Minister's open palm.

"Not an appropriate decoration for a Westerner to be wearing, do you think?"

The Justice Minister looked impatient suddenly. He tapped on the window glass beside him, and the driver did a quick U-turn and began taking them back toward town.

⠿ ⠃ ⠿

Trowbridge assumed they were returning to Pont Noir, but when they reached Jacquesville, the car pulled off the highway and moved through pot-holed streets, stopping before a low, rambling building. Above the door a faded sign announced this as the local *Gendarmerie*. They went through an entry foyer past a frightened-looking desk sergeant into what appeared to be the office of the *Capitaine de la Gendarmerie*, who looked up in annoyance at the interruption, then goggled and leaped to his feet, saluting furiously.

"My office is at your disposal, Excellency. If you prefer, I can leave."

"Stay," the Justice Minister said. "I need your help. Sit," he said, glancing at Trowbridge.

"If I'm under arrest I want to contact my embassy."

"You're not under arrest—not yet, anyway. And if we *do* arrest you, our obligation is to inform your embassy within twenty-four hours. Sometimes that slips to forty-eight hours. Isn't that right, *mon Capitaine?*"

"Absolutely," the gendarme said.

Silence descended over the room. They seemed to be waiting for something. The *Capitaine*, in a fit of bureaucratic courage, shifted the fan on his desk so that its slight breeze, which he had formerly enjoyed, was directed at the Justice Minister. Trowbridge wiped the sweat from his face. There was something wrong about what was happening here; this was not the lead-up, in his limited experience, to being deported. A car pulled up out front, and he heard doors open and someone walking into the station. Two people came into the room. The first wore a righteous, officious expression; it took Trowbridge a minute to recognize him as the director of Customs at the port. The man who followed him in—a short man in a green leisure suit, looking extremely unhappy—Trowbridge recognized more quickly. It was Alain's expeditor.

Ten minutes later he was under arrest, charged with offering a bribe to a Diamantien official, fraudulently importing controlled goods, and violating immigration regulations. The Justice Minister had asked the expeditor only one question—had he seen Trowbridge offer money to the Customs chief? When the expeditor said, "Yes, but—" the Justice Minister told him that was all, and added that he would be lucky if he weren't prosecuted as an accessory to the crime. The gendarme captain put a pair of handcuffs on Trowbridge, the modern variety made of two plastic loops which had to be cut to be removed. He considered resisting, but realized it would probably just earn him a beating, after which he would end up wearing the cuffs anyway. The gendarme captain asked if Trowbridge should be put into a cell. The Justice Minister said no, that he would be detained elsewhere. Someone would be arriving shortly to take charge of him.

While they waited, Trowbridge considered the situation of a white foreigner in sub-Saharan Africa. There was a certain immunity attached to that status, but the immunity was far from inviolate. Plenty of white foreigners had died in the course of coups and tribal warfare. A group of journalists had rowed across Lake Victoria into Uganda during Idi Amin's day, been given tea by a group of soldiers, then stood against the wall of a hut and shot. And plenty of whites like Jean Luc had died, at least officially, as victims of crime.

But this was not Uganda, and there was no war going on, and this was not some hut on the shores of Lake Victoria—nor was it some remote clearing in the park. He was surrounded by people who worked for a government which prided itself on being moderate and relatively progressive; one of those people was the second most powerful man in the country, someone who spoke on a regular basis with international bankers and heads of state and high-level visitors from the United Nations. There was no way the Justice Minister—whatever his involvement with Moneyboy and Foote—could be serious about trying to make this stick. It would never work, not once Gordon and the embassy got involved. He might spend a few days, even a couple of weeks, in prison, but it couldn't get any worse than that.

He felt oddly naked without the fetish bag at his throat.

Another car pulled up outside. The Justice Minister walked briskly to the window, and said, "Good. My assistant."

Trowbridge was led outside, his cuffed hands before him. A white Citroën had pulled in beside the Justice Minister's Mercedes; a man wearing mirrored sunglasses was getting out of the passenger seat. Trowbridge recognized him even before he took his glasses off. He stopped, and looked behind himself. The expeditor saw his face, and spoke up with astounding bravery.

"May I ask a question?" he said. "May I ask what jail Monsieur Trowbridge will be held in?"

In the silence Moneyboy closed his car door and walked past Trowbridge and hit the expeditor in the face, hard, with an open palm. The gendarme captain and the Customs chief looked away nervously. The Justice Minister glanced at the expeditor without much interest. The expeditor put his hand to his nose, which was bleeding. *I'm getting too many people in trouble,* Trowbridge thought. The expeditor's eyes met his for a moment, and he saw real fear in them, and then he felt a jerk on his handcuffs and found out how awkward it is to climb into the back seat of a car when your wrists are bound.

░ ▓ ░

The Mercedes accelerated toward Pont Noir, bearing the Justice Minister, and, Trowbridge remembered with a hollow feeling, his passport. It occurred to him that for all intents and purposes he had ceased to exist. The gendarmes in Jacquesville would ask no questions about what had happened. Certainly the Customs chief wouldn't. The people who'd seen him taken off the bus, even assuming they had any interest, were scattering to the upcountry winds—and the cost of interference had been made abundantly clear to the expeditor, who, in any case, would probably have dared only to tell Alain, who was out of the country.

He looked over at Moneyboy, sitting beside him in the back seat. Moneyboy wore a bored expression, and glanced occasionally at the dirt roads which led off the highway into the bush. Trowbridge had an image, suddenly, of the station—the utter silence, the bodies strewn about—and realized he wasn't going back to Pont Noir. Panic washed through him, and he closed his eyes, squeezing his stomach muscles tight, trying to stay in control, trying to think. Even if he managed to get the door open, there was no way he could jump out of a car going fifty miles an hour. And Moneyboy had a gun tucked into his waistband.

They approached the village where the celebration was taking place. The Citroën slowed, hemmed in by traffic as other cars stopped to see what was going on. Moneyboy, with an annoyed expression, turned and looked out the rear window, as if considering whether to go back the way they'd come, but there were already cars behind them. Moneyboy looked forward again; Trowbridge saw his eyes flick across him to his door lock to be sure it was down.

A sound of drumming came from the village, where a troupe of young girls was dancing. People carried last-minute flowers and palm fronds to add to the archway at the village entrance. Across from them, on the other side of the highway, a black Jaguar stopped and U-turned, cutting into traffic beside them. Above each headlight on pencil-thin poles fluttered a Union Jack; in the back seat, a large, important-looking woman in a rather foolish pillbox hat was studying a piece of paper, oblivious to the traffic around her. There was only one country in the world that would import a Jaguar to West Africa; this had to be the British ambassador, no doubt reviewing her notes for a speech inaugurating a well or warehouse or covered market. The woman looked up from her notes and glanced over at him. Moneyboy had leaned forward and was cursing the driver. Trowbridge reached for the door lock and got two fingers beneath it and flipped it up, then squeezed the door handle. As Moneyboy grabbed at him he slammed his elbow hard to the left, hitting Moneyboy in the face, then kicked the door open and rolled out onto the concrete between the two cars. Scrambling to his feet, he tried the door of the Jaguar, which was locked. The British ambassador looked at him in indignant disbelief; then she looked past him, and her eyes grew wide, and she lay down onto her seat in an inelegant but very practical movement. Moneyboy must have the gun out, but was afraid to fire it with Trowbridge between him and the ambassador. In front of him, the driver of the Jaguar had flung his door open and was struggling to undo his seat belt. He heard other car doors opening around them, and someone yelling, and he ran.

⁂

He dodged between cars and ran beneath the archway into the village, which was filled with milling people. He was gulping air from fear and exertion; smells of food cooking and dust and palm wine filled his nostrils. He shoved and darted through the thickest part of the crowd, keeping his head low, then broke out into the open. A pair of goats skittered beneath his feet, and he leaped over them, nearly falling. It was hard to run in handcuffs. He heard someone go down behind him, and a goat bleating; a woman began yelling in indignation, then suddenly began to scream. The sound died away as he ducked behind a row of huts, moving away from the center of the village, hoping the huts would block the vision of whoever was chasing him. He put his cuffed hands onto a low fence, vaulted into a pen filled with pigs, and stumbled through in an explosion of squealing. He kicked his way through the low gate on the far end of the pen and ducked around a mud-and-wattle hut. This part of the village had not been spruced up for the official visit; an old woman wearing only a wraparound *pagne* skirt sat in the door of her house washing out a plastic tub. She looked up in astonishment as he stopped before her, his chest heaving. To his left was a narrow ravine bridged by a rickety structure made of cable and twisted vines and irregular planks. Beyond the bridge there were trees. He pounded across the bridge, nearly losing his balance as it bounced beneath him, then ducked past a huge *fromager* tree, and stopped.

A man stood before him, staring, naked from the waist up and heavily muscled, with a machete in a raised hand. One of his legs was withered and in a brace of some kind with leather straps. There was a pile of loose foliage—animal fodder—beside him, and a cart piled high with branches. The man lowered his machete with a slow movement and looked at Trowbridge. His expression was doubtful. Trowbridge, gasping for breath, held up his cuffed hands in an appeal, then set them on the side of the wooden cart. The man studied him a moment, then looked past him toward the village, where yelling had become audible. He looked back at Trowbridge and raised the machete. Trowbridge closed his eyes, straining to separate his hands as far as possible. There was maybe an inch between his open palms, no more. He sensed movement, and then the machete came down with a *whack* atop the cart—no pain, no blade biting into his flesh—and he was free, and running deeper into the trees.

43

"I need to talk to the consul," he said. "It's an emergency."

"Are you an American?"

The voice on the other end of the line had a Texas accent and a military correctness.

"Yes."

"Hold the line. I think Ms. Rizzman's still in the building."

He waited, standing with his back to the rest of the darkened bar so the loops of stiff plastic hanging from his wrists wouldn't be so obvious. He'd ridden back to Pont Noir after dark in a covered truck filled with tired-looking men who worked on a banana plantation. When the others had climbed out, he'd given the driver a few extra *befa* to bring him to this bar near the soccer stadium.

Someone picked up the line. "Consular section."

A familiar voice. He could visualize the no-nonsense expression.

"This is David Trowbridge. I'm an American."

"Registered with us?"

"Yes. I'm the one with the package."

There was a silence. "I remember you. There are no more packages here for you, if that's why you're calling."

"It isn't," Trowbridge said, and he relayed a terse summary of what had happened. It was difficult to tell if the consul believed him, but her reaction, when he'd finished, was prompt.

"You've got to get in here. That's an astonishing story, and you've clearly left out a good deal of what led up to it, but we can sort that out once you're in my office."

"They'll be looking for me to show up at the embassy. I don't think I'd make it to the front door."

"I'll send someone for you. An Amcit in trouble is my responsibility."

It took him a moment to realize what "Amcit" meant.

"No," he said. "I'll be better off hiding out in the city."

"Listen to me carefully," the consul said. "Our phone lines are tapped. We've known it for a long time. If someone's listening in, presumably—"

"I know, they can trace the call. I'm about to hang up."

"Wait—" the consul said, and Trowbridge hung up.

⠶ ⠿ ⠶

Najla's mechanic let him into the courtyard, widening his eyes slightly at his appearance, and disappeared upstairs. When he came back down he motioned Trowbridge into the shadows behind a pair of engineless cars. Trowbridge sat on a three-legged stool, leaned back against the wall, and closed his eyes. A few minutes later three people came down the stairs from the terrace—Najla, an older woman who must have been her mother, and a teenage girl, probably her sister—and climbed into the Mercedes. By the brief illumination of the dome light he saw three beautiful Middle Eastern faces, one a prediction, one a memory, of Najla's. The gate was rolled back and the Mercedes swept out of the courtyard. The mechanic cut away the remnants of his handcuffs with a pair of tin snips. A while later the Mercedes pulled back into the courtyard and Najla took him upstairs.

⠶ ⠿ ⠶

She looked at him in the light of the living room and propelled him straight into the shower. Collecting a towel and some of her brother's clothes, she leaned against the bathroom wall and asked him questions above the sound of the running water. He got out and dried off and put on the clothes, and they went and sat in the living room and he finished telling her what had happened.

Something about a sympathetic face allowed the panic to well up inside him. He felt shaky, and couldn't keep that out of his voice, and stopped talking.

"It's all right," she said. "You're all right now. You must have been terrified."

"I was. I am."

He took a deep breath, and released it slowly. "I probably shouldn't have come here. It might be dangerous for you."

"I don't think so—if anyone had followed you, they'd be here by now. What could the Justice Minister possibly have in mind? Aside from having you disappear somewhere."

"I don't know. Until a few days ago I thought it was just something to do with illegal logging in the park. It looks bigger than that now."

"I'd say so. The freighter we talked about? The *Tsar Simeon*? It's filled with guns, not logging equipment."

It took a moment for this to sink in.

"Guns?"

"Weapons, and pickup trucks. Whatever that means."

"How solid is the information?"

"More than a rumor. Less than a certainty. It came from someone in Cyprus who's pretty reliable. I'm beginning to wonder if the Justice Minister plans to invade Denkyara."

"That's crazy. Why would he want to do that?"

"You just told me he's got beachfront property there. Maybe he wants to protect his interests."

He leaned his head back on the couch, and nearly laughed. "You're not taking this very seriously."

"Oh, you're wrong there. I just hate to let it show when I take something seriously."

She went to the kitchen, poured them glasses of wine, and returned, putting one into his hand.

"I can fly you to Accra. I have a brother there who'll put you on a flight to London. You'll be there tomorrow night."

"No," he said. "I have to go back out to the park."

"That's a *terrible* idea. It's exactly where you shouldn't go."

"There's something I have to do for one of my leopards. And there's someone out there who'll be in trouble if they come looking for me."

She looked at him.

"Another scientist," he said. "She worked for Jean Luc."

Najla studied him a moment longer, then stood and went into the kitchen.

"So," she said, "I fly you out to the park. Then what?"

"Then I get Alberto to fly us to Accra. If he's willing."

"All right," she said coolly. "If that's what you really want."

⊞ ⊟ ⊞

Najla kept her plane at a strip an hour's drive outside the city. They left before sunrise, and he didn't get to see much, since he made the trip lying in the trunk under a blanket atop which was piled a shovel and a pair of pineapples. The precaution proved unnecessary; Najla drove fast on a paved road for a while, and then he felt the car leave the pavement and bounce along a dirt road for a while longer, and then she stopped and let him out.

There was just enough light in the sky to make out a row of small hangars and a number of private planes on tie-downs. Najla waved to a sleepy old man in shorts who emerged from the office.

"The *gardien*," she explained. "And relax, I'm a good pilot."

"It isn't that."

"I know. But it's all right. No one knows you're here."

She unhooked the tie-downs on her plane, poured them *café au lait* from a thermos, and went calmly and methodically through her preflight checklist. A few minutes later they taxied down the runway, a paved corridor through a grove of rubber trees. Right up until the last minute he expected jeeps to pour onto the runway and stop them at gunpoint. It was a miracle when they didn't, and the plane skimmed up over a dark green curtain of trees into an enormous sky just beginning to turn orange.

⊞ ⊟ ⊞

When they reached the park he saw the inselberg standing in the distance, partially obscured by a rain squall. It looked like something out of a myth—a great stone tooth thrusting upward into the sky. He touched her on the shoulder and pointed.

"That's where you live?"

"Yes."

"It's beautiful. I should have met you before you got into all this trouble."

She flashed him a smile, and because he was afraid, he recognized a bravery in her he might not otherwise have perceived. Beneath them he saw an opening in the forest. In it was the skeleton of a downed tree, white and sharp against the forest floor. Drops of water began whacking the windshield in tiny precise points.

"Looks like the rainy season will be right on time," she said.

"Do you care?"

"Sure. A prosperous country is good for us."

"It must be strange. Always thinking in terms of 'us.'"

"I've never known anything else. It's hard to imagine not having nine brothers and sisters and a hundred aunts and uncles and cousins. Not having people around all the time, criticizing and helping and putting pressure on. Sometimes it gets oppressive."

She paused, then said, "I wouldn't have minded someone like you in my life. Someone outside the family. I'm just telling you this. It doesn't change anything, not in practical terms."

"I know."

The park boundary passed beneath them. Villages and open fields appeared. Najla began to look a little preoccupied.

"Can you land all right when it's raining?"

"The grass gets a little slick, but yes, I can land the plane all right. Are you sure you want to do this, though? I have plenty of fuel—we could just keep going to Accra."

He shook his head. The *piste* came up beneath them, and they turned south, following it until they flew over the sawmill and Alberto's compound, where the bungalows looked like toys and his swimming pool shone an artificial blue against the surrounding green. Najla circled and flew low over the mill, then circled back, flying low again. Trowbridge saw a figure come out of a small office building beside the mill and look up. Najla waggled the wings briefly, then turned south toward Alberto's airstrip.

He was seized by doubts, suddenly, at involving Alberto this way, but he didn't know what else to do. The plane was jolted by a blast of turbulence, and he felt his muscles tighten.

"Are we okay?"

"We're okay." Her voice was tense. "But we'll to have to make this fast."

She pointed ahead, where an ugly squall loomed within the overall gray of the sky. A few minutes later the airstrip became visible beneath them. She circled over it once, then brought the plane in, floating it down smoothly onto the rain-soaked grass.

44

Najla didn't turn off the engine, and she didn't get out of the plane. She kissed him quickly, narrowed her eyes and waited a moment, as if giving him a chance to say something, then said, "I have to go. Take care of yourself."

She taxied back down the runway, turned the plane in a tight circle, and took off in a blast of wind and engine noise. He watched the plane grow smaller and disappear into clouds, then stood against Alberto's hangar, taking partial shelter against the rain until the familiar Land Rover emerged from the trees.

Alberto leaned across the seat and opened the passenger-side door.

"David?" he said. "What—"

"It's a long story," he said, climbing in. "I'm in trouble, and Claire may be in trouble as well. I need you to fly us to Accra tomorrow. If you're willing, and if you think you can do that without anyone finding out."

"Yes, and yes. What happened?"

He told Alberto about seeing Moneyboy at the Justice Ministry. About the scarred tire, his arrest and escape, the load of weapons on the Bulgarian freighter.

When he was finished, Alberto let out a long slow breath.

"My God, you had a busy couple of days. Wouldn't it be better if I flew you to Accra right now?"

"I have to go to the inselberg. And Claire will be out with the chimps until this evening. I'll leave her a note and come back through in the morning to pick her up."

"Won't they be looking for you in the park?"

"I don't think so—I said something on a tapped phone line which ought to make them think I'm still in the capital. But I'm worried you might get into trouble later if you're seen with me."

Alberto protested, briefly, that he could handle any such problem; then he agreed to lend Trowbridge an old pickup truck at the mill compound that wasn't registered and couldn't be traced to him.

"What can the Justice Minister be up to?" Alberto said, as they headed toward the mill in torrential rain.

"Najla thinks he may be planning to invade Denkyara."

"An invasion makes some sense, actually. He could probably take the western third of the country, the Ebrio part, fairly easily. But there are a dozen different tribes in the center and east, none of which would want to be ruled by an Ebrio, especially one from Terre Dia-mantée. It would be a bloody, dirty fight, and a long one. A single shipload of weapons wouldn't be enough to pull it off."

"What about a coup here?"

"That makes no sense at all. Not with several hundred Belgian marines in the capital, and not when he stands a good chance of in-heriting this country anyway, if he waits a little longer. Plus he knows the government would collapse tomorrow without money from the World Bank and IMF."

"Whatever's happening, it's happening soon. I think you should stay on in Accra for a few days. Let this blow over, whatever it is."

Alberto looked doubtful. "There's no one else to run the mill."

"Shut it down for a while."

"We'll see," Alberto said. He pulled to a stop outside his office, dis-appeared inside, emerged a moment later with a key, and drove them behind the mill to where the truck was parked.

"I'll see you tomorrow morning," Alberto said. "Eleven o'clock, at the airstrip."

"We'll be there. Listen, I'm sorry I never saw elephants. I would have liked to be able to tell you about that."

"At the moment," Alberto said dryly, "I'd say that's the least of your worries."

⁂

He was nervous as he drove into the park, but there were no road-blocks, and no one was waiting when he reached the station and hid the truck and plunged into the dripping forest.

Twenty minutes later he walked into what he thought would be an empty camp. Claire was sitting beneath a tarp in shorts and a T-shirt, tapping away at her computer.

"Seydou's out with the chimps," she explained, looking up with a cheerful smile. Then, seeing his face, she said, "David, what happened?"

He told her, and gave her a minute to absorb it. Then he said, "I'm sorry to do this to you. It's my fault. But we have to leave. They'll be all over this place when they can't find me in the capital."

"This is unbelievable. You're all right, though?"

"I'm all right."

The implications of what he'd said began to sink in. She looked around at the forest, and at the makeshift camp that had been her movable home.

"That's it? We just walk away?"

"I'm afraid so."

"Are we going to be able to come back?"

"I don't know. I doubt it. Listen, I'm going to the inselberg to bring out as much gear as I can. And I have to dehabituate *L1* and the cubs—I don't want her vulnerable to poachers. I'll be back through in the morning. Can you be ready by then?"

"I'm coming with you."

When he started to object, she said, "I can help you bring out your equipment. And we had a deal. You promised me a leopard sighting."

He didn't argue.

Five hours later, after a hard, wet hike, they reached the inselberg and followed the narrow trail up to the platform. The wide-open, rainy-season sky around them was a labyrinth of dark clouds, shafts of sunlight, and shifting patches of blue. Beneath them, an expanse of water-soaked canopy curved dark green to the horizon. He opened the computer, took down *L1*'s coordinates, and plugged them into the GPS. She was at one of her lying-up places not far from the inselberg, which was good news; there wasn't much time if they were going to catch her before she went out for the evening hunt.

⁂

Rain spattered down while they walked. When they were close, he touched her shoulder and said, "From here on we shouldn't talk any more. They're habituated to human presence, not human voices."

"Okay."

She looked a little tight.

"Are you all right?"

"I'm all right."

He studied her a moment, then said, "Do you love your little girl?"

She looked at him curiously. "You know I do."

"If it's any help, you and *L1* are both quite beautiful and quite stubborn. You both have your behavior shaped by the fact you have offspring. You have a lot in common. Think of her as a colleague. Maybe a kindred spirit."

She made an attempt to smile that didn't quite come off.

"Thanks," she said.

"I'm guessing that when I start toward her she'll turn and bolt into the den. That would be normal leopard behavior in daylight. But she's got cubs, so she's less predictable. Once we see her, keep your eyes on her. It isn't like chimps—she's less likely to attack if we're making eye contact. If she does attack, do me a favor and hit her with a stump or something. I understand you've very good at taking on leopards."

"You can't possibly be this calm."

"I'm not," he said. "Come on."

They covered the last hundred meters in silence.

"There," he breathed.

In the dimness beneath the canopy, only *L1*'s head and shoulders were visible. Her dark-rimmed, elegant eyes opened lazily, and she blinked and yawned, watching them where they stood fifteen meters away. The cubs, presumably, were somewhere behind her in that root system.

They moved forward until they were about eight meters from the den, closer than he'd ever been before. *L1*'s eyes became narrow slits, and her gaze flicked between the two of them. Moving this close violated the rules of the habituation agreement, and she knew it as well as he did. With slow, deliberate movements, he took a container of waterproof matches from his pocket, then something that looked like a hard cherry with a fuse.

As he handed Claire the matches a small round face, wide-eyed and curious, appeared at *L1*'s shoulder. Without hesitation, *L1* cuffed her cub straight back into a dark opening in the roots. She was sitting now, staring at them intently.

"Now," he said quietly, apologizing silently to the leopard before him.

Claire struck a match. The crisp sound caused *L1*'s ears to stand up, and in a movement too quick to follow she was no longer sitting but crouching, in a position that suggested both threat and defense. She made a peculiar hissing, then growled an unmistakable warning.

"Okay," he said. Claire held the match to the fuse. It caught immediately, and he held it out before him, then rolled it directly toward *L1*, raising his arms and shouting and running forward. *L1* crouched lower, snarling and indecisive, as the cherry bomb—something brought to him from Mexico by one of his former grad students— went off in a blinding flash. *L1* whirled and disappeared, a yellow-black streak beneath the roots. Trowbridge stood with his ears ringing and an acrid smell of gunpowder in his nostrils, considering how quickly four months of work could be thrown away. He realized he would probably never see *L1* and the cubs again, and noticed there were tears running down his face.

The silence in the empty clearing before him was deafening, the ringing in his ears an insistent pain.

***

Claire handed him a cup of tea.

"You all right?" she asked.

"Not great."

In the aftermath of the explosion, Claire had come up and stood next to him, saying nothing, her arm touching his. He'd been grateful for the physical contact, the silent understanding.

You could get accustomed to that, he thought.

"I guess I haven't said thank you," Claire said. "She was beautiful. Terrifying and beautiful at the same time. It's going to be easier for me to walk through the forest, assuming I ever get another opportunity."

She stirred her tea thoughtfully, and then he saw her stiffen, and heard a flat sound that shouldn't be there. A faint whack, like the sound of a machete, followed by something that might be a voice drifting up through treetops.

There it was again, this time answered by another voice. For a brief moment he thought, Alberto. Then he dismissed that possibility, set the cup of tea down, and went to the edge of the platform. He looked down on the darkening canopy.

Was that a flicker of light?

Claire was standing beside him. "Can they see us?" she asked quietly.

He glanced behind himself at the rock wall of the inselberg. A few minutes earlier the granite had been shining nearly red in the reflected light of sunset. Now it was fading quickly, the color gone.

"I don't think so. It's pretty difficult to see up through the canopy, even during the day."

"How did they find us?"

"I don't know."

Only Alberto and Najla knew about the inselberg—he hadn't even told Alain. Had he said something careless to someone else, perhaps the Justice Minister? He remembered their first conversation, his instinctive reticence about the specifics of where he worked, then remembered saying something about having a view. For anyone looking at a decent map of the park, that wouldn't prove too difficult a riddle.

Another flicker of light beneath the canopy. It was dark down there, but in that darkness people were looking for them. Looking, rather, for the trail that would give them away. They wouldn't find it immediately, but it wouldn't take all night. Eventually they would come across the bathing pool, see footprints around it, and follow the trail upward.

The flickering lights already made a loose pattern around the place where the trail started up the inselberg. Like fireflies in the darkness, only less innocent.

Claire said, "Can we slip past them? If we leave now?"

"They're already pretty close to the trail. And we'd make too much noise if we went off it."

"Is there another way down?"

"No."

"Any ideas?"

He was silent a moment. Then he said, "Only one. And I don't much like it."

45

In the fading light he took a knife and a spool of fishline and went partway down the trail and rigged a taut line at about knee level, marking the place carefully in his mind. Then he went back up a ways and tied a second line. When he returned to the platform, Claire, who'd been working with a file on a handful of his practice darts, held one up for him to see. The tip of the dart was now sharp instead of blunt.

He thought her hand might be shaking slightly, but it was hard to tell in the near darkness.

"I guess we're not going back out to meet Alberto," she said.

"I guess not."

She set the darts down and began putting camping gear, food, and clothes into their packs. He pulled a bag from beneath the cot, put on the scope, and went to work. He mixed the remaining Kezol and loaded four of the syringe darts, then looked at the two remaining syringes and the small amount of Kezol solution left over. Less than half a dose. He hesitated, then poured out the Kezol, mixed a batch of Tagamine, loaded the remaining two darts, and set them with the others.

He took off the scope and went to the edge of the platform. The lights stood out more clearly beneath the trees, and seemed to be drawing together in a cluster around the bathing pool. He ducked beneath the tarp, dimmed the computer screen before opening it, and clicked on a menu file called *Parameters*. Studying the technical specifications, he changed the wakeup interval from *1/1* to *1/24*. The computer asked him if he was sure he wanted to do this; he tapped in a yes. From now on, the six radio collars would continue beaming their positions into the sky once an hour, and *Atlantic East* would continue to receive that information, process it, and shoot it down here, but the computer would wake up only once a day to listen. If he or someone else was able to come back later the quality of data would be drastically reduced; he would know little more than whether each leopard was still alive and living in its current home range. But the batteries in the computer and transceiver, the two weakest links in his system—especially given what the oncoming rainy season would do to his solar panels—would last much longer.

Some data would be better than none at all.

Here's to the rainy season, he thought, remembering what Komo had said. What could that have meant?

He closed the tracking program, clicked on *Maps*, and plotted a route down through the park to Granville. Their only realistic chance, now, was to reach the coast and get out by water. Nowhere in Terre Diamantée was safe, and the western half of Denkyara, Ebrio territory, was actively dangerous. If they could borrow or steal a boat in Granville, it was barely seventy kilometers by water to Denkyara City, more or less neutral ground. Another eighty kilometers would take them to Takoradi, in Ghana.

The map of Terre Diamantée floated dimly before him on the screen. Granville, on the coast, with its lighthouse and harbor; nearby, the old city, set on a tiny finger of sand. North of Granville, several kilometers of rubber plantations, then the southern boundary of the park, and sixty kilometers of forest stretching to the inselberg. They had a decent hike in front of them.

The map, suddenly, began scrolling left across the screen; his finger—probably because of the tension he was feeling—had been pressing down too hard. He was about to scroll back when Claire, looking over his shoulder, said, "Wait."

He glanced at her, then looked back at the computer. The river which formed the border, a slender blue line, curved up through the center of the screen, dividing it in two. On one side, a good chunk of Terre Diamantée was visible; on the other side, about half of Denkyara.

"David," she said urgently. "That's it. That's what the Justice Minister is doing. He's not going to attack Denkyara. He's going to carve out a new country in the middle."

"Jesus," Trowbridge said, staring at the screen.

A shout floated up from beneath them. Someone had found the trail. Working quickly, he tapped a final set of coordinates into the GPS, shut down the computer, and picked up the night scope.

"It's time," he said.

⛆ ⛋ ⛆

He stepped carefully over the upper line, moved down to the lower, and stepped over that. Then he crouched and peered beneath him. The trail angled steeply downward and disappeared into the canopy, which pressed close against the inselberg.

Like descending a steep slope into a nighttime ocean.

Voices drifted up; lights flickered almost directly beneath him. The men were at the base of the inselberg, and had found the trail, but were talking, not moving. What were they waiting for? He moved down into the canopy, far enough that he could see through it but would still be screened in case someone hit him with a flashlight beam.

There they were. Through successive filters of vegetation he counted four figures holding flashlights. No, there were five; a dark shape stood without a light. That was bad news. Then a flicker appeared off to the left, and he watched another light and another shape come in through the vegetation and join the others. This one wore a headlamp instead of carrying a flashlight, and looked more like a poacher than a soldier, someone who was accustomed to working in the forest.

Six, he thought. That meant all six darts. All six darts if he was lucky. He closed his eyes and felt a faint trembling in his hands. He couldn't do this. There were too many, and they had guns; it was an impossible plan made more impossible by the fact he was losing his nerve. He couldn't aim and shoot in this condition. Then something tiny and stubborn in him came alive, and he remembered how he'd stood in Gordon's backyard with the crossbow and a paper target on the lawn, practicing until he could hit the target every time.

You trained for this, he told himself. *Just do your job.*

He opened his eyes and saw six figures starting up the trail. Taking the crossbow from his bag, he loaded the first Kezol dart, and set a second dart beside him. He raised the bow and studied the trail through its sight. He would have to wait until they were within fifteen or twenty meters; he had no experience shooting from a greater distance. Realizing his chances of success would be better if the target weren't moving, he looked around himself, found a piece of rotten wood the size of his forearm, shook it to knock the ants off, and held it, balanced lightly, in his right hand.

They were coming up slowly, scanning the trail, no doubt believing they were close to their destination. Closer than you know, he thought. He held the piece of wood until the first shape was nearly to the place he'd chosen, then flipped it down so that it made a crashing sound through mid-levels of canopy. The man dropped into a crouch and turned sideways, shining his flashlight toward the forest floor. Trowbridge raised the bow, aimed, and squeezed the trigger. There was a hiss, then a choked-off gasp of surprise; the man fell to one side, dropping his flashlight and swatting at his leg. Then he leaped to his feet and began screaming something in Ebrio.

If I knew the Ebrio word for snake, Trowbridge thought, I'd be hearing it now.

He reloaded and took aim at the next man, who was pointing his flashlight nervously down at the trail, and standing with his feet together, as if he wished he could float. He squeezed the trigger, and then there were two people howling they'd been bitten by snakes.

In the din, he retreated. Moved quietly back up the trail, out of range of flashlights and semi-automatic weapons. The men beneath him might, or might not, realize what had actually happened; it would depend on whether the two syringe darts had been kicked away in their initial flailing. He glanced at his watch as he climbed and nearly tripped over the first fishline.

Ten meters higher up, where the trail made a tight turn, he crouched, made his preparations, and waited.

They came more cautiously this time, playing their flashlights before them. The two men he'd darted had fallen back to the end of the line. Trowbridge raised the bow and sighted on the place where he knew the fishline stretched across the trail. When the lead man pitched forward onto his hands and knees he fired. There was yelling; flashlight beams darted wildly. He squinted against the light, reloaded quickly, waited for the second man to stop moving, and aimed at his thigh. When he squeezed the trigger he saw the dart do something it shouldn't, jump sideways on impact; it must have hit a seam on the man's fatigues. The man whipped his flashlight beam onto his leg, then began sweeping it in frantic patterns on the trail around him.

Four darts, and only three hits. It didn't add up. Swearing quietly to himself, he loaded the fifth dart—the first with Tagamine in it—and took a deep breath, trying not to think about what he was going to do. The lead man had crouched and picked up the syringe dart that had bounced off his leg, and was talking urgently to the men behind him. Trowbridge aimed, squeezed the trigger, and saw the dart go home where it should. Then he retreated again.

Fifteen meters up he knelt behind a granite extrusion which extended into the trail. This was the last real shelter before the platform, and he used it to shoot his final dart, hitting the man with the head-lamp. The dart took the man squarely in the thigh, and he cried out the way the others had, and then the firing began, ripping the night open with sound. They didn't have a specific direction, but they knew that whoever was tormenting them was somewhere above. They sprayed the trail with flashlight beams, and fired wildly at every bit of brush and vine which hung from the side of the inselberg. He was afraid they would keep coming while they fired, trapping him behind the granite outcropping, but after a minute the firing stopped. Someone near the back was yelling. He raised his head cautiously and saw that there were only five men now. He recognized Moneyboy standing with a rifle in one hand and a flashlight in the other, yelling furious instructions at the men before him. He would have presented a good target if there had been any more darts.

Seven minutes. The second man ought to be out of action soon. Not long after that, two more, and then a fifth. But that still left Moneyboy. He pulled the slingshot and the bag of ball bearings from his pocket. His heart was pounding, and he had a terrible sense that things had unraveled around him; he didn't have a clear plan any more. Some frightened part of him simply wanted Moneyboy to give up and retreat down the trail. But that was no good either. As long as Moneyboy was waiting at the base of the inselberg they were trapped. And three of the five men would shake off the effects of the drugs by sunrise.

He heard Moneyboy's voice falter, as if he were confused. Trowbridge risked another glance and saw that one of the men was lying peacefully on the trail on his side. Another wobbled, then sat down abruptly. The two remaining looked around nervously, shining their flashlights against the inselberg.

He leaned back out of sight and listened to Moneyboy urging them up the trail. There was a dangerous quality to his voice. Nine minutes now. He set a ball bearing in the pad of the slingshot, put his head around the outcropping, sighted on Moneyboy's temple—the one with scarification—and shot. Moneyboy's head jerked, and he put another ball bearing in, and fired again. Moneyboy was on his knees, one hand to his head. The second shot made the flashlight explode in his hand, cutting short his howl of pain. Then Trowbridge put his head down, because there were bullets everywhere, random bursts of firing by frightened men who were swearing and yelling at one another.

Moneyboy's voice cut through the yelling with recognizable authority and an undertone of rage. The ball bearing had hurt him, but it hadn't hurt him enough. Trowbridge looked at the slingshot in his hand, rubbing his thumb over the little carved leopard at the joint, and felt the fear inside grow until it was nearly overwhelming.

Beneath him he heard a moan, a quiet sound at first, growing louder into something that expressed pure terror. When he looked he saw one of the two men he'd darted with Tagamine set his flashlight down and back away from it as if it were a live creature. The man turned and staggered down through the darkness, stumbling over the other Tagamine hit, who was sitting in the trail, trying to take his shirt off, getting tangled in it as if it were something he'd never done before.

Moneyboy looked back in disbelief. Looked forward, then back again.

He's alone now, Trowbridge thought, and he knows it. Maybe he'll run. Panic, and go back down the trail. Maybe if he does that and doesn't think to pick up the rifles lying there I can pick one up and follow him.

Both Tagamine hits were screaming. The sound got under his skin, made him want to run as well. He thought about the narrow places on the trail, places you had to be careful even when it was daylight and you weren't drugged. The pair of screams became one, suddenly. There was a quick thrashing, a whirring of wings and a cry of barbets. A heavier crashing, lower down in the canopy, and then nothing. He held still a moment, listening to one man screaming, listening to his own breathing. He set down the slingshot and pulled a plastic bag from his chest pocket and took out a pair of cherry bombs. He doubted it would be enough, but it was all he had left.

When he looked back down the trail Moneyboy had made a decision. He was coming up fast, rifle and flashlight held low before him, a desperate, determined look on his face. Not a coward after all, not this time, anyway. Trowbridge felt adrenaline surge in him and lit a match, hands shaking, hurrying, holding the flame to the fuses. He'd waited too long; Moneyboy would be on top of him before the fuses burned down.

The fuses took, flaring brightly. A shout came from above him, Claire's voice. Moneyboy was suddenly visible, only a few meters down the trail, standing transfixed by the beam of a flashlight. His rifle was coming up, pointing up past Trowbridge toward the platform; then he stumbled and groaned, and Trowbridge saw a crossbow dart jut from his collarbone.

He remembered what was in his hand, and flicked the bombs down the trail, turning his face away, scrambling to his feet after the double report and the flashes of light. Claire was already coming down behind him, carrying a flashlight and the two packs. Moneyboy lay on his side at the outside edge of the trail, hands to his collarbone, a dark trickle of blood coming through his fingers. Trowbridge picked up Moneyboy's rifle, reversed it quickly, feeling the barrel hot in his hand, and thumped Moneyboy on the head, once, with the metal stock. Then he put the toe of his boot beneath Moneyboy's hip and looked out into a free fall of darkness and empty space. He could have tipped him over the edge, easily. He hesitated, then picked up the rifle of the second man—who was scuttling backward down the trail, weeping and talking to himself—and stepped past him, Claire close behind him, the two of them moving together down toward the forest floor.

46

They followed the dim tunnels of elephant lanes, using a compass to keep their direction south toward the coast. After four hours of walking, when the GPS told them they were seven kilometers from the inselberg, Claire collapsed, overwhelmed by sudden, uncontrolled shaking. There was naked fear on her face, a delayed reaction to what had happened. He put his arms around her, wordlessly, until the shaking stopped. Then they continued on, passing like ghosts through the rainy vegetation.

With nothing to focus on but their movement through the forest, Trowbridge began to feel not merely exhaustion, but some kind of rising sickness. He wasn't capable of collapsing cleanly and completely the way Claire had; he felt, instead, as if he would come apart slowly for years.

Stopping, he put his hand on the hard trunk of a *fromager* tree, and closed his eyes.

"David," she said. "We need something to eat. And I think we should try to sleep some."

He nodded. They found a place to string the tarp, and Claire prepared dried soup and opened a packet of crackers. They drank the warm soup, listening to the water dripping on the tarp above their heads.

"How long does the Tagamine go on?" she asked.

"Five or six hours. I'm not really sure."

"It isn't necessarily fatal, though. The other one—"

"If he stays on the trail, he might be all right."

"You didn't have any choice."

"I know."

He paused, struggling with what had happened.

"Moneyboy was right there, right by the edge. I could have tipped him over. Probably should have."

"You can't beat yourself up because one person died, and feel bad at the same time you didn't kill someone else. We'll be off the continent in a few days, and this will all be over. It'll be better, then, you didn't kill Moneyboy."

"Even if he killed Jean Luc and the others?"

"Even so. Even if you could have justified it."

⠿ ⠿ ⠿

They were moving again at dawn. It rained intermittently throughout the morning, and solidly all afternoon, coming down so hard the water seemed to be not merely pouring down from the sky but exploding from the vegetation itself, as if the forest were a giant network of plumbing that was bursting at the joints. When the root system of a fallen tree offered too perfect a shelter to pass up they finally stopped for a few minutes, and ate something, and talked for the first time since they'd left the inselberg about what they thought the Justice Minister was doing.

His plan, they guessed, was to take a piece of both Terre Diamantée and Denkyara, dissolve the border between them, and set up an independent state. The new country would have a solid economic base, with two good ports in Granville and Denkyara City, a lot of untouched forest, and the phosphate mines in northern Denkyara. The two sitting presidents, one feeble and one crazy, would retain their capitals and enough of their countries to be reasonably happy, thus minimizing the threat to the political order, which might have prompted the other countries in the region toward military intervention.

"And the World Bank won't be telling him what to do," Trowbridge said, "which it would have if he'd waited to become president here. No debts, no loans, no leverage. Just a lot of forest to cut down and sell to people like Randy Foote, and let the environmentalists scream all they want. He can claim he's simply redrawing illogical old borders imposed on Africa by the colonialists—"

"Which is true."

"—and set up the first single-ethnic state in Africa."

"On a continent with several hundred ethnic groups, it's everyone's worst nightmare. Can he actually do it, though? Can he pull this off?"

"I don't know," Trowbridge said. "It depends on whether he can hold on to the territory he grabs. It looks like Moneyboy's been rallying support among the Ebrio on this side of the border—and the Justice Minister is already influential in Denkyara. But he's got the other ethnic groups to worry about, and the Diamantien army, and the Belgian marines in Pont Noir."

The rain came down steadily around them.

"I guess we're going all the way to Ghana, then," Claire said. "Not just to Denkyara City."

"I guess so."

They covered another five kilometers before darkness fell, set up camp, and pushed on again in the morning, making good time until they ran out of elephant lanes, at which point the going became slower and more difficult. At this pace it would take five more days, easily, to reach the coast.

It rained hard, all night long, and he woke several times, listening to it come down.

When watery gray light filtered through the trees they put on the same soggy clothes they'd taken off the night before—there was little point changing, since dry clothes would be soaked immediately—and set out again. They talked occasionally, voices drifting between the sound of the rain and the noise they made pushing through the undergrowth, but mostly they were silent; they alternated taking the lead, which was harder work, and stopped only briefly for lunch. Their progress remained slow, and was slow again the following day, until late in the afternoon, when they noticed a change in the quality of the forest. Something was different about the light and the vegetation, and the canopy was lower. They'd reached coastal lowland forest. Soon afterward the rain stopped for the first time in thirty-six hours, and they emerged into a network of fresh elephant lanes, allowing them to move more quickly and easily.

He thought about Alberto, who would like to have known there were at least two places left in the park where elephants lived.

"David," Claire said, pointing left off the trail, down an long-disused elephant lane so grown over it was barely recognizable. *"Look."*

He realized she was pointing above the trail, and exclaimed quietly at what he saw there. They pushed their way down the path and stood looking up at a substantial log, fifty kilos at least, suspended above the trail by a vegetation-entangled vine. The log's lower end was sharpened to a wicked point.

"Poachers use guns now," he said wonderingly. "This is a relic. Must be years old."

He found a stick with a forked end and poked around in the leaf litter beneath the log, keeping a wary eye above him. When he unearthed a straight length of vine he pushed at it, but the stick went right through. He studied the vine by which the log was suspended, then found a heavier branch, took careful aim, and slung it at the log. The first time he missed. The second time the vine parted and the log came down in a straight silent rush, burying itself a foot deep in the forest floor like an enormous upright pencil.

"Wow," she said quietly.

"I wonder how they knew. The elephants, I mean. It looks like they stopped using this trail because this was here."

He reached out and touched the rough wood of the log, then heard something, and both he and Claire froze.

Elephants, even those born to the forest, moving on lanes they've made themselves, cannot move in utter silence; there was a crashing sound in the near distance, coming closer down the trail on which they'd been walking. The slight movement of forest air must be in their favor, he realized; otherwise the elephants would have caught their scent. The crashing grew nearer, and he heard another sound, the rough, sandpapery noise of skin scraping on skin—elephants were contact animals, and touched one another even when they walked. In the dim light a trunk came into view, and a pair of short tusks, nearly straight and aimed toward the ground; then small oval ears, a sloping forehead, and the wrinkled, wise, sad face of a forest elephant.

They held perfectly still. The elephant stopped, raising her trunk in a question mark, as if she sensed something wasn't quite right. This would be the matriarchal cow, the leader of a family group of seven or eight; forest elephants lived in smaller bands than their savannah cousins. She was barely two meters at the shoulder, and full grown. One of her ears was notched with little holes, probably from parasites.

The matriarch swung her head from side to side, rumbling uncertainly. In the dim light, he could see the pinkish tone of her tusks, and thought of the inselberg. She took two steps, swaying slightly, then turned as a pair of smaller elephants crowded into view. Adolescents, with new tusks smaller than his forearm. The smaller tusks made a clonking noise as the young elephants jostled one another, then leaned into the matriarch, who touched them each in turn with her trunk, as if counting them. He looked at the watchful expression on the ancient face, the dark, recessed eyes, gleaming and deep amid the wrinkles. This was a creature that had managed to safeguard her family for years against old threats like suspended logs and newer threats like automatic weapons; this was a being deeply careful in her essence.

A smaller cow pushed into view, touching her trunk to the matriarch's mouth in greeting. Then all four animals froze simultaneously. One of them must have spotted him and Claire, or perhaps a shift in the breeze had brought them their smell. A moment later they were gone, leaving an image of baggy gray rumps and comical small tails crashing into a wall of green.

"Lord," he said, releasing a long breath. "They were so small. They looked like pure *cyclotis.*"

Loxodonta africana cyclotis were so different from their larger cousins they'd been assumed to be a different species until it became clear the two could interbreed. As forests had shrunk and the savannahs expanded, interbreeding had become more common; now most forest elephants were hybrids. But the elephants they'd just seen looked as purely and distinctively forest as any he had ever known reported.

Claire looked so happy as to be on the verge of tears.

"This forest has been intact since before the Ice Age," she said. "That means this family goes back several hundred generations, maybe more."

The idea that a population of elephants had survived the Ice Age in a core of this forest, then expanded, recolonizing the surrounding habitat, should have been a cheering thought. A national park could function the same way, as a repository for plant and animal species that could serve, someday—as people and their governments slowly grew more enlightened—to repopulate the ruined land around the park.

Only there was no trend toward enlightenment in this region. With a sinking heart, he realized that if the Justice Minister succeeded in his scheme, the section of forest they were walking through—given its proximity to Granville—would probably be the first to be logged. With the timber crews would come the elephant hunters, and this family line of elephants, unbroken for more than ten thousand years, would come to an end.

They returned to the trail and headed south, stepping over elephant droppings that were still warm.

⠒ ⠃ ⠒

"Jeeves says we're still three miles from the coast," Claire said, looking up from the GPS, which she'd rechristened in honor of its faithful and loyal service.

She was smiling, but the exhaustion showed in her face. They'd spent most of the day struggling through high stands of raffia palm, impenetrable explosions of vegetation rooted in low swamps which exuded heat, moisture, and voracious biting insects. Late in the afternoon, when they'd been ready to give up and make camp, they'd emerged from beneath the trees, and stood—soggy and scratched and itching—with forest at their backs, and a kind of miracle before them. Rubber trees, in neat endless rows, narrow white trunks scarred with tapping and distinguished by plastic bowls attached at waist height.

The light was dying around them; the trees formed dim straight corridors, long and open.

"Shall we try for Granville tonight?"

She nodded, and they pushed on through the twilight between the straight rows of trees. The turned soil was a new hardship, and relatively slow going, and it was almost eight o'clock when they first smelled smoke and human smells, and stood where the rubber trees ended and the dark trailing edge of Granville's shantytown began, marked by flickering lanterns and cook fires.

47

They followed a muddy footpath between tumbledown huts made of palm thatch and plastic sheeting, working their way down toward the more established section of town. Coming in through the forest had allowed them to avoid any roadblocks that might have been set up; they'd left backpacks and the rifle hidden in the trees, and there were enough aid workers and Belgian *coopérants* and Foote-type Western businessmen floating around, even in Granville, that a pair of white faces, while noticeable, wasn't necessarily remarkable. They tried to look confident and normal and anything but out of place.

People stared, nonetheless. Young women holding babies, and groups of children, and men standing in wraparound *pagne* and rubber sandals stopped what they were doing, their faces becoming frowns, or worse, going expressionless. A young boy selling grilled meat on wooden skewers watched them, openmouthed, making no effort to get their attention or their business.

"No one's smiling," he said.

"It isn't normal."

"They aren't Ebrio, anyway."

"No, they're Lagoon. That's something in our favor."

They passed from the narrow footpath into an open dirt street. There were houses on either side, mostly cinderblock with corrugated roofs, some with electric wires running into them and the glow of electric light coming from inside.

"Do you know where you are?"

"This way," she said, and they moved down through the sloping streets.

The friend who'd loaned Claire the Peugeot was Lagoon tribe, not Ebrio; Claire was friendly with the mother, who she was confident would be able to arrange a boat for them. Trowbridge wasn't entirely happy with this plan, but didn't see they had much choice. Stealing a boat had sounded the lesser of two challenges when they were trapped by a group of armed men. Now it seemed a formidable difficulty, particularly since the port was likely to be heavily guarded.

Claire led them across a low footbridge over a drainage ditch and down a long straight street. At the corner she hesitated, peering around herself in darkness. He felt his nervousness increase—was she lost? Then she turned right, and said, "Yes, this is it." A moment later they stepped through a gate beneath a high mango tree, and she knocked quietly on a closed door. Through a wooden shutter, a female voice said, *"Qui est là?"* Claire said, *"Assa, c'est Claire."* A deadbolt was undone from inside, and an older woman with a lined face opened the door and looked at Claire in disbelief.

The woman pulled Claire inside quickly, then glanced at Trowbridge with an unhappy expression before drawing him in as well. The room was simple, but very clean, lit by a single bulb hanging from the ceiling. Three wide-eyed children were shooed into a back room of the house, and they sat at a rough wooden table, amid plates of orange *foutou* and fish bones, while Assa and Claire spoke quickly in low voices. Assa neglected to offer them something to eat, a breach of West African hospitality that could be attributed to the fact she was scared.

A curfew had been imposed, she said, and roadblocks set up outside the city, and the phone lines to the capital hadn't worked for two days. There had been rumors of some kind of uprising at the military base, followed by reassurances from the Ebrio mayor that everything was normal—but all the soldiers on the street were Ebrio, and the Ebrio elders had been throwing their weight around.

Claire told Assa what they knew, what they suspected was going on. If they could get to Accra they would go to the Swiss and American embassies. Maybe something could be done to stop this. Assa was still a moment, then said she knew a Lagoon fisherman, a cousin with a boat, who might be willing to help. But it couldn't be tonight, and they couldn't leave from here—the port had been declared off limits, and police were conducting random house checks. She would try to set it up for tomorrow night at ten o'clock, in the narrow lagoon behind old Granville, the abandoned city.

There was a silence. Trowbridge heard footsteps pass on the street outside, and said quietly, "What time does the curfew start?"

"Eight-thirty," Assa said.

Trowbridge looked at his watch. It was almost eight-thirty now.

Assa said to Claire, "You're going home? To Switzerland?"

When Claire nodded, Assa said, "Call my little girl. Tell her we're all right."

Claire nodded again; then she and Assa hugged quickly, and Assa went out to be sure the street was clear, and waved them out the door and away from her house.

⊞ ⊟ ⊞

They walked back through the streets to the shantytown, retracing their steps, enduring the stares again. He would have liked to take a different route, but was afraid of getting lost and not finding their gear.

When they walked in beneath the trees, they found they hadn't hidden their things well enough. The rifle was gone, and the packs had been opened; one tarp was missing, and a flashlight, and one of their sleeping bags. The losses were less serious than the fact that someone knew they were here and making an effort to be secret about it—although there was some comfort in the fact that it obviously hadn't been police or soldiers; if so, they wouldn't be standing here by themselves. They picked up the packs, consulted Jeeves, and made their way east through the rubber plantation, emerging an hour later on a narrow beach.

Dark water lapped at the sand; the lagoon before them, maybe two hundred meters across, was mirrored on its far side by a similar beach. Beyond that, the shadowy, irregular outlines of buildings, the old city of Granville.

They stood a while in silence. Claire said, "I don't think we can wade this."

"We could go around. If my map is right, there's a place where the sand connects. But it's five kilometers down the beach, and five back."

"That would take all night. We have to swim."

They found downed branches and driftwood and fashioned a raft for the packs, then stripped and waded into the brackish water. As the bottom slipped away they hung from the makeshift raft, kicking their way forward. He was intensely conscious of the blackness beneath him, and relieved, ten minutes later, when they touched sand, and waded up onto the beach, and stood naked and dripping, holding their clothes and boots. They took the raft apart, scattered the wood, and moved like a pair of newly born creatures into the ruined structures of an old and crumbling place. Cautiously, at first, in case someone might be there—a fisherman, perhaps, or someone else who had his own reasons for staying out of sight—but there was no sound, no light or movement. Just the dark outlines of overgrown gardens and collapsing two-story houses with gaping holes in their walls and roofs. They walked through one such house—climbing over a pile of rubble that had formerly been a wall, moving through a high-ceilinged room—and stepped out through an opening that must once have contained double doors.

Before them, the ocean, a black expanse beneath a cloudy black sky. Occasional shafts of moonlight knifed down through the turmoil of rainy-season clouds, making the waist-high waves into crumbling, ethereal walls. The sound of the waves was clear and crisp, the openness before them, after five days in closed forest, a physical shock. They stood a moment, then walked back into the house of some long-dead wealthy colonialist, feeling their way up a set of stone stairs without a balustrade to the second story.

An enormous hardwood table, too heavy to carry away when the city had been abandoned and stripped, stood beneath a broad window with no glass in it. The roof above them was mostly intact; there was only a single ragged gap in the ceiling at the far end of the room, a pool of water on the floor beneath it.

"We're home," she said. "What do you say we not have sardines for dinner, and go to sleep?"

They spread the remaining sleeping bag on the table for a bed. A bat flitted into the room, then out, then in again, and it began to rain. He could hear the rain's soft touch coming in through the roof onto standing water. Claire's breathing was close by, and he could feel her shoulder touching his. Beyond this, the steady sound of the surf.

4 8

He woke at the first hint of dawn, and went down the stairs and stood looking back across the lagoon. The water was a wavy, steely blue; beyond it, dim lines of rubber trees stretched away into night. He looked to the east, where clouds lay on the horizon like a jagged black mountain range. Above the horizon was another mass of clouds; in the band of open sky between, Venus hung like a tiny lamp. He was about to turn and go back when he saw movement, something animal, not human, a low familiar shape, more than he could believe. He was sure he'd seen his last leopard in this country, and yet here was *Panthera pardus*, slipping out from the trees, stopping a moment, going motionless—a dark icon against the sand—then moving out onto the open beach with steady, fastidious steps. The leopard stopped and began digging for something, probably turtle eggs. It seemed confident in what it was doing, and took no notice of him, and he watched it until the sky began to grow light and the leopard turned and slipped back into the trees the way it had come.

⚏ ䷜ ⚏

An airplane went by in the early afternoon, but it was small, and high up, and didn't make a second pass.

Trowbridge found a rusty fishhook lodged in a piece of driftwood, and a length of tangled line; baiting the hook with a small sea crab, he took it over to the lagoon, and pulled out an ugly but more than edible *tilapia*. They made a fire on the floor of their second-story room. The rain came down steadily while they cooked the fish on the grill of an abandoned Land Rover. They sat beneath the window to eat, leaning against the wall.

"Some butter would be nice," Claire said.

"Butter, lemon, capers, sliced tomato, some decent bread, a glass of white wine—"

"Stop. We'll get some real food in Accra. I know a good Chinese restaurant there. We can eat and drink ourselves unconscious." She hesitated, then said, "It's going to be strange saying goodbye to you. I feel like we're partners, somehow."

Her khaki pants were rolled up above her knees. He reached out with his left forearm and brushed it against her calf, his leopard scars touching hers. She looked down, not getting it at first. Then she smiled a little doubtfully, as if she weren't sure what he meant by this.

"Couple of veterans," she said.

"We have the rest of today, and then a boat ride, and a hotel in Accra, and that Chinese restaurant."

"You make it sound like a package tour."

"I hope it goes that smoothly."

⸸ ⸸ ⸸

When the rain stopped he climbed to the roof of a three-story building and aimed his binoculars toward Granville. He could see the stone lighthouse, and the breakwater enclosing the port like a crooked arm. A freighter was tied up beside a row of cranes. Individual dark shapes—what looked like some kind of small vehicle—were being hoisted from freighter to dock, where they stood in lines beside a row of covered pallets.

Four-wheel-drive trucks, and weapons to go with them.

Here's to the rainy season, he thought, finally deciphering what Komo had said.

A single paved road, the coast highway, connected Granville to the rest of the country. North of Granville, the park formed an enormous natural barrier, and the *piste* which ran up around the park—like every other dirt road in Terre Diamantée—was currently a river of mud, and would stay that way for the next two months. If the Justice Minister's men could hold the coast highway—and in the rain, with four-wheel-drive vehicles and some rocket launchers and machine guns, that shouldn't be too difficult—it would be impossible for the Diamantien army to mount an effective counterattack. At least until the rain stopped, which would give the Justice Minister time to consolidate a defensive perimeter.

He walked back to the mansion, wondering if they would reach Accra in time to make a difference, wishing he'd known all this when he talked to the embassy.

Claire was lying on her side on the table. Her eyes were closed. A smell of smoke from dinner was mingled with a salty ocean breeze; rainy light came in the window. He was sleepy and not sleepy at the same time, and climbed up onto the table, and lay beside her. She opened her eyes, then closed them, and he lay facing her, listening to her breathing. He didn't think she was asleep, and sensed she was conscious of him even though they weren't touching. He felt oddly breathless. They lay like that a while; then he heard her breathing change, and she made a moaning noise, and opened her eyes, and said, "Lord, are we going to do this?" and put her arms around him, pulling him close like they were long separated lovers, pulling his shirt up out of his pants.

When it was over they were both breathing hard and there was a sheen of sweat on their skin. Outside it was raining again. It seemed to him the sound of the surf had gotten louder. He felt happier and more at peace than he had in a long time. Claire, unexpectedly, started laughing, a sound that was low and contented. She propped herself on an elbow, kissed his temple, and said, "That happened pretty fast. I must have been waiting for it longer than I knew. You're not going to sleep on me, are you?"

"No."

"I always wanted a big house on the beach, and a handsome biologist boyfriend installed on the second floor. Someone I could talk to afterward."

"You've got everything but handsome."

"You're handsome," she said. "Don't kid yourself."

They were silent a minute. Then he said, "What are we going to do?"

"I don't know," she said honestly. "We're likely to be living on different continents."

There was nothing to say to that. She laid her head on his chest, then raised it, and kissed his neck, and said, "Not going to sleep?"

"Definitely not going to sleep."
"You're a trouper," she said.

⠿ ⠿ ⠿

When he woke it was dark. His left arm was asleep beneath her, painful in the places he could feel it. A heavy sound of surf came in the window, and he felt a stab of worry. The boat had to find its way through a narrow channel into the lagoon, then back out again once they were aboard. Would that channel be navigable in high surf?

Claire woke, and they slid down off the table-bed and walked down to the beach. The waves, big dim shapes coming in through the darkness, were much larger than before. A storm somewhere in the South Atlantic. The wind blew mist toward them as they stood beneath a row of thatch-headed palms. He heard a faint sound, something above and behind the waves as they crashed and rolled toward them. The sound disappeared, then floated in again, rising and falling with a logic that was almost musical. As if the ocean were singing at the shore.

He realized it *was* singing, distant and faint. Human voices, drifting out of the darkness, in through the surf line.

"Ghanaian fishermen," she said. "They sing when they set their nets."

He strained to make them out, but all he could see was darkness and mist and the vague shapes of waves.

49

He put her passport, the money they had between them, and the GPS into the smaller of the two waterproof stuff sacks, then added his Swiss Army knife and a waterproof flashlight. Into the larger sack he put the night scope, the remaining sleeping bag, the last of their food, and that was it. The backpacks would stay; they were pretty beat up, and wouldn't be much use any more.

He looked at his watch—a full hour, yet, before the boat was supposed to come in—and went to the window.

It was raining hard. Beneath the heavy cloud cover there was neither moonlight nor starlight. Just a lot of darkness and noisy ocean out there. The Atlantic, which had seemed a relatively calm body of water during the day, had become a wilder place.

"Maybe we should go down to the lagoon," she said. "In case the boat gets here early."

He nodded and picked up his poncho, and then he heard something that was neither singing nor the sound of surf. He lost it, and concentrated, trying to separate it from the sound of crashing waves and the wind.

There it was again.

"David," she said urgently.

The noise was unmistakable. A high whine, the sound of an engine, coming from the far side of the lagoon. He started down the stairs at a run, then came back and scooped up the stuff sacks, and they went down together.

███ ██ ███

"Wait for me," he said, leaving her in the darkness of the ground floor. He went out through the back of the mansion, into the garden, and stood in a gap in the crumbling wall. The engine sound was louder. On the far side of the lagoon were two sets of yellow headlights, coming along the beach from the direction of Granville, moving fast. When the trucks were directly across the lagoon they slowed; a searchlight came on, and began playing across the buildings around him.

He crouched behind the wall, blinking at the light. The trucks were idling; he could hear voices across the water. The engines revved, and he stood cautiously and watched two sets of red taillights tearing away through the darkness.

Five kilometers along the lagoon, five kilometers back along the beach. The trucks could do sixty kilometers an hour on sand, maybe a little more. He looked at his watch. They had about ten minutes.

He was breathing hard when he rejoined Claire, more from fear than exertion.

"Two pickups, going around the lagoon. We don't have a lot of time."

"You think they're coming for us?"

"They have to be. And I don't see any sign of the boat."

"I don't think it's coming in."

She pointed out into the darkness. Beyond the surf line, he saw a faint pulse of illumination. Someone was waving a light out there.

"The surf's probably too high for them to get in through the channel," he said.

"We could swim for it. Signal the boat with the flashlight once we're beyond the surf line."

He hesitated. "I'm not much of a swimmer. Not in this kind of surf, anyway."

"I'll help you. I used to swim in waves much bigger than this."

Almost two minutes had passed. He hated this idea, but didn't see an alternative.

"Okay," he said, and they ran down the beach, then crushed down through a steep ledge of caved-away sand, wading out until the cool water came to their knees. There had to be reefs out there, or sandbars, to make the waves break so far from shore. Claire took the smaller stuff sack and tied it around her waist. She was the better swimmer; it made sense. He flung the other sack into the water and watched it disappear beneath the foam, feeling unhappy. No fetish bag, and now no night scope; just Claire, and a lot of dark water.

"The waves come in sets," she said evenly. "Usually three or four. Once in a while you get five or six. But eventually there will be a break. The trick is to be as far away from the beach as possible when that break comes—and then to go like hell, make it out beyond the surf line before the next set. If we don't make it the first time, it's all right. We get knocked around a bit, and pushed back a bit, and we try again."

"Okay."

"See that white water? There are no big waves behind it. That's the end of a set."

He saw the white water. He didn't like the looks of it at all. He said, "How much time between sets?"

"Four or five minutes. Sometimes a little more. If it goes much longer, though, there will be a couple of smaller waves in the gap."

"How do you know all this?"

"I spent a lot of time in California, remember?"

He looked at his watch. Six minutes since the trucks had accelerated away from the far side of the lagoon. Claire was already wading out ahead of him. As he followed her out, he was shocked at the heavy insidious pull of the water, even here, waist deep.

After a while a heavy booming came from the darkness in front of them.

"First wave," she said.

::: 8: :::

The wall of white water became visible, rolling toward them like a slow avalanche, reaching them in waist-deep water. He was knocked down, but stood determinedly and pushed his way forward, parting the water with his hands, half swimming and half running to catch up. Somehow Claire had kept her feet. They were maybe fifty meters from the beach now. There was a new booming, and a second wall of white water came toward them, high enough that he couldn't see anything over it. Just rainy, unspecific darkness. He heard a crack, and a more distant wall of white water rose behind the one that was drawing near.

Claire said urgently, "Go *under* the white water this time. It's too rough to fight directly. And blow air out your nose. Slow and steady, so you don't use it up all at once. We're lucky. I don't think there are any rocks here."

He hadn't even considered rocks. He was having trouble keeping his feet in the current, and the biggest wall of white water he'd ever seen was maybe ten meters away, coming fast. He didn't feel lucky at all.

"Ready?" she said. "Dive when I dive. Remember to blow air out your nose."

The white water was almost on them. Claire made a little forward arc and disappeared. He took a deep breath and followed, swimming down and forward. Too much down, not enough forward; his face scraped on sand, and there was salt water in his nose, and he was choking. The world exploded and began whirling him in mad circles. He blew air out his nose in a frantic burst, clearing it, and then there was nothing left, either to blow or to breathe. His lungs were empty and he was on the verge of panic when his head popped out of the water. He took a deep, shuddering breath, and found his feet.

Currents swirled heavily around him, as if he were in a tank filled with heavy fish. Claire was farther out. How had she managed that?

"You okay?" she called out.

"Okay," he called back, and began wading toward her. It was hard to move through water this deep. A hollow crack came from the darkness ahead of them, another wave breaking.

"Swim," she said urgently. "It's faster when the water's this deep."

He swam. Put his head down and churned forward as best he could, his barely healed collarbone aching. He felt her grab his arm, and he lifted his head, spitting and gasping, finding his feet on the sandy bottom.

Chest deep now.

"All right?"

"Yes."

"The wave that just broke was probably the last of the set. You're doing great. When the white water hits this time, dive sooner, and swim along the bottom—you'll cover more ground that way. And keep breathing. When you come up we're going to have to sprint for it."

He saw her look behind him, and followed her gaze. Yellow headlights were coming along the beach, maybe a kilometer away. A spotlight was playing across the ruined structures of the town.

"Not our problem," she said forcefully. "Our problem is to get out beyond the surf line."

The next wall of white water—hopefully the last—was coming at them.

"Now," she said.

This time was better. He blew air out his nose steadily, and swam and crawled his way along the sandy bottom until the water picked him up and spun him. He rolled into a loose ball until the force lessened. Then he opened his body, and his feet touched bottom, and he pushed off. He was learning.

Claire, once again, was farther out. She appeared to be treading water, not standing.

"That's the end of the set. *Swim*, David. Swim hard now."

He swam, wishing to God he hadn't ditched swimming lessons in high school. His stroke, he could tell, was inefficient, and the shoulder injured by *L6* was still weak; it seemed like he was beating at the water instead of dividing and pushing through it. The main thing was to keep going. It would be all right if he kept going.

Something touched his shoulder and he jerked his head up.

"Watch your direction—you're swimming almost sideways."

"Okay," he said, breathing hard, realizing she'd come a good distance back for him. "But *go*. You've got the flashlight to take care of— and you can't help me any more. I'll catch you."

She went, towing the bag, and he followed, looking up every few strokes to correct his course. He'd assumed the water between the sets of big waves would be flat, but it wasn't; it was bumpy, and roiling, filled with swirling currents and thick foam. He swallowed water unexpectedly, and stopped, spitting and coughing, and looked back.

Two spotlights now, one of them playing across the water. He could hear engines.

"David," she called out. "There's another set coming. Swim hard now. Give it everything."

He heard in her voice that she was afraid he wouldn't make it. He swam hard for what seemed like a long time. It seemed like he was doing all right, but when he put his head up for air, feeling hopeful, the dark horizon was lifting steeply in front of him.

⠿ ⠃ ⠿

He had a close-up view of the wave as it pitched down toward him from a high place in the darkness. Its heavy lip hung a moment— unimaginably heavy in midair, forming a fat barrel as it fell—then landed with a cannonlike crack a body's length in front of him. He took a desperate breath, went for the bottom, and felt a giant hand pluck him up, then fling him down. He hit the bottom hard and lost most of his air; then he was up again, whirling and tumbling with a violence that made the previous waves seem easy. It was difficult even to pull himself into a ball. The violent swirl seemed endless, and he had no idea where the surface was, and felt overcome by the need for oxygen. His lungs were screaming, and he kicked out desperately. Nothing but more whirling water. His forehead ground unexpectedly into sand, snapping his head back; something in his neck began to burn, and he felt himself about to go limp, to give up and breathe water simply because he had to breathe something. The whirl grew calmer, suddenly, and he felt himself rising, and then his face broke the surface. He opened his mouth, managing a convulsive gasp before he was pulled down again, but he had air now, and a direction. He kicked furiously, and his face broke the surface again, and he breathed deeply before the water took him down one last time. His feet touched bottom, and he pushed off, and when he came up it was over. He took deep, shuddering breaths, treading water a moment before he realized he could stand.

The water was only chest deep, which meant he'd been pushed a long way toward the beach. Something threw light against him, and he saw the shadow of his upper body flung out across the dark water and the wind-strewn foam.

The spotlight slipped off him, then came back and stayed. He began thrashing his way back out, wondering when they would begin shooting.

The devil and the deep blue sea. Another big wave was breaking out there—but he had to get away from the beach. An engine gunned behind him, and grew louder. They must have driven one of the trucks right down to the edge of the water.

Your problem is to get beyond the surf line. Concentrate on that. Don't look back; it can't help.

He dove under a mass of white water, fighting it hard, scrabbling forward through it, but he was tired now and could feel it pulling him toward the beach. When he came up for air the sound of the motor was louder. He heard one of the trucks rev hard, and heard a heavy splashing, and was just turning around to see what it was when something smacked him from behind, and a new darkness settled over the darkness he knew, and he felt himself slipping down into water.

5 0

He lay on a pile of burlap bags in the back of a covered pickup. He couldn't see much, but he could hear rain drumming on the canvas cover, and feel the truck slewing in the mud. His hands were cuffed behind him, and his ankles were weighed down by a set of heavy manacles.

He wondered again why they hadn't simply shot him on the beach.

The damp burlap was rough against his face and smelled of green coffee beans. There was something sticky on his neck, and an intense, disconnected pain in his right shoulder. Drawing his knees up carefully, he rolled onto his back. Feeling returned slowly to his shoulder in a painful, tingling cascade. The pickup swerved abruptly, then bounced over a deep pothole; pain drilled deeply into his head.

A pair of fatigue-clad soldiers sat on low benches on either side of the truck bed. They didn't look at him, and in the near darkness he couldn't see their faces. When he asked for a drink of water, one of them glanced at him briefly, as if he were an animal who'd made an unexpected noise, then looked away. A while later one of the soldiers reached out and raised the canvas flap on the back of the truck. The darkness outside was a deluge; little was distinguishable by the red taillights but rain and the dim shapes of trees. Then he heard the sound of other engines. A moment later they pulled out and passed a convoy of similar trucks, with the difference that the beds of these trucks were open, not covered, and in those beds, wrapped in plastic shrouds, were shapes that were unmistakably military. The covers had blown off a couple; one was some kind of heavy machine gun, and another was simpler, just a tube on a stand, a grenade launcher.

Mud splattered in, and the soldier pulled the flap down with a quiet curse.

He lay back and closed his eyes. Foote's timber machinery. It might have been funny, under other circumstances. The pickups, with their grenade launchers and machine guns mounted in the beds—long beds, he remembered Najla specifying—looked deadly serious. But they also had roll bars and fog lights and racing stripes, and their steering wheels were on the wrong side. The Justice Minister's odd little rainy season war would be waged with leftover Warsaw Pact weapons, purchased in Bulgaria and mounted on Japanese sport utility vehicles intended originally for off-road enthusiasts in Cyprus.

The sound of other engines faded.

A while later he roused himself with a start. Faint light was coming in—dawn, or at least the watery and indistinct version of dawn which occurred during the rainy season. He noticed that the bouncing and lurching had grown worse; it hurt his shoulder more, and his head. They must have turned off the north-south *piste* onto a smaller track. They crossed a small bridge, and then another. When they crossed a third, and he heard a familiar xylophone sound of tires on timbers, recognition edged into his brain. They were going to the station.

⠿ ⠻ ⠿

"This is the first time," someone said, "that I've been sorry to see you walk in the door of my dwelling."

It was gloomy inside Jean Luc's hut. He'd had only a brief view of the station before being dragged in through the outer room and flung onto a cot in the study, but it appeared to have been transformed into a kind of command post. A lot of people were moving about, some in camouflage fatigues who must have been Diamantien military, others who looked like irregulars from Denkyara, still others in gendarme uniforms. Nearly all were Ebrio.

It took a minute for his eyes to adjust, to be sure it was Alberto sitting on the other cot. Alberto's hands were held together before him in a way which suggested handcuffs. He was wearing only underpants and a thin T-shirt. His face was puffy, one eye swollen almost shut.

Trowbridge said, "Are you all right?"

"I was better until I saw you. I assumed you'd escaped."

"Claire did. I'm pretty sure she did, anyway."

"Ah," Alberto said, and took a deep, audible breath. "That's good, isn't it?"

"I'm sorry you got dragged into this."

Alberto shrugged almost imperceptibly. "I had every chance to avoid doing so. When you didn't show up I called your embassy and told them you were missing somewhere in the forest. The consul suggested I go to my own embassy immediately. I could have done that, or I could have flown to Accra. Instead, I had lunch, chatted with Therese for a few minutes, and went back to the mill. They came and got me about an hour later."

"The embassy's phones were tapped."

Alberto nodded. "I've had several days to consider that fact."

Raising his cuffed hands to his face, Alberto touched his cheek beneath one eye. "There's something sharp here," he observed. "I think they broke my cheekbone."

Trowbridge could hear orders being shouted outside. They sounded like orders, anyway; more Ebrio was being spoken than French.

Alberto said, "I think we have a full-fledged war going."

"Why here, and not Granville?"

"Presumably he's worried about an attack by sea, or an air strike. The Diamantien air force isn't much, but it could probably drop bombs on a headquarters building out in the open. I haven't been able to figure out what he hopes to *achieve* by all this, though. He can't possibly attack the capital in this weather."

"I don't think he plans to attack anything," Trowbridge said, and told Alberto what he and Claire believed to be going on.

Alberto listened carefully, then nodded with an unhappy face. "I suppose that makes us the first official guests of the new president of a new country. I have to say the guest residence leaves something to be desired."

Alberto was trying hard to be brave, and not entirely succeeding. Trowbridge saw that his bare feet were unadorned by manacles. He gestured at the manacles weighing down his own feet, and said, "They must think you're more trustworthy than me."

Albert tipped his hands toward his right foot, which Trowbridge now saw looked swollen.

"An old man with his hands tied might try to run, but an old man with his hands tied and a broken foot isn't going anywhere. I think the two of us are here for the duration."

⸻ ⸻ ⸻

A soldier brought them a plate of rice and a bucket of water. Trowbridge's hands were still cuffed behind his back, so Alberto limped over to his cot, and fed him and helped him drink. The food and water made him feel better, and for a while he felt a degree of optimism about their situation. The possibility of rescue seemed remote, but they were alive, and their physical condition could have been worse. He had a filthy headache which made it hard to concentrate, but that would go away; Alberto's injuries were serious, but not life-threatening; and Alberto's phone call, however much trouble it had gotten him into, was probably now helping to keep the two of them alive. If the Justice Minister was successful in carving out his new country, one of his first diplomatic challenges would be fielding inquiries from the Americans and Italians as to his and Alberto's whereabouts. If he could produce the two of them with a humanitarian flourish—claiming he'd been protecting them during the hostilities—it would help his cause a good deal more than producing a pair of bodies, or claiming, implausibly, that he had no idea where they might be.

Then he considered the converse of this argument, and felt some of his optimism ebb. If the Justice Minister failed in his bid to create a new country, he and Alberto would be significantly less useful. Which led him to the unpleasant conclusion that they had a personal stake in the Justice Minister's success—a personal stake in the success of Foote, and Moneyboy, and the *Chef des Gendarmes*, in the blood that was being shed and the probable destruction of the park.

Rainy light streamed into the outer room, what had once been the sleeping quarters for Jean Luc and Pascale and the children, but it was gloomy here in the study, where the single shuttered window was closed. He was tired of having his hands behind his back. He thought about his leopards, what would happen to them if the Justice Minister won his war, and then he slept.

51

He was roused by a painful tug on his hands and ankles and the whack of a machete blade against the cot beside his face. Someone took him by the hair and hauled him to a sitting position. The pain in his head and neck was extreme; he gritted his teeth to avoid crying out, and looked up, feeling a pure, exhausted rage, a lust to hurt someone back, whoever it was.

A soldier looked down at him, expressionless in the gloom. Kneeling, he inserted a rusty key into the manacles, then stood and jerked his head toward the door. Trowbridge stepped out of the manacles and glanced at Alberto. Some tattered darkness flickered at the edges of his comprehension as the soldier moved in behind him, lifting his cuffed wrists in a quick movement; pain shot through his shoulders, and he was propelled through the outer room of the hut, out the door and into the rain and up beneath the *paillote*.

There were a lot of people there, mostly soldiers of one type or another, none paying him much attention. One was talking on a short-wave radio; others were looking at maps. Someone dressed in forest clothes instead of fatigues was sitting on the couch, staring at him with a peculiar expression. Trowbridge tried to place him, and failed. Moneyboy appeared from one side of the *paillote*, walking stiffly in a way Trowbridge remembered from when his sister had been thrown from a horse and broken her collarbone.

At the center of all this activity, dressed in fatigues that looked cleaner and neater than those around him, sitting at a table where Trowbridge had shared meals with Guy and Jean Luc and Pascale, was the Justice Minister. The fatigues, and the pistol lying on the table before him, didn't entirely erase the impression of a man who would be more comfortable in the capital.

The Justice Minister looked up.

"Well," he said, "it's the leopard man. I thought we'd lost you. You seem to have picked up some of the qualities of the animal you study—you're very good at slipping away and disappearing."

"Not good enough," Trowbridge said.

"You know what I'm doing?"

"I think so."

"As soon as the rain stops and we've stabilized the borders," the Justice Minister said, gesturing at the forest, "these trees will start coming down. When I see *Le Vieux* one of these days I'll have to thank him for keeping so much timber for me until I needed it to fund my start-up operations."

Trowbridge said nothing.

"It's my observation," the Justice Minister went on calmly, "that two types of Westerners come to Africa. The colonialists, who make no bones about the fact they want to lord it over the natives, and the sensitive types like yourself, who want us to appreciate them, and who want us to turn out, in the end, to be like them. The second category is easier to delude. Your friend Juvigny was in the first."

"Is that why you had him killed?"

The Justice Minister raised his eyebrows slightly. "That's a breathtaking accusation."

Trowbridge felt naked, suddenly, without his fetish bag.

The Justice Minister said, "Your other friend, the one who got away, has apparently been talking in Accra. The Diamantien navy launched an attack this morning on my troops in Granville. Rather ineffectual, but I didn't expect an attack for a couple of days, and would have preferred to use those troops someplace else."

Moneyboy, he saw, had sat down on the couch beside the man in forest clothes.

The Justice Minister's gaze was steady. "You've proven to be very adept at causing trouble."

"I don't think I'm in a position to cause much more trouble," Trowbridge said, which was true.

The Justice Minister ignored him, and looked at Moneyboy. "You've let him get away twice now. Surely there must be a way to prevent it from happening again."

Moneyboy nodded, and in that moment Trowbridge recognized the man sitting on the couch. It was the poacher from the forest, the one who'd been standing with a shotgun watching as he drove off in Foote's truck.

The Justice Minister stood, picked up the pistol from the table and put it in a holster, and gathered some of the papers before him.

"I've done everything possible," he said briskly, "under difficult circumstances, to ensure your safety. If some kind of accident takes place, it won't have happened when I was there to see it, which will make things easier to explain to your embassy."

The Justice Minister nodded at one of his assistants, stepped down from the *paillote*, and walked through the rain to a pickup truck. The assistant followed, climbed in the driver's side, and drove them away. It grew very quiet beneath the *paillote*. Trowbridge considered his situation, then tried to break and run. Several pairs of arms grabbed him, and someone hit him in the face with a rifle butt. They held him down, tying his arms tightly against his body so he couldn't struggle, then lifted him off the edge of the *paillote* and laid him on his back, propping up his legs on the edge of the concrete slab. As if he were lying on his back in the street, heels on a high curb. It took a number of them to hold him down, and he heard himself begging them not to do it. Moneyboy was standing over him. He asked Moneyboy at least to turn him over, so he wouldn't see it happen. Moneyboy seemed amused at this; they turned him over so his face was in the mud. From the corner of his eye he saw the poacher step up onto the concrete slab beneath the *paillote*, and put a hand on one of the support posts, and balance a second, looking downward, before he jumped out and away, pushing off from the post, kicking downward as he dropped.

Now one of his legs was broken, lying on the ground at an angle that shouldn't be possible. Moneyboy was leaning down to tell him that if he begged, they wouldn't do the other one, and he was sobbing, begging them not to, when the poacher came up on his blind side and did the other leg.

52

The next two days were a hallucinogenic blur. The pain was unrelenting, even when he slept. He dreamed he was in a narrow boat, wandering the dim corridors of a hospital as if they were waterways. Another dream started in the mountains, him watching a herd of blue sheep, their coats shining in the thin sunlight, their breath quick cones of steam. When the herd spooked and began streaming down the mountainside in great wild leaps he wanted to follow, but couldn't, because his legs were quiet fire, shapes of embers and ash that flickered with pain.

He was conscious that Alberto talked to him, sometimes, when he wasn't sleeping; on the third morning the voice began to seem less distant, and he felt some of the delirium going away. Alberto had arranged blankets under his legs to keep them elevated, and covered them with a light sheet because it was better not to look at them; the sheet was also useful in that it kept the flies off the places where bone splinters had come through skin. As his faculties came back, he wondered dimly why he didn't simply die. His legs beneath the sheet were a broken rack of flesh and snapped bone and torn nerve endings. With so much pain, and so little prospect of an improvement, it seemed the physical organism ought simply to shut down; he wondered why it didn't work that way.

Alberto kept talking to him, and he didn't die, and eventually he began to take some minimal level of interest in what was going on around him.

The war, apparently, was going well, at least on the Denkyara side of the border. The guard who brought them food and water twice a day had been telling Alberto the news.

"Apparently the Denkyarans haven't even organized a credible counterattack," Alberto said. "The Justice Minister's people will probably keep pushing east until they reach the limits of Ebrio country. Then things will peter out in a spate of village massacres, and something like a border will come into being."

Trowbridge nodded, eyes closed.

"It isn't going quite as well here in Terre Diamantée. They've been holding the Diamantien army, with the help of the rain. But have you noticed? The rain has stopped."

He hadn't noticed, but he did now. There were sounds of people talking, orders being shouted. Occasionally a truck driving in, or out. But no sound of rain.

He opened his eyes. "When?"

"This morning at dawn. And no, it isn't normal—not in my twenty-five years here. Normally during the season the rain never stops for more than an hour or two. Never for six hours straight."

He drew a deep breath, trying to hold on against the pain. It came in a complicated, steady attack from different places in both legs, and it changed all the time—no doubt there were various interesting processes of swelling and infection and tissue breakdown taking place—and there was no controlling it. You couldn't focus on it and make it go away; there was simply too much. All you could do was distract yourself.

"Alberto, how old is your daughter?"

"Thirty-two."

"Claire has a little girl, did you know that? She left her with her mother in Switzerland to come here."

"Are you serious?"

"Yes."

"God in heaven," Alberto said, looking calmer. "It's even more wonderful, then, that she got away."

⸭ ⸭ ⸭

The rain started up that afternoon in fitful bursts that spattered the hut roof, then tapered off again. Trowbridge could tell by the quality of light outside the door that the sky was cloudy, but no rain touched the hut, or the trees around them. Alberto was sleeping. He thought about Komo, and the fact that the Justice Minister had been sleeping with her. Was he infected? If so, did he know? Had that been one of his reasons for attempting this, instead of simply waiting to inherit Terre Diamantée?

A while later the light was gone, and still there was no rain.

Morning saw a steady increase in the amount of activity in the clearing. It hadn't rained since the brief showers yesterday afternoon. Voices carried through the walls of the hut in urgent tones, and there were repeated bursts of static from the shortwave radio, which seemed to be in constant use. The guard who'd been telling them about the war refused to do so any more, and looked unhappy. It rained some during the course of the day, but not much. In the late afternoon there was yelling, and then shots fired. High, individual spitting sounds, the sound of a handgun. The Justice Minister came into the hut in a rage, carrying a pistol which he put to Trowbridge's head. There was a hot smell from the barrel of the gun, and a smell of palm wine, and an acrid smell of sweat, the smell of fear.

The Justice Minister wasn't drunk, but he'd been drinking, which Trowbridge found astonishing.

"You're a scientist," the Justice Minister said, "why isn't it raining—it has to rain!"

Trowbridge looked at him and said nothing. The Justice Minister was sweating heavily. He turned away, then turned back and pointed the pistol at him again.

"It has to rain," he repeated, and walked out of the hut.

Trowbridge waited a few moments, then said quietly, "Alberto, how long would it take the roads to dry out? Assuming the rain holds off."

"Two days. Maybe three, as wet as they were, before the army could drive their trucks on them."

"Is there anyone in the outer room?"

"Not right now."

"Can they see you from outside the hut if you're standing at the desk?"

"I don't think so."

"There's a machete beneath the desk—I'm pretty sure there is, anyway. Jammed up between the middle drawer and the backing."

Alberto considered this a moment. Then he stood, an old man with spindly legs and one broken foot and his hands held together by a plastic thong, and limped to the desk. Looking over his shoulder, he squinted against the light which came in through the door. Then he knelt and put his joined hands up beneath the desk drawer.

"You're right," he said. "There is a machete here."

He worked at it a minute, loosening it, then pulled it out in a smooth motion which made Trowbridge think of the King Arthur story. He would have laughed if he weren't afraid it would lower his defenses against the pain and leave him crying. Alberto, holding the machete against his leg, limped back to his own cot and slipped it beneath the blanket.

He was sitting now, looking at Trowbridge.

"I suppose if they find this," Alberto said, "we could get into more trouble."

"I'm not sure how much more trouble we can get into."

"It's a point. What now?"

"I don't know," he said. "Probably nothing."

There was a fair amount of firing that night, people shooting off their weapons, presumably into the sky. Either they were drunk and releasing tension, or they were frustrated by the heavy clouds which hung so low and promisingly in the sky, but refused to release the rain within them. No one brought them food or water.

Sometime before dawn it rained for a few minutes. The sound woke him, but as he came to consciousness, listening, it stopped again, and there was only the sound of fat drops plopping off the trees, something familiar that took him back to better days at the inselberg. By first light even that had stopped.

He was wakened again an hour later by the popping of semiautomatic weapons. Someone shooting off their rifles again, for the hell of it. Then he heard what sounded like a helicopter, a long way up. Instinctively, he pushed himself to a sitting position, a movement which caused a pulling on his wrecked legs. He held still a moment, letting the pain peak and subside, then said, "Alberto, are you awake?"

Alberto was awake. They talked quietly, making a plan, then sat in silence. While they waited, the rain began. Tentatively, at first, then more solidly, filling in like a waterfall. They heard yells of exultation from outside, and more shooting. The rain didn't stop, and the shooting died down. The sound of the helicopter died away; the rain came down in a steady torrent.

"Well," Alberto said finally, "that would be normal, of course. It was surprising the rain stopped for as long as it did."

There seemed to be a lot of shooting, suddenly, from different directions, and yelling in the distance, yelling which was not exultant, but urgent and confused. They heard truck engines gunned, and a sudden upsurge in the number of rifles being fired, and then they heard the helicopter coming back. Its heavy thudding sound was closer, a steady ratchet against the rain, something they could feel in their bones.

"Alberto," he said, but Alberto was already reaching beneath the blanket.

⠿ ⠿ ⠿

Alberto heard it, where Trowbridge didn't, an order snapped out among the other orders: *"Tuez-les."*

The soldier who came in to kill them was wet from the rain, and looked both angry and scared, as if he wanted to get this over with and go back outside as quickly as possible, either so he could participate in what sounded like an increasingly serious battle, or run away. He stood between the two cots, hesitated, then looked at Alberto and raised the rifle, waiting a moment to let his eyes adjust to the gloom. There hadn't been time for Alberto to saw through his plastic handcuffs, something that had been part of their plan. Alberto stared back at the soldier with shocked eyes. His joined hands were resting on the blanket to one side of his naked thigh. Trowbridge could see the flat profile of the machete beneath the cloth; the soldier could not, but it wouldn't make any difference once he fired.

"Smallboy," he said urgently. "Listen, you bastard, kill me first. I don't want to watch my friend die."

The soldier looked over his shoulder. Trowbridge spat at him, and he turned, raising his rifle. Behind him Alberto pulled the machete from beneath the blanket.

It was relatively difficult to hurt someone seriously, swinging a machete with a dull blade, standing on a broken foot, and having one's hands held together. For all that, Alberto did a credible job. The machete took the soldier across the side of the head at the level of his ear, hooking around across one eye. The rifle went off, but the soldier was already going down and the bullet went into the hut wall. The soldier was on his knees, one hand to his head; he cried out for help, but it wasn't a sound which would carry above the noise outside. The rifle was still in his left hand. Alberto had fallen as he finished his awkward swing, and was lying on the hut floor near the soldier. As he tried to crawl away, the soldier twisted to his left, holding the rifle one-handed, and fired blindly, two shots. Now Alberto was hunched over. The soldier had dropped the rifle, and was making a noise that was something between a wail and a growl. He had both hands to his face; he'd lost most of one ear, and probably an eye; there was blood pouring through his hands. He staggered to his feet and stumbled blindly into the outer room of the hut.

I have to shoot him, Trowbridge thought. If he goes out the door of the hut it will be obvious what's happened and someone else will come in. He pulled himself sideways and down off the cot, dragging his legs with him—nearly losing consciousness when his legs flopped onto the floor—and picked up the rifle. He raised it and pointed it at the staggering soldier, but was unable to pull the trigger. His heart was thudding and his hands shook, and he knew this was necessary, and yet somehow he was incapable.

Someone appeared in the doorway beyond the soldier. A rifle came up; there was a quick stitch of firing, and the soldier went down and lay still. The figure in the doorway, backlit and unrecognizable, remained motionless a moment, then came in fast, moving at a crouch through the outer room. Trowbridge recognized something familiar in the movement. Saw the man stop, eyes adjusting, and make out Trowbridge's shape on the floor, and raise the rifle. This time he was able to pull the trigger without difficulty, and he did so three times, once for each stripe of scarification, once each for Jean Luc and Guy and Gregoire, pointing the rifle muzzle at the dark shape until it stuttered oddly and went down.

He dropped the rifle, feeling nothing but a stinging in his hands.

"Alberto," he said, but Alberto was absorbed in a private drama of his own. His arms were wrapped over his stomach, and he was rocking slightly. Trowbridge had a roaring in his ears that blocked out everything except a voice which said you don't survive a stomach wound unless it happens in a hospital. There was blood coming out around Alberto's left hand, and he was breathing fast, making a whistling noise. Bullets were zipping through the walls of the hut. Trowbridge pulled himself around and propped himself against the desk. A huge amount of firing and yelling was taking place around the hut, and the helicopter sound was louder. If someone came into the hut now he wouldn't know if it was one of the Justice Minister's men or someone coming to help them. He could see people running past the outer doorway, moving through the clearing past the *paillote*. The shooting seemed to be further away now, muffled by trees. A big wind blew up suddenly, and the hut seemed to shake, and a blast of wet leaves skidded past the doorway. Someone appeared, a dark shape looking in cautiously, and he raised the rifle. Then suddenly behind him and to one side the shutter window was jerked open, and light flooded in, and he saw the shapes of rifle barrels poking in at him, and then he heard Douli ba's voice, calmly saying, "David, put that fucking gun down before someone shoots you."

5 3

When he woke it was raining outside, and the sky, what he could see of it through the two windows, was filled with charcoal clouds and an occasional patch of blue. He was alone, lying in a hospital bed on clean sheets.

He lifted his head and looked toward the foot of the bed. His legs were suspended above the bedclothes, wrapped in plaster and gauze. There was a dull pain below his thighs. When he tried to tighten his leg muscles nothing happened, and he let his head collapse back on the pillow, feeling utter despair. Then he noticed an odd familiar pressure at his throat. Bringing a hand up, he touched his fetish bag.

He tried to make sense of this, failed, and fell asleep. When he woke again a nurse was standing beside the bed. She was African, which answered the question of where he was. He wondered how long he'd been sedated; his mouth was uncomfortably dry.

He noticed the nurse had gone away.

There was a quiet knock at the door, and someone came in.

"You've had a good sleep," Douli ba said.

Trowbridge had some trouble finding his voice.

"Where's Alberto?"

"Still in intensive care. One kidney's gone, but he's going to be all right."

Trowbridge touched the *juju* bag at his throat. "Are you responsible for this?"

Douli ba nodded. "We found it in the pocket of the Justice Minister."

"Where is he?"

"With his ancestors, if they'll have him. He died with a pistol in his hand and a single bullet in his head."

Douli ba glanced at Trowbridge's legs. "The surgeon who worked on you guessed you must have been lying on your stomach when they did this."

Trowbridge nodded.

"He said it would have been worse if you'd been lying on your back. Blown-out ligaments, permanent knee damage, instead of what's mostly a question of shattered tibia."

"They were going to do it that way."

"Why didn't they?"

"I asked them."

"My God," Douli ba said unhappily.

"How long before I can walk?"

Douli ba hesitated. "The surgeon's going to come talk to you himself. He's Belgian, one of the best in the field. You were lucky, he just happened to be vacationing at the local Club Med."

"Tell me what you know."

Douli ba shifted uneasily, then said, "You should be up on crutches in a couple of months, and eventually be able to get around more or less normally. But you may never again be capable of sustained, serious walking."

Trowbridge took a deep breath. "I guess we should have talked about family first. And crops, and the weather."

"I'm sorry," Douli ba said. "Truly."

He moved to the window, looked out a moment, and turned. "Actually, I do have something to tell you about the weather. I ran into a friend of yours, someone named Nobila. He told me that when the villagers realized the Justice Minister was using the rain to cover his attack, they weren't pleased. He and the other elders went to one of the sacred groves and made a ceremony asking that the rain stop for a few days."

A faint smile crossed Douli ba's face. "I'm just telling you this so you don't attach a scientific explanation to what happened."

⠿ ⠿ ⠿

He slept restlessly for several hours, waking and dozing repeatedly. Each time he rose toward consciousness he heard Douli ba's words.

You may never again be capable of sustained, serious walking.

He visualized himself in the director's office of the Society, a pair of crutches leaning against the wall, then pushed the image aside. He felt immensely lonely.

He hadn't realized he was sleeping again until he was wakened by someone taking his hand.

Claire was sitting beside the bed.

"Hey," she said.

"Hey," he said, after a moment. "It's the swimmer."

"I should have tried harder to help you through that wave."

He realized she was crying.

"Claire, I'm alive. You're alive, and Alberto's alive, and it looks like the park may not be cut down after all. Right now that seems pretty good."

She wiped her eyes, and nodded.

"I hear you did good work in Accra."

"I talked to every diplomat who would listen. It helped me keep from thinking about what might be happening to you." She paused, then said, "They're flying you out in the morning, did you know that?"

He felt a pang of unhappiness. "What about you?"

"I'm going back out to the park to check on the chimps. I thought I might collect the rest of your equipment while I was there. I could hand deliver it, one of these days, to New York."

"I'd like that," he said. "I'd like that a lot."

"Maybe," she said, "if your legs are better, we could find something more comfortable than a table. I had nothing against the table, but—"

"I'd like that, too."

"What are you going to do?"

"I don't know. I won't be doing fieldwork anytime soon."

"What about the directorship?"

"Claire, I'm not suited to the directorship."

"Why not? It'd be tough, but you'd be good at it. And you could do some good things. Maybe that's the silver lining in all this."

"I decided a long time ago never to do that kind of work."

"Decisions can't be reversed?"

"I'm not sure this one can." He started to explain, and found himself telling her things about his father he'd never told anyone, not even Nima.

When he stopped talking, she said, "I think you can do your father's work without becoming your father."

"You think so?"

"I'm sure of it."

He heard voices raised in the corridor, two people arguing in French. One of the voices insisted she didn't care if visiting hours were about to end, or if the rules said only one visitor at a time, she was going in that room.

Najla came in wearing high heels and a short skirt. Her hair was up, and she was wearing a lot of gold jewelry.

"Claire," Trowbridge said, "This is Najla, the woman who flew me out to the park."

He'd described Najla to Claire as a middle-aged Lebanese woman who ran an auto parts store, and suspected this wasn't quite what Claire had visualized.

She raised her eyebrows, then leaned down and kissed him. "I'll see you in the morning."

She nodded politely to Najla on the way out.

Najla looked at him disapprovingly.

"So that's the other scientist. Well, I suppose you have something professional in common. But tell her she needs to put on a little makeup. She's a skinny, pale European. She can't afford to—"

"I'll tell her."

He put his hand out. Najla took it begrudgingly. "I'm glad you came," he said, and meant it, feeling grateful for what had happened between them. "I'm not sure I ever thanked you for the plane ride. And for everything. You've been incredible."

"It was fun," Najla allowed. "Although it looks like it only got you into more trouble."

∷ ⯑ ∷

They flew him out first class, with his legs immobilized and propped against the bulkhead, and his head against a pillow so he could see out the window. He was given an escort, an embassy nurse who was apparently due out for some kind of rotation. The nurse made sure he survived takeoff, and that he had his various medications and something to read, then fell asleep in her seat across the aisle with the practicality of an experienced traveler.

For a while, as the plane angled upward, there was nothing to see but streaming gray; then they broke into sunlight, and he looked down on the rainy season. Great heavy reefs of dark cloud shifted and churned beneath them. An occasional jagged-edged well leading down through the clouds gave up glimpses of brilliant green. After a while the clouds began to break up, and the green became patchy and intermittent, and disappeared altogether. The few remaining cloud structures drifted like unhooked islands above what was now savannah. He saw a narrow straight line, a solitary road through the straw-colored landscape; then a city that seemed to have been made of baked mud and pressed against the Niger, a fat brown snake twisting across the land. Then no more roads or cities, just straight-on desert, three thousand kilometers of Sahara, a pale expanse that hurt his eyes, a place without trees or greenness or shadow, a place where darkness, when it came, came empty and only at night.

A Note About the Author

Steven Voien grew up in Southern California and earned a bachelor's degree in literature from the College of Creative Studies at the University of California at Santa Barbara. In 1989 he joined the Foreign Service and served two tours, one in the Côte d'Ivoire and one in Bulgaria. He resigned from the State Department in 1994 to devote his time to writing fiction. He lives in Alameda, California, with his wife, Lydia Bird, also a writer.

A Note on the Type

This book is set in a typeface called Méridien, a classic roman
designed by Adrian Frutiger for the French type foundry Deberny
et Peignot in 1957. Adrian Frutiger was born in Interlaken,
Switzerland, in 1928 and studied type design there and at the
Kunstgewerbeschule in Zurich. In 1953 he moved to Paris, where
he joined Deberny et Peignot as a member of the design staff.
Méridien, as well as his other typeface of world reknown,
Univers, was created for the Lumitype photo-set machine.

Composed by Crane Typesetting Service, Inc.,
Charlotte Harbor, Florida

Printed and bound by R. R. Donnelley & Sons,
Harrisonburg, Virginia

Designed by Iris Weinstein